THE WOLF AND THE WILD KING

K. V. JOHANSEN

Praise for *The Wolf and the Wild King*

"K.V. Johansen's THE WOLF AND THE WILD KING is a lyrically rendered tale of intrigue and war enriched by two compelling central characters in a world that is both mythic and fully realised. A darkly beautiful book crafted in some of the finest prose it's been my pleasure to read. Can't wait for the sequel."

~ Anthony Ryan, author of *The Traitor*

"A wonderful and timeless epic fantasy—a book with wisdom, beauty and claws."

~ Tom Lloyd, author of *Stranger of Tempest*

"With beautiful prose reminiscent of Patricia McKillip, Johansen paints a bleak and devastating picture of a cold world where humans, fey, and near-fey struggle for control of an unforgiving land. The magical system is deep and well thought out, haunting and resonant. The dual plotlines of the main protagonists braid together into an intriguing narrative that leads to an explosive conclusion. *The Wolf and the Wild King* will fulfill your desires for epic dark fantasy that is original and fascinating. I can't wait for the second book in the duology!"

~ Jo Graham, author of *Black Ships* and *The Emperor's Agent*

DEDICATION

In memory of Marina C. Mooney, who read every draft of every story from the start of it all, but never got to find out how this one was going to end. The very first thing she ever said to me was, "Cool dragons, babe."

THE SEA

Far Arrisnaar

Lann Leda

Lann Naar

THE LAKE

N
W E
S

Lann Warnavon
The Fells
Warnavon

Lann Laitellon

Island of Laikyn

5

Borlinn

Long Sound

Lann Krada

6.

THE FOREST

The Holy Isle

Arrunlinn

Bay of Fogs

The Merkal

Lann Estyn

Lower Lann Lathrun

1. Arrunmouth
2. Queensborg/
   Queen's Arrun
3. Fallborg
4. Borharbour
5. Mair Laikyn
6. Goslack
7. North Cape/
   Singersborg

Upper Lann Lathrun

Lann Rath

The Falls

Lann Rawla

50 miles   150
100

Skagga Mts.

copyright K.V. Johansen 2024

~MAIRRAN~

The old songs tell how the Queen my mother came down from the ice of the north, flying in the shape of a great dragon, silver as hoarfrost under the moon. I had always thought it might be true. As fair and frail as frost and starlight, she was, looking as though a strong breath might blow her away, but her eyes, cold and palest ice-blue, held always a white fire in their depths that had nothing human about it.

In the halls of the earls and the landtheyns of the Forest, in the borg of the Queen herself, the Singers did not offer those songs.

A panting hall-runner found me in the yard of the horse-barns, about to ride out with Nowa. The child came skittering through the gateway and across the straw-strewn stones, startling the ravens into flight. She offered a hasty bow, not meeting my eyes even once she straightened up.

"My lord, your mother the blessed Queen asks that you attend on her at once in her chambers." And to Nowa, plaintive, "I've searched half the castle for the prince, theyn. My lady did say, at once."

Well she might have searched. My shield-companion and I lodged alone in a watchtower in an angle of the old curtain wall, fallen into disuse after my mother had a new yard, a barn-ward with barn and dairy, built beyond and a new wall flung out to encompass it. Hallcarls brought firewood to stack by the tower door for the soapstone stove in the first-floor room, where we mostly lived, and kept the water-butt by the door filled, but that was it. Nowa, myself, and my ravens. Nobody to tell where we'd gone or pass messages on. Ill luck the runner had managed to find us at all.

"Say you just missed us," I told the little runner, as Thunder and Lighting flapped back down from the ridgepole of the barn on which they'd taken undignified refuge.

Lie to the Queen? No, even I never thought I could get away with that. The runner's eyes widened and she glanced at Nowa, who sighed and frowned at me. "He'll come," she said. "Run now, and say the prince will follow."

The child gave another bobbing bow, more to Nowa than to me, and pelted off again.

They liked Nowa, the hallcarls and barnfolk. Big and calm and reassuring, plain and ordinary with her weathered face and her hair the colour of old hay standing up like a dandelion gone to seed. In her youth, she had left the Forest and fought as a mercenary among Outlanders, and had been initiated into the Outlander cult of the Ascendant, too, with the tiny silvery scar of the brand between her brows to prove it. Returned home again, she had served as a road-warden, keeping the stone highways safe, until she and the handful of spears of her remote waystation on the upper Lann Lathrun hunted down a much larger band of well-armed and -mounted outlaws who were preying on travellers all through that region, tracking them to their hidden stronghold. Nowa took it by challenging and killing in single combat their leader, the disgraced and banished son of an earl. The sort of thing only a fool expects will rescue her outnumbered spears from inevitable slaughter, save that while she and her small company held the outlaws' attention before their gates, the rather larger company of Forest levies she had gathered—foresters and landcarls and countryfolk who had gone too many months in fear of the outlaws' raiding—were able to scale the steep bluffs at the castle's unguarded rear and take it from within. This brought her to the Queen's attention, at a time when the Queen was looking for a tutor in arms for a child growing too old to be kept as a pet underfoot any longer. A minor hero, given minor favour, an honour no one of greater status, seeing the waning of the Queen's interest in her latest offspring, feral and already, castle rumour had it, halfway mad, had envied her.

I think without Nowa, I might have been swallowed by that burgeoning madness, with its dreams and voices, combined with the grieving conviction that—strange, small, and apparently no longer wanted where once I had been at least offhandedly petted—I had somehow failed my mother.

I wasn't a child any longer. Despite the Queen's summons, I considered riding out regardless. Nowa could hardly catch me by my pony's bridle and turn me home again. Late in the Month of Falling Leaves but the lands of the Forest were having a long and unusually mild autumn, only the lightest of nighttime frosts as yet. A clear, bright day, and the woods on the lower slopes of the inland fells were still all gold and scarlet and shivering in the wind. The horses wanted a run; so did I.

"Ignoring your mother rarely turns out well," Nowa said.

I shrugged, twitching Lighting off my fist, gathering the reins in my hand. The bird only walked up my arm. Thunder, on my other shoulder, suddenly beat his wings and cried, "Craaaawwr," which was not something one wanted bellowed in one's ear at close range. I flicked his beak for silence and the raven snatched at a gloved finger. We played a tug of war for it, for a moment. I won.

"Mairran."

"I'm not her dog."

"If not, what are you? Do as she asks, my lord. Have it over with, and maybe we can still be away before noon."

"Fine, but we might as well tell them to turn the horses back out. You know this is going to be about washing my hair and prettying up to be charming to that stout Outlander trader again."

"You do need to wash your hair, or at least let me comb it. I've seen wild ponies look better groomed than you."

"You're one to talk, with your hair cropped like a drover-boy's."

She ignored that. "How did you end up with your braid full of sticklewort, or do I want to know? And if by 'stout Outlander trader' you mean the wine merchant of Julliac, she's already sold her cargo and taken ship for the Rath, as you'd know if you dined more often in the hall and paid the attention you should to what's going on around you. There are those found her charming in her own right and her plumpness—and good humour—rather attractive than otherwise."

I doubted Nowa had really been romancing the Outlander wine-trader. She had her Bran, who kept the Red Cat alehouse with his sister by the river-gate of the borg, and she hadn't, at least not since I'd been of an age to notice such things, looked aside from him. And the wine-merchant might have been selling barrelled Outland wines, but she had also been nosing about in Arrunmouth among those who dealt in bluestone from the Lann Lathrun, and within the Queensborg with those who had connections to the earls of the Upper and Lower Lathrun both. A rare thing, bluestone, deep and vivid as squill blooming beneath the birches in the spring forest, a much-prized gem and useful too as artists' pigments when ground; the valleys of the headwaters of the Lathrun were one of the few places it could be mined. Trade in bluestone was by the Queen's licence alone; it was as well to keep an eye on Outlanders taking too great an interest. Hence my mother's reasons for trying to nudge me into bed with the supposed wine-merchant. Wanting to know who stood behind her and what their intentions might be.

But by those days I chose whom I slept with, whatever my mother might have wanted, or so I told himself, though it didn't always work out that way.

"I don't want to know." I picked at the tail of my braid, which, yes, held the tiny burrs of sticklewort, and so did my cloak. I'd been roaming up the course of the little Meull brook with a red-haired fiddler the evening before, to play a few tunes together and watch the sun setting through a poplar wood at its bright amber perfection, and what else we might have gotten up to up there was the fiddler's own affair and mine and none of Nowa's. Besides, it had given her an evening's leave to visit her man at the Cat.

"Don't sulk," she said.

"I'm not sulking." When I sulked—as Nowa would have it—I bolted alone for the high fells and stayed there, till my mother sent

Nowa to find and drag me back, to play the dutiful swordtheyn and devoted son again.

"Pouting?" Nowa suggested.

"Scowling," I said. "I'm allowed scowling."

"You're not."

"You know you like me, really," I told her.

"You think? Sometimes I wonder."

Nowa called herself my keeper for a reason, and not just because it was what the folk of Queen's Arrun believed. I hadn't had to name her my shield-companion when I was made swordtheyn, but who else was there I could trust? Who else would dare—or bother—to nag about the snarls and burrs in my hair or sit up with me the night through, when I couldn't speak for dreaming of the Dark Beyond and all the world felt like nothing but shadows and the knife's edge?

I'd had twin sisters, Unn and Ullin, both dead long ago, and an older brother, Lorne. Prince Lorne was born with a strong Forest-blessing. A Seer. He fell lost into the Dreaming Dark when he had seen but seventeen winters. By the time I was born, Lorne had spent the past forty in raving incoherence or empty-eyed silence, kept away from sight in a hunting lodge in a remote valley up in the central fells, tended by a succession of patient keepers. The Queen had taken me to see him once in a while. I don't know if it had been meant as a kindness to my brother, some variation in the routine of his day, or a warning to myself. No more visits, now. In the depths of the winter past the lodge, though stone-built and slate-roofed, had been gutted by fire. Only charred bones remained, of the dream-drowned Seer prince and his keepers.

The Queen's public mourning had been brief. I suspected her rage still smouldered. Not a grief born of affection, not that I had ever seen, but Lorne had been hers, as I was hers, and whether by mischance or through the work of her enemies, he had been taken from her.

What he might have foreseen and told of warning, I did not know; Lorne had so rarely spoken two coherent words together in my hearing. But it had been after the burning of the lodge that my mother sent me, twice, to hunt in the Warnavon.

My sister Ullin had died by her own hand at the age of sixteen winters, almost a hundred years before I was ever thought of. Flung herself from the roof of a tower. The Queensborg had many towers. The songs of it, which were not sung in Queen's Arrun, did not settle on which one she chose. Some said, she flung herself into the Lake. This one could not do from any tower of the Queensborg. Few songs went so far as to offer a reason why, beyond the bland ballad possibilities of a love betrayed or a lover lost. I wondered if she had been trying to fly. Unn, not long after her twin's death, set the Queen's Great Hall alight and perished in the fire.

I was not a Seer, yet I dreamed, and in some of my dreams the Dark reached out arms, like a great winged figure all shadows and sleeping fires, and wrapped them hot around me, and drew me in, and I didn't know if I was dreaming, or drowning, or dying…

So you see, Nowa had reason, to fear for me when the nights grew choking dark.

Sometimes I suspected that I was mad as all my mother's children. I just hid it better.

Nowa dismounted and took my bridle with a scowl of her own, whistling to catch the attention of one of the barncarls. "Look to these, would you? If we're not back shortly, unsaddle them, but leave them in. We'll be wanting to ride out again later."

I sighed and swung down, and leaned a moment on Smoke's warm and solid pewter-coloured shoulder. The horse turned his head to nose at me, a comforting shove.

"Sorry," I told him, putting my head close, scratching the hairy cheek and the thick mane, clipped to stand erect and bristling, showing off the black stripe amid the silver. Whispering, because the servingcarls found me worrying enough as it was, without my talking to animals. Surely better than talking to myself. Or arguing with the voices in my head. "Later. I promise."

Nowa shook her head at me and handed over the reins of her own pale-gold Thorn, who sighed gustily. Speaking for us all.

Haste, my mother presumably wanted, so I tossed the ravens to the sky and we headed through the lanes and yards of the castle as we were, without bothering to change tunics and rough cloaks for finer hall-gowns.

The Queen's apartments were over the New Hall, reached from a flight of stairs hidden by carved panelling and the mass of the chimney behind the dais of the high table. We went in by the great double doors in the porch, which were carved with two dragons grappling one another, surrounded by oaks with branches snarling and tangling like the dragons' furious claws, and crossed the length of the hall, empty and echoing. Queen's Arrun, sometimes called the Queensborg, was far greater and grander than any mere earl's castle, built all of stone, the hall not a lodging-place for spearcarls or swordtheyns but reserved for dining and music and the ceremonies of court. It was hung with embroideries and painted cloths showing scenes of the wars fought by the Queen against rebel earls and Outland invaders—the latter mostly Coastlanders and fire-worshipping Southlanders, who had tried the mountain passes from east and south on more than one occasion, thinking to seize some Lakeside port and fortify it as their own. They had never yet succeeded, but that didn't—probably never would—stop earls of the south and east taking bribes, to turn a blind eye to smugglers and scouting parties. Though the Queen had her ways of finding those out.

No guard challenged us, not till we came to the top of the stairs, where the Queen's shield-companion, Swordtheyn Rabi, frowned at our boots and plucked a stray wisp of hay from my cloak. She gestured Nowa to a bench in the antechamber and showed me through to the private room beyond the bedchamber, where, according to the whispers of the castle folk, the Queen worked her most secret magics. There was a table set against the wall, like an altar, with beeswax candles in silver holders to either side of the stand holding the polished stone mirror of her visions. Obsidian framed in silver, a moon eclipsed.

Unexpected, to those who might have thought to see darker secrets if they were admitted so far, would be the walking wheel by the wall, with about it the everyday clutter of baskets, some with carded wool, some with flax. My mother did her best thinking while spinning, she once told me, and had ordered the wheel brought from some Outland beyond the Falls not long before I was born, though often she would walk about the castle yards and gardens with a distaff in hand and the old clay-weighted spindle, like any landcarl. No idle hands in any common Forest household through the long winter evenings, when the work of the outdoors and the hearth was done. It was at the great wheel she was standing as I came in, right hand setting it in motion, tick-tick-tick as it turned; she stepped away, feeding a slate-dark wool to the whirling spindle.

She left the weaving to others, but I suspected I rarely wore cloth, linen or woollen, that had not passed through her hands.

Some, I suppose, might have taken that for love.

The Queen tilted her face, presenting a cheek to be kissed. I gave her the briefest brush of lips in passing. Dry, cool skin, perfumed. She wore a hall-gown of rich blue and a diadem of red gold with dangling beads of bluestone and pearl and jet black as raven's eye, as if she presided over the hall, which made me think I should have at least combed my hair that day after all, her mood being such. From beneath the diadem her own hair, pale white-gold, fell past her hips in a single long braid wound through with scarlet ribbon. Beautiful, fragile, and like a mountain in her implacable and waiting strength.

"The Earl of Laikyn is dead," my mother said.

"Yes?" I asked, and crossed to the gable window. The shutters were wide open. The air smelt of bread from the nearby bakehouse and the water-weed scent of the little river, the Arrunlinn, that coiled its way out of the forested lower hills. Even the miles-distant Lake, I could smell. I wanted to be out under the trees, riding beyond the pollarded wood-pastures and the tended forest and up into the high wild calling wind. An earl dead was nothing to do with me. Not this earl, anyhow.

An earl living, whom my mother wanted dead, would be a different matter. As the woods of the Warnavon might witness, if they could.

I couldn't even bring to mind a face for Laikyn, though the earls had a duty of attendance on the Queen—and remittance of their taxes—in the festival season around Kingsday in the Month of Golden Nights, and I must have seen her at some point. Or him—there were a few earls who were men, though by custom it was women who held the land.

Safe to assume, though, that Laikyn had not died quietly in her bed of the complaints of old age, or the Queen would hardly have bothered to tell me of it.

So I waited, watching out the window. Thunder and Lightning would sometimes follow and find me in whatever hall I entered, but they never came to the windows of the Queen's apartments. My eye found them, circling high, and as I watched the ravens swooped away towards the river and were gone from sight.

"She died at Harvesttide," my mother said, and took a seat in the wooden armchair, draped in wolfskins and carved with oak-leaves like a throne. It turned my stomach, those pelts, every time, though they were old, and smelt mostly of bread and woodsmoke, and of the Queen. She wore perfumes brought by Outlander traders, scents I didn't know, except that they were hers, and more valuable, ounce for ounce, than bluestone.

I did not wear fur save that of prey—hare and squirrel, sheepskin or shaggy goat—and I never let Nowa do so, either, and my mother knew how those damned wolfskins made me feel.

"Sit, Mairran," she said. "Don't loom there as if you're about to take flight. Come here and sit."

I didn't loom. I stood a bare inch or so taller than she, and shared her light build and fine bones, a small, slight young man who would have made a very pretty girl, my first lover Dove had told me. Too much condescension in that for her to have meant it as a compliment.

Anyhow, I couldn't loom if I tried.

Lurking, that, I could do.

But I sat, obedient, on the low stool at the Queen's knee, like a child—there being no second chair in that private place, where even Swordtheyn Rabi was a rare visitor.

"And?" I asked, because I still didn't know how the death of the Earl of Laikyn might concern me.

For a ship to bring news from Laikyn to the Holy Isle could take five or six days at best, with good weather, and usually rather more, if there were storms or contrary winds, or none at all. A quick calculation—Harvesttide this year had fallen late, since the equinox sat more or less square between two full moons, and usually the Harvest festival was celebrated at the nearest. So even though we were almost to Slaughtermonth, we were only three weeks past Harvesttide and to be hearing of this death after three weeks was not so great a delay at all.

"Earl Raynellin's daughter, her heir Rikenza, has not yet sent a message. The word was carried by a quacksalver coming from summer travels among the villages of the Lann Laitellon."

"One of your eyes-and-ears among the tribes?"

"He is, yes. And he tells me that the earl apparently rode out early with some of her household folk on Harvesttide Eve, and was separated from them, and though they searched all the night, she was not found till the morning. Dead, and lying at a remote heartstone's foot, her blood soaking the earth about it. And when my man left—he stayed some few days, to see if any murderer would be taken—when he left, the killer had not yet been found, or even named. I do not like this, Mairran."

"No," I said. I did not like it either. Not a murder done within the bounds of a fane, at a heartstone's foot. And on a lesser holy day, at that. "Are you thinking this merely a murder, or—something more?"

"That, I expect you to discover. That the earl's heir has not seen fit to inform me of the death does not set my mind at ease."

"Three weeks—a ship can take so long easily enough. The heir might have waited before sending her messenger, expecting to be able to tell you the murderer was found."

There was nonetheless a chill prickling along my spine, like a cold claw trailing down, but I did not particularly want to go to Laikyn, not then, almost Slaughtermonth, to be on the Lake with the first storms of winter blowing out of the east.

Come, I thought one of my dream-haunts was saying. *Come soon.* I could not, with my mother there, listen closely enough to tell which one. No knowing what she might overhear. And besides, waking, I tried to pretend such voices were only my dreams.

I had not been sleeping well for some time.

Since Harvesttide?

But my dreams had been all of horses, and wolves, and hounds yipping high and distant, running on the wind, which anyone might dream, hearing geese.

Not horses. *A* horse, the colour of burnished copper, and the rider — the rider only a shadow, a memory I could not hold. A voice that called me, but I could not answer. The name it called was not my own.

Fly to him. Fly, before it is too late —

I was no Seer. It was important to remember that.

"The heir may have wanted to wait till she had a murderer in hand, perhaps," the Queen agreed. "But nonetheless my earl is dead, and to confirm her daughter in her place lies with me, and were it not for my man thinking this matter urgent I would not even know of this killing yet. And I may not have any formal notice of it till into Yearsturn and deep winter, if Lady Rikenza puts off sending much longer and uses the uncertainty of waiting for freeze-up as excuse for her delay. Mairran, I do not, I very much do not want this to be unresolved still when Huntersnight comes."

There was always a time, spring and autumn alike, when news did not travel well, or at all. Nor soldiers. Roads turned to bogs, brooks and rivers flooded, and the spring break-up of the Lake made it impassible. In the autumn, there would be roads and tracks alternating between stone-hard frost and sun-thawed muck, and rain, and snow maybe sudden and deep, and the Lake icing over, hazard to ships not taken from the water in time, but not yet reliably bearing for horse and sleigh or even a courier on skis.

This was not, I suspected, going to be a journey I could make by other means. It was the Queen's son that would be wanted, her carrion crow, prince and executioner sent as envoy and threat in one.

Not her assassin, her dealer-out of secret death in the shadows.

"No," I agreed. "Better not to leave it till Huntersnight." Best not to go into the dark and the turn of the year with such a death as Earl Raynellin's unresolved. "But if it is kinslaying — the earl's daughter?

Why kill to gain what would come to her in time anyway, when she must know she would be suspected?"

"I don't know. If I knew for certain who had done it, I might know what they thought to gain."

"Beyond an earldom, you mean."

"A slip on the stairs, a spooked horse, a dish of bad mussels, would do the job as well, if greed for an inheritance were all. No need to make a sacrifice of it."

I had never poisoned anyone.

And I was distracted, wondering whom she had poisoned, and when, that such a death came to her mind, among more plausible ways to rid oneself of a troublesome earl.

And also, I was wondering what, beyond an earldom, one might think to gain, by offering an earl's blood to the Forest. Even on a lesser holy day. Though I did not want to believe the power of the land might be so easily won.

"You've seen—nothing?" I nodded towards the mirror. I did not know for certain what, or how, my mother saw, if ever she really did see at all. I did not know if she was really a witch, to partake of vision not as Seers do, possessed by their Forest-blessing without warning, but as witches may, in some reflecting surface, through prayer or meditation and an offering of their blood to the Dark Mother. True or not, it was common knowledge that she did. Just, I suppose, as it was common knowledge that I was fathered by a fayling out of the hollow hills and no human man at all, so maybe the mirror was only there to catch and throw back the light of her candles when she sat to read of an evening. What did I know?

"I don't need to seek vision, to be worried by a woman bled and killed at a heartstone," my mother said.

That, I did note, was not an answer. I waited.

"A man," she said.

Still I waited.

"There is a man," she said. "There will be a man?" She smiled, briefly, at me, but her eyes were distant. Remembering, I thought, or seeing again, what the mirror had shown her. If it had.

It was a chilling thought, that she might be not a witch but a true Seer herself. A witch was much more…ordinary a thing, in the end. But that she had a Seer's Forest-blessing had never been said of her. Maybe that was why she lay with a Seer, I sometimes thought: to get me.

Though I did not have that blessing—she told me so herself. And one would think, given the fate of my brother Lorne—his madness, not his recent death—she would have decided that trying to breed a Seer was a work foredoomed to failure.

Maybe she had just fancied Immellain's black-silk hair, or the music of his Forest-harp. That was my preferred belief. Ordinary folk went to bed for such reasons all the time; why not a Queen?

"Begotten of autumn," the Queen said, as if some line of a song had come to her, but it was no ballad nor lay that I had ever heard. "Born into winter. Sunset on his hair, fire at his blade's edge, and he rides a horse as red as flame. Kill him."

Red horse running, bright against the snow, and overhead a falcon flies into a burning sky.

Suddenly I was tired.

"What do you want?" I asked, to have it said and done with. "Regarding the earl's heirs, and Laikyn, what do you want?" What I wanted was to get out of that room, outside the walls and up to the wild heights. Away from the faint scent of wolves long dead, warmed by her body.

"Go to Laikyn. Find out who killed the earl. Find what they thought to gain by it, and consider whether there are any threads that lead back to the Warnavon, or to Outlander troublemaking, however unlikely that may be. Do whatever you must. You act with my will in all you do, even to the death of Lady Rikenza the heir, if that is your judgement. The *Snow Goose* is at your disposal. Theyn Rabi will tell shipmaster Ermintrud to make ready. You should leave tomorrow. No later than the day after tomorrow. And the crew's lodging and board must be borne by the earldom of Laikyn through the winter, if you can't return by ship before the freeze-up and they need to pull the *Goose* out till the thaw. I appoint you high reeve of Laikyn Province, until such time as I am satisfied and can either confirm Lady Rikenza in the earldom or name another to hold it. Take this, in token."

This was a heavy ring of red gold, the signet a squared bluestone carved with the Queen's emblem of the dragon in flight. She took it from her thumb; it fit my third finger well enough, though I would give it to Nowa to keep for me as soon as I was out of the hall. "I'll send letters with you to inform the heir and her officers of this."

"Yes," I said.

A high reeve stood in the Queen's stead, and was usually some law-reeve or swordtheyn of her court set to oversee the affairs of a province if an earl were taken in rebellion, or died without a clear heir, or when a child inherited the earldom. A temporary position, but it could mean taking over the whole mess of overseeing and accounting for tithes and tolls and taxes, and the village levies, and the muster of spears of the landtheyns... No, I told myself, it meant harassing the various clerks and reeves and sergeants who already had charge of such things to ensure they kept on doing them, and ensuring likewise that the accounts and the keys of the storehouses and treasury were in my — Nowa's—hands, not Lady Rikenza's. I had no need to feel a child's panic at the thought of my sums not adding up.

"Though you will not," the Queen went on, "carry Rikenza's confirmation as earl. Say to her, that remains in doubt, until I am satisfied that she is innocent of any involvement in this death. And there is an elder brother as well, Lord Raynar, whom you must not discount."

"I won't be back for Huntersnight," I warned.

"You might," she said. "It may be a simple matter to resolve." As if she had forgotten her vision, or dismissed it, now. Or as if on that, there were no more to be said. "Bring me the earl's murderer for the Huntersnight sacrifice, if you settle the matter so soon. Or hold the full rite there, if you cannot get home in time. We will make shift without you here."

She did not need to say that for the earl's killer there would be no trial before the travelling justices who administered the Queen's law, not once I had made my judgement. I had that right, which was hers.

She had given me that with the sacred knives I bore and no one would dare speak against me. Life and death, in my hands, on the edge of a stone blade.

I had never travelled far down the Lann Rath, never even so far as Head of the Falls, where lakers put in and cargoes were carted to the high-walled Fallborg and down the steep-slanting road of the escarpment, to the surging tides of the Bay of Fogs and the ships of the Coastlanders and their outland trade. I had never seen the Falls. But sometimes I dreamed I was flying over them, the river white and roaring.

I fly on and on over the broad dark water, and the salt sea opens out, like a lake without a shore and the sun rising from it, and though I fly till wings fail and I fall into the sea, I never look back...

"And Mairran," the Queen said.

"Mother?"

"Wash. Comb your hair. You look like a tramp."

My mother rose, and I did, and gave her the kiss of parting. I glanced back as I opened the door, thinking, I didn't even know what — to see something in her face of regret at this necessity, or concern. Maybe even I meant to argue that she should wait for the letter from Earl Raynellin's heir, which was more likely than not merely delayed by the usual chances of the Lake. But she was standing at the wheel again, pale, serene, only the slightest of frowns troubling her face, looking down to unwind a span of the yarn already on the spindle, as if it held some flaw.

~LANNESK~

There is the Lake, vast as a sea, and all about lies the Forest, and the countless rivers and river-valleys of the Forest. And in the Lake, or beneath the Lake, in the long and long ago, there was the Dragon, Erryth the Golden.

Long and long ago, the story begins, the way it always begins in his mother's telling. Long and long ago, the Kings stood for the tribes of the Forest under the Dragon, and the earls governed the tribes of the Forest under the Kings. There were three Kings, or five, or nine. It varies. Some nights she says twelve, or two. Sometimes, only one.

Long and long ago, there were the Kings and they lived and died for the folk of the Forest, under the rule of the Dragon.

Seven years, a holy chosen King had. Seven years of blessing in the service of their folk, under the Dragon. And then they served one last time, and died by the stone knives of the sorcerer-priests, to renew the bond between the tribes and the Dragon of the Lake.

There were Forest-folk, who were humankind, and Forest-faylings, who were not. The faylings had their own bargain with the Dragon, of which they do not speak.

There were dragon-kin who served the Dragon, and some were sorcerers, and some were the sons and daughters and remoter kin of the Dragon, and some, perhaps, were only men and women who left family and tribe and gave themselves to serve the Dragon.

And there were those who belonged to the Forest, and were none of those things, and some of those were numbered in after times among the Immortals.

There was a King chosen. A human. A man of the Warnavon, a land on the eastern shore of the Lake, northerly, where the limestone bones of the hills thrust through the thin clay.

Just the other side of those mountains, Harlev says, and waves a hand westerly, towards the great hills that rise to block the sunset horizon from the Coastlands. It's all a fireside tale to Lannesk. He's small; he has no notion of geography, or of time beyond the last winter. He thinks the Dragon might lurk there, just beyond the hills, and come floating down in the night on wings of shadow to eat them all.

"Don't tell the child such stories," his father says. "You'll give him nightmares."

"It's his heritage," Mother says, rocking the baby's cradle with her foot, needle in her hand, twisting and knotting the yarn to make a sock while Lannesk sits on his father's lap, head against his chest, half drowsing, warm and safe and held. "Every child of the Forest needs to know this tale."

"He's not a child of the Forest," Father says. "He's a Coastlander, and he'll be a seafarer like his daddy, won't you, my little man? No dragons to fear in the great ocean."

But his mother goes on with the tale.

There came a time when that man was chosen to be the next King. If he had a name of his own, no one remembers it. A man of the Warnavon. Perhaps. Perhaps not. A wanderer, he had been. Not a Singer, because there were no Singers in those days, only musicians and poets and folk who sang, who wandered between the tribes. Or perhaps he was a warrior, champion of a tribe, an earl's son. Who, now, remembers? What matters more was that he was beloved of a creature of the Forest, a shapeshifter and an Immortal, who was wolf and falcon and human-seeming woman. Dangerous, to give your heart to such a one. Dangerous to draw such an eye.

The dragon-kin sorcerers hunted such folk, who were powers of the Forest, neither human nor fayling; they slew them as enemies to Erryth, because even such as they can be slain, though not easily. The Dark Beyond holds them only lightly, and they might in time be called back. (The Dragon herself had been only one among those creatures of the

Forest inhuman and undying, only one among the fellowship of the Immortals of the Forest, in the long and long ago, till she rose to be greater than all, and rule the Forest. But that's another story, Harlev his mother says, and no one remembers now how it is meant to go.) So for a King to be the beloved of a creature like the shapeshifter, who was called the Grey Hunter, was a dangerous thing, and a defiance, because the Kings belonged to the Dragon Erryth, and spoke to the Dragon on behalf of the tribes, and rode in her train as swordtheyns more honoured than earls or even the great lords of the dragon-kin, until their time came to serve her by their death.

Seven years, this King served. And when his time was over, he was summoned to the Holy Isle, to renew the bond between Dragon and folk with the pledge of his life's blood, given to the stone knives of the sorcerer-priests of the dragon-kin. This was the way of Kings, and the bargain made between the tribes and the Dragon.

But this King, who had no name, because to be a King meant to put aside name and kinship, spouse and child, to stand alone and to stand for all, went in secret to the anchorstone called the Heart of the Holy Isle, the night before the day of his sacrifice was come, and with his own knife he offered his life's blood, not to Erryth the Golden to whom it was owed, but to the Forest.

And he died there. The Grey Hunter who loved him was with him, and held his head in her lap, and wept over him. And afterwards the sorcerer-priests, afraid, said that his blood had been spilt for the Dragon, but that was a lie, for the Grey Hunter had carried the King's body away on the back of his red horse before ever the time of the Dragon's rite was come.

And when the ritual of the crowning of the next King was begun, a King came riding, armed for war and crowned with oak and roses, for it was three weeks into the Month of Golden Nights, and he slew the sorcerer-priests, and the great wolf who ran at his side slew the dragon-kin who had gathered, and that was the beginning of the war of the Forest tribes and the earls of the tribes against the Dragon and the dragon-kin. And after long and bloody years of war, when even poets and harpers fought by the magic of their song, the dragon-kin were driven out of the land, and they fled to the far north beyond the headwaters of the Lann Leda. And the Dragon was driven into the depths of the Lake that had given her birth and bound there by the song and the magic of the Wild King and the Grey Hunter. And still, Harlev says, her voice gone soft and low and ominous, so that Lannesk shivers and hides his face against his father's chest, half in earnest, because fear is a part of the story, still the dragon-kin wait in their northern exile for the day that Golden Erryth will return, to claim the Forest once more.

There are other things he remembers, from before the Forest. Hazy things. A little dark stone-built house they share with no one else, no grandmother and aunts and cousins, just their family alone, and a couple of shaggy she-goats, half a dozen hens. Raspberries red and juicy and the summer sun beating on his head as he picks them, careful not to crush, so proud when he's filled his basket.

Their little house is part of a straggling village on a restless, barren shore, and it's half a day's walk to the walled town where the big ships come in. Low stone houses with roofs of saltmarsh thatch, red-sailed fishing boats, waves that crash and comb back through slippery black weed and bladderwrack that pops under bare feet. The great gulls wail. Salt tang of the air, salt taste of the sea.

A wave breaks over his head, knocking him off his feet, and he chokes and splutters, half crying, half laughing. Father swings him up and sets him on his feet again. Almost, remembering, he can hear his voice. Looking up. Impression of blue eyes, tawny gold beard and wind-whipped hair, white teeth laughing, so laughter wins and their brown-haired mother laughs, standing poised on a rock with the baby on her back. She's wearing a long gown, Outlander-style, that the waves have splashed dark, though she's kilted the skirts up through her belt. Her feet are black with muck up over the ankles, as though she's wearing boots.

Vast stretch of muddy sand and weed-covered rock. The tide is out. They're digging quahogs for chowder. Tide creeping in, each wave that little bit farther. Father has taught him from babyhood to watch the waves, to watch the change. To have that rhythm always in mind, till it's part of him, like his blood.

Tide on the Lake is a small thing. You can notice it on a calm day, a little stain of waves travelling up and down on the shore, but ships need take no heed of it. And there's no salt in the air.

Sometimes he dreams, still, of the salt wind, when he hears gulls, the little white ones of the Lake, whose cries turn them to the great black-backed gulls in his dreams.

Their father is a shipcarl who goes over the sea, voyaging between Coastlander ports and out to the Far Islands, and down away to Outlands strange and mysterious, from which he brings back odd things. Sometimes it is spices that only the wealthy in their great high houses in the town could afford to eat every day, resinous nuts and twists of bark and dried buds. Their mother pounds them up to use in stews and pies. Sometimes it is bright strange shells like nothing they ever find on the beach of home. Once, a blue scarf for their mother's hair, a cloth so fine it feels like baby's skin, like water, and once a string of beads, polished and glittering in all colours like a rainbow, as fine as any Master of the town might wear. Their father isn't a ship-owner or shipmaster, but Father's sister is both, and his brother, and they live in the town. Their father has disgraced himself, left his wife to live with a Forest-born singer, who is Mother, and he serves on ships that do not belong to his family. Folk of Father's family speak to Mother sometimes when, some neighbour having given Mother and Lannesk and the baby a lift in a pony-cart, she goes in to the market of the town; those kin of Father's say unkind things. But when Father is home he laughs, and brings them pretty shells from far away, and it does not matter.

Mother is a singer, a Singer, that Forest word meaning so much more than someone who sings. Someone who knows the songs, who carries the history and the lore of the Forest lands, who passes between valley and valley, hall and hall, tribe and tribe, free of all hindrance, owing loyalty to no clan, no earl. She says, she has a right to call herself that, even though she has not been awarded the braided silver ring of her three years' study under the Master-Singers on the Holy Isle. She should have had both title and ring, she says. But she travelled down beyond the Falls on her first solitary summer-wandering, and rather than returning in the autumn, to sing for the Masters the tale of her travels and be rewarded with her ring, she fell in love with a Coastlander shipmaster, and for him she gave up what she might have been, and for her he gave up what he was, and they became Mother and Father in the little dark house in the fishing village on the shore of the sea.

There's an autumn storm, a great three-day hammering of black skies at noon and wind that tears away the thatch despite all the ropes and hanging stones that hold it down, and the sea leaps over the rocks and throws itself up about the walls of the house, and they climb the rocky hill, carrying what they can on their backs, even little Anzimor, and the goats pull against the ropes by which Lannesk is meant to lead them and run off into the hills, and the hens blow away.

The ship Father sails on should have been returning. Another ship, running in just before the storm, has told that it had set out from an Islander port just behind them. But it hasn't come. It never does.

Driftwood. Planks.

Mother goes to the house in town, where Father's mother and father live, and one of his younger sisters. They will help, she says, because Lannesk and Anzimor are their kin. But though a girl, big-eyed and worried, opens the door and lets them in, an angry old man pushes them out again and slams it, and a woman comes out and yells at them, and Mother yells back, and they go away.

Some bigger boys find them as they go through the town; they throw stones and clods of dog-dirt. The names they call Mother mean bad things. People watch, but nobody stops them.

Lannesk doesn't remember how he knows, but he does know. They are his brothers, those boys, his brothers and Anzimor's. They're Father's other family.

A man with a great wagon full of barrels and crates of grey salt-cakes takes them on the coast road, through bright gentle warm autumn days under a sky that seems as if it could never be angry bruise-black, beside a sea that sparkles at noon as if it's scattered with stars. The man lets Lannesk hold the reins and teaches him to really drive the six-horse team, not just pretending with the rein-ends like a baby. That man shares his quilts under the wagon with mother at night, so she's not cold, though she's very quiet, and Lannesk and Anzimor sleep in the wagon itself, curled under the driver's bench, where it is cold, because the quilt they have is worn thin. Lannesk wraps himself about little Anzimor to try to keep him warm. And after the wagon, there is a ship, a small, fat, wallowing ship, that sails up the great Bay of Fogs, but the Mothers Above and Below are kind and the heavy blinding fogs of the tales, which swallow ships and shipfolk and leave them broken on the cliffs, are only small things, which wrap the world in white as dusk settles and burn away again with the dawn.

The Rath is a great wide river, too wide for any bridge, and it flows dark and swift. The hills rise high on either side, breaking into barren stone where trees hang as if their roots are claws digging in, and then there's a town, which does not belong to the Forest or the Coast, and the Falls, pounding white, like the sky is falling, and the steep, steep road up, twisting and turning, and stone towers above, and that is where the Forest begins.

~MAIRRAN~

I had seen a great poet, a Singer with the gold ring of the full seven winters at North Cape, whipped at the chief heartstone of the Holy Isle till his back bled, when I was small. A tall man, as I remembered my first sight of him, lean and lanky. Grey-eyed, darker-skinned than the usual tawny complexion of Forest-folk, and uncommon black hair, like my own. A handsome man, and terrible in his courage, standing before the Queen.

It wasn't only that he had sung a song of the Immortals returning to ride the Forestways and lead the folk against a dragon come again out of the Dark, but that he had made it. Dragon-heart, he had sung. All knew it was the Queen whom he meant, and it might have been only the usual sort of poet's accusation: that she was cold, and severe in her justice, and levied taxes that the earls did not want to pay. Crime enough. But dragon-heart, destroyer of kings and heroes, had been his words, and, dragon, he had cried, or so his accusers testified, will not stand against dragon, when the Great Dragon, when Erryth the Golden, comes again. The earl of the Lower Lann Lathrun, in the marketplace of whose very borg the Singer had sung this reckless song, had no choice but to seize him and carry him with her when she sailed to the Golden Nights Court, the annual gathering of the earls before the Queen ahead of the rites of Kingsday.

"The King must ride," the Singer said, when he was brought before the Queen's judgement. His eyes were dilated black. I had been afraid to look at him, standing by my mother's great chair, meekly observing, my hands, small and crossed with scratches from some misadventure or other, clutching the arm of it, sternly not fidgeting.

"The King must ride," the Singer said, and maybe he could not help himself, lost in vision. He was a Seer, drowning in the Dreaming Dark.

I had likely not been the only one who expected the Singer's death, in that moment.

But the Queen had him stripped, and whipped, and then she burned his harp and banished him not only from the Holy Isle, but from the Forest lands altogether, giving him till the next new moon to be gone, never to return, and not even the Masters of North Cape spoke up to defend him.

His name was Immellain of the High Lathrun, Singer and Seer. And he was my father.

Nowa—she was guardian and tutor in those days, not yet my shield-companion—told me so. I had been pestering her on that point, having worked out that most children, even sons with no land-right, even bastards, knew their fathers, and I was convinced that Nowa, being so old and wise, must hold all the secrets of the world. That one, at least, she did.

I wondered, afterwards, whether my mother had loved Immellain, in the days when they begot me. Sometimes I thought she must have, as much as her cold dragon's heart could love anyone. I knew my mother, even then. I couldn't think of any other reason that she would have left Immellain alive.

Some years later, at the Huntersnight dawn that was the seventeenth anniversary of my birth, the sacrifice at the heartstone was another Singer. Like Immellain, she had made songs that told of the last of the Immortals called back from the Dark Beyond, and the Wild King riding the Forest again, the Grey Hunter and all their Forest-blessed Riders in his train. A dragon nests in the heart of holiness, that young Singer sang, and who will set the Forest free?

For that young fool of a silver-ring Singer there was no mercy, no mere flogging. She faced her own death bravely, died swiftly.

I made sure of that.

That was the year, the start of my eighteenth winter, that I became my mother's executioner. Flint-king, knife-king, priest of the sacrifices, as once, or so I was taught, the true Kings had been.

Though it had been their own blood they offered to the Forest.

So the Singers said.

That isn't how it was, at all, the voice of the dream-haunt I most trusted told me. *You know it wasn't.* But I was not sure I knew any such thing. I had so many dreams.

The night after my mother told me of the murder of Earl Raynellin of Laikyn, I dreamed.

My mother stands at her window, looking out over the Lake.

One couldn't see the Lake from the Queensborg; the stone castle was eight miles up the Arrunlinn from the harbour at the river's mouth. But that was my dream.

In the moonlight, she stands looking over the Lake, combing and combing and combing her hair. The comb is carved of bog-oak polished glossy black as the hilts of my flint knives, and she sings, softly, as she combs, but I cannot understand what she sings. I think I should. It sounds like a tongue I should know, something twisted just aside from my own. But understanding does not come.

She sings, and she watches over the Lake in the moonlight, and she draws out the loose hairs caught in the comb, long and fine and coiling, hardly thicker than gossamer, hardly warmer in colour, and winds them about her thumb.

~LANNESK~

Anzimor is crying, silent, as he has learnt to cry. Lannesk's tears dried up long ago. He puts an arm over his brother, pulls him close and tight, hums, softly, an old song from the sea they have lost, till Anzi is still and sleeping, salt drying on his bruised cheek like spray. Tries to fall into that place where Father was alive and Mother was patient and kind, but it isn't there anymore. Even the memories are broken and dull.

A long road, and a winding, a dark road and a long. They measure it, month after month after year, and they never count the strides. Mother, Lannesk, Anzimor. Bundles on their backs. That first winter they drift up to an earl's tower. Mother spins, and washes pots, and Lannesk drives the dash of the churn up and down and up and down till his arms ache and his shoulders burn and the butter comes, until the cows dry off for the winter and when he isn't churning he spins too, and even little Anzi has to sit in a corner and pick dirt and straw out of the fleeces, squinting in the grudging light that comes through the scraped hide over the window. They have their share of the bread and kale, and the fermented summer vegetables once the kale is done, and scraps of meat and cheese, but a scant share, because they came as beggars, though the earl is distant kin to Mother's father, or so Mother says. In the spring they leave that place early one morning, before anyone else is stirring.

Mother has a new harp in a fine waxed-leather bag, but that bag goes into the heart of Lannesk's bundle, which is the rolled-up quilt they all sleep under and a piece of waxed leather big enough to keep the rain off if they all sit up with it over their heads all night. Lannesk doesn't think the earl's son, whose harp it was, gave it to her.

They go by little winding Forest paths high over hills and into the shadow of another earl's tower, and then another's, before Mother begins to play the harp, and to sing, and to call herself, not a Singer, because she has no braided silver ring, but a minstrel of the coast. She teaches them to sing, and to dance, and to juggle. They sing Father's songs, because they are strange and new, and people will listen and give them supper and shelter.

Aren't the little boys sweet, people say, and a lady, an earl's sister, tries to buy Anzimor, because he is so beautiful, with his soft red-gold curls and big blue eyes, and she has no child of her own.

Sometimes they stay with a man or a woman who wants Mother in their bed, and sometimes that's good, because there's plentiful food and a warm fire. Sometimes it's not so good.

Mother's bad-tempered, because things are so hard. She's angry, when Anzimor cries because he's tired, or he's hungry, or—most often, Lannesk thinks, because he's sad and scared and too young to properly remember back to when they were happy, only he knows that something is lost and can't be found again. I should have sold you to the lady, Mother says, more than once, but she doesn't mean it.

She hits, when they're slow or stupid, when they're practising their juggling, and they drop one of the carved wooden pins they throw back and forth. She hits when Lannesk doesn't learn on the first telling-through the words of a new song, or Anzimor muddles the chorus. She doesn't mean to, but she does, and sometimes, when she's drunk too much of the strong Outlander spirit that she buys whenever someone pays them with a broken sliver of thin silver Coastlander ship-penny, she hits hard. Lannesk manages to palm a slip of silver, now and then, and keep it from her, to buy food and a place for them by a fire in the lean times. Mother pretends not to know.

Slowly, season by season, year by year, they work their way around and up the west of the Lake, never settling longer than from frost to dry roads. Winters are the worst. Cold and dark and hard, hard, hard. Anzimor can wear what Lannesk outgrows but Lannesk has to beg cast-offs almost every autumn. They don't look like minstrels, bright and defiant; they look like beggars, which they are, patched, ragged, and dull, and his boots are always worn thin and leak; he hobbles with chilblains.

Winters are snow and ice, dark days, and hunger, and huddling together in a draughty corner, while Mother finds some warmer bed to share. She almost always does. She's pretty, still, and mostly she saves her temper for Lannesk, who stands between it and Anzimor as much as he can.

Summers are better. Never mind the mosquitoes. Green roads and clean winds, and folk happy and generous at summer markets and the fairs, and dancing at Kingsday, when the women weave a birch-king and deck him with flowers and give him to the fire, to claim the Forest-blessing for clan and tribe through the coming season. Folk make vows and prayers, pricking a finger and pressing a smear of blood to the stone in offering. They make birch-kings and winter thorn-kings, Mother says, because the dragon-kin were driven into exile and the Dragon bound beneath the Lake by the other Immortals many generations ago, and there is no longer any need for a living King to give themselves to the Dragon. She tells them old tales, sings the old, old lays that no one much remembers any more, she says, save the Singers of the Holy Isle. Those tell of such Kings and heroes, such grim, dark times, when dragons that were not Erryth the Dragon of the Forest came, or famines, and the black years in which the sun was dark and the winter never ended till the Month of Golden Nights and even then there was snow and frost in Haymonth and Harvesting. That was when the Winter King, who had hair like frost and eyes like night and was antlered like a reindeer from the headwaters of the Leda, fought the dragons who came from the ice to challenge Erryth the Golden, whom she served. The Winter King defeated them and drove them back into the northern wastes from which they came, and by her own freely offered death sealed the ways against their returning. But that was in another age.

Lannesk loves best the stories of the Wild King, because he's a musician as well as a warrior, and he defeated Erryth, who was the first and last and greatest of the dragons. The Wild King still rides the Forestways and keeps the land safe. It was he who rallied the tribes and their earls against the enemies who came north through the Skagga Mountains seeking to conquer the free folk of the Forest and take the land for their own, back when Mother's grandfather was a boy, and great-grandfather went with them, though he was not yet old enough to shave, as a servant of his earl's son, and saw the great deeds of the King and his Riders and the spearcarls of the Forest. Those who offered themselves as sacrifice in those days, going to a certain death, still return even now to ride with the King as heroes among the Immortals. And if such enemies and such dark times should come again, if the Dragon beneath the Lake should wake, the King will summon his Riding again.

So her stories tell.

~MAIRRAN~

Nowa and I sailed from Arrunmouth the second morning after my mother spoke with me. The *Snow Goose* had carried us before, though I didn't always go out from the Holy Isle openly, nor with Nowa at my side. But this was official, the prince sent as an envoy of the Queen's displeasure to the province of Laikyn, and after arguing it over, we were even taking our own horses, though I could certainly commandeer whatever I wanted, and from whomever, once we were in Laikyn. But strange horses and I were sometimes an uneasy thing, and Nowa eventually gave in, perhaps more for the consideration that we didn't know what we were heading into, and that it might be as well to prepare to have no welcome at all when we arrived. So we took Smoke and Thorn along, and Mouse, to carry our baggage, and Ermintrud grumbled, as she did whenever she had horses cluttering up the midship hold. She grumbled even more when Thunder and Lightning came swooping down to join us.

It was not as if their fascination with knots and strings and dangling ties had ever done any *great* harm.

The wind was light, but against us. We kept to the coast of the Holy Isle, and for the first day we were rowing—*Snow Goose* had four pair of great oars, fore and aft of the hold amidships where the horses stood, cross-tied and peevish, and their legs wrapped against the bruising and battering of stumbles and rough water. We would have been faster walking along the shore, which yes, was done on the lower stretches on some of the rivers, taking lakers up to an inland harbour by towpaths. Nowa and I took our turn at the great oars too, and I had the blisters and the aching back to prove it. On the second morning, which came with grey skies and a chilling fine drizzle, we—Ermintrud and her shipcarls, with Nowa and I standing well out of the way entirely failing to be useful—raised the yard and angled the oxblood-red sail to catch the wind. It was all slow tacking, making our way out to round South Cape, and no closer to Laikyn than when we'd started. The ravens flew circles, squabbled with gulls, perched on the yard and mocked us, but "as the raven flies" is not as direct as all that and they couldn't have done any better on their own. From even the northern coast of the Holy Isle, North Cape of the Singers, to Laikyn was farther than Thunder and Lightning could manage in unbroken flight. A goose, now, that was a different matter…or a pigeon, but who wants to be prey?

Regardless of what true birds might do, for *Snow Goose*, lacking wings, it was a long run out of sight of land, across the width of the lake to the north-west, once we were able to catch a more favourable wind. Laikyn was the largest island of the Lake, four times the size of the Holy Isle, with a lake of its own, the Fairnmere, at its heart. Only a narrow strait cut it off from the mainland province of the Lann Laitellon. A quiet place, making no trouble for the Queen. I had never been there, openly or in secret.

A long unbroken voyaging, as Lake sailing goes, though Seafolk and Islanders would scoff at the notion of any voyage on the great inland sea as long, even from the mouth of the Rawla in the south to the Leda in the north. Try crossing the ocean, they would say, sail to Illandra or Massenwai, and then you can talk. It felt long enough to me. We ate dry oatcakes and hard cheese and apples through the day, and dark ale, with the usual ship's fare of porridge and stewed smoked fish or bacon with potatoes and cabbage, all cooked together on a sandbox fire for our suppers. When we were drearily rowing and tacking, the crew would make a tent before the mast, where all slept together rolled in blankets and sheepskins on the deck, with one on duty at the steering-oar and a drift-anchor out to stop us being pushed too far astray. I didn't sleep well, those nights, with so many people about. I would crawl out from Nowa's side and go to keep company with the horses. The weather had cleared, so I would watch the waxing moon climb the sky, watch the slow-turning stars, counting the hours of the dark and trying to feel the currents of the Forest, which sometimes I could, moving like shifting waters in the depths of the Lake. But whatever I was looking for—I wasn't sure I even knew—I didn't find it. I couldn't even take out my flute because nobody—Nowa first and foremost of all—wanted to listen to the long wandering music—Nowa would add, if you could call it that—which was what I chased alone at night, when there was nothing but the moon and the stars and the faint heavy presence of the Dark Mother to hear.

Not that I had ever yet managed to capture the song I hunted.

The third night out I fell asleep there, curled up alone and perilously close to the hooves that might not do me harm on purpose, but easily could through no fault of their own. I dreamt of a fox among birches.

Bare trees, the last bright yellow leaves swirling free to fall on a blanket of new snow. The fox is dancing, darting and leaping at the sky as the northern lights burn slow, twisting, flaring and dimming overhead. The raven—who is myself, or is not myself but some dreaming other—spreads black wings to fly to it, and her landing shakes snow from the fine whippy twigs of the birch. The fox stares up at her with brilliant amber eyes and flees into a heap of snow-covered brush.

She, that dreaming other, dreams of hooves, drumming, drumming, pounding the earth. A path worn deep beneath trees, tall smooth ashes and vast elms. The leaves fall and settle, till they come. Riders, and she cannot count them. Men and women, ponies and horses, dogs coursing alongside, and wolves, and other folk running afoot and yet all coming swift together. They run to battle, she knows it, armed with spear and bow and sword and axe. A fox running that is not the fox of the birches. A black mare riderless. A white gyrfalcon and something twists then in her heart and she spread her wings to follow—but before them all rides a man.

Red horse, with a flaxen mane and tail, and the man's hair bronze and copper, streaked as if it catches firelight, and his beard, and his tattered cloak all scraps of multicoloured silk—the costume of a dancer playing the Wild King in a Kingsday pageant. It flies back like a banner with the speed of his riding.

The King rides. I-Mairran, I-she is with him; she-not-I, she-falcon flies at his shoulder. Gold rings like beasts coiling on his bare arms. He carries no spear, only shield at his shoulder, sword at his hip, its pommel a bluestone the size of a duck's egg, rounded and smooth, clutched in gilded raptor's claws. Reins slack, the King holds his harp cradled in his arm, fingers of his left hand just touching to mute the unwanted strings, and with his right he strikes a chord that swells and grows as if a hundred voices join. I am the falcon and still the rider outspeeds me, and his host behind him. But the King checks in his riding, and turns the red horse, and there are only the two of us in all the Forest, and a gale blowing, stripping the leaves from the trees, blowing all the ghosts away, and the trees turn black. Soft white ash is driven like snow in the wind.

The King wears the mask of a pageant-dancer, a thing of leaves and flowers, garland-crowned, but snow, ash, swirls between us and then it is the Huntersnight mask of the priest of sacrifices, the flint-king, white bark and black feathers, stark and lifeless, and there are no eyes looking back at me, only the emptiness of the Dark Beyond, and the strings of the harp are broken, and I know, I know that there is something waiting, there in the Dark, and it is hungry.

I might have yelled. Maybe I only dreamed I did.

I woke tucked beneath the cape of sheepskin I had abandoned, with Nowa sitting by, between me and Smoke's blue-black legs, her hand resting on my shoulder.

"You were dreaming," she said.

Even when I don't remember dreaming, I toss and mutter in my sleep. Still. More than one bedmate has complained of it. In the worst dreams, I used to yell—I've been told I still do—with dreaming rather worse things than a mask with no eyes behind it—and bite at my own hands and arms.

That, at least, I've left behind.

"She burnt his harp," I said. Maybe I was thinking of my father. Long and long ago.

"Whose?" Nowa asked. "You're dreaming, love. Come on, wake now." She passed a hand over my forehead, brushed loose hair from my face. She was only so gentle when she thought I wouldn't know.

"I can't find him," I said, plaintive as a child, as if she would understand that any better, but it was the oldest haunt of my dreams I answered.

Wake him. Call him. We must ride, we must ride—

Frost in the air and breath making clouds. Water froze to a treacherous gloss on the decking. Maybe it was only the weight of winter's approach troubled my sleep, and Huntersnight with it.

The wind changed that day, coming from the east, and the ship was able to run with it cold on the shoulder, making for the north-west, sailing day and night. The crew of twelve kept three watches, but I had nothing to do other than gaze out at the sky and the waves, and whistle the ravens back when it looked as if they might venture beyond sight. Foolish, maybe, but I could feel the water closing over me, in that dream I had of flying out to sea. When I did sleep—beneath the awning on the foredeck and not under the horses' feet—it was fitful, and dream-troubled, and I would twitch awake, knowing how they would whisper, the crew. The shipmaster had had to turn off two of her sailors after the last time she'd carried me, for their talk in the harbour towns that I was haunted by the ghosts of those given to the Forest at my hand, ill-luck to have aboard.

Mostly I seemed to be dreaming of the fox, though, the young vixen furtive and solitary beneath the trees. Not dancing now. Lost, I thought, and afraid, and something in me hurt, that I could do nothing to comfort her.

The eighth day out from Arrunmouth, with the wind gusting east and north, we lost the sun beneath heavy cloud.

"Snow coming," I told Nowa. But there was a thin dark line on the western horizon: the Lakeshore in sight again at last. The island of Laikyn, unless we were badly astray and still below Long Sound, but I did not think so. Even as a boy, I'd had a strong Forest-sense. I always knew, more or less, where I was. Ermintrud, herself taking the steering-oar, called a few orders to those who knew what they were doing with the sheets—tightening this rope and slackening that—and *Snow Goose* swung more directly west, running fast, almost leaping the waves, it felt, like a horse with its barn before it. The shipmaster would take us in close enough to read the coastline and see where we were, turn north or south—and hope the wind was still in a quarter to be some use, because I did not want to row again, or struggle tacking along the coast looking for the mouth of the little Borlinn, which flowed from the Fairnmere.

Or to be on the Lake at all, on a lee shore, if this blew into a gale, though of course lakers could be run aground, no need for a wharf, if the bottom was kind, and there were plenty of creeks into which we might nose our way for shelter, if we could see our way.

I kept my place in the bow, and the ravens came to me, one on each shoulder. I took them on my fists and tossed them aloft, first Lightning, then Thunder. Wished them, *Go, see.*

They flew.

They said the birds of prey were my mother's eyes and ears. That was not true.

But sometimes the ravens were mine.

It was not seeing. It was not…anything I could name, but a certainty in the feel of the land, a taste on the wind, a knowing. Maybe it was only some deepening of the Forest-sense that those who lived or wandered in it deep and alone could learn, as a shipmaster learned the subtle moods and changes of the Lake. But they flew, drawing steadily away, over the Lake and into the Forest, and I felt as though I stretched, not flying with them, but taking up a greater space, breathing more deeply…something like that.

Felt the Forest, a living thing.

We were south of the Borlinn—which Ermintrud would soon be telling us, as the low dark smudge of the trees grew and the shape of the land, the rising hills, became known to her—and I wanted ashore.

"My lord, we're not ten miles from the bay and we'll easily make the mouth of the Bor before nightfall. There's no danger, if the wind doesn't shift northerly, and I think it will hold—"

"Put me ashore," I repeated. "I think—I would rather come to Mair Laikyn overland, and unheralded."

"But my lord, the Queen commanded me to wait on you, through the winter if need be. *Snow Goose* is a Queen's ship; we fly her banner, and besides, we're known. If you aren't there to speak for us, we can hardly put into harbour and pretend we've come to trade, when we're carrying no cargo. And we've no means to support ourselves without your word for our provisioning, if we do get winter-bound."

"The weather's cause enough," I said. "You could have been heading for the Lann Leda, or even over to the Warnavon. Invent some repairs. I'll either come myself or, if I go straight to Mair Laikyn, send a message down to the harbour-reeve to be sure you're given lodging and provisions, and a place to haul out before the ice, trust me. I'll be only few days behind you."

"If you find a road at all, my lord. If you aren't lost and Forest-wildered by nightfall."

"My lord," said Nowa, "is the son of the Queen and Forest-blessed. He does not get himself lost." But she would have been arguing with me, if there had been any place she could have done so without being overheard. "If he says he'll send to you within a few days, he will."

"And if you don't hear anything—wait a week, and then go back to the Holy Isle. Tell the Queen it was my command you do so. She'll know it no lie. She'll not expect you to have disobeyed me."

She would, of course, in such a matter, but her displeasure would mostly be stored up against my return. She was cold, maybe, but fair, by her own lights, when it came to her folk, and those who served her did so without fear of arbitrary cruelty, which is more than one could say for some earls and landtheyns and village elders I'd met in my time.

When it came to her child...that was another matter entirely, but I could not let myself think about that.

Ermintrud shook her head, but frowned at the shore and pointed to a distant hog-backed hill. A creek just a little to the north, she knew, and marshy ground about it, a small cove. She could run in to the shallows and we could get the horses ashore, but the ship would be having to row against the wind to get far enough out to sail again, even tacking. Or moor and wait for it to change.

If that was a play for pity, it didn't work. An urgency tugged at me, and I didn't think it was just the sight of land and the hope of getting off the close quarters of the ship.

Getting the horses to clatter up a little ramp to the afterdeck, and then plunge over the side into the waves—the keel brushing bottom in the muddy shallows of the cove and the ship canting over, wind against broadside and part-reefed sail, nearly dipping the top strake—was no easy matter, and nor was getting *Snow Goose* turned out to the Lake again, though Ermintrud managed it without capsizing or running aground. No one but Nowa and I—and the horses—ended up soaked, either. The ravens came back to find us and circled, croaking laughter.

So prince and swordtheyn, we carried our belongings and weapons on our shoulders to shore after the horses, and waved Ermintrud off, shouting assurances we would get word to her in the harbour of the Borlinn in a few days, and—given the wind she would have to fight to get offshore again—maybe reach the river ahead of her.

"If you don't take a chill and catch your death before then, my lord," she called through cupped hands.

I shrugged that off without comment. I was not utterly a fool. We had our axe, and found a good site for a camp a little up the brook, sheltered from the east by a stand of young spruces. It didn't take long to start a fire; there was always lots of fine dry deadwood for kindling where evergreens choked out their own inner branches from the sun, and old-man's-beard growing plentiful for tinder. Not much longer to fell some birch saplings and make a shelter, low and open-fronted, back to the wind and facing the fire, roofed and floored with spruce boughs. We'd done this before. Dried off the horses, who hadn't taken much harm and were glad enough to have solid ground under their hooves again. Forest horses are a tough breed. Satisfied with a few handfuls of grain, they wandered along the brookside, finding enough to graze and browse on to keep them going. Nowa and I weren't prepared to supply ourselves for long, but the horses could make do till they came to farmed countryside again. Then dry socks, steaming boots, steaming everything, much of which we were still wearing. We made a meal off oatcakes and cheese, feeding the hard rinds to the ravens, heated water in the little copper self-boiler we always lugged along—much faster than using a kettle hanging over the campfire, and useful when we didn't want to make a big fire, or any at all, which—was sometimes a consideration—and sat companionably drinking hot snaps-and-water shoulder to shoulder, wrapped in cloaks and sheepskin capes, warming ourselves from both inside and out.

It was after noon by then. The wind dropped a little, but it carried fat white feather-flakes, and the sky was heavy and grey with the promise of more. I had a flask of red snaps, too—I always did—infused with the root of kingswort, which flowers late in the Month of Golden Nights. I took a swallow or two of that, icy-cold in the mouth and burning bitter heat going down. Nowa gave me a disapproving look, but it wasn't as if I'd taken enough to make myself tipsy or clumsy, certainly not drunk, even on top of the watered-down cup we'd shared earlier. But I felt as though dreams were hovering, waiting for me. I wanted to forestall them.

The dusk came on rapidly under the thick cloud. I had an almanac along—it was a part of my duty to be sure of the heavens—but didn't bother to consult it for this; I'd looked up the tables and been watching the stars as we'd come up the Lake. We would have a good fifteen hours of darkness here, in this season. Dry and warm, now, but there was no point moving on until morning. Thunder and Lightning were settled for the night, roosting sheltered in the spruces.

"So why are we here, rather than snug aboard the *Snow Goose* and arriving under the White Dragon as the Queen's envoy should?" Nowa asked.

I shrugged. I didn't know.

Nowa was good at silence. One of the many things I liked about her. And she knew when there was no point pushing. All she said to that lack of answer was, "Should we keep a watch?" and then, "Do we want to sleep in our mail?"

"I don't know," I said. "No. And no. I think not."

She grunted, not much liking either answer, but she'd hardly have liked a "yes," either.

"Should have brought one of your pet minstrels along to pass the time," she said.

"Not with you in the bed too."

She jabbed me with an elbow.

"I could sing," I offered.

"Don't."

Which was hardly fair. She was the one who couldn't carry a tune.

"And no wailing on that flute, either."

I protested that I hadn't even thought of suggesting it.

"I swear, someday that's going to be ash."

"Don't," I said, because the flute, made from some exotic wood of Illandra, golden with a strong dark grain, had been a gift, some years back, from the Outlander minstrel who was my first lover, exotically far-travelled and wise with many winters—she had been twice my age at the time, all of thirty. Dove played the bronze-strung harp of the Islanders, many-stringed, shaped like the profile of a billowing sail and held on the knee to be plucked with both hands—a completely different instrument from the six or seven-stringed Forest-harps, gut-strung. Hers was a beautiful thing that could sing like all the birds of the Forest on a spring morning, but that didn't give her the right to scoff at the Forest-harp or call it by an Outlander name, denying it its own.

It had been my mother who put me in Dove's way, and maybe the minstrel had her own reasons for taking the Queen's half-feral offspring to her bed, but I wanted to think Dove had come to like me, that summer, well enough in my own right. I had liked her, too. And so I treasured her gift.

Before Nowa could suggest breaking out the bag of coloured pebbles and the leather square on which she had burnt the lines of fox-

and-raven—she complained I never thought ahead, and then gloated when she won but called it luck if I did—I took the axe and went to cut more wood from what I could find that was dry and dead. Mostly spruce, poplars, birch, and red maple there, and fairly young growth, the greatest trunks no more than a foot across, as if a fire had passed through some years back. Jackpines on the higher ground. Bracken stood as dead brown stalks, frost-blighted. The last few leaves of the trees hung heavy, clumped with the falling snow. Lots of wind-broken deadwood, so close to the shore. Charred stumps and massive fallen trunks I found, as well, though too far gone in decay for burning, grown over with red-capped lichen. Nowa rounded up the straying horses and tethered them where they could still browse, though not on maple, before she made up a bed. Boots and belts off, but otherwise we lay down as we were, close together for warmth. Nowa could sleep anywhere. She would say it was a skill learnt as a road-warden, but I'm sure I must have spent as much time as she ranging wild in the Forest, and I still haven't found the knack of it.

I wanted to be off, roaming.

The horses shuffled and stamped, bunched together, tails to the wind. The spruces whined and hissed, and the snowflakes sizzled over the fire.

I dreamed of birch trees.

I didn't think I'd been asleep, but I woke, and ragged islands of clear stars were breaking through torn clouds. The full moon hung bright in the south, silvering birch-trunks, sparkling on the snow. I wormed out of the heap of bedding without waking Nowa—which, sound sleeper though she was, nonetheless took some doing—and pulled on my boots and the hooded shoulder-cape lined with eastern shore black squirrel. Took the flint knives which I never left behind, their sheaths fastened to the belt that cinched my tunic, always, but left off my sword-belt. Nowa had rolled more than her share of the blankets around herself, including my cloak, so I took one of the sheepskin capes that had been an extra layer over our feet, cautiously, lest the change in weight wake her. She didn't stir.

I didn't reach for the spear leaning against the shelter roof, either.

I thought I smelled fox.

Pawprints in the new-fallen snow.

The horses were alert, ears pricked, and all turned together, like ships nudged by the wind, to stare in the same direction. Smoke rumbled softly and pawed at the snow, nostrils flaring.

Nowa had hoisted the bags of our provision higher than I could reach, a rope cast over the branch of a red maple and tied to a lower, safe from wolverines, raccoons, wolves, and bears not yet denned up. But not, apparently, from more agile thieves.

She perched on the branch over which the rope was slung. A naked girl, midway between child and adult. Bony, too-thin face, a spiky mane of short light hair. Jutting bones—collarbones, ribs, hipbones, knobby elbows showing sharp-shadowed in the moonlight. She clung with her toes, one hand grabbing to steady herself as she let fall the bags she had pulled up. They bounced and swung while she stared, eyes wide, pools of shadow. Chewing hastily, swallowing whatever she had crammed into her mouth.

Then she dropped, caught the branch, swung out and leapt, and was on four legs running, dodging through the trees and the broad stumps, jumping the crumbling logs.

I leapt after her, but on two legs I couldn't overtake a fox, lumbered with clothes and boots and sheepskin. No point running, and a fox could, and would, go where Smoke could not follow. I settled into a steady jog-trot along her trail.

~LANNESK~

Shouting in the night. Lannesk and Anzimor wake together. Sometimes there's arguing, when they've been promised a payment and cheated of it, or when too much ale drives Mother and a lover to quarrelling. This is different. Her voice goes high and shrill and frightened. The man's a widower who inherited his wife's longhouse because there were no daughters or sisters, and the household's only him and his sons, who are bigger than Lannesk but not yet grown and married. It's a small household, only one cow and an ox to drag the logs and pull the cart, and a field of buckwheat around the coppice-stools, somewhere in the south of a great island called Laikyn. The man's bed is by the hearth beyond the wattle screen that divides the house into an end for people and an end for beasts, while the boys sleep in the haymow with the cow and ox brought in for the night beneath, the calf penned in a corner.

The man's sons lie quiet and unhappy, but they don't do anything. He beats them when they're slow at their work and they're afraid of him, because he hits so hard. He's beaten Lannesk, too, more than a few times, and Mother shouted at him, but they didn't leave. It's late in the Month of Falling Leaves and there's hard frost at night. Likely they'll spend the winter; that's the way of things. It's not so bad save for the man's heavy fists. There's enough to eat, anyway, and Anzimor doesn't get hit. It's his job to take the cow out to graze along the Forest paths, to meet up with the village herd, to work in the garden and then to go to fetch her home again, while Lannesk and the father and sons cut wood and Mother grinds buckwheat with the quern and makes heavy sour hearth-bread.

Now he and Anzimor lie still and afraid like the man's own sons. But then mother cries out again, and Lannesk goes like a kingfisher diving down the ladder, so fast he doesn't know it, only he's on the bracken-strewn floor by the startled cow, and he takes the stick Anzimor uses to drive the cow, though he never beats her as the man's sons do, because Anzimor says cows do what you want if you sing to them—and anyway, the cow knows where she's supposed to go and why shouldn't she go at her own pace—and he vaults over the dividing screen rather than going around, and Mother is on the floor beside the bed as if she's trying to crawl away and the man has hold of her by her hair and is trying to bang her head on the floor.

Lannesk swings the stick, hard, as if it's the broadaxe that's still too heavy for him to use with any skill, and the man flings up an arm so that he hits that instead of the man's head.

The man yells, but he's let go of Mother. He grabs and wrenches the stick away from Lannesk, and swings a fist that knocks him back onto his rump and Anzimor's there, going low to grab the man around the leg and bite him, hard, like a dog, on his naked thigh—the man's only wearing a shirt, nothing else, and he grabs Anzimor with both hands and hurls him away so he hits one of the posts that hold up the rafters. Mother shrieks, jumping to her feet. She's not wearing even a shirt. The man swings the stick at Mother. She ducks. Lannesk lunges at the man and kicks him where he's dangling still half-stiff and swollen. The man falls down yelling and clutching himself, but he puts his heel into the fire in his falling and that sends him rolling back up to his feet, calling Lannesk things he's never heard even when folk are fighting outside an alehouse.

Mother's crouching over Anzimor, who's crying, but these days Anzi cries when he gets angry, not when he's hurt, and he's struggling to get free and Lannesk doesn't want him to. Lannesk thinks the man might kill someone, he's so enraged, and Anzimor is the smallest. He puts himself in front of the man again, so he can't get at Anzimor and Mother, and the man lunges and grabs him by the throat with both hands and he's shouting that he'll wring his neck like a fowl's, dirty little Mothers-sucking Outland bastard that he is. Doesn't remember falling but he's on his back on the cold earthen floor with the man heavy over him and his throat's on fire and he can't breathe, and the tide's rushing over him, hot and burning, red as sunset light.

~Mairran~

The little vixen was cunning, after the first panicked dash for cover. Snow and moonlight showed her tracks plain, wide-spaced as she stretched, running. Led me into a clump of balsam fir, and I wasn't quite enough of a fool to follow, because even a naked starveling child could bash me over the head with a rock or a broken branch. I circled around the evergreens till I had the whiff of fox plain to my nose again, and no tracks, but a disruption of shaken snow. She'd gone up the trees, but not to hide. Along through more maples, precarious tree to tree, and down—cunning, yes—into the black chiming water of the ice-fringed brook. No scent of her on the wind, which still came from the Lake, up the little valley. So I went upstream, soft-foot in the snow, watching for tracks and the disturbance she would make scrambling out on either bank, but the clouds tumbled together again and the moon dimmed to a faint grey smudge, the dark eating even the snow. I could still see as well as any fox—tree-trunks, snow, humps and hollows—but the fine detail of tracks was washed away. And without the moon Nowa wasn't going to find even my tracks to follow. Too late to worry about that now.

Snow began to fall again, smaller, finer flakes. The night was growing colder. Birch trees and rising ground beyond the brook. Shallow, chiming over stones to hide any incautious splashing as I waded across, and I had not greased my boots since they'd been in the Lake and dried, so they leaked, icy water seeping into my socks, and in the cold and a walk of a couple of miles back, even if following the brook would be shorter than the roundabout way the little fox had led me, that risked frostbite. Should have thought of that sooner, shouldn't I?

Without Nowa at my side, I had to nag myself.

And there, not yet buried in snow, fox tracks, and on a well-trodden path at that, back and forth to the water's edge. Human shoes had made it.

Smoke, too, in the air.

I walked very softly and warily. New snow, not cold enough to squeak or hard enough to crunch, and the fallen leaves tramped to mould, and silent. Stood still and watchful among the trunks with the snow falling around me and the wind strengthening. Pile of brush, in my dream. A small domed brush-hut, here, bowed saplings covered over with boughs of fir and spruce, and smoke leaking through. Heap of broken deadfall by it, and much tramping back and forth and into the woods where she'd gone gathering wood, fearing winter's approach. She'd be much warmer, snugger in her little den, keeping as a fox, but there'd be a fear in that, too. Wolves kill foxes. Lynx will, and so can eagles, if the fox is caught out in the open.

And there'd be the fear of losing herself. Of finding it all too easy for Fox to fade into mere fox, and the self that was Fox and Girl together to become a dream.

I went carefully weaving through the trees. I was upwind, and that wind should have carried my scent, but she would smell nothing but smoke, inside. I circled to the doorway. I couldn't have stood upright within the hut, and the door was only a low opening blocked with a bundle of fir-boughs. She'd been in and out as both human and fox, but I could smell her now, vixen, girl, something faint of both, and subtle tang of whatever it was that made her whatever she was, a thing beyond mere Forest-blessing. Maybe it wasn't even smelling. There was just no better word for it, that sense of something … not quite human.

Of course, by then I was so close that despite the smoke she could smell — or whatever one should call it — me, too, even if she didn't know what it was that she was suddenly aware of, there prowling to her very door, and she burst out through and past the screen of branches, fox trailing a ragged shirt, tangled in it, too panicked to strip off the bit of clothing she had begun to pull on. I was ready and dropped my sheepskin cape over her, flung myself down, grabbing her under it, bundling her up, she squirming and snapping and squealing as if I were skinning her alive. Held her fast and tight through all her thrashing and yipping and snapping, held her tight when her teeth sharp as needles closed in my forearm, and held her tight still when she went limp. Then I knocked the door-screen fully aside and crawled into the hut on knees and elbows, holding her fast, tight to my chest.

My toes were growing numb and I wanted her fire. Also my arm hurt.

"Hush now," I said. "Hush, and listen. I'm not going to hurt you, little vixen. You're safe with me."

So long as she hadn't murdered any earls, anyway, but it seemed unlikely.

"I'm not your enemy."

She whimpered. The poor thing was shivering. And she was going to bite me again, and bolt out and be gone and lost and die in the Forest, afraid and alone, if I let go of her.

"I'm truly not your enemy. Here you are alone, and afraid, and hungry. Raiding our camp like that—half starved, aren't you? Can you not hunt?" Still she shivered. Well, a fox, no less than a human, has to learn, and learning comes easier if taught. And not so easy, for one hunted out of their home. If one was a thing that was a wonder and a Forest-blessed hero in a ballad but an unnatural monster when it's born to some everyday hearth. I could guess at her story, and it wasn't *The Lay of the Fox-lad and the Daughter of Snows*. How old might she be? Thirteen, fourteen winters?

"Believe I'm your friend, little cub. Believe I can protect you. All right? Will you stay, if I let you go? Here, I'm going to set you down, here by the door, and I'll go back and sit on your bed. See? You'll be able to be out the door and away before I can stop you."

And if she did, I would strip and be off and after her, and overtake her too, because I was not leaving the child to die here alone, as seemed all too likely to be her fate. If that meant carrying her back to Nowa by the scruff of her neck I would do it.

I set her down, as I'd said. Such a slight weight. I might almost have thought she had slipped away and gone. It was the sort of trick the Fox-lad would pull, in one of the more light-hearted ballads.

But when I shuffled back on my knees, around the small fire smouldering in the ashy firepit, and sat, with an unnecessary amount of rustling and crackling, on the heap of bracken over boughs that did for her bed, too close to the fire for safety, the sheepskin stirred and heaved and a small pointed head and enormous ears poked out, amber eyes gleaming in the firelight. She bared her teeth at me.

"We could talk," I said. I sat cross-legged, hands on knees, trying very much to be not a threat. My arm hurt. It was bleeding: warm, wet, growing stain. "I'd like to take my boots off, get my feet dry. If you wouldn't mind?"

And of course someone in their sock feet, or barefoot, was even less of a threat when it came to chasing down a fox in a winter forest, yes? So I unfolded myself, slowly and cautiously, and worked off one boot and sock, and then the other, and propped them closer to the sullen fire. Tucked my feet up again, rubbing my toes. They ached and burned, beginning to warm.

"My name's Mairran," I said. "Tell me yours? I'll look away while you dress, if you'd rather." I turned his head to show earnest, but I could see movement in the corner of my eye. Fox, still wrapped in the sheepskin. The space of a breath, no more, a shape larger, hunched, arms stirring, wrapping the cape around herself. A thin, tan-skinned face, the fox's amber eyes, a spiky head of coppery hair gleaming in the firelight. Crouched, ready to run, to shift again, to hurl half-burned and smouldering sticks at my face—it was what I might have done, anyway.

"You're sitting on my clothes," she said, her voice hoarse with disuse, barely more than a whisper, and sullen as her fire.

So I was, and the shirt that had been all she wore when she shifted to run was half out the door at her back. She remembered, and reached around to drag it in, and then the screen of brush, though she left a fox-sized gap in setting it in place. Clutched the shirt to her, and other clothes, ragged much-worn things, when I leaned to give them to her snatching hand. No cloak, no blanket, no caped hood, not even a shawl or headscarf. She had run, I guessed. Run to the Forest without the chance even to grab a wrap. And the shoes were poor thin things stuffed with dry grass for warmth; she'd tried to repair the holes with a lining of birchbark. At least she had a knife, a little blade in a worn sheath, of a size fit for minor household chores, and probably she'd been using it for everything from hacking the saplings till they would break for her hut to skinning and gutting prey—I suspected she hadn't yet brought herself to eat much while in fox's form. It's hard, at first, to swallow down gobbets of slick raw hot meat, or a mouse still squirming.

The knife, I stayed sitting on.

"How long have you been out here on your own?" I asked. "Look, it's safe, truly. Get dressed." I made himself busy, leaning to feed the fire with broken deadwood from another heap of twigs and branches by the wall, then pushing up the sleeve of tunic and shirt, frowning at the bite. It wasn't deep. She had snapped and let go. Shocked, maybe, at the realization of teeth in human flesh. The blood welled up, which was better than not, cleansing. I put my mouth to it, till I thought what Nowa would say.

The girl didn't want to get dressed. She wanted to be able to shift and run. She stayed as she was, hunkered down by the door, clutching her rags, with my cape, which was no longer than would come down to my hips and not a lot longer on her, wrapped close. Staring, with the sort of dull fear that a deer shows when it's been run to exhaustion.

"Or don't," I said obligingly. "What's your name? I'm Mairran."

"You said." Her voice still wasn't much more than a whisper. "Like the prince. The Queen's carrion crow."

"Yes, very like. What are you called?"

They say magic could be worked with a name. It isn't true. Knowing the truth of a thing, that's what mattered, not what one calls it. I thought I had her truth, but I wasn't going to magic her to submission. Not if there were any other way.

"Sage," she said. Reluctant. Too exhausted, I thought, to lie. But her teeth nipped off something more. Sage of—I didn't much care which tribe she belonged to or what village or forester's camp had spawned her and driven her out, nor yet which landtheyn might have claimed her family's service. She was mine, now.

I didn't like to think what Nowa was going to say. Or my mother.

It was suddenly very important that my mother not know.

"Sage," I said. "Good. Sage, I'm not going to hurt you. I'm not, truly. I think we should go back to my camp, before my shield-companion wakes up and finds me gone. And then we make breakfast, and find you some warmer clothes, and—" I shrugged. "—go on from there."

"I'm a fox," she said, as if I might not have noticed.

"You're not," I said. "The Fox-lad wasn't a fox, or a man. The Grey Hunter wasn't a wolf, or a falcon, or a woman. The Fisher wasn't man or mare or otter. They were shapeshifters. It's not a bad thing. It just...is. Really. It's a blessing that they say is gone, faded out of the Forest, but—here you are."

"They're dead," she said. "They died and they left us, they left the Forest, they're gone. That's what the songs say. But the Immortals were never true, not the Wild King, not the Fox-lad, not even the mortal faylings. None of them."

"You are," I said. "Those are real fangs. You bit me."

She hunched lower, as if she could make herself even smaller. I rolled my sleeves down, pulled my socks on, and my boots. They were not dry, but damp and warm was better than not.

"Put your clothes on. Get your things together while I put out the fire," I ordered. "You can't stay here, though it's a very good hut; you're already starving and winter's barely begun. I'll take you into my service. How are you with horses? Do you like birds? Not for eating, I mean. As pets. Sort of pets. Ravens. They're more...pests that follow me around. They don't really need looking after, but they like to have someone make a fuss over them. You could do that."

Sage didn't bolt. I thought she might, then, the way she froze, staring, eyes all horror. What had I said? I reached a hand, drew it back when she flinched.

Didn't want to watch as she unfolded and drew on her clothes, awkward, hands shaking, trying to keep the cape about her and never taking her eyes off me. Made a show of poking about to see what other small treasures she might have stashed, beyond that poor excuse for a knife. No firesteel, and not a chip of flint. She must have managed to start a fire by the wearying means of drilling with a stick, and keeping it alive would have been the core of her existence since then, I expected. No cup, no spoon, no comb. A basket of folded birchbark which she must have made to take foraging. Autumn would not have been so desperate as what would come. There would have been hazelnuts, mushrooms, berries, haws, and the astringent little fruit of the thorny wild crabapples. A long branch sharpened to a two-pronged spear. She had been fishing. Maybe she would have done all right, if she had grown more confident in her hunting as a vixen, learnt at least to dig out the mice and voles running beneath the snow. Maybe. I didn't think she would have had the time.

She didn't even have a blanket.

I used the birchbark basket to smother the fire with deep ashes, and then crawled out and back to throw on some snow, which melted hissing and filled the hut with steam like a sweat-house. Sage was dressed by then. She held the sheepskin cape out to me mutely.

"You'd better keep that on," I told her. It had an antler toggle at the neck, and I fastened it for her, as if she were a little child. She seemed to have gone that way, utterly meek and broken, and for all her chill shivering she sweated fear. I didn't know what to do about that, except be very gentle and careful, as with a frightened horse. Didn't know what I'd done to make her so. She'd been frightened, yes, but not so devastatingly, surly but not broken, when I'd caught her.

Took her by the hand and set off, not keeping to the track I had made following her but crossing the brook where there were stones enough to keep our feet dry, then going along with the water at our right hand, not too close, to avoid the underbrush thick and tangling along the bank.

The snow blew into our faces, cut through my quilted tunic, so that I was shivering too, before very long. Sage stumbled, tripped over branches, fell into hollows, though I had no doubt but that she could see in the dark almost as well as I could. Legs weakened with her fear. She became a drag on my hand, until after I fell too, through not letting go of her, I scooped her up in my arms. Shivering and passive and not much of a weight at all. But heavy enough as I trudged on, with her head against my shoulder.

"You'd be lighter, and warmer, too, as the vixen," I said. But she shook her head, face turned away. I sighed. "All right. Up on my back, though, or I'm going to end up falling on top of you next time I trip."

Docile, she obeyed, and I took her up piggyback. The night was wearing on, the broken clouds had thickened to a solid low sky again, and still the snow fell. My tracks, leaving our camp, would be vanishing beneath it, even if Nowa could see them at all in that overcast night, which I doubted. Yet I kept my ears pricked, as it were. I'd laid on more wood before I left, but still, the cold of my absence and the dying fire should have woken her by now.

I smelt the horse before I heard him, knew the scent for Thorn. Whistled, and heard its echo answer. Whistled again, calling, *safe*, and *come to me*, and leaned a shoulder against a tree, waiting. We were back in the deep humps and hollows of the old burn scar, and I was starting to feel it had been a very long night. And a cold one, also.

Splashing in the brook as Nowa crossed back, then soft thudding of hooves and Thorn whickered, a pale shape taking form, rising from a dip in the land, plunging eagerly forward and then tossing his head, reaching out to blow and snuffle at the stranger on my back. Thorn was bridled, not saddled. Nowa had no spear, in the dark and the trees, but her own sword belted on and mine slung by its belt over her shoulder; she had carried my cloak draped over the horse's withers and her knees.

"My lord, Mothers be my witness, if I don't put an end to you myself one of these days—Do you want it to be *my* heart's blood they give the Forest come Huntersnight, when I have to go back and say I've let you run off to die in the snow?" But she leapt down and reached to take Sage from me. "Where did this come from?"

The girl struggled, not to escape, only a little protest at being handled about, and Nowa set her on her feet, keeping a grip on her shoulders.

"It was raiding our provisions."

"And you had to chase it halfway across the island to catch it?"

"Hardly that," I said, Laikyn being well over a hundred miles across. "And it's a she. Both ways." That was known of those with the shapeshifters' Forest-blessing in all the tales, that they might be in male in one of their forms and female in another. "Yes, she did take some chasing. She's a nippy thing, when she goes on all fours. A Forest-blessed shapeshifter, Nowa. Her name's Sage, and she's a vixen, too. Sage, this is my shield-companion, Swordtheyn Nowa. Don't mind her. She's all right once you get used to her."

Sage said nothing, only hung her head. And all Nowa said, on a long breath, was, "Ahh."

I supposed it was exhaustion, hunger, cold, the aftermath of terror...all of that, turning time into a baffling nightmare for the girl. We bundled her up in Nowa's cloak over the sheepskin cape, and Nowa gave me my sword and bundled me in my own cloak and scolded some more, and gave me a leg up on Thorn, hoisting the girl up to carry before me. We went back so, not all that far now, with the horse warm beneath me. The fire was burning cheerfully and our smaller pot of beaten copper keeping warm on the chimney of the self-boiler, squatting in a patch of melting snow on its four clawed feet. I could smell that some strips of dry ham were being steeped into a sort of salt broth, no doubt meant to revive me once Nowa had fished me out of whatever trouble she presumed I'd fallen into.

Thunder and Lighting, who'd been told that ravens weren't nocturnal but had a natural disdain for authority, had both come down from their roost to perch on what was left of my pile of firewood, to be close to anything happening that might involve food.

Nowa left it to me to tend to Thorn and make a little fuss over Smoke and Mouse to apologize for their having been left behind, while she dug through a bag and put my woollen single-layer tunic on Sage over her own, and a pair of my socks, too, before tucking her around with blankets, sitting just inside the open front of the shelter, feet to the fire. Hot water and snaps to warm her belly, and a wooden bowl of the steaming broth, oatcakes crumbled into it to make a porridge and a horn spoon to eat it with. Nowa had to take the mazer back, Sage's hands shook so. Frowning, setting it aside and putting the back of her hand to the girl's forehead. But I didn't think she was fevered. I crawled into the shelter too, squatting on my heels to consider. All the fight had gone out of her, back there in her own hut, and I hadn't done anything to cause it.

"Sage…"

"Are you going to kill me?" The words were an unsteady whisper.

"No!" I said. "I don't kill children."

"You're him." Her face looked terrible, pinched and sickly pale now, and her eyes brimming with tears. "The prince. With the ravens. With the knives. For the offerings. You kill people. For the Queen."

"Only when she tells me to," I said, as if that made it any better. "Not for fun." Should have bitten my tongue, rather than speak at all, but I babbled on. "Any earl has some armscarl who wields the axe when the justices find a person guilty to the death under the law. It's no different." Scowled at the look Nowa was giving me, but just try thinking of something reassuring to say when a child looks at you like that. The sickness in your belly drives out all common sense.

Nowa would of course say, I never had much to start with.

I took the girl's hands. They were so cold. Rubbed them between my own, as if those weren't as bad, because had I thought to put on my mittens before setting off? Only long cuffs and keeping my hands within the sheepskin had kept my fingers from freezing. Common sense, lack of… Lightning chose then to come flapping in to perch on my head, talons pricking, leaning and twisting to take a better look at the girl. Probably considering whether she could get away with snatching a strand of ham from the dish. Nowa shooed the bird away.

"Sage. Sage, look at me? Sweetheart, little sister, I'm not going to hurt you. I am not. I'm not going to let anyone else hurt you, either. You're mine, I said, if you've no home worth going back to. My carl, of my household. Your landtheyn, your village elders, your family, whoever it was drove you out here—the Queen herself won't take you from me."

That last was one promise better not to make, one I couldn't keep. But I didn't see why it should come up, if we were careful and kept the fact that she was Forest-blessed, and the rare nature of her blessing, to ourselves. My mother was always saying I needed better service, more of a household than Nowa alone.

The tears rolled down Sage's face and I didn't know whether she believed me or not, but I had the sense then to back off and leave her to Nowa and her bowl of mushy oatcakes and shredded ham.

I took the flask of kingswort snaps, and my cloak, and went to brood on the other side of the fire, to warm my feet and finish drying my boots.

The Queen's carrion crow.

~LANNESK~

Red panic, and he strikes out, struggling, drowning, can't breathe — "Shh, shh, Lan, Lan, it's me, it's all right, don't thrash around or you'll choke again, shh…"

It's Anzimor, and there's a taste in his mouth, honey. Lannesk lies still. Breathing hurts. Breathing's hard. He has to drag the air in, as if it's something almost too big to shift, as if he has to brace his heels, every muscle straining. There's a horrid whistling wheeze, in and out. Mother, he wants to ask, and Anzimor seems to read his mind.

"She killed him," Anzimor says. "She hit him with an axe, and she told the boys, they could help her bury him and say he'd gone off with her, and keep the house and land-right as their proper inheritance from their mother, or they could face the village grandmothers and explain how they'd stood by and watched their father strangle a child to death. They said they'd help. Mother told them what to do. They never were very clever, themselves, were they? They chopped a hole through the ice in the swamp away up through the alders and weighted him with the quern-stones so he doesn't float come spring—I guess they'll be eating groats all the winter—and we put him in it. I don't think they minded much, really. I think maybe their mother died of too much beating. So he's gone. She wrapped your neck all up in wool and splints to keep your head still so you could breathe and—and you didn't die. So when we came back with the ox from the swamp, she told them again what they had to say, and they helped her put you on her back like a baby, and we walked away. I thought you really were dead, Lan."

And he starts crying then.

Lannesk wants to tell him to stop, but it's hard enough to breathe. He can't force a word out. He moves a hand, feebly, and squeezes Anzimor's, and Anzimor wipes his face on his sleeve.

"You need to eat," he says. And he swipes a finger into the little pot he holds and sticks it into Lannesk's mouth, rubs it on his tongue.

Honey.

He tries to suck, to swallow. It hurts. It burns. It feels, not like a bruise, but like he's all ripped and raw, and all that raw flesh smashed together into a knot. He tries to turn his head away and Anzimor says, "Don't," his voice going all high and shaky, so he doesn't. He sucks, and swallows, which hurts so much he has to think himself through it, and the honey goes into him, slowly, slowly, one finger's-worth at a time. Water and weak ale, too, a horn made of birchbark and a teat stitched of leather, and he sucks that, again and again, until he's so tired he can't, and then Anzi lets him be, and lies down next to him, an arm over him, as if he's the elder brother now.

Honey, water, ale. Honey, ale, the thinnest of gruels sweetened with honey and maple sugar and strained through a sieve of woven straw. There's a fire. There's a roof. There's Anzimor. He panics when he wakes and Mother isn't there, but each time, Anzi tells him that she's gone to find a friend to help.

He's glad Anzimor believes it. He's ashamed he does not. He thinks it would be easier to die, but Anzimor is still so young, only nine winters. He can't survive on his own.

They're not on their own in this place, which is a cave with a lean-to built over the front of it, where the fire is. There's an old woman. She has dark, dark eyes, almost black, and wears a long gown of tanned deerskin and ties her hair up in loops with red and blue threads and dangling beads of pink mud-snail shells out of the Lake, which even the poorest folk of the Forest can afford. A witch and holy hermit, Anzimor whispers. She's gone all day, harvesting mushrooms, which hang drying in the smoke of the fire, and buds and shrivelling berries, not all of which are good to eat. She makes medicines, or charms for good fortune or blessings or curses, who knows. Once she takes a deep basket on her back and a staff in her hand and strides away for several days. When she comes back, she has half a dozen eggs wrapped in straw, though how she found anyone with hens still laying in this dark of the year is a wonder, and Anzimor stirs them up with lots of butter over the fire till they're just slightly set, and Lannesk eats that a little bit at a time out of a horn spoon.

She sings, sometimes, but not in any language they know, Forest or Coastlander. She's from far in the north, Anzimor says, though how he knows, Lannesk never learns, since she doesn't speak any language they know, either. But she and Anzimor understand each other well enough. She found them on a Forestway, Anzimor said, and brought them here, and then Mother went. It was as if she knew to find them, where they were walking, slow and weary beyond thought, slogging through deep snow, Anzimor breaking trail without skis or snowshoes, and Mother leaning on a staff, bent nearly double, with Lannesk tied to her back, his legs dragging. Winter has come early.

You can tell the Forestways because they're narrow, not a road fit for wagons, and they don't grow up in trees and brambles even though no one ever clears them. Villages and farmsteads avoid them; foresters never use them to haul timber. Sometimes sunken deep, and sometimes marked by waystones, like anchorstones but smaller, set up to mean something long ago, though no one remembers what. Often the snow hides the stones. The little fayling-folk ride their moon-pale ponies along them, when they come out from their hollow hills, the songs say, and the Riders may come down them like a storm when the Wild King calls a Riding, and if you are so foolish as to be travelling on a Forestway when he rides, you may be swept up in his train and fall out of the living world, and be doomed to run forever through the Forest and through the stars with his Riders and his wolves and his hounds.

But that's another song they learnt from Mother. Anzimor says it would have been good, if there had been Riders like a storm, to trample a hard road for them through the drifts. He laughs.

Folk don't travel on Forestways, generally. They're for festival days, when folk will follow them to the fanes, singing and dancing, or with singing and torches and sleighs decorated with evergreen boughs at Huntersnight, the only time one may drive on them, or they'll take the herds along them a mile or two in the spring at Pasturing, for blessing. But they run far, the Forestways, far beyond villages and pastures and assarts, into the deepest, most secret hearts of the Forest; they weave a web all through the Forest, fane to fane, anchorstone to anchorstone. Mother told them that, in her Singer's voice, when first they came to the Forest.

Lannesk wonders if they've done something against Forest lore, by travelling on the Way for a reason that's far from holy, fleeing with a murdered man behind them. There's no other track near the hermit's cave, only the Forestway, and the waystone below the cave is hung about with red and blue threads and beads of pink shell like her hair.

Maybe she's what a fayling really is. Just a woman who's gone to the Forest, which seems not such a bad way to live, far from other folk, quiet and alone. He thinks of himself and Anzimor becoming hermits with her. Apprentice hermits. It's a thought that makes a laugh bubble in his chest, but there's only pain when it tries to come out, and he can't tell Anzimor. A hollow hill might be just another name for a cave.

Lannesk eats what he can, and tries to walk around, to get his strength back, so that, apprentice hermits or not, they can be useful to the holy woman through the winter, in return for her kindness. Breathing, swallowing, those grow slowly easier, but it hurts when he tries to make a word, and the sound is just a wheezing like a bagpipe deflating.

Then one cold white morning, there are hooves stamping, harness creaking and jingling. Riders, ordinary human riders, on the Forestway. It's Mother.

Mother, wearing high boots and a warm cloak and fur mittens, and armed men and women with her, and a wiry little man with dark hair, they all make way for, and the hilt of his sword is gilded.

Brux, he says. *Earl* Brux.

Long ago, he was a student at the Singersborg with Mother. But his sister died, and his cousin Lady Tannis, who is, he says, a greedy fool who treats her folk like cattle, took his mother's earldom in a part of Laikyn north of the Fairnmere, being her nearest female kin and land-heir. So he left the Singersborg on the Holy Isle to claim the earldom for himself. And Mother, who was his sweetheart, wouldn't go with him, but went to make her summer-wandering instead and be a Singer, and...

"You should have sent to me," he said. "As soon as you came back to the Forest, you should have sent to me."

"I was a fool," Mother says. "I was ashamed."

It's obviously the sort of thing they've said to one another before, and now they say it again, because Lannesk and Anzimor and the hermit are there to hear. Lannesk doesn't know if it's true; Mother has that bright smile she gets when she's talking to a person she thinks might keep them for the winter. And he wonders, was it them she was ashamed of? Was it Father? Or was the shame for what she had to do, to get herself and them back to the Forest?

"Any child of Harlev's has a place at my hearth," Earl Brux says to them, or to reassure the hermit, who is watching and not saying anything, though maybe she doesn't even understand the Forest tongue, or maybe he's telling all the folk standing about.

And he picks Lannesk up, though he's nearly tall as the earl and able to get up and walk about, only he's so very, very weak and thin. Earl Brux hands him up before another man still on his horse, and Anzimor, big-eyed with delight, is put up behind a laughing red-haired woman and told to cling to her belt, and Mother has her own horse.

One of the spearcarls throws a purse to the hermit, and they ride, hooves crunching, breath puffing, along the Forestway beneath trees bowed with snow.

~MAIRRAN~

The late dawn came with the snow fading to sparse scattered pellets, but the wind kept up. The cold had driven me back into the shelter once the girl was asleep, curled up against Nowa, even her head hidden under the blankets. Snaps only goes so far to warm a body, and it's better flavoured with pepper and ginger for that. Maybe I'd slept. Maybe I hadn't. I thought I'd seen a dragon, golden as dawn, dark as night, flying low over the familiar skyline of the fells of the Holy Isle, and from the towers of Queen's Arrun the red flames rising.

Let it burn, says the woman who is sometimes a grey he-wolf in my dreams, but I don't always listen to her.

"What do we do with the girl?" Nowa asked me, low-voiced, coming to help as if I weren't capable of doling out a little grain to the horses on my own.

Sage might still have been afraid, but she squatted by the fire, stirring the porridge, her copper-bright hair wrapped in a shawl of Nowa's. Fearful, still, but not any longer overwhelmed by terror.

"Serving-carl? Groom? Shieldling?" I didn't bother to murmur. She would have heard anyway. Sharp ears, sharp nose.

Nowa snorted at "shieldling," but I didn't see why a skinny little feral child shouldn't make as good a swordtheyn, in the end, as any landtheyn's brat. Or any forester's fosterling, which was the story Nowa told of her childhood. The girl would get some meat on her bones if we fed her.

Sage looked up. "My mother was a herder of the Far Arrisnaar, my lord, my lady. She brought half-broke ponies from the hills of the Naar in the northwest, to sell at the summer fairs all through the Lann

Laitellon and Laikyn. I can look after your horses, my lord. I can...I can do whatever you want."

"I'm not 'my lady,'" Nowa was quick to say. "Used to be a road-warden. 'Theyn' is more than lofty enough for me. So why aren't you with your mother now, my girl?"

That hunching again, and a scowl at the porridge, which was beginning to belch and spit, and would burn if she didn't take it from the fire. "She died. We were on our way back to the mainland after the fair at Fairnshore and she fell ill and died, four summers back, and I was sick, too, and her partner in the horse-dealing—her brother, my uncle—left me in the village where we'd pitched our tents, when my mother fell too fevered to ride. He paid the elders a little, I think, to nurse me, and said if I lived I'd work for my keep till he came again the next summer, but he didn't. He didn't come. I thought maybe he'd caught the fever too, and died. But then I heard he was at Fairnshore Fair the next summer. The smith's son went, and he said. But my uncle didn't send for me, and he didn't come. They said, the elders, I was given to them as a bondservant to pay a debt, and they had that set down in the village tally, when the justices and their clerks came for the next law-court that year. I said it was a lie but they said I was a child and didn't understand such things and the justices didn't listen to me, and no one, not one, spoke up to the truth. I served in the smith's house, a little, but he didn't like me around his son, so they set me to herding the geese in the summers and passed me around in the winters, to spin and scrub pots for my bread, and—I tried to stop it coming on me. I do try. My mama said—it started when I was little, and she said, never tell, and if I prayed to the Bright Mother and the Queen, and was good, and didn't think bad thoughts and go alone into the Forest, it would stop. But it didn't. It got worse."

"Your Fox, you mean. Here." I brought the dishes, a couple of wooden platters and one of the shallow drinking bowls, steadied them on the snow while she scraped out the porridge into them, not looking at me—trying not to, but flicking sidelong glances.

"I used to go off into the Forest. When I felt I couldn't—when it was going to come on me, when I knew it was. When I felt I had to—to just go. To run. To hunt." She ducked her head down, whispered that, small and ashamed.

"Foxes hunt," I said. "So do human folk. Teeth, bows, they're both fair means to feed yourself."

A wary look from under the scarf and the fringe of her hair. "They said I was lazy. Shirking. Hiding in the woods to get out of work. That I owed them service, for food and fire, for taking me in. A good-for-nothing tramp's brat, they said, when she was—she had half a dozen carls in her service, and their families, and twenty mares plus the range rights over two wild herds—and then they said I was a fayling, a cursed thing, because the smith's boy found where I'd left my clothes and took them, and I sneaked back into the village and tried to take a shirt where it was hung drying and someone saw, and they chased me, and I—the fox ran."

"The Fox is you," I said. "You can say, I." She flinched when I raised a hand, about to lay it against her cheek, to comfort, so I didn't touch her after all. But Nowa, coming to join us with the remainder of last night's round of cheese and a horn-handled knife stuck into it, put a hand on the tensed shoulder a moment. Sage eased and took a deep breath.

"And they turned the dogs loose, and shouted them on and—and one of the dogs got me, and they threw stones, and—I think they hit my head. It was—all—I don't remember." She rubbed her temple. A reddened scar there, under her hand. Small puckered flecks of other scars over her face, and I would have been willing to bet her neck would have shown more of the same, where excited dogs had grabbed and shaken. "They shut me in the sweat-house and wedged the door from outside. They said they were going to send to the earl's law-reeve, and that the earl would hold me chained in gaol till the Queen's justices next came. They said I'd be given to the Forest, my throat cut for a fayling."

"The Queen's Law doesn't execute faylings," I said. The Queen's Law didn't admit faylings existed. Maybe the law was right. I'd certainly never seen one in my times of wild Forest roaming, for all that there were those called me one myself. "And there's no offence against the law, the Queen's Law or the old Forest Law, in a shapeshifter."

Which didn't mean she would have found any justice. There had been a shapeshifter in a village south of the Lann Rath, when I was a youth. A girl a few years older than I was then, who had also had the form of a young bull aurochs. Those great wild cattle still live in the far western reaches of the Forest and around the headwaters of the Lann Estyn, south of Long Sound, and even the cows stand five foot tall at the shoulder. A yearling, or so she—he in his aurochs form—had seemed, the Singer who brought the tale had said, though she—the Singer—hadn't ever seen the shapeshifter living. She, he, that-one... I wish we had some better word, in our Forest tongue, for one who contains male and female by turns in their being, rather than the "they" of one who faces the world as neither or something of both at once—he, she, that shapeshifter had died as the aurochs. The folk of that-one's own village had flayed him, and burned his carcass and hung his skull and hide from a tree by a heartstone as an offering to the Forest. A daughter of their own kinship.

The Queen had levied a heavy fine on the village, when word of it came to her attention, though the law-reeves of the earl of the Lann Rath seemed uncertain what crime, if any, had been committed; not one person was ever brought to trial before the Queen's justices.

It might be chance that most of the elders of that village died, a few years later, over one bright summer. Something came out of the Forest on moonless nights, hunting them, and dragged them away, one by one. A wolf, maybe.

There were crevices and sinkholes aplenty, in the stony hills of the Lann Rath. Their bodies were never found.

Sage shrugged.

"You were right to be afraid, though," I said. "There's a lot goes on that's no justice of the Queen's, and people are forgetting the truth of our own Forest. You escaped?"

"Someone let me out," she said. "That night. One of the girls. She wasn't even a friend, really. But she came in the dark, and dragged away the wedges that held the door. She left some clothes, and a knife, and a bit of bread and cheese, and she ran home. She didn't stay to say anything. Just—let me out. She was afraid. Of course she was afraid. But she let me out." Sage scrubbed at her eyes with the back of a hand. "So I went into the Forest, away from roads, away even from foresters' tracks. I followed an old Forestway a long time, I think, that only the animals used. Days and days. Weeks, just—going, not thinking where. And I've tried to live. I've tried not to be a beast—"

"Hey." Nowa, with an arm around her shoulders now. "Nothing wrong with beasts. Nothing wrong with a shapeshifter, either. The old heroes, the Immortals—the Grey Hunter, the Fox-lad, the Fisher—you're among them, girl. Those who went before you ran as companions to the Wild King. That's something for pride, something to live up to. Not a matter for shame. And you did well, surviving as you did so long, and on your own. There's not many your age could do so."

"What's this village your uncle left you in?" I asked.

"No," Nowa said.

"I want its name."

"Mairran—no."

Sage looked between us, and down at her heaped dish. Shook her head wearily. "It doesn't matter, my lord."

I took my porridge off to eat by the horses, leaning against Smoke's warm and steady shoulder. Yes, sometimes I sulk. It's that or smash things.

The earl of the Warnavon watches the stars and sends letters to the university at Goslack about the patterns of the northern lights and the passage of the straying stars that have neither name nor fixed place, all entirely harmless, but in other letters to certain of her fellow earls she writes of such bright outlaw stars as portents of change and chances to be seized. Her servants have crept into the forbidden cellars and passageways beneath the castle of Queen's

Arrun, and all of what they sought I did not know, but what they found stalking them on silent paws was death.

Was me.

The earl of the Warnavon watches the stars on a cold night in Springsturn. She calls it her star-tower, but it's only a platform atop tall posts, like the watchtower of some small harbour. It has a flight of stairs angling around three sides instead of a ladder in a concession to her maturing years.

The earl of the Warnavon watches the stars, and she hears movement behind, the rasp of feathers, wings folding. "Just a little longer," she says. She must think it's one of her spearcarls, come soft-footed up the stairs to the platform of her star-tower to urge her down to warmth and light. "A wanderer is rising in the mouth of the Serpent, just as I calculated it would. Just as it did in the last days of the Wild King. Would you like to see?"

"No," I say. I don't know why I speak. I shouldn't. I should strike while she still has her back to me, seize and choke her—it's safer so. I've done it before. But as in a dream, I can't help it. She asks a question and I answer, and now she looks around, blinking vaguely, star-dazzled.

Frowns in confusion. Not one of her own folk. What's she seeing? Naked human, all wild hair and shadows, perched like a squirrel on the top split-log rail that fences the platform of her tower? Less than that, only a shape, a darkness? I can only guess what ordinary human eyes can see by night; I've never seen that way. She doesn't cry out, name me, though she's seen me before, braided and gowned and tame at my mother's side, at the yearly Kingsday assembling of the earls.

I would rather not have done it this way. I would rather not be seen. Not see myself, being seen, in the terror of dying eyes.

An accident, that's what this will be. Though people do slip and stumble and fall down stairs all the time without necessarily breaking their necks.

One blow, if it's the right one. I didn't learn that from Nowa. There was a man, an Outlander mercenary. My mother took me away from Nowa and gave me to that man for six months, off in a half-ruined tower in the remote upper Lann Rawla far in the south, after I had healed from fighting the bear. He drank and I was bruised and battered, angry and sometimes frightened, the whole of the time, but he taught me what the Queen asked of him, and at the end I killed him as a wolf kills and dragged his body out to be claimed by the carrion-eaters, *the wolverines and the ravens, because that was what my mother asked of me, and anyway I had come to hate that man.*

One blow to the throat, if it's the right one. The earl drops soundless. I catch her under the arms before she can make a thump and a clatter on the boards of the tower roof, hold on to her while her throat closes and her mouth gapes, trying to drag air as uselessly as if I've stuffed and choked her full of wool, and her lips go grey and her eyes empty. I hold the body, limp, heavy, swaying, all soft cushiony flesh still horribly warm, haul it upright at the top of the stairs, steep and narrow and with only a single handhold rail, and give it a little push away.

The planks underfoot are greasy with settling frost, but it's not so thick yet that I've left any prints of bare human feet, I don't think. Nothing that will show by daylight, once they've charged up and down and made all the fuss that must follow.

She's still tumbling and thumping her way down, the spearcarls keeping warm at a fire below only just calling out, "My lady?" at the noise of her, when I leap and she, the raven that I am, flies.

Ravens don't like the dark. Thunder and Lightning are waiting for me, roosting in a pine a mile down the valley.

That was murder.

That earl's only child, son and successor, dies early in the spring, horse run away with him into the Forest, found with his neck broken at the foot of a tree. Such things will happen, if one will send agents to attempt to steal relics from the caverns beneath Queen's Arrun, where the dead of a long-ago battle are interred, bones heaped and stacked, at least one stone tomb, as well, bearing no name nor sign of whose bones may lie within. Such things as sudden falls and runaway horses may happen, if the Singers who pass through one's hall carry too many songs that praise the age of the Wild King and the Masters of Singersborg and the so-called free earls of the tribes. If one meets in secret with traders of Julliac, to talk of dealing in northern jet that has not passed through the accounting of the Queen's Master of Duties and Tariffs at Head of the Falls. And if one shelters, for the Queen suspects the Warnavon does, somewhere she and I have not yet found, a Seer who defames the Forest-blessed Queen as born with a dragon's heart, and foretells the rising of the Forest against her.

There's a ghost flying wingtip to wingtip, white gyrfalcon to my raven black, but she can't slow to keep pace with me, or won't, arches away, banks, diving back, falcon rolling under the raven as I fly onwards, stolid, strong, steady flight, with every instinct saying to land, fold close, shut my eyes and wait, for dawn will come.

The falcon is pale; she's a mist, a thought swallow-swift, a dream.

I know it was murder, I tell her. I've never told myself it wasn't.

~LANNESK~

The stealthy crackle of brush warns him, almost too late, and without looking for the source Lannesk goes sideways and down, rolling, dropping off the undercut bank of the brook's curve and onto a shoal of dry gritty silt, the water being low. A hot summer, this, and little rain. Could be a deer, oblivious of his careful winding way through the dense greenery. Isn't. Arrow hisses past and into the tangle of wild cucumber vine clothing the skeleton of a once-drowned spruce on the other side. No voices, no discussion. One? A hunting party? No new rustling. He goes downstream, hands and knees, spear in his fist, keeping low, not quite on his belly. Comes up, warily, kneeling, peering through touch-me-not and rasping tall grasses. Mosquitoes whine and he can't slap at them; dragonflies spin and dart overhead. Beaver-meadow, growing up in the rich-earthed clearing that had been their pond, now that the dam has broken, the beavers taken for their fur, some, and the rest moved on when they had felled and stripped most of the nearby trees.

Good fishing here, brook-trout where the water still pools deep in a bend above the green-grown remains of the dam. But they aren't here for that today.

Nothing moves. A deerfly bites and he doesn't flinch, glances down and away, moves one hand stealthy and slow to the back of the other to crush it without looking again. He smeared a bit of goose-grease ground with yarrow and fleamint over his face and neck before setting out to look around, but nothing puts off a deerfly set on biting.

Still nothing moves. Then a warbler, small blur of black-barred wings, flashes out from behind the high mound of the weed-grown old lodge, green island in a lake of green, lush and rank, high as his shoulders if he stands, and he's a tall man.

He could cross the brook, get up the steep slope, get into trees and be well away before his stalker knows he's gone. No chance encounter this. A forester, a hunter—those would not have shot at him. And Anzimor, laggard-waking, will come looking for him once he's dragged his eyes open and tended to his bird. Hawking, scouting...a bit of both, this expedition, wandering easterly towards the chain of hills called the Arris Menlaw, where Earl Tannis has her tower. This is still their own ground, this little side valley, well within the boundary agreed between Earl Brux and his cousin at the Kingsday Fair at Fairnshore two months past, a peace made between them by three gold-ring Singers, who came from the Seer of the Holy Isle in answer to the pleas of the landfolk and the six other earls of the island of Laikyn, to end the long years of warring back and forth across these hills. Peace, they have made, for the sake of the landfolk of the island. Peace, as the whole of the Forest stirs uneasy, rumours of dragon-kin blowing down from the north in the talk of wanderers and shipfolk.

Some say the Seer of the Holy Isle has foretold the return of the Dragon. Some say the Wild King will rise to ride against the dragon-kin.

Another stirring in the grass, a wind-sway softness. Lannesk risks bobbing up, a swift glance. Anzimor, pale red-blond head, spear canted back over his shoulder, picking his way around the sharp hidden stumps, grass rippling like water. Lannesk drops again but betrays his own position with a shrill warning whistle. He's already moving, a low scramble, towards where he's seen his brother.

Rustling. Rushing. Crack of a branch. Muffled shout.

Freezes a moment. Listening. Further scuffling, abruptly stilled.

"You—Lannesk!" a man's voice shouts, a stranger's. "I know you— Brux's Coastlander boys. I have your brother. Show yourself!"

Lannesk stays where he is, crouching, lost in green. A stump to his left, black relic of the pond, long-drowned, but not yet soft with rot. There'll be more like that, hazard to any wild rush, and purple-flowered vetch growing in a great tripping tangle.

"Call him," the man says, not shouting, not meant for him to hear, which gives him a better fix on how close they are. "Go on. He's dumb, not deaf, and not witless either, I'm told. Call him."

An animal sound, grunt of pain stifled, and Lannesk shifts his grip along his spear, slow, careful, shortening it.

"Call him!" A bellow, then. "You, Lannesk! Come out, or your brother dies. Don't be a fool."

Does the man think he can make them believe they'll come to no harm? Dead now or used against their lord and stepfather, made hostage, their torment set against—what, the ceding of territory, the renouncing of Brux's claim, which he's fought for longer than they've been alive? They're not so valuable as Earl Tannis might think. Their mother Harlev is four years dead of a wasting disease and their sister Swanlight, who would have been Brux's heir, of croup in her infancy. Brux has remarried, with promise of a child growing big in Lady Islyn's belly this summer.

One of them dead now, or both dead later. Some might weigh the matter so and creep silently away, save one of two and carry warning to Brux.

"Lan—run!" Anzimor shouts. "Get out of here. I'll—" Words break off in another grunt and the goshawk beats noisy wings.

Mothers, let it be a fist, not a knife. Something he feels too deep for fear, hot hard knot within him, but his hands are cold and steady. Creeping, careful. The man is shouting again in not quite the right direction, facing down towards the brook, and he holds Anzimor before him. Knife at his throat, maybe, or pricking hard against his ribs. Can't see, only heads above the grass. Anzi has dropped his spear but he'll have the hawk to his wrist still. Their enemy wears a leather hood, a young, unweathered face light-bearded, shorter than Anzi by half a head. The man's searching for the telltale stirring of the grass, down where Lannesk first dove and vanished.

Lannesk whistles, two notes—high and a tone lower, which is, just, *I'm here*—as he rises like a trout and the hooded hawk is flung blind into the air as Anzimor seizes in both strong hands the wrist that holds the knife pricking into his ribs, the man close like a lover behind with his other arm crooked around his captive's throat. Anzimor flings himself and his captor both over sideways, and Lannesk is atop them as they struggle. Only the briefest moment's hesitation—reverse the spear, strike his head, kick him senseless so they have time to run... Doesn't. No one would shoot at them but a spearcarl of Tannis's, and no spearcarl of Tannis should be creeping about all the length of this brook. Stabs, and the man wears leather vest as well as his hood, but it's no half-hearted blow, all Lannesk's strength behind it. It goes deep. The man makes a sound like a cough and lies staring at him, face twisted. Blood leaks from his mouth when he tries to speak. Anzimor rolls away and to his knees. With the man's own knife he stabs into man's neck above the collar of his leather vest, which finishes the matter, if there had been any doubting.

"Bright Mother flay me," Anzimor breathes, gasping. Hands on his knees, head bowed a moment. "Lan—" Looks up, blood-spattered, and doesn't say anything, just reaches a shaking bloody hand, and Lannesk grips it. Teeth bared, not in humour. Still in the grip of that fierce anger, that a knife was set to his brother.

They've ridden cattle-raiding almost every summer since Brux claimed them, though their mother hadn't liked it. They've killed before, but that was open battle, a clash of spears and swords, company and company, when Tannis came in force over the Larchbrook ford to burn the standing grain in the valleys, and they rode to thrust her back, and did, in a hot bloody afternoon in the month of First Harvesting, last year.

After a moment he can breathe again, can look. The man's eyes, blue as Anzimor's, stare at the sky, empty, and his blood-drooling mouth hangs open as if he would still shout.

The goshawk, unharmed, has floundered to a perch on one of the rotting stumps.

Lannesk raises a finger. Something he wants to say.

"Knew he'd find us here, didn't he?" Anzimor is good at understanding him, after so long; their thoughts pull and turn together, like oxen yoked. Lannesk nods. Not here, precisely, perhaps, but along this brook, this valley? A spy in the land would avoid them, slip away if he discovered his path crossing that of a couple of Brux's hunters, hoping to go undiscovered himself.

"Seen him before?"

Lannesk takes a second look, shrugs. He couldn't swear he took the measure of every man and woman who rode with Earl Tannis to attend that Summonsing of the Singers. They're more easily known, themselves—the Coastlander brothers, the stepsons, light-haired, gangle-limbed, and a head taller than most.

Though the man, balding under his hood, isn't quite a stranger, now he thinks about it. He has seen him...

"Told we were coming out this way...or crossed our trail by chance, and watched, and followed?" Anzimor watches his face. Lannesk shakes his head, still chasing recognition that eludes him, the memory like a robin diving into brush, himself the goshawk twisting, turning, plunging after it...

"Scout," Anzimor says. "A spy, and his bad luck meeting us."

It was the Sun's own blessing the bad luck wasn't theirs. A rueful smile says that.

Anzimor makes a face, acknowledging that point. "She's planning something," he says.

That's true enough, whoever the man is. Tannis is a schemer, never satisfied, and—a truth loyalty can't deny, Brux is the same. Through summer and autumn they raid back and forth over the hills, driving cattle that maybe no one knows any more who truly owns, and the landfolk, some of them, have gone south of the Fairnmere, to the lands of other earls, where their few cattle and sheep won't be seized by one lord or the other and the fields of oats and barley and rye ridden over, their kaleyards and very houses plundered, and their young folk summoned to carry a spear for this earl or that, to die for their quarrel. Wise lords would take and welcome the settlement decreed by the Singers and their fellow earls of the island, the wisdom brought by the Masters from the Holy Isle; wise lords with a care for their folk would keep the boundary set between them, two earldoms where there had been one, for the good of the land and the landfolk. Oaths were sworn, hands and blood, on the anchorstone of the Summerfair fane, calling the Mothers Above and Below to witness.

Brux says he'll abide by those oaths, keep that peace, and yet, here they are, his stepsons, his trusted theyns, out scouting. Spying. Wandering a remote valley, two young men and a hawk, taking here a duck and there a hare or squirrel, camping at their leisure, singing, no real work to do, the earl's almost-sons, his most trusted theyns, idling in this summer of negotiated peace when the rest of the tower and village folk are at the second haying…

"Go and take a look over those hills, why don't you?" Brux has said. "Islyn's got a feeling…"

Islyn's father is a witch. Islyn is not, not that she's ever admitted, but she gets feelings.

"And if you happen to fly your hawk over beyond the Upper Larchbrook…" said Brux, and grinned at Anzimor. But they haven't gone so far yet.

Squatting there with the dead man between them, fools, and it's more a change in the sound of the wind than anything else that warns them, the voice of the grass.

The second man comes rushing low, spear levelled, and they spring away in opposite directions and he shouts, stumbling over his own comrade's corpse. No hesitating. Anzimor's caught up his own spear again, and whirled back, stabbing down and Lannesk is only a moment behind him.

The man's very dead, prone in the grass. A stranger, again.

They wait, kneeling, spears braced, facing opposite directions. Wait, and wait, and the flies buzz and bite and the mosquitoes whine— why don't they go for fresh-spilt blood and leave the living alone—and the birds begin at last to sing again. Only the wind, rustling grass and distant hissing in the spruces, and the purling water. It's hot, the air muggy, heavy, down here in the close thick grass. The goshawk beats her wings, restless.

Anzimor takes a great breath, lets it out a sigh.

"Think we'd better stop mucking about and take a serious look over the Larchbrook?"

That or bolt for home, warn Brux that his cousin is no more meaning to keep the peace than he is. Lannesk considers. Points away to the east, towards Earl Tannis's lands beyond the hills.

They leave the dead lying, after searching them and finding nothing worth burdening themselves with beyond the short bow and the quiver, nothing to show what the mission of these men might have been. Anzimor takes up the restless hawk on his gauntlet again. A few mouthfuls of fermented buttermilk, the last, from the skin, a few bites of oatcake. They have only a couple of blankets, a bag of food, Lannesk's harp in its waxed-leather sack. It's the work of a few moments to pack up their camp and set out, walking soft and light and wary, along a deer-track that angles more or less the way they want to go, in the warm green dimness beneath the broad and ancient trees.

~MAIRRAN~

We travelled up the coast through trackless woodland, slow going and the new snow cloaking everything in deceiving waves, until I found us one of the old sunken Forest tracks that more often linked heartstones than settlements. It was narrow and overhung, but took us northerly, cutting inland below the bay of the Borlinn's mouth, while avoiding villages and foresters' or charcoal-burners' camps. Away from the regrowing burn, the trees stood broad and high, shaggy with moss and liverwort and old man's beard. Deer used the Forestway, and moose, and wolves, but there were no signs of humans.

No signs of the Wild King's riding, either, but maybe the ghost-horses and hounds of the lost Immortals did not mark the snow.

We didn't even smell the smoke of any solitary assart. After three days, I took us along another little valley and found a road, beaten earth fit for carts in dry weather, with causeways of split logs laid over boggy ground and fords made firm with stones. Nowa and I wore helm and byrnie, went with spears canted to shoulders and shields pushed up to shoulders, ready to shift down to a forearm. Sage followed on Mouse with the baggage. Now we were coming nearer to settled places and neither I nor Nowa forgot that an earl had died and rebels or brigands of some kind might be roaming.

We came to the harbour town at the mouth of the Borlinn near sunset on the fourth day since we'd come ashore. It was not a defended borg with a ditch and palisade but a long scatter of houses, with their fenced yards and outbuildings, along both sides of the river for a mile or so, with the stone Queen's Road that ran northwesterly up the Borlinn valley to the castle of Mair Laikyn on the Fairnmere on the northerly bank, like the harbour. More houses were strung along the shore of the Lake, with sheds and boathouses, smokehouses and flakes for drying fish.

That there was no gate to guard didn't mean my little party escaped notice. A watchtower looked over the harbour and the roads, the sort that was more a shed on tall posts than anything grander, and while we were still on the ferry and the two burly men who poled it across the river were trying and failing to learn from Nowa who we were and what our business was, I saw a youngster come scampering down the ladder. They went running off to a nearby longhouse, from which a little white-haired woman, presumably the harbour-reeve, promptly emerged, trailed by a much taller and younger woman with a spear laid over her shoulder, and an older man wearing leather vest and sword beneath his cloak. I spotted *Snow Goose*, too, bobbing at one of the grey wharves. The Queen's banner, white dragon on blue, hung limp from the naked mast, and the shipcarls clustered about the little smoke of the sandbox and the big stewkettle. The awning was stretched over the foredeck. It didn't look as though Ermintrud had turned anyone loose to the comfort of alehouse or guest-hall. Well and good. It wasn't that I begrudged them a few days of comfort, only that I wanted to be sure word didn't run to Mair Laikyn and the earl's heir ahead of my coming. If the crew had kept mum on their true reason for putting into Borharbour, and I left from here early in the morning, it wasn't likely anyone would ride out before me and Nowa—the Queen's carrion crow might be exciting gossip, but I was hardly an outlaw raid out of the deep hills, to warrant a frantic ride by night.

So, as the red twilight sky faded into darkness I spoke with Ermintrud and settled matters with the old harbour-reeve under the eye of her taciturn spearcarl on my crew's behalf, claiming the use of one of the guest-halls, which were mostly shut up in the winter once the season of trading and fairs ended. It was a log-built longhouse with a central hearth and a smoke-hole in the sod roof above rather than a soapstone stove or fireplace and chimney, benches along the wainscoted walls broad enough for comfortable sleeping and its own bath- and sweat-house, built with an adjoining wall and one stove of heaped stone between, as was common. The family who ran the guest-hall were charged with arranging supply of food and drink and firing for as long as need be, and a place to haul up the *Goose* if the freeze came before my return from inland. All to be paid, and duly accounted for, out of the hearth-tax and fees of harbourage and cargo-landing before those revenues were remitted, in coin or kind, to the earl, who would keep back her own share and pass on what remained owing to the Queen. Doubtless no matter what my mother said about the province bearing the ship's keep the earl's treasurer would contrive to hold back from the royal exchequer the better part of whatever we had cost the earl twice over, when the earl, whoever that might then be, rendered their accounts at the Golden Nights court. Or not. I forgot. I was high reeve of this place.

We should have brought our own trustworthy royal clerks with us, if my mother truly expected that of me. Which I knew she did not. I was only a knife in her hand, and she would be amused, with that indulgent curl to her lip, to think I was bothering to worry over the rendering of accounts implied in the position she had given me here.

Or had she meant me to think of clerks myself? Truly meant me to take on a lord's proper responsibilities? A new game, if so.

Responsibility for the *Snow Goose*, at least, was something I could deal with, and that done—it took some while, for the harbour-reeve wanted to tell the letter over herself, sounding out a slow word at a time, but it was a rare thing one of the class of carls could read at all so I allowed her that pride in her skill—there was water to heat in the bathhouse so we could all scrub off the sweat and grime of two weeks aboard ship. A chance to shave, as well, for those of us so inclined, and Nowa's combing of my hair to be endured—loosed from a braid it curled wildly, and damp, it snarled like briers. And then the sweathouse to fill with steam, to drive out the aches and bone-deep chill of winter's first bite. Even better was to be in our own hall afterwards, with dark ale and autumn vegetables, fresh bread, fresher char that had been swimming that morning, and more than a few songs and tales as someone's battered Forest-harp went round, at which I was glad to take my turn; I left off spinning the sweet rich thread of the wooden flute through the music to sing a song of the Fox-lad, his wise cunning and his gay courage, to hearten Sage. Didn't know if she took it that way, though, or heard it as teasing.

Ermintrud did report that there had been a man of the earl heir's come to the town that morning, asking questions that an earl's servant might reasonably ask of a Queen's ship put in, but she had given him a tale of needing to replenish some supplies—which she had in fact done, in case he asked—and replace some worn ropes. He had gone away satisfied, she thought. At least, she hadn't seen him about after that. Since no one showed up to ask questions of me, it seemed that spearcarl had returned already to his lady.

Perhaps I should have moved faster, ridden to the castle rather than to Borharbour, even had it meant going with Sage dressed in rags and riding pillion. If I'd been sent hunting I would have done so, if I'd been riding at all...but I wasn't hunting. I was going as my mother's emissary, not her secret killer. No need to arrive unheralded had sent me ashore; that had only been my excuse, because I could hardly tell Ermintrud I dreamed of my little lost vixen.

We scrounged about among the smaller folk of the crew, and spent a few coins around the harbour, to came up with some warmer and less tattered clothes for my new groom, and a pair of sheepskin boots outgrown by a son of the hall-keepers, not too badly down at heel. A mount, too, though there wasn't much choice now that the fairs were past. They weren't horsebreeders along the coast. Someone offered an underfed pony gelding, black with white feet, of the wild hill stock such as Sage said her mother had dealt in. The beast apparently had a reputation for a contrary nature, but Sage seemed well pleased with him. Maybe it was that stopped her shying at my nearness. I'd hardly be buying horses for someone if I meant to cut their throat to see the year out.

Or maybe she was only planning how she might escape and elude us all, now she was well-fed, well-shod and warm, with a pony and the road inland to her own hills before her.

I had Nowa, and Sage, too, keep their ears open, for what gossip there might be of affairs at the earl's borg. But maybe even Sage was recognized as belonging to me. Borharbour was not a large place. I dropped a few careless comments myself, on another matter, to see what gossip rose to my bait, but there didn't seem much talk of the prophecies, none that took the talk of the unknown Seer in the Warnavon, who foretold Immortals returning to overthrow the Queen, as more than a tale out of a ballad, as if that Seer and those rumours were a story long ago and far away. Well and good.

I might have slipped out, after my folk had gone to their beds. We'd passed a house with a board hanging over the door, a bunch of splayed seedheads, crudely painted, which could have been caraway or dill, or maybe meant for elderflower, but either way the sign of a still-keeper. It might be that I filled my flask of kingswort snaps again, and bought another of the common clear caraway.

The Queen stands at her altar. Her hands are fisted, propping her as she leans forward, towards the black mirror. The flames of the sweet yellow candles burn pale, white, blue at their heart, which seems...right, and yet I know flame should not burn so. White, and blue as my mother's silver-edged eyes.

"Mairran," she says. She doesn't turn around, still staring into her mirror. It fails to reflect her face, or the room, or me, though I watch over her shoulder, trying to catch her gaze in it.

"What?" I sound like a sulky child.

"Look at me."

"I am looking at you."

"Mairran," she repeats.

Something blinks, in the depths of the polished black. Flicker of golden light. A candle, a hearth, a glint of the sun.

No, says the woman who is sometimes a wolf. Look away.

I can't look away.

"Mairran!" my mother says, and each word falls like a blow. "Look — at — me!"

She-I shut my eyes, tuck my nose under my tail, curl into a warm knot.

"She'll go away if she can't see us," the woman says, and the grey wolf curls up with the black one, he with me, close and warm.

I'm very small. A puppy, soft and weak. But she, who is Mairran, the small black pup, feels safe when he's with me, he, I, the great grey wolf who is sometimes a woman. The grey wolf guards the black wolf's dreams, my dreams. But Nowa says the grey wolf's not real, the woman's not real. She says, a lonely little boy makes up friends for himself, that's all. But before Nowa came, it was Kallyn sang the songs that kept me safe, when there were dreams and I cried in the night.

I never did sleep well, as the nights closed in towards the winter solstice.

~LANNESK~

They never make it over the border into the lands of Earl Tannis.

"Mothers Below," Anzimor whispers, and they stay where they are, crouched low among great trunks, watching, waiting. The woods are still. Nothing moves, only leaves, birds, a crow crying alarm, telling on them, if there is anyone to hear.

It's been a day and a night since they left their camp in the spruces above the beaver-meadow and headed towards the east. Not hard marching, but swift travel, and breaking once to fly the hawk for her own feeding, not risking a fire to cook for themselves, sleeping with no shelter more than dew-damp blankets. Oatcakes, cheese going greasy, raspberries plucked from the canes in sun-spangled clearings as they walk. Now there's a foresters' track below, which they should cross to strike over to the Larchbrook. This road snakes along the valley, a road no use in spring's floods and built up with logs in many places to keep it dry in summer, though mostly it sees winter service, oxen and timber-sleds. It ought to be green, undisturbed, now, showing only the passage of a few landfolk out Forest-foraging, or the passing of a pedlar's pony. Instead, it's been churned to dust, and where it crosses a rivulet from a hillside spring, thick mud, by the passage of horses.

The crow is quiet. A veery sings; another answers. They go down, slipping wary, tree to tree.

There's an autumn fair at the Fairnshore, which lies now within Brux's lands, and all the tolls and fees of that in his coffers, which may be a good half of Tannis's quarrel with him, though she has the harbour at the mouth of the Borlinn. But horse-dealers out of the west coming to the autumn fair would take the road through Earl Karna's lands, coming from the ferry, not this.

Heading south. Too many for an ordinary raid.

"Yesterday," Anzimor says, prodding a scatter of drying dung with the toe of his boot. "Early yesterday?" Looks at Lannesk for his nod.

Aye, he judges the same.

"Our two fellows were scouts, scattered far out." Anzimor frowns. "So far?"

Lannesk shakes his head. That's it, that's who. The balding young man. Saw him at the peace-making. Saw him once before that, unnamed, a man among a small crowd, spearcarls turned out in welcome when they rode in the Month of Falling Leaves not quite a year past, rode to a wedding...

Fist thumps lightly on Anzimor's shoulder.

"What is it?"

He drags his hair back, flat and tight. Stabs at his chest, makes a screwed-up face, a child's mockery of a dead man.

"The bald scout?" Anzimor isn't certain.

Yes, he nods. Fingers walk. Hands make a flattened boat, bobbing on waves.

"Cutting across to the ferry?"

Shakes his head. He repeats the ferry. Nods, to say, ferry, aye. They both mean the ferry to the west, over the Strait, crossing from Laikyn to the Lann Laitellon, not the little scows that might cross the Borrlinn, of which there are several. He runs a finger across his brow. An earl's diadem. Shapes the words.

"Earl Karna of the Ferry? He was...Karna's carl? Not Tannis's?"

Lannesk nods, grim.

"The Mothers Below take the pair of them, Karna's conspiring with Tannis? Tannis has bought her?"

Lannesk thinks so. Fears it.

Anzimor is outraged. "I saw them together. Kingsday. Evening, while the fire burned. Tannis and Karna. Walking, talking. But that's what the Summonsing was for, earls gathering, talking. Making peace. Come to talk peace and used it to cover their treachery? Conspiring against us, east and west? Karna's sworn friendship with Brux. Islyn is her *sister*..." Anzimor's voice trails off. "No," he says. "Not Islyn, Lan. Not her. She's no traitor."

Awkward, being in love with your stepfather's new wife, which Anzi is, a clumsy, adoring first love. Lannesk shakes his head, then shrugs. He doesn't think Islyn a traitor either, or doesn't want to think it. Could be she's betrayed with the rest of them.

They don't need to discuss it. Home to Bruxestorr. Deer-paths and Forestways. Wary of scouts, aye, but swift as they can go, marching, jogging, through long twilight. Might even get ahead of the war-band.

That hope fades. They're spotted, treading too close on the heels of what turns out to be a mounted patrol on another foresters' track. There's close pursuit, four dismounted to follow when they take to steep and thickly wooded hillside. Fair shots, but they're neither of them foremost among Brux's archers; Lannesk shoots, arrow tumbling, knocked askew by a branch, and again, and maybe wounds one, maybe not. There's a cry, but then glimpse of figures moving, closing on them. The delay's not worth it in this dense cover, only making capture more certain. Anzimor tugs him on. Up, down, along a ravine. Good cover there, and they catch their breath, wait, watching, to see if they've lost the pursuit. Lannesk pulls a fold of his hood's cape up over his face to muffle the noise of his breathing, which troubles him when he runs. Two men, a woman, making their way along, glimpsed and gone again, but still on their track. Anzimor, grimly, cuts the hawk's jesses free, takes her hood. Scratches the back of her neck where she likes it. A farewell. She sits, looking about, blinking. His pride and joy.

You might call her to you again, Lannesk thinks. Come back here, when this is over. Or come looking in the spring, take a nestling, her daughter, maybe. But it's the right thing to do. There's no time to fly her, to take game. She can't feed on oatcakes, and it's going to be an all-fours scramble along the face of the ravine, hidden in dense hemlocks. Clasps his brother's shoulders, rocks him a little. Sympathy.

"She'll be fine," Anzimor murmurs, reassuring himself, and the goshawk flies.

A shout says she's been seen. They haven't lost the bastards yet.

Into the hemlocks, along, down rough crumbling stone like squirrels down a tree. Over a narrow stream and up again, and cutting through a woods of red maple and birch, trackless. There's a trick to moving through bracken without leaving a crushed trail, weaving like a dance, like foxes, down on all fours for a while, and it's so dry, if their pursuit gets low they'll see the crushed moss, not sinking and rising as it would in a wetter season, but it begins to seem they've lost them, so they rise and walk, still weaving, dancing, swinging through the bracken stalks and breaking none, and down into another valley, another brook, another track, where a dog-trot carries them miles into full dark. Lannesk is short of breath, has sometimes to crouch and just breathe, trying not to wheeze.

Miles and miles out of their way. Chill damp night, sleeping turn and turn about under a whispering oak, stiff-leafed with summer's decline. They rest only the few hours of deepest dark, and are on their way so soon as the thinning night lets them walk without putting an eye out on a broken twig or turning an ankle on uneven ground.

But Earl Tannis will have done the same, and she has the clear road, and her company is mounted, raider-fashion, even the archers on ponies.

Smoke, boiling black and dirty against the sky and there's no hoping it's something other than what it is. Bruxestorr stands clear of trees atop a hill, and within the encircling earthworks there are barns and lodging-halls, the granary, the smithy, and the last of the hay just coming in. That's hay burning, that black. That's the barns going, empty of beasts in this season.

They keep their heads. They don't rush. Go sidelong around through the more open Forest, trees coppiced, and wood-pasture of broad scattered trees with cattle still grazing beneath, though they've clumped up, the herd they pass by, uneasy. No cowherd. No stranger there to drive them off, either. Not raiding, this.

Long evening shadows give some cover. For a while he and Anzimor hide in a ditch dug to edge and drain the hay-meadow, sheltered in hazel bushes and high-springing canes of the little white roses, sprays of small glossy hips beginning to brighten to red. Wary and watchful. There must be pickets out, scouts roaming lest some counterattack come from the Forest, landfolk gathering to their lord.

But landfolk lie low, in such times. There's hay to get in, vegetable crocks to salt and fill against the winter. Bring the cattle and the flocks of the little brown short-tail sheep in close to the home yards or send them far to the hills and your young folk with them, watch to defend your own. Let the earls and the folk who eat their bread settle it, do the dying.

Little sign of battle. The meadows about the hill's foot are tawny silver, some raked to windrows, some already dry and in, one wagon abandoned, lacking a team but its bed piled high in a great silvery-green mound. Peaceful. Flock of goldfinches flies, twittering, descends on a patch of goatsbeard gone to seed. Crickets chirp. In an elm standing over the ditch a haymaker buzzes, buzzes, then flies clicking in a flash of black and yellow wings. A jay arrows over them, brilliant blue. Ordinary summer's day drawing to ordinary evening.

So little time the tower had, so little warning. They've come just too late. Wouldn't have been this morning, with dew on the hay, wouldn't have been loading a wagon then. Nearing noon, maybe, or after. They'd almost overtaken, but almost wasn't good enough. Earl Tannis's company has come along the north track swift as flood, capturing, maybe killing, anyone unlucky enough to be in their path. Seize the cottages there and roll over them. Aye, that was it. Come in the afternoon, when kitchen-folk were preparing for the late supper, when everyone would turn towards home, or maybe that had been the last load, that wagon, and most folk within the walls already, and trestle tables out in the yard, all the earl's folk dining together, or about to, hot and hay-prickly, dusty or fresh-bathed in the brook that curls about the hill's foot, barrels of summer ale, the last of last fall's barley...

But they'd still have seen the warband coming. They'd still have had time to rush in, up the twisting track between ditches and banks, though the gateway, wide enough for a haywagon. Time to close the gate, to string bows, to sound the horns and summon the folk from the Forest, spread the word of raiders...

Earl Karna's folk. Come to visit her sister, in this season of good roads and plenty. Come to visit as she swells, to talk of the things women talk about at such times. Come, maybe, not long after he and Anzimor left.

And a pair sent out after them, close behind...with or without Islyn's knowing?

All the folk of the tower, all Earl Brux's following, out haying, in this hot summer that's not so dry but what it's given a second cut from the aftermath. And their guests, too, ought to have been sharing the labour, but if they were not...folk come and go, in and out, and they're marriage-kin, not enemies, not rivals, no keen close eye on them.

Word comes of the approaching raiders, no raiders but a warband, cattle not the prize they seek.

Horns sound alarm, but even so they'd think it Earl Tannis raiding as she's ever done in summer seasons, they'd abandon the fields, they'd pull folk and teams inside...

Their own defences close on them, trap rather than shelter. Their own gate, the fighting-platforms over the gate, held by Karna's carls, the tower closed up, maybe, and Islyn within...?

The earl seized as he strides through, hayfork changed for spear, and his theyns then swiftly disarmed.

Islyn in the tower, with her sister.

Islyn hostage, the lady and the unborn child.

Hostage, or seeming so?

Send Lannesk and Anzimor, she says. It's not witch's divination, Brux, it's not a dream, only a feeling...send them up the Larchbrook, away from here. And her eyes rest on Anzimor where he leans against the mantel of the fireplace, and she smiles, and Lannesk thinks, we should go away. We used to talk about finding a ship, serving a free-captain, a shipmaster serving no earl. We should do that.

Why does it seem something he already knows, something he's seen, learned, remembered...?

Here, now, they don't know this. They only know that the gate stands open and guarded, but the barns are aflame, and the halls. Later, they speculate. Later they hear rumour, word gone round the farmsteads and the deep-woods assarts and the foresters' summer settlements. Later, they put together a story of how it was, the treachery of a hot summer's day. And in the end they learn the truth, of Karna's alliance with Tannis, her treachery. But Islyn's part in it—that's never to be known. She's renounced all claim on the earldom on her child's behalf before it's ever born, gone back to Karnastorr at the ferry, folded safe into her sister's household. What she wanted, or survival?

Did she mean them to find the warband, bring word in time, betray her sister's ally Tannis without betraying her sister?

Did she mean them to be away, to be left orphaned and lordless, but alive, and ignorant of her betrayal?

Did she not know what she meant, only that she wanted Anzimor not to be at the tower, not to die defending Brux, as he would have, as they both would have?

And did she then betray that, to her sister's asking—where are your stepsons gone, where are Brux's Outlander boys?

"Islyn," Anzimor says, a whisper, a gasp.

There's a dark shape on the roof, then, struggling against others that hold it.

There's a man.

Small man, smaller than he used to be, now that they're taller. Small and agile and fierce, a bright kestrel of a man. Lannesk understands how their mother came to love him. But he's bound; they see it when he's thrown to his knees and hauled up again. Figures about him, spears, axes, a couple with swords. A small woman, heavy-bellied, who turns her head but does not go to him. Another close by her. Holding her? Karna, he thinks.

Lannesk has the bow strung. Anzimor doesn't ask, only hands him the arrow.

It's a long shot for the short Forest bow. Karna's too close to Islyn and at this range—he's no marksman, won't risk that, not Brux's child. Another woman in lordly bright long gown and a short-sleeved byrnie over it, the conical helmet any spearcarl might wear, but the browband is enamelled blue, and that's Earl Tannis, though she's no swordtheyn—women who hold the land do not train as warriors. Sensible precaution, though, to go armoured. Lannesk rises up on a knee on the edge of the ditch, half-hidden still in the hazels. He takes careful aim—

Sudden surge of movement, and Brux is falling. Their lord, their stepfather, who made a pair of feral beggar boys theyns of his tower.

Not falling. Sudden jerk, brought up by the rope about his neck.

Dark, against the red stones. Thrashing, twitching. Lannesk has loosed and the arrow flies and Anzimor is handing another but then Anzi clutches and drags him down because it seems he's flung himself upright, as if he could run, could fly, to hold Brux, to cut him away from his choking death—

But his shot has dropped Earl Tannis.

No. She's up, though a spearcarl stands before her, shielding her, and Islyn is struggling now, wrapped in her sister's arms, and spearcarls are pointing—

"Mothers damn them, Mothers flay them, dragons eat their souls—" Anzimor's voice breaks and he puts his face to Lannesk's shoulder a moment, as if he's a child again and his brother can take away his pain, and Lannesk's arm is around him, as if that might be.

Then he takes the arrow from Anzimor's hand, and aims—

Brux is still. A dead weight, hanging.

So he shoots the man nearest, whoever he might be. The one whose hands were on him, who sent him over the drop. Clear shot to his pointing, staring face. And that one goes down and does not get up.

Third arrow. Strikes the parapet, falls, and now there are bows strung among those on the tower top and orders doubtless being shouted down the stairs.

They need to go. Dead, prisoner, forsworn, or tamed by threat to Islyn's child, to Brux's heir, their fellows aren't fighting, there's no attack to join, and none joining them. Anzimor's fingers dig into his arms. "Lan," he says, and pulls him back into cover.

This isn't a ballad. Islyn does not stab her sister and fling herself over the parapet to follow her husband to the Dark Mother. She's only standing there, passive again, embraced by, held up by, maybe, the woman beside her. That they don't hustle her away down to safety says something. He's not sure what.

Shadows are joining, the sun going down in smoke.

"Come on," Anzimor says. "We can't do anything more but die, here."

Aye. He bows his head to Anzimor's shoulder a moment. Touch. Comfort.

An arrow thuds into the earth not six feet from the hedge. Another hisses through the hazels over their heads.

They scurry like voles down the ditch.

But already Lannesk is thinking of roads and ways. He didn't know he had so much of their mother in him. Her teaching, isn't it? Well, that's over, time to move on. Never look back.

Karna to the west, Tannis to north and east. Not the fells, and not the road west to the ferry. Nor southeast down the Borrlinn to the harbour, through Tannis's lands. Better they steal a boat, head out across the Fairnmere. Some earl of southern Laikyn will take them into her following. Though they have feud with Tannis now, and Karna too, and he can't see Anzimor letting that go, Anzimor passing by either earl or her theyns at any fair or Golden Nights gathering without violence ensuing. Or himself, either? He doesn't know. And what follows then but their own deaths? Nothing saved from the ruin. Nothing to be saved but themselves.

"I'll kill her," Anzimor says, looking back over his shoulder. "If Islyn betrayed Brux, I'll kill her."

Lannesk wants to feel the same anger. Doesn't.

Caught between her sister and her husband—if she was. What might a mother do, to save her child? If that was the choice her sister gave her.

Doesn't know how to tell Anzimor, the tower, a theyn's place in it, had always the feel of a cage for him.

Not sure what else he can offer Anzi for their future. The beggar's roads of their childhood, a tramp's unlearned claim to minstrelsy? Anzimor's adult voice is fair enough, but no better than any casual singer at the fireside, and he's never had Lannesk's interest in learning new songs, never his memory for the long lays of the Singers who come even to a rebel earl's hall, the great cycles of the quest of the Bright Mother for her son lost in the Dark Beyond, the Riding of the Wild King and the Grey Hunter against the priest-sworn hordes from the Outlands or how their song defeated and bound the Dragon Erryth the Golden beneath the Lake from which she had been born, or the Winter King's hunting of the ice dragon…

To be spearcarls of some tower is all they're fitted for, now. But better they leave this island altogether, go down to the Lann Estyn or the Lann Lathrun, seek some service there. They need to get over or around the Fairnmere first, though.

End of the ditch's cover and they abandon it, run, crossing the bottom corner of the field, through the pole-barred gap there, across the lane, down into dense green, across a curl of the brook. There are riders crossing the hayfield, hooves loud on dry earth.

Into woods, tended, open, but there's steep ground beyond, and a spur of wild Forest thrusting down between wood-pastures. Tannis's carls don't know this ground.

Night falls slow and the afterglow of sunset lingers in a long smoke-hazed twilight, as the Forest takes them.

~Mairran~

The highway along the Borlinn, the snow trampled and dirtied with use, passed mostly through hedged pasture and croplands, skirting by hamlets of a few houses and their outbuildings, with occasional tendrils of the Forest feeling their way to the river. A dozen miles or so from the harbour town and among one of those long thrustings of trees, thick cedars where a stream ran in a deep ravine, we were coming out of the darkness of a covered bridge when I heard the whispering hiss of an arrow in flight, the thunk of its striking. Nowa cried out.

The next arrow spat by my ear, but I was low, shield raised, Smoke at a gallop, spear swung down ready by the time the third arrow missed and I was into the deep shadows of the close-grown trees. Maybe they thought me blinded by the snow-dazzle dapple of sun and shade, because they came to meet me running reckless, the archer's bow abandoned. Both carried spears. I turned Smoke to plunge crashing along the bushy cedars to the right. The thrust that had been meant to take the horse in the chest missed, changed its angle to follow him again, rising—if the archer had been going to kill Smoke she should have aimed at the horse while she was still shooting from cover—and I knocked it aside with my shield, clipping the woman alongside the head, turning hard about to come on her again as she turned and skidded on snowy stones. My point took her under the jaw, snapping her head back. I jerked the spear free as we passed. Bright blood spattered the snow. The horse wheeled around again. A big man, round spearcarl's shield, nothing painted to show his service, but then, we had covered my wicked raven on our own with scrap linen and hasty flour-paste back on the ship when I decided to go ashore.

The man charged, yelling, and I went aside from him, twisted and struck down along my own spear-side. The attacker folded to a knee, neck bloodied, Smoke turning like a hare and I had to let go my spear then as we pivoted about it. Drew my sword and brought the horse about again to face the scene, but the woman was still and the man making only a feeble effort to push himself up off the road.

Smell of human sweat, of horse, of—not dog, but wolf, and my hackles rose, or would have. Skin prickled.

The third came out of the cedars to my right, but that one moved too slow, thrust going wide. I struck his arm aside and then spun Smoke circling around to have him on the shield-side. Slashed sleeve, bloodied. The man's hand was flowering red where blade's edge had opened a long furrow to his wrist. Bad angle, too glancing a blow. Not enough to ruin him. To weaken his grip, maybe. To slicken shaft. The man came close in thrusting over his shield, teeth bared in grin, pain—whatever—and I took the strike on my own shield, turned about and crossed back to him, slashed and split his face. It had looked briefly familiar, before I destroyed it. Thought I saw something, flash of bright foxy copper moving, ahead, aside, and that was when the fourth man came leaping from the trees with sword raised two-handed.

Zing of arrow, and that man pitched down onto the stones of the road and did not move. I didn't waste time looking at him, kept Smoke moving, watching—shadows, flicker of the broad flattened scale-sprays of the cedar boughs, wind-stir of cloth and hair. Could smell little, now, but death and horse and sweet broken cedars. Whiff, still, of a horse not my own? The ravens were coming down through the trees, branch to branch, excited, croaking. I didn't think they'd be so bold if there were still strangers lurking, and yet...

Nothing moved in the trees. Nothing now to smell but death and my own sweat, and Smoke's.

The woman, the archer with the quiver at her belt, was dead. A leg looked as though Smoke's hoof would have doomed her anyway, if more slowly. The second attacker had stilled; blood pooled about him.

Now I looked for the other archer, my unexpected ally, who had been back behind me, not ahead in the woods, where I had for a moment thought there was another horse.

Sage. Face set, and the bow—where had she got a bow?—drawn again.

The man with the split face was somehow still moving, a dreadful slow random reaching of arms and legs where he lay in the dirty snow. Mindless, and his animal whimpering was not to be borne. Another glance at Sage—it didn't seem she was going to shoot me as well—I slid down and stabbed through to the wounded man's heart, to the road beneath, all my weight behind it. Cleaned my sword. Reclaimed my spear, and cleaned that, too.

Nowa rode up, wary, watchful, and Sage, her black pony sidling and blowing—not actually baulking, though, and the reins loose on his neck. Apparently a horse-master as well as an archer, my new retainer. Mouse followed, stolid and calm through all. Sage kept an arrow nocked, eyes wide, watching for movement behind. Her extended arm was beginning to shake, though.

"Is that the lot?" Nowa asked.

"I think so."

"We should have had one alive."

"Better they're dead than I am."

She hadn't meant it as a reproof to Sage, I didn't think, but I'd seen the girl flinch.

I looked at the man I'd killed on the ground. Not just his nose, the flesh of his face. I had split his skull.

I'd thought they had shot Nowa, and I would have killed them all regardless of how useful they might be, for that. Now, her calm, and her careful speaking—I did not like that. I ducked around under Thorn's nose and felt as though my heart stuttered, because the long skirt of her tunic was dark with blood, and it was seeping down her trousers past her knee. The arrow still stood from her thigh, just below the bottom edge of her byrnie.

"That," said Nowa, "is starting to hurt. A bit."

"A bit," I said. "Yes." And we couldn't stand around here waiting for the ambushers' reserve to creep up and start shooting, if this wasn't, as Nowa had said, the lot. "Sage!"

She brought her pony over, arrow and strung bow held together in one hand now, and a birchbark quiver slung as if in haste about her neck. Her face was pallid, a spatter of brown freckles standing out across her nose.

"Is anyone else in this wood?"

She blinked at me. "My lord? I don't know—"

"If you can't smell from here, go find out," I said. Of course she couldn't smell anything but the stink of the dead, standing next to them.

"My lord." She gathered the reins to urge the pony on.

"Strip," I said, impatient, and she stared, big-eyed. "Now."

"I—my lord."

"Don't yell at the child," Nowa said, which was a bit much, because what example of child-rearing did I have but hers? My mother aside, and I would far rather be just shouted at. "Dark take you, Mairran, she's twelve years old and she just killed a man for you."

"I've fourteen winters," Sage protested weakly.

I had been perfectly capable of killing that last man on my own, but that wasn't Nowa's point. On the other hand, my shield-companion was bleeding heavily, the hot sweet reek of blood was in my nose till I could taste it and someone had just nearly killed her. I wasn't thinking clearly.

But Sage, with a look at Nowa then, said, "Yes, my lord," and swung down from the pony, unstringing her bow. She wasted little time, boots and hood and cloak, and then the rest in haste, bundled and shoved among Mouse's bags to keep off the wet snow. And away, a flashing fluffy russet coat darting into the trees.

"That wasn't—" Nowa abandoned words, hissing in pain. I had my hands on her, trying to feel through sodden layers of cloth how bad it might be. The arrow seemed well-lodged. It wasn't going to come out gently.

"It was necessary," I said, to her bowed head and gritted teeth. "There might be another pair, further on, lest one of us breaks through."

We neither of us thought the attackers were likely to be chance brigands, not here.

"Go on, one of you. Watch over the little vixen." I flapped a bloody hand at the ravens, who were taking too great an interest in the mess of the last man's head. Lightning croaked and took off, flying low down the clear tunnel of the road. Thunder disappeared into the trees. I tried to let a little of myself fly with them, but it was hard to set that apart, with the reek of Nowa's wounding so close and hot and urgent.

"Where did she get the bow?"

"No idea. Snatched it from Mouse and rode off after you to get closer. Ermintrud, maybe. Bows on the *Snow Goose*. No idea she could shoot."

"Not that we asked her. This isn't going to just pull out. It looks — bad. A broad head. Going to break it off," I said. "Don't fall on me."

I gripped the arrow's shaft hard in both hands, careful, fearful, not to let it move, snapped it above my grip. Nowa made a faint noise, not really a squeak. A handspan left, to draw it out by, once I — or better, some surgeon — could see what wanted doing. I feared very much it was barbed — but at least now there was less weight tearing at it to widen the wound. Nowa braced herself, hand on my shoulder, head bowed.

"Want down?"

"No. You'd have to heave me up again."

"Want to try to get this out of you now after all?"

"Bright Mother keep me, no! Not unless you think it's not safe, going on to Mair Laikyn."

"It's the castle or back to the harbour, with you in this state. Hold on there, then."

I went to rummage through the bags on Mouse, found some clean linen, Nowa's supplies, not mine. Sluiced the wound with snaps, because physicians did use it so, though maybe not flavoured with caraway — and she yelped and hissed at that — and fastened pads of the cloth around the base of the shaft, wrapping a scarf about her thigh to hold them in place. Blood stained the pads and bandage, but slowly, a seepage now, not a gush. To the bone, maybe, but I didn't think the bone itself was broken. Not a lot of fat on her, though she had her womanly curves. Some meat there to take the arrowhead. Not the inner thigh, not a killing wound, if it didn't turn bad. I told myself all those things, for comfort, and then I poked around the dead and took a few tokens. A man's thick silver ring, patterned with a double harvest-knot, which was usually a wedding-gift, the oblong brooch, enamelled with a curling fish, that held the woman's tunic closed, the little belt-knife of the man I had killed on the ground, which had a handle made from antler, incised with a running stag, very crude, just a few lines, but done with care and stained with something black to bring it out. Distinctive.

They waited. I picked at edges, peeling the starchy cloth away from my shield, spread-winged raven floating black on sky's blue, then did Nowa's. Not much point to concealment now. We really should not have gone to the harbour, even for one night. Without warning—she circled downwind, which was maybe instinct, or possibly chance— Sage was back, her pony snorting and pulling away, but for the stolid anchor of Mouse. It would take more than a bold fox to startle one of my horses. Vixen shifted into girl in an eye's blink, keeping the brown dun's bulk between us and her nakedness.

"They came on skis," she said. "And my lord, there's another dead man. You'd better come and see."

~LANNESK~

Eight, Lannesk tells Anzimor, holding up fingers, and Anzi slides down beside him. Too many. They've no arrows. Eight coming up the hillside through the ashwood, and riders along the brookside track, and more, spearcarls and archers both, to the west, which is what drove them back this morning. And Anzimor limping, though Lannesk has bound his brother's ankle up tight, slit the side of his boot to take the binding and tied it again over that. Turned it slithering on lakeside stone, three evenings back, when the boat they tried to take turned out to be bait in a trap. They knew that Earl Karna had the lakeshore patrolled, all boats watched or taken into winter sheds, but it had seemed this shabby fisher's rowing-boat had been forgotten, pulled up on the shore at a creek-mouth. Only night's darkness had saved them, lying in water jammed in against the undercut bank, cold, shivering with it, waiting for the searchers to pass; water seeping into everything, into even the little buckwheat and salt butter they had, gift of an assarter who didn't know or didn't care they were named rebels and outlaws, assassins of Earl Tannis—who wasn't dead last they've heard but said to have taken a fever in her wounded arm.

Abandoned his harp, which was his mother's. Gave it to the assarter. It was become only one more thing to carry. At least that saved it from ruin the night they spent near-drowned. The assarter had not only fed them, but told them tales come down from the north of dragons flying on the wings of storm, and a late-summer battle against dragon-kin raiders somewhere far up the Lann Leda. He seemed a man who could make good use of music to carry his tales.

Meanwhile they're dirty, ragged, clothes thorn-plucked and covered in clinging beggar-ticks and sticklewort, mud and moss and lichen-stained, all ground into clothing and skin alike. Wild men of the woods, Anzimor has joked, but he's grey about the eyes, too often leaning on Lannesk as well as his spear as he hobbles. That ankle's bad, even if it's not broken.

There's a ring closed about them, as if they're quarry in some autumn hunt of lords, not a mere moose but a great bull aurochs strayed out of the west across the strait, something earls will come together for, making a festival of its inevitable doom.

"You should leave me," Anzimor says. "I'll say you've drowned. You can find a canoe, once they stop searching. Get across the Fairnmere and to some other coast, get out to the Lake at last and off this cursed island. Go home."

He means the Coastlands. Lannesk feels for his wrist, and then his forehead. Anzimor bats his hand away. He's not feverish. Forces a grin for the joke. Likely Anzi doesn't even remember that first home, the salt air and the ceaseless roar of the waves. Lannesk hugs him close, to say he won't leave, won't even think about it, ever. To say, he knows that was a joke too, Anzimor pretending to think he might do so.

Eight coming up the hill. He tugs at his brother's sleeve. Anzimor nods. They crawl.

There's a track wide enough for two horses, maybe. Not rutted, just a deep sunken green, all wire-grass and hawkweed, pale asters where sun breaks through, and ferns and moss in the dark shade. Blackberry canes overhang the sunny patches, snatching at cloaks and trousers when they crawl down into it. Birds have stripped any berries away. They dare to stand upright, there being no sound of anyone near. Not that Anzimor goes much faster on two legs than on four.

Poplars have given way to red oaks along the banks here, great broad trees and saplings between, waiting their day, a dense screen of them, tinged with russet. More or less a month, they've been on the run. Harvesttide, soon.

There's a quiet here. A deep stillness. Only the leaves rasp together. Small birds dart across, warblers, finches, sparrows, but no jay or crow calls a betraying alarm.

Forestway, not an ordinary track. There's a waystone set, and another facing it, just the local red sandstone roughly shaped to an upright, waist high. A shape carved into one. A crow, might be, or a raven.

This is still their land, Brux's land, yet Lannesk has never walked this Way before. Isn't quite sure, now, how they came on it, or where it might take them. His arm is around Anzimor's waist, taking his weight, Anzi's arm over his shoulder. Their mother's stories would have faylings ride here on their moon-white ponies, but nothing has passed here, not even a deer, that he can see.

Breath slows, eases, grows less rasping. He wonders if they might sleep here and be safe. Might fade away into some other time, be boys again, walk home laughing to the tower, talking of taking a hawk—in his memory, in his dreams, he speaks with Anzimor in his own voice, but then when he wakes he can't remember what that man's voice sounds like.

Dreams he sings. Wakes up feeling it in his chest.

He's dreaming now. So tired, he's out on his feet. There's a horse alongside them. A rider, and Anzimor's breath catches. He sees it, too. Or they're dreaming together. Fever-madness, brought on by the assarter's tales.

Red horse, with a long cream-pale mane unclipped, and the rider's hair and beard are red as his horse's flank. He wears leather, and a sword with a bluestone the size of a duck's egg for its pommel.

"The Forest," he says, and his voice is rich and deep and alive beyond anything Lannesk could dream, "is waking. The Forest must rise. And you are hunted, young men of the coast. You are the quarry and the pack draws in. Will you join with me? There are dragons in the north. The Seer of the Holy Isle dreams of fire and death."

Maybe that's not what he says. Maybe there's more, or less, or maybe he only looks at them, and they understand.

A falcon plunges from the sky, grey-barred white gyrfalcon, and she cries, and the sound is like the crying of gulls over the waves. She swoops not to the rider on the red horse but to Lannesk, who raises his fist to her. The falcon lands, wings beating, folding, talons digging deep and he bleeds, red pearls rising about every claw.

The falcon stares at him. Stone-grey eyes, wave-grey, cloud-grey, flecked with amber, and wings unfurl and she leaps to the air. A small feather falls and he catches it, white, barred grey. The falcon goes like an arrow down the darkening tunnel of oaks and the King, who wears a crown of oak-leaves, nods to them and touches spurless heels to the red stallion's flanks. The horse leaps after and for a moment, just a moment, there is a great throng about them, horses, people, dogs, wolves, running, riding, rushing like the wind, and then there is only the wind, a wild gust smelling of rain, leaves rattling and tearing, and they cling together as the night falls sudden, sunset come without their noticing.

Lannesk is still clutching the feather.

They go on. Anzimor's gait is stronger, less awkward, less of his weight on Lannesk. But they're both so tired.

The Forestway climbs along a ridge and dips into a hollow, entering a clear ring of squat, wide-spaced stones. There's a tall grey boulder for anchorstone, its daylight pallor a dark shadow in the moonlight, and a big oak standing tall and straight over it.

He knows this place. Oakridge fane. Not far south of Bruxestorr. They've circled back, over the weeks, and did they mean to…? He does not see how they did. But he knows this place.

And Anzimor turns loose from him and limps to the anchorstone, shrugs off the pack from his shoulders and sits down, spear laid by his feet with his back to the stone, beneath the carving of an aurochs-horned man, who might be some earlier King even the songs have forgotten, or only some other Immortal of the Forest. Lannesk joins his brother and they share water from the skin that once held fermented buttermilk. That's all they have. Yesterday there were hazelnuts gathered while they walked, but those were few. Squirrels take the most of them before they ripen. They haven't stayed put long enough to fish, to set a snare, haven't found a friendly roof since the assarter. Lannesk turns the feather in his fingers, holding it delicately by the quill. Anzimor strokes a finger up the shaft, looks at him. Moonlight catches the movement.

He doesn't speak, to ask, is it real, did we dream? If they dreamed, they dreamed together.

They sleep, sitting, leaning together, backs against the stone.

Sanctuary, a fane offers. Three days' grace, during which someone may offer to buy their bond-service—for three years, seven years, or even three times seven. And the choice is, accept that, whatever is offered, and banishment to follow after, or accept the death they're fleeing.

But they can't run any longer.

Grey dawn, and the sky gone cloudy and cold when their hunters come on them, chance, having lost them long before. They ride an ordinary village track to the fane, not the Forestway. Lannesk can't even see where it lies. Confused, turned around in the night. He'd thought them sixty miles west of here, but was either far out of his reckoning, Forest-wildered, or the Forestway had proven as unchancy as any fayling ballad would have it, and turned them about and swept them here all unwitting.

"Sanctuary," Anzimor says, when the first men enter the fane, and it looks as if they're going to be hauled to their feet and dragged out to die. "We claim the right of sanctuary, and—" a look at Lannesk, who nods, with the feather he's never let go held in his hand as if it's the plectrum of his harp, "—our service is already claimed."

The price, of course, is meant to be paid to the earl, not to the outlaws who have bound themselves. What is a feather's worth?

Their lives, maybe.

The spearcarls are inclined to argue, and threaten, but it's a hard thing to kill a pair of battered and near-broken boys who only sit on the ground looking at you, maybe, or maybe the earl's folk remember respect for the holiness of the place.

A young woman gives them a wooden cup of cider to share between them, and the heel of a loaf, which is kindness. It's near noon before the earls come, both of them, Karna and Tannis, the latter's face leaner than before, sick-bed aged, but with full use of both hands, which she proves by striding to them and striking them, first one, then the other, across the mouth. To show them taken.

The earls, and Islyn, huge-bellied and a month from delivering. She rides a led pony with a woman spearcarl striding close at her side, helping her down, holding her arm. One of Karna's folk, a stranger. Attendant. Guard? Islyn looks at the ground, or rather, down at her belly, not at them. Not at Anzimor. She was never much interested in looking at Lannesk.

"Not one landtheyn in all of north Laikyn would buy your service even to shovel muck," Earl Tannis says. "You are dead men. Rebels, outlaws, murderers. Foreigners." Oh, the contempt she puts into that last.

"Who did we murder?" Anzimor demands, indignant. "We haven't killed a one but those who came in arms against us, and in defence of our lord, our stepfather."

"Your so-called lord was a rebel against his rightful earl, and a cattle-thief, and a murderer, and declared outlaw twenty years since."

"Our lord was acknowledged earl of all this land about so far as the Larchbrook just this Kingsday past, as Earl Karna witnessed and you yourself, lady, agreed to."

"He broke the terms. He sent raiders over the Larchbrook and into Hawdale."

"That's a lie!"

It is, because if Brux had done so, not only would they have known of it, they'd have been riding chief among them.

But Lannesk elbows Anzimor. Nothing to be gained by arguing, and push her much more, she'll profane the sanctity of the fane and the sanctuary they've claimed; she's proven treacherous, a liar, a woman with no honour or respect for the Mothers before whom all oaths are sworn. Anzimor bows his head.

"Lady," he says. "We've come to the fane to claim sanctuary, by Forest-law, and our service has been offered, and accepted."

She snorts. "There's no price I'll take, but your heads."

"The Wild King claims us," Anzimor says.

It sounds mad, said aloud. Deluded. Like something out of a song.

"To ride with him, lady," Anzimor says, "to war against the dragon-kin."

Lannesk holds up the feather, as if any but they might read it.

"Yes." Speaking for Lannesk, now. "The Wild King, and the Grey Hunter. They came—we met them on a Forestway in the night."

"Are you children, to give me such tales?"

But Islyn has raised her head, and her blue eyes look nearly black, which might be the shadow of her hood, or tears, or vision taking her.

"The Wild King," she says. "He rode last night. I heard him. I heard him call them by their names."

Just that. Then she's silent, and her head droops again, like a frail-stalked flower heavy with rain.

"There's a Singer come to Borharbour," a theyn says, a grey-haired man with a sword. "She's sent by the Seer of the Holy Isle herself, asking the earls to make ready to sail in the spring to fight the dragon-kin who have seized the towers of the upper Lann Leda. Asking the free-captains, too, to ready their ships. The Wild King will ride, they say. And some are not waiting for spring to answer the summons but are travelling already to muster on the Holy Isle, to form a company of mortal spears who will join the King's own riding."

"That Singer came to my tower, too," Tannis says, dismissive, "I've said any fools who want to may go, and come spring, if by then we know these tales from the north to be true, I'll give ships and a company of spears as Forest-law demands, if my sister-earls of Laikyn are willing to do likewise. But if this pair of scoundrels thinks I'll take such a children's tale as excuse to withhold my hand and let them go free—"

Earl Karna has been frowning at her drooping sister. "Let them go," she says abruptly.

"What?" Tannis demands.

"They're sworn to the Wild King and the Grey Hunter, they say. That's not a vow even a fool would falsely claim, and not a vow any of us should dare to deny them. Let them go."

Islyn's hand is clutching her sister's sleeve.

"You're not serious," says Tannis.

"I heard wolves, last night." Islyn says, hardly above a whisper. "Wolves and hounds, calling together."

"Geese," Earl Tannis says, sneering.

"Have you sworn to do this?" Earl Karna asks of Anzimor. "To go to the Holy Isle and join the Wild King's Riding, to fight the dragon-kin?"

"Yes, lady," Anzimor says. "I have. We have."

"And your brother?"

Lannesk nods, to answer for himself.

"I won't—" Tannis begins to say.

There's a shadow flowing, slinking, between the boundary stones. Horses snort and shy.

Great grey he-wolf stands, hackles raised, between them and the earls, swinging his head this way and that, taking them all in. He stalks slowly over, so close they see teeth, whiskers, every golden fleck in his storm-grey eyes. And for a moment the wolf is a naked woman, white-threaded pale brown hair, tawny-skinned, grey-eyed, so close to where they kneel that Lannesk can't help but see even the fine hairs of her smooth thigh, the curve of her hip, the darker curling hair that he and Anzimor have no business taking notice of, and his heart is pounding, but not for that. Lifts his gaze, which feels less offensive, breasts being that shade less private. One should see without looking, as if they're comrades, family, in a sweat-house together, not a stranger and a holy Immortal of the Forest.

He may be about to die and he's worrying his noticing her nakedness may offend her? Anzimor would laugh. But he is noticing, mostly, her eyes, which have snared his gaze so there's nothing else. The gyrfalcon's burning gaze, the wolf's. She looks into him, through him, down to the shadowed heart of him and what he feels is—music, half-formed, something like rain promised on the wind, the tension of an awaited dawn, the sun not yet at the horizon. Still-hanging leaves, summer-heavy green, wind-wakened into wild silver rustle—

"Ours," the Grey Hunter says, looking back over her shoulder at the gathered hunters, and Lannesk breathes again, not sure where he's been. Here. Only here. The Grey Hunter rests her hand on his head. "They give themselves freely. Do not you dare to come between us and what now we claim." And the grey wolf shows his teeth, and even the earls and their armed theyns back away. The wolf looks them over again, the pair of them, stares eye to eye, hot breath on their faces. Anzimor offers a shaking hand, as if to a strange dog, and the wolf touches his damp black nose to it. Swipes a tongue over Lannesk's startled cheek, grinning. Turns and bounds away and is birch-pale gyrfalcon, rising, circling high, lost in the grey clouds gathering.

It doesn't seem that even Tannis will order them taken and killed now. She's silent, mouth clenched to a thin line, fists bunched on her belt. Lannesk draws a shaking breath that sears in the raw old way, as if the scars of his throat and voice-box are broken open, but it's only the damp and the cold and the dryness of his mouth. He makes a fine braid behind his ear from out of the woods-draggled mess of his hair, binds the falcon's feather into it. Plenty of ragged ends to tear from his clothing, to tie it off with. Earl Karna watches this.

Traitor, he thinks to her. Oath-breaker. Traitor, and cruel beyond belief, to put your sister to this. Karna looks away.

"I'll go to Borharbour with the Coastlanders, to join the Riding of the King," the grey-haired swordtheyn says.

"And I," says the spearcarl who gave them cider.

Islyn stirs as if she would speak. Earl Karna grips her shoulder. She droops silent again.

"And I," says a young man their own age. They know him, met him at the Kingsday festival, circling wary and bristling, like the testing of strange dogs. Ekkard, his name. Lord Ekkard. And he glowers at Earl Tannis his mother.

"No!" she says. But Ekkard lifts his chin and crosses over to stand by them, looking down at them expressionless, and only they see how pale his knuckles, from the grip he has on his sword.

Anzimor, slowly, struggles to his feet beside Ekkard, propped on his spear. Reaches a hand to Lannesk, who rises, too. Cold, and feeling weary and stiff as an old man.

So that's decided. They'll join the company assembling to follow the Wild King against the dragon-kin. Like falling into one of their mother's songs. But Lannesk did that when the Grey Hunter flew to him out of the shadowy green. Black scabs mark his wrist, the root of his thumb. He feels it burning, not pain, exactly, but an awareness. As if she's set some sign on him.

~MAIRRAN~

"Dead?" Nowa asked. "How?"

Sage was pulling on her drawers as she spoke, and her shirt. "Killed, theyn. A spear, I think. He's just beyond these trees, the dead man. But there's no one else in the woods that I can tell, not anymore."

"Well done," I said. "And Sage—thank you. That was good shooting."

She ducked her head, a flush darkening her cheeks. "If I'd a bow, there in the Forest where you found me, I'd have been fine. I've practised since I was small—my mother taught me. To be a guard for the road, in the summer trading. But it's good we were close. I'm not very strong."

"Yet. You're still growing. Strength will come. Better to be accurate, which you are. Unless you were aiming for me."

"My lord—" A smile, then, a fleeting glance up at me under the hair, fluffy now that it was washed, and a fox's glint of teeth. That was the look that should be dancing free under the stars.

"But you shouldn't have let Nowa know. She'll have you in the practice-yard till you have shoulders like hers."

A laugh, an actual bubbling chortle.

"Come on, then, my vixen. Show me this dead man."

We left Nowa sitting Thorn very erect and alert, spear at the ready, and pushed our way through the cedars.

Much trampling and scuffling, where the attackers had come down on the road. The ones who'd lurked on the other side must have crossed farther on. Where the snow was undisturbed, fox-tracks ran, and older, a bit wind-softened, hare, squirrel, a grouse stitching a wandering line. And then—dog? No, wolf. Out of nowhere.

"Sage?"

She looked where I pointed. Frowned. "I didn't see that." Pointed aside to where her own fox-tracks ran, small and dainty, and no, she wouldn't have seen.

"Did you smell it?"

"A dog? No. I don't think so. No. I'd have noticed. I've—I like dogs, but they're dangerous, I know they're dangerous, when I'm—"

"It wasn't a dog," I said.

She didn't notice that the tracks came from nowhere. Or had wind, or snowfall from a bough above, broken the trail?

And there was the fifth attacker, a swordtheyn sprawled on his back in the churned and scarlet-spattered snow, arms spread. Shield, unblooded sword, open-faced helmet, and a byrnie, which had not saved him, because the spear had taken him with brutal precision through the eye.

"Why didn't you come back when you found this?" I asked, and then held up a hand, seeing how she flinched. "No, I'm not saying you should have. But tell me your reasoning."

"I—He was dead, my lord. He wasn't going anywhere. And you and Theyn Nowa were there, and Nowa was hurt and you'd said to find if there were any others in the woods—"

"Well enough. Don't worry. I was only wondering." But she could have shifted back to her human form for a moment and called out to us; a voice briefly calling wouldn't have told anyone hiding in the woods anything they didn't know and she'd have been Fox and gone before any could come looking for her. Still afraid—ashamed, maybe— of her changing. I wasn't sure how best to approach that. Left it for later.

I do that a lot, with things I don't want to think about. I do know it.

The man wore a fine heavy cloak which, if we had been just passing through, I would have pinched for Sage, good shearling boots that would have been far too large for her, and a big bronze disc-brooch to clasp the cloak.

That, I took. It wasn't any lord's device, but a pattern of dotted whorls, very old, and not in common use. Someone would recognize it.

A man of middle age, grey-bearded, light-skinned, face gone slack, open-mouthed. The blood in the snow had not yet frozen, but it was not a cold day. His shield—I did lift it to look—was white, newly whitewashed. He was still warm, but cooling. Lightning hopped down and studied the hollow pit of his eye and brains like a woodcarver looking over another artist's work, forbearing from comment but certain she could do better. I scooped her up and put her in Sage's arms.

Our brigands had come on skis, as Sage said. Short and broad, the skis stood neatly upright, waiting. One could make good time on skis, even through trackless Forest, but they had come down the road, of course, and gone aside only a little west of where they meant to lay their ambush.

But a mounted attacker—there were hoofprints trampling about. Large. Unshod.

I'd heard nothing. That was—I stared through the cedars, then shouted.

"Nowa?"

"My lord?"

"Nothing, just wanted to know if you could hear. Stay there."

"I should have heard," I told Sage. "He was killed while I was just the other side of these trees."

Sage eyed me. "You were busy, my lord."

That was true enough. And this was the commander, I was certain. Sending his spearcarls to deal with me—with all of us—no. I coursed back and forth, following bootprints. The swordtheyn had gone to the roadside, he had been there with the others in hiding but had then turned back. Had heard something, seen something—thought the others could deal with me, rushing rash ahead of my retainers. The theyn had turned back, not in outright alarm or he wouldn't have gone alone, but disturbed—to die.

"Did you follow the horse?" I asked.

"I tried. The snow's blown to cover the tracks and—horses are strong, the scent of them, but I guess the wind carried it away."

I followed her dainty fox-tracks. Horse, weaving, pushing through dense trees agile as a deer. Wisp of gossamer, silver in a ray of sunlight piercing through the bronze-green foliage. Hardly the season for spiders, and well over my head. I reached, and it was still too high.

"Sage, come here. Do you see that?"

Squinting, she finally said she did, once I told her what she was looking for.

"Going to boost you up." No point trying to send Lightning to retrieve it. Ravens were not dogs, eager to serve.

I hoisted Sage, wobbling, by her braced legs, and set her down again with our prize. Such as it was. Not one but three long strands of hair, fine as silk thread, tangled and caught in a spray of scaly leaves.

"A noble," Sage said, watching as I drew them straight. Pale. No good reason for my mind to expect the glint of red. A light brown, but one was flaxen-blond.

"Maybe," I agreed, wrapping the hairs around my finger, like a ring. Which was only going to lose them. I wrapped them back around the bit of cedar instead, and put that with the tokens of the dead in the purse at my belt.

The two of us followed the hoofprints a little farther. Wolves and a big dog, two and one, wove around the trail. And they faded away and were gone, tracks and scent and all. Snow still lay heavy overhead on the thick rafts of the cedar boughs. In some places it had shaken down. So maybe Sage was right.

Any sensible rider should have broken through onto the road as soon as the need for concealment was over. Even I would have, and you know what Nowa thought of my common sense.

No scent of horse lingered under the cedars. Only death and broken twigs.

Sage and I returned to Nowa, and mounted, and rode through the cedarwoods, out into farmlands again, pastures or cropland deserted in this season, hedged and marked with a few tall standing trees and copses, because it's never good to clear a field entirely. One does not want to lose the blessing, by pushing the Forest out entirely.

"What about the mess we've left behind?" Nowa asked. "Turn aside, find a reeve? There'll be a village there, up the brook. See the smoke?"

"You good to ride?"

"If you need me to."

I shrugged. "Then we can send someone for the bodies once we come to Mair Laikyn. I've got what I need from them. Let the crows look to the dead, till then."

The castle of Mair Laikyn filled a small island in the lake called the Fairn. It was timber-built, as was usual. By the law—Queen's law, not Forest—only the Queen might build walls and towers in stone, though one might find the ruins of old towers still standing a few courses high, in remote corners. Remnants, it was said, of the old lawless times, when earl warred on earl and the folk starved for the burning of their summer fields and the plundering of their herds. The Forest did not even breed masons, any longer, save in the eastern fells. They were one of the travelling trades, and their work was mostly the building of chimneys for fireplaces and for the soapstone stoves of the timber-built halls of earls and tower-houses of landtheyns.

We saw few others on the road, though I watched for a red horse and a tall rider. Only a girl driving cattle and an old man trudging with a staff in hand, a couple of dogs by his side. Neither of them admitted to seeing a rider ahead of our small company, and despite the quiet then there had been enough traffic since the snowfall to leave the road a trampled confusion. Only blank looks and shaken heads, when I asked about a red horse, in particular. It was not a common colour among Forest horses.

We attracted some attention, riding through the village that stretched along the lakeside. Fairnshore, where Sage had come to a great summer fair with her mother and their ponies. Strangers, unknown swordtheyns, and Nowa's bloodied leg. And then the device of the shields, making us known. I saw the heads put together, the wary distance folk gave us, with none of the children or the dogs allowed to chase after, none of the gossip-hungry closing in to ask where the strangers had come from, what our business might be.

Nowa put Thorn ahead as we neared the bridge. She had ridden those last miles grimly upright and glowering at Sage and me with equal force as we traded off hovering close with scouting ahead, Sage, at least, obviously sniffing the air, turning sharp eyes from side to side. Once we were out of the cedar woods, the ravens spread wings and flew circling over the fields beyond. Sage, unasked, had her bow strung and in her hand. As we approached the castle she watched the platform where a pair of spearcarls lounged over the open gate.

The girl really needed a month's feeding up. Despite bathing and being decently dressed she still looked like some starveling brigand's brat from the deep wilds, not any honourable lord's groom, all bones and hollow, bruised eyes. Her new quilted tunic—by chance a rich unfaded russet, which amused me—was too large, the cuffs hiding her hands, which must despite that have been numb with cold.

I shrugged off an uneasy wish to have either sent Sage safely back to Ermintrud the shipmaster, or to have brought all the crew of the *Snow Goose* with me, to have more spears, a proper retinue, at my back. Too late now. I had known I was riding into—if not a trap, at least an unfriendly hall, since the first arrow flew. And Nowa was shivering, with an ugly pallor to her skin.

"Sage," I said, and she brought her pony up alongside. "If things go badly—run. Don't take the pony. Don't even take Smoke, and he's the fastest we have. Just get outside the walls, hide when you must, wait for darkness if you must, but be Vixen and run to Ermintrud. Don't do anything heroic or desperate, don't come looking for me or Nowa, don't stay to defend us. You understand? You'll be safe with the shipmaster and she'll know what she must do. She's a trusted servant of the Queen, and no one will kill you for a fayling, which you are not, nor a shapeshifter and Forest-blessed, which you are. Give me your word you'll obey."

"My lord."

"Tell me."

"Yes, my lord. I'll—run. If I have to."

"Good."

Hooves echoed hollow on the planks of the bridge. It was wide enough for a team and hay-wagon and zigzagged between several stony islets. We were, of course, watched, and some of the folk of the village followed, though none set foot on the bridge behind.

The castle gates stood open, but the guards had come down by the time we crossed the last span—a drawbridge, that.

Nowa straightened her back. "Tell Lady Rikenza that the Queen's son Prince Mairran, by the Queen's word and writ the High Reeve of Laikyn, is come."

"And we'll need your surgeon," I added. "At once."

"My lord prince." A nodding bow from the elder of the pair, and raised eyebrows at Nowa's leg, with the arrow's stump still standing in it. There was new blood staining the bandages, and her face had taken on a grey cast about eyes and lips I did not much like. "Run to the earl—" He addressed the younger spearcarl, but I interrupted.

"Earl Raynellin is dead at Harvesttide, or so the Queen was told. Is this not the case?"

"My lord, yes, my lord, the old earl has gone to the halls of the Dark Mother, but her daughter—"

"The Queen has not yet confirmed that succession. I want Lady Rikenza, and I want a surgeon to see to my shield-companion. Not necessarily in that order. Go—run." The younger spearcarl bowed more deeply, cast her partner a worried sidelong glance, and dashed away across the ward beyond. I couldn't see which hall she was making for. As was usual with such strongholds, the outer ward was a crowded place, filled with halls and workshops and storehouses, hens and geese and dogs, even a few swine roaming, most of the buildings wooden-shingled and all more close-packed than usual, constricted as the castle was by its island site.

Fire would go through Mair Laikyn like the flood when a spring ice-dam gives.

"You were attacked, my lord?"

"Not ten miles from here. Is Laikyn short of spearcarls or just courage, that it leaves outlaws and brigands roaming free and bold enough to attack armed travellers on the Queen's highway, and so close to the earl's castle? How do your landcarls get their crops in or drive their cattle home in peace, when swordtheyns can't ride through open farmland? Small wonder your earl died such a death."

The man's face was a blank mask. So was Nowa's, but I could feel her disapproval. Save my anger for the lords and commanders over them, she would say.

The spearcarl's lack of disbelief, or shocked outrage, I found—say, interesting. Worry, maybe, is what I read in that face.

I wondered if the man was making a quick survey in his mind of who had come carrying tales from Borharbour the night before, and who had gone out in the dark before the dawn.

Who had not come back, of his barracks-mates?

I touched heels to Smoke and rode forward, which sent the guard skipping out of the way. Maybe the guard hadn't actually intended to block our entry, but he hadn't exactly been clearing the road, either.

The keep was a squat, square, log-built tower on a knoll of rock, surrounded by its own palisade, and it had the deserted look of most such inner strongholds, too comfortless for everyday use, but we chose a lane angling towards it, around a smithy where a pair that looked like father and daughter were beating out the runner of a sleigh. The earl's hall, I thought, would be the long, high-gabled building we saw then on the slightly higher ground to the east of the gate, one of the few to boast chimneys. A broad-antlered moose-skull was mounted at the peak, old and weathered, and the antlers gilded. Both the ravens settled there. I turned to where there was a stirring in the little crowd that had gathered to gawp, a woman stooping.

"I will see the heart's blood of any fool who throws so much as a pebble at my birds," I said.

Seems I was not in a good mood.

We headed towards the hall. It was early afternoon, and a fine day for all the taste of winter in the air. The window-shutters were still open, and sometimes the half-doors of the small halls and bowers, though the shadows already stretched long, the light gone evening yellow. More folk emerged to eye us, whispering together. Not dangerous. Not yet.

Lady Rikenza herself came out to meet us, standing on the steps of the great hall's porch. A woman maybe a handful of winters older than myself and no taller, brown hair caught up in loops of one of the more ornate patterns of braiding, of which, though I remain wilfully ignorant of such things, Nowa could probably have told you the name. White ribbons woven in. She had warm tawny skin and unusual light brown eyes. Her hall-gown was the unrelieved black of mourning and she wore few jewels save a small disc of bluestone set in braided gold wires as diadem, plain gold hoops in her ears, and her seal-ring. There were two spearcarls behind her, a young hall-runner, and a man to her left, also in mourning black. Lord Raynar, the brother. Tall and broad-shouldered, beard trimmed fashionably short. He was handsome, very like his sister in colouring, though he wore his hair in a simpler braid. More rings to his fingers, though, some set with minor gems, and beads of jet for his ears.

I had never laid eyes on either of them before, if ever they had come with their mother the earl to the Kingsday Fair and the Golden Nights court at Queen's Arrun. Raynar was a swordtheyn, I presumed. The Queen would have mentioned if he had followed some calling less usual for a lord's male and landless offspring, and there was, not quite aggression in his stance, but something close to it, legs braced, hand resting on the gilded hilt of his sword. Rikenza introduced him as her shield-companion, a bit stiffly, as if expecting comment. That was not the usual thing, for one sibling to serve another in such a position, which was meant to honour a close companion among swordtheyns. Not always a lover, but often enough to be a recurring element in the sort of ballads that told of the made-up adventures of made-up heroes.

No, I've never slept with Nowa, other than in the ordinary way of a shared bed at need. I give short shrift to those who suggest otherwise.

"My lord prince." The lady bowed, and the lord as well, all very proper. "We're honoured, my lord. We had no word of your coming to Laikyn—"

"Did you not? I asked for a surgeon's attendance, Lady Rikenza. We were attacked from ambush on the road, not many miles from your gate, and my shield-companion is gravely wounded."

"My lord, yes—come inside, and be welcome. I've sent for Mistress Glinn, who is physician and surgeon both, and travelled in her youth to the outlands to study at the school at Goslack." Lady Rikenza peered around us, caught sight of someone. "Ah good. Henning will help your girl stable your horses."

The barncarl was an older man, red-haired as Sage, elbowing through the onlookers. He gave Sage a companionable nod, reaching for Thorn's bridle, stroking the stallion's nose, but looking up to Nowa, too. "If you'd allow, swordtheyn?"

I dismounted and went to steady Nowa down myself, tossing my reins to Sage, who gave me a worried frown.

"See to the horses and then have our bags brought to our chamber," I said, taking over my own shoulder the one bag Nowa would not let out of her sight. We had better have been provided some lodging place by the time Sage had the horses seen to. I wanted Nowa settled with her leg up, and quite possibly Sage and her bow by her to watch the door. Crooked a finger to the girl, spoke softly in her ear, when she came, obedient, and let them wonder what private orders she was getting.

"Remember what I said before, little vixen. Keep your eyes and ears open. And remember, too: you're the carrion crow's own and you take orders from none but me and Nowa. Be courteous, be respectful, but be certain no one, not the lady and lord themselves, has any right to set you aside from what I've commanded or send you off on any errand whatsoever, save you hear it confirmed by one of us two."

"Yes, my lord."

Nowa was, I thought, in too much pain by then to be fuming at either the indignity of having to hobble using me as a crutch or her helplessness to defend me if some second attack came.

And probably shamed, deeply, at having no share in my defence, during the ambush.

"Are you sulking that Sage and I had all the fun?" I murmured, which got a grunt out of her, and fingers digging into my shoulder as she forced herself a little more upright. But still, the two steps up to the level of the porch left her mouth pinched and pale, and brought out a sweat on her face.

The private apartments of the earl's family would be above the hall, but I did not think Nowa would manage the stairs with only me to lean on. Lord Raynar must have felt the same, because he looked me over, dismissed me as too frail a thing for the task—a mistake of which I'm generally not at all averse to taking advantage—and summoned a couple of sturdy servants of the hall to get their shoulders under Nowa's arms, more carrying than supporting her. And thus we all went up the stairs, which were at the side, hidden by a wall of bright-painted panelling.

"My brother's chambers are being made ready for you, my lord," Lady Rikenza said. "If we'd had more warning of your visit...but it won't be long."

A couple of servants were bustling various chests and baskets and armloads of bedding out as we all staggered in. Lord Raynar himself, with an apologetic smile, cleared a small shelf of books, half a dozen of them at least, and took them away stacked between arms and chin. A pity. I wouldn't have minded getting a look at those. There was, every now and then, a telling entirely different of an old lay to discover, set down in some book that had never found its way to the library at Queen's Arrun, and what a Singer wouldn't do for you, seduced by a tale they'd never heard... Oh laugh, but it was true.

Anyway, we sat Nowa on the low bed in the anteroom which would have belonged to Raynar's attendant or shieldling, to wait as the last baskets went out and fresh bedding and fine wax candles to replace the grease-lamps—which were all we usually burned in my own tower—brought in. There was a fireplace in the inner room. I ordered Nowa to be helped into the warmth and settled, when she protested at the high, curtained bed, on a chair, got her boots and sword-belt off her myself. By then the grey-haired surgeon and her apprentices, a man my age pale-skinned as a Sealander and a freckled girl smaller than Sage, had appeared; Mistress Glinn at once set these assistants about heating water and cleaning in the fire her various needles and probes and blades.

"Out," Nowa told me, and, recalling witnesses, "There's no need for you to stay, my lord."

The surgeon, too, was politely suggesting that all those with no business here should remove themselves. I wasn't entirely easy about leaving Nowa alone with unknown people and knives, but I was fairly sure she had one or two of her own up her sleeve, and Mistress Glinn did not seem any more murderous than the average surgeon. I took myself off, but no further than the antechamber, shutting the door behind me and raising a hand to summon the earl's heir back when she would have gone out to the landing of the stairs beyond.

"Wait."

"My lord, I'll order wash-water, and bread and ale brought for you. You'll want to refresh yourself—"

"Thank you," I said. Nowa did do her best to bring me up properly and sometimes I remembered. "Later. The Queen, my lady, is most disturbed. She is not pleased at having had to learn of your mother's death from traveller's gossip. And they were certain, at the gate, that 'earl' was your right title."

Nowa used to tell me not to make people angry and not to make people afraid, especially when I was cornered alone. She never understood that somewhere in my head I was always alone, always cornered, and that fear tasted better channelled into rage—which was rather more useful to my mother's hand anyway.

I dropped the bronze brooch on a table, and from my purse, took out the other trophies as well. The cedar spray holding the hairs was among them.

"I took these off the brigands we killed," I said. "Recognize anything?"

Rikenza frowned, taking up the heavy brooch of the man Sage and I had found dead. Then her hand went to her mouth, eyes wide, and her face, I thought, shone suddenly with sweat, though the light was very dim. But I have good vision even in the dark. I thought she might faint, in truth. She dropped it and looked at me, swallowed, gripping the edge of the table. Too late now for her to deny it.

"What will I find," I asked, "when the bodies are brought back? Will there be grief and wailing among your folk of the hall? People to cry out their names?"

Lady Rikenza was shaking her head. Abruptly, she thumped her fists on the little table, so that the candles swayed and set the shadows swirling in the windowless room.

"No," she said. "No."

"What is it?" her brother asked, coming in. He must not have gone far.

"Harilan," she said. Her knees folded and she dropped to the floor.

I was before her brother in catching her, though almost we knocked heads.

"What have you done?" Raynar snarled, dragging Rikenza from me, sweeping her to the narrow bed against the opposite wall. Frantic. Calling her name, patting her cheek, raising his voice, shouting for Physician Glinn. The older apprentice popped his head out the door, scowling.

"The lady's fainted, nothing to concern you," I said and didn't quite shove him back to do whatever he was doing that might aid Nowa, but nearly. Lady Rikenza was already stirring, trying to sit up and push her brother away.

Raynar demanded again to know what I had done, shouted out the door for the spearcarls who were hanging about on the landing, and Rikenza moaned the dead man's name again. I ignored the uneasy armed pair who crowded in. They weren't quite fools enough to draw on the Queen's son, luckily for them. Eventually I got lord and lady both to shut up and sent the hall-runner to fetch her something to drink. The boy was quickly back from Rikenza's own rooms with a cup, which she sipped. Some healthier colour came back into her face.

"Harilan," she said. "Swordtheyn Harilan. That's his—" A shaking hand. "Where is he? I haven't seen him in the hall since last night."

"If that was his brooch, he's dead in the cedar woods this side of the covered bridge on the stone road to Borharbour," I said. "He and four with him attacked us. They shot at us and wounded my swordtheyn, which you've seen for yourselves, and then attacked us, there among the trees. But him, at least, I didn't kill. It looked as if one of his own had turned on him."

No, I didn't actually think that.

I gave them the bare outline of the ambush. The spearcarls attacking as I rode to confront the archer who had shot from cover before rushing at me, the fifth man, this Harilan, found dead in the trees, the half-glimpsed red horse.

"Him!" Raynar said. "With the red horse! The outlaw. The wild man. Our mother's murderer. My lord, they weren't hunting you, they didn't attack you—"

"They most surely did."

Yes, I felt sick for a moment then, because what if—but no. Even Thorn's golden coat couldn't be mistaken for red, and three riders openly on the Queen's stone road—yes, even with their shields covered and maybe I had better have not done that—should not shout "outlaw" at anyone.

And a swordtheyn of the earl's hall should neither shoot from cover nor attack without declaring himself. Nor whitewash his shield.

"He was our mother's shield-companion," Lady Rikenza said. "He was—her friend, very dear to her, in the years since our father died. Like a second father to us, growing up. He—why?"

And other such unenlightening mumbling. Her shock and grief seemed real enough.

Lord Raynar had left his sister to frown down at what I had flung on the table. He hefted the swordtheyn's brooch in his hand.

"The Dark Mother take you!" he shouted, and swept the litter of clasps and knife clattering to the floor. Failed to knock over the candles. Turned on me with a clenched fist raised. "You murdering little—"

I hit him, before he could do anything more stupid, like reach for a weapon. Fist to his face and turning with a sweeping kick as he reeled, so that he went crashing sideways into the spearcarl who had started forward.

"Lady, control your hallfolk!" My shield and helmet I had set aside earlier, but my sword was drawn by the time Raynar hit the floor, and I still wore my byrnie. I did not want to have to kill the lady's brother here, or the spearcarls.

Shouts in the bedchamber, too, and that door was flung open. One glance behind showed me Nowa, clad only in breast-band and drawers with one leg cut away, and about her neck the silver amulet she always wore, the spread-winged eagle of the Bright Mother, the disc of her son the Ascendant borne between the eagle's shoulders. A thick bandaging about Nowa's leg, and her sword in her hand. The physician and her young man caught Nowa as she staggered and began to fall. They had her. Well enough. Couldn't be my problem just then.

But one spearcarl was hesitant, looking at his lady, and the other had hit her head in falling and was swaying on hands and knees and still tangled with Lord Raynar, who sat splayed like a frog with his mouth swelling.

"Stop!" the lady shouted, on her feet. "Lower your weapon." And the hesitant spearcarl did.

I, pointedly, did not. Because she could not give me orders, and I was still watching her brother, who was picking himself up, rather cautiously.

He said nothing, hand to his mouth. Then he bowed, very low.

"My lord prince. I apologize. I was—upset." He bowed a second time, even lower. "Forgive me," Lord Raynar said. Didn't look repentant in the last. He turned to the door, as if he would leave.

"No." The gall of the man. I pointed to the bench-bed. "Sit. Both of you, sit."

They did, brother and sister not touching, not looking at one another. The little hall-runner helped the fallen spearcarl up.

"Swordtheyn Nowa," I said, because she was on her feet again, swaying braced in the doorway, sword wavering in her hand. I think they must have drugged her, and by the ashy pallor of her face, just as well. "Go back to bed, before you tear that wound worse or catch your death of cold."

They did get her away, and the door shut again. I sighed, and sat down on the settle. Did keep my sword out, though, across my knees. Waved a hand to the guards to take a place by the door. The young boy shuffled aside, trying not to be noticed, but when his foot slipped on the antler-handled knife in its sheath he squatted down to pick up the things Raynar had scattered and set them softly again on the table between the candles. I gave him a nod and told him to sit down on the floor out of the way once he had done that. There wasn't another chair.

"This ambush was treason," I said, and I tapped the flat of my blade with each word. "High treason. An attack on me, here on my mother's service, is high treason. The swordtheyn Harilan, if that was who wore this brooch, is dead. The spearcarls he doomed and damned by leading to their deaths—I might, if Nowa takes no lasting harm, have had the mercy to enquire whether they knew what he led them to or not, should any of them have lived, but they are beyond the reach of the Queen's law now. You, Lady Rikenza, are not. You were his liege-lady—not as earl, but as your mother's land-heir. Did you send him against me?"

"No, my lord prince. The Mothers Above and Below, the Bright Mother and the Dark Mother and the Sun Ascending be my witness and leave my soul to wander the Dark Beyond forever nameless and voiceless if I lie, I did not." She was afraid, terribly afraid, and miserable, not defiant. Which did not mean she was not lying, despite the weighty oath. "I didn't even know Harilan had ridden out from the castle."

That they hadn't ridden was perhaps a point in favour of her truthfulness. Perhaps.

But I thought I believed her.

"Lord Raynar."

"No, my lord. I say as my sister did. I swear—he mistook you, my lord. Surely he mistook you. You said yourself, you saw a man on a red horse."

I had not said that, only that someone other than myself had slain the man who wore that brooch while he hid in the trees, and that I had thought I saw the flash of a bright hide among those trees, and had found the marks of hooves, fading under drifted snow. And to what was Raynar swearing, and by what? Words are tricky things, and some know enough to be careful with them.

"We're hunting such a one, my lord prince. A wild man."

I ignored that, and Raynar, once more. "Lady Rikenza. Who was it came bearing word of me from Borharbour?"

She shook her head. "My lord, there was no one."

Both denied they had any warning of me, before the armscarl ran from the gate. Obviously I chose not to believe that. Some man of the earl's service had been in Borharbour asking questions of Ermintrud, probably summoned by a perfectly reasonable and innocent message from the harbour-reeve when the ship first put in…

The armed man I'd seen with the harbour-reeve. Whom I had not seen with her again…

Not one of the old reeve's household. Fool.

I had recognized him, almost, then. Did, now. The man I'd given that final mercy to on the ground.

There were questions to be asked among the folk of the castle— barncarls and armscarls and the servants of the hall. Had he gone to lady or lord or straight to Harilan… I could think of utterly no reason a swordtheyn I had never met, shield-companion and leman of a murdered earl, would choose to waylay me with murder in mind himself, unless he had slain his own lady, which—did not smell right. No, someone had ordered this Harilan out, in haste. In panic, even, dared I think, and I could hope that they might now be reconsidering the folly of my death, and what might follow on it.

I would set Sage to answering that question, I decided. The girl came into the room then, while I sat frowning in thought. Scowling, Nowa would say.

Letting sister and brother fidget and sweat. Or think and fix their lies in their minds. The groom Henning was with Sage, both burdened with the baggage. I had them set things down out of the way, dismissed Henning with my thanks. Noted that he gave Sage a friendly nod after he bowed, with a wary glance at his distressed lady, and that Sage smiled back. Not the polite, wary smile of a young person being sensibly cautious of someone older, bigger, stronger, of greater authority. Just a comfortable smile, and the man's look at her had been just…comfortable, too. Matter-of-fact kindness and fellowship, not like someone eyeing up a pretty youth. Decided I'd have another look at the man, later. It wouldn't come amiss for the girl to have someone she could trust belonging to this place, who would keep a parental eye on her among the serving-folk. But for the time being, I sent her in to watch over Nowa.

"Tell me," I said to brother and sister, "about this wild man."

~LANNESK~

Diving and rising. He's a bird, storm-buffeted. No, it's the Lake, rolling and heaving and throwing them to the sky, black night and the Lake wild as the sea, as if the Dragon herself is waking and rising beneath their hull. The storm comes on in the grey before the dawn and drives them all the day and into the night. They run hard before it, the sail reefed, just enough left for steerageway, and it takes three big men to hold the steering-oar. Lannesk was set to that himself earlier, he and Anzi with the shipmaster's brother, till grip grew numb and muscles burned and limbs trembled and another watch relieved them. Others bail with oxhide buckets, and they've had a turn at that, too. There's been cheese and leathery smoked fish for those who could keep it down, which didn't include him at the time, and he hadn't thought to sleep, but somehow he has, rolled up between the benches, soaked to the skin and shivering cold. Dreaming he's a bird.

He thinks that's what's woken him, the shivering, the marrow-deep chill, till he misses Anzimor at his back. Thinks Anzimor's iron belly has finally rebelled, though his own head feels clearer now and he's hollow and light and no longer compulsively retching. People have been sick everywhere, even the shipcarls, not making it to the side, not daring to, puking where they huddle, too many of them, and the water sloshing down between the ribs must be filthy. Someone went overboard, a woman of Earl Karna's, gone and no turning back to look for her, though they threw ropes. Daylight, then. She must have sunk like a stone. There was no frantic flailing, no bobbing head struggling above the waves. She was just…gone.

A jolt like lightning burns through him, remembering that, and he's on his feet, crouching, braced on the rowing-bench where a shipcarl is lying, and that woman grunts at his weight on her. Where did he go? he would demand of her, but it's black dark and he'd call, shout over the wind and the creak and the crash, but all he can manage is a faint breathy moan himself.

Anzi—as if thought could call him and be answered.

A sound then, a scuffling, near, and a muffled sound. Something thumps, and Lannesk goes scrambling over another bench and into something yielding, slick wet leather, a body beneath. Hands grab him. He thinks it someone struggling for balance like himself and they cling together a moment, till another body crashes into him and he falls to his knees. Anzimor cries out his name, and the hands that have clutched him force him down, face into water, filth, a weight on him and someone says, voice raised to be heard but not meant to carry, "Got the other one here, I—" Breaks off in a grunt as he flings the man back. Reaching, not daring to use his knife. Pulls the arm he finds.

"Lannesk!" Anzimor bellows above the wind but a hand has found his face, Anzimor's because it doesn't clutch and try to push or drag. "Is that you, Lan?" and he nods against the hand. "Where are they? Bastards dragged me off—tried to heave me over—"

Scuffle, and he strikes out, hard, with Anzimor's back set to his. A grunt and a crash, someone falling. There's another body dropping onto them, and a shout, "What is this?" Lord Ekkard's voice, sharp.

Someone moves, stealthily, away, so Lannesk scrambles after that sound, grabs and brings them down—down hard, the ship's roll helping him.

"I was attacked, my lord," Anzimor says. "Someone—more than one—tried to shove me overboard. Lan, where are you?" His voice isn't going shrill in panic, but it's a close thing.

This night is a fever-dream, a madness. Cold wet shivering eyeless noise, thudding and roaring. Lannesk whistles, their old two-note signal, feels Anzimor set himself against him once more. Hauls his captive upright. They lurch and pull away but not before he's swung, fist connecting with a rough-bearded face. That'll mark him. He'll know that one, when the dawn comes. If ever it does.

"If anyone's plotting murder this night, it's those Mothers-rejected outlaws," a man says, somewhere out of reach. "My lord, come away up here. Don't give them a chance—"

"Shut up, Tolla," Ekkard says. Tolla is one of Earl Tannis's spearcarls, sent, he and his brother Ovan, as shield-companions to the young lord. "Where's Ovan?"

"Here," Ovan says out of the night, blacker than the Dark Beyond. A thick and surly growl, and Lannesk knows who was on the other end of his fist.

"Then listen. Listen well. Listen, all of you!" Lord Ekkard shouts over the wind, over the creak and slam and the waves. "I will not have this! We're all sworn to answer the call of the Wild King. These men and women, Earl Brux's spearcarls—" There are almost two dozen of them, who chose to join this autumn muster rather than swear oaths to Earl Tannis, and as many of Tannis's and Karna's followings, counting the shipcarls. "—and these two, his stepsons Anzimor and Lannesk, they are our comrades, our brothers and sisters. I will not have fighting. I will not have this—this profaning of our oaths. I will not have the quarrel between my mother and her cousin carried on among us. Not here, not when we come to the Holy Isle and our winter camp, not when the army sails north in the spring. Do you hear me, all of you? You are not theyns and carls of Tannis or of Karna or of Brux. You are all of you carls of the King, now. You serve the Forest, no one earl. Anyone who raises a hand against another does so against their brother, their sister. Do you hear?"

There are voices that answer, some. Lannesk wonders how many even heard.

"Tolla," Ekkard says. "Ovan." His voice is lowered, and the anger is something else. Something cold. "I don't ask you what orders my mother gave—"

"My lord—"

"Be quiet. Does she truly believe Anzimor could raise Brux's folk against her? Against me? He's not even Forest-born. He's no danger to me. He's certainly none to her or to my sister's inheritance. So. I don't ask you what orders my mother gave, but I swear to you, if either Anzimor or Lannesk die on this journey to the Holy Isle, be it open murder or supposed accident, the both of you will hang, Mothers Above and Below be my witness. They are my brothers in this company, as they are yours; they are my cousins, my kin by their mother's marriage to my cousin, and you will defend them as you would me."

"My lord, I might have stumbled against him in the dark, but I never—"

"We heard a fight starting, my lord, only that, the Coastlanders were quarrelling with someone, we didn't—"

"Shut up, before you damn yourselves with even more lies. This is over, you understand? No more. Go lie down and get what rest you can. The fewer people moving about, the safer we'll all be."

"Aye, my lord, the Bright Mother being merciful, and thank you." That from Myrild, the shipmaster.

"Yes, my lord," says Tolla, or maybe Ovan, grudging. "Will you come away forward, my lord?"

"I'm fine where I am," Ekkard says. "Go, and we'll say no more of this."

"My lord?" Anzimor begins to speak.

"No more on it from you, either," Ekkard says to Anzimor. He doesn't address Lannesk. Few of them do. It's not deliberate slight, only a discounting they hardly realize they make.

"Ah, Lan," Anzimor says then, and leans on him, swaying with the ship's sway. "Nearly went for the long swim then."

Lannesk pulls Anzimor close in a one-armed hug, a hand still free for their enemies. He wonders, was it like this for their father, the long dark of the storm and the waves piling higher and higher? Did the ship plunge down and fail to rise, or was there the crack of broken timbers? Was it swift, or was there this long terror, before the weight of the water, smashing over, dragging down—

Don't think of that.

"Bright Mother bless and keep us and send the dawn," Ekkard mutters, and his teeth are chattering. "Let's get some sleep, if we can."

They find their place again and lie down, warmer, crowded, three of them together, and it's too wet and cold and terrible for it to be anything but the little sharing of warmth and Ekkard making certain no servant of his mother's is going to try murder in the night again. But Lannesk wonders, and wonders if he's sorry for Ekkard, who does watch Anzimor in unguarded moments, or for Anzi, who doesn't seem to notice it.

They don't sleep, only wait out the hours in what seems an unending nightmare of cold and noise and wet, but the dawn comes grey, with the winds growing weak and the clouds breaking. Folk who've only been able to help by keeping out of the way come back to life; they stir, slow and heavy, like the dead waking. They can see what they are doing to bail and to mend what's broken, set straight what's out of place. It's a bad time of year to make a Lake-crossing. The Dragon, as the shipcarls like to say, sleeps lightly. But Earl Tannis refused to allow Lannesk and Anzimor to winter in Borharbour and travel to the Holy Isle in the spring, which left them needing to find some way down over the Lake or pay with their lives, and Lord Ekkard swore he'd go with them, and—rather than back down and let them stay the winter in Borharbour, as if honour were at stake in her cold rage against them, she gave her son this ship and crew, and they set out.

With orders given to murder Lannesk and Anzimor, it seems.

In time, the waves calm enough to make a fire in the sandbox and boil a great cauldron of porridge, so they can warm in turn hands and feet numb or swollen, throbbing with the cold. No land in sight in any direction, but Myrild knows the Lake, its wind and currents, and he says they'll have been driven far and hard and could maybe count a day or two off their journey, only they've come too far south too soon and need to bear hard to the east now, if the winds will be kind.

The Singer who carried the message that brought them here is a woman with grey in her short-cropped hair and the gold ring of seven years' study. She brings out a swan-bone flute and plays a song meant to draw the kinder winds. Maybe it works, because the wind veers round to the southwest over that day, fresh but not furious, and they angle the sail and scud over the Lake like a leaf riding the swift current of a flooded brook, and find the hills of the Holy Isle already on their horizon, a smear of autumn gold against the east.

Tolla has a split lip and Ovan a black eye and swollen cheek, and they are sullen and careful around Anzimor and Lannesk and their lord all three, by which Lannesk decides they believe Ekkard's threat to hang them. Maybe a bit relieved, themselves, to be spared having the weight of murder on their souls?

He worries, though, what will become of Islyn's baby.

A hazy windless dusk with frost sharp in the air when they come nosing into the Holy Isle, rowing hard as much to make a good show for Laikyn's pride as to reach harbour before the smoking mist thickens to hide the southern rocks and northern marsh of the rivermouth. An oar-song of the Wild King's first Riding keeps their rhythm. Lord Ekkard's is far from the only shipload of spearcarls who've not waited for spring to answer the Seers' call. The sheltered landing-beach with its log rollers is fringed with ships, and the others are moored at the few wharves. New boat-sheds loom yellow and the air smells of fresh lumber. The folk are not unwelcoming, but not over-friendly, either. Wary. But the folk of the Isle are few, and suspicious of armed strangers. There have been earls before who tried to claim mastery here. None that ever succeeded. Nothing unites the earls so swiftly against one of their own as fear that she may come to rule the Singers.

The Holy Isle is a fringe of coast around a steep central rise of fells thrusting above wooded hills; the scattered landcarls and foresters owe service only to the Masters of Singersborg. Inland, there's the village of Arrunstead on the northern shore of the little river, sheltered below a bluff of soft yellow sandstone, which itself lies below a great ridge of harder grey rock running from a sharp headland towards the northwest, climbing in a rising spur to the fells. The Singersborg perches on that ridge above bluff and village and the swift-running Arrun, a collection of stone-built halls and towers within a stone wall said to have been raised in the Dragon's day, though what that fortress guarded, Lannesk wonders. Not the river, set high and as far back as it is, and anyway, you can't get anything but a canoe up the shallow little river so far; it's eight miles or so from the harbour.

The smell of that autumn is new-felled timber, halls built in haste of bark-stripped green wood. They lay out a settlement above the bluff, above Arrunstead strung out along the river's edge, but below the western flank of the ridge crowned by Singersborg. The Masters have set aside this land, which was a fairground, and given timber-right to build their shelters and fire-right till they sail again. So the companies build a village-worth of longhouses, and raise an earthwork and palisade as if they will need to defend it against outlaw raids or earls' warring, but it is only that the commander set over them all—a southern earl's sister, Lady Lauran, who went, it is said, as a mercenary among Outland folk in her youth—wants to keep them busy. And to teach them to think as a fellowship in one service, Lannesk suspects, with rivalries and feuds set aside, though they keep to their ship's companies in their longhouses.

The Masters of the Singers had not expected their summons to draw so many to the Isle so soon, to batten on their land through the winter. Some have come under the command of lords, earls' sons and their spearcarls, like Lord Ekkard; some arrive singly, or in small furtive bands. Wanderers, tramps, outcasts and outlaws, telling that the Wild King, the Grey Hunter, or some ghostly Rider half-seen came upon them in the Forest, by chance or in answer to some desperate moment, and sent them here. Some may be seeking only bread and a winter fire, planning to desert come spring. Lady Lauran sets such strays in companies under a captain, to share a longhouse and work and train together. There are fights and thefts, and one attempt at rape that ends in a killing the assembled captains of the longhouses declare justified, one murder and soon after, a hanging. They have a smith, fletchers, bowyers. They settle together into a community.

The feather Lannesk braided into his hair at the anchorstone in Laikyn—it seems so long ago—was lost in the storm on the Lake.

Maybe it didn't mean anything, after all. Birds moult.

~MAIRRAN~

This is the story Rikenza and Raynar told me, sitting side by side on the bed in the antechamber of Raynar's chamber like children enduring a scolding.

A hunting party from the castle had ridden out in the afternoon the day before Harvesttide, the earl and Lord Raynar, but not Lady Rikenza, among them. And of course, because that's how tales of this sort go, they became separated, and a fog came up into the Forest off the Fairnmere, or perhaps a great fog rolled in off the Lake itself, and though most returned safely to Mair Laikyn, horses and hounds and hunters and all, the earl was not among them. It was hardly unusual, a fog off the water in such a season, and the Forest-cunning expect such things. Raynar, discovering his mother was still astray, rode out again without his shieldling or spearcarl or hound, without even taking a fresh horse, and was quickly Forest-wildered himself, roaming lost without sight or sound of any other wanderer.

"Without coming upon any known road or track either, my lord, that would have led me to some safe familiar village or even some forester's assart where I could spend the night, as I hoped my mother was doing. I've been lost before—who has not? But never Forest-wildered as the songs have it, with all the familiar grown strange and fayling-touched."

So in the end, like a sensible person of the Forest, he gave up on riding aimless in the dark and settled for the night in the hollow between the roots of a great elm, with a little fire to warm him and keep the wild things off. Raynar did not truly sleep, he claimed, but dozed, and shivered, and started awake thinking he heard voices, but waking, he would hear none. His horse was uneasy.

In the grey dimness before dawn he mounted and rode again, and found a narrow, sunken track. A Forestway. Naturally, he followed it.

"Of course," I said, because that's what one does, especially if one is the hero of a ballad. Rikenza sat in silence, twisting her hands together.

I wondered, if she were not guilty of murder, or of not doing worse than failing at once to inform the Queen of Earl Raynellin's death, was I also meant to judge her fitness to succeed her mother as earl? Because it was her brother seemed to dominate, when one took them as a pair. But there had been earls ruled by kinsfolk, or by friends or spouses or shield-companions, before, and no doubt would be again.

I wondered if her brother had been her own choice to stand at her shoulder and guard her door, or if the earl, dead and gone, might still be shaping her offspring's lives.

Raynar did recognize, then, the woods he rode through. He was far from Mair Laikyn, high in the red-oak hills to the north, but he also saw the marks of a solitary horse, galloping, deep-dug in the leaf-mould, and so he went on, winding higher, and then down again.

I would have asked myself, why was she galloping? What was she chasing, or what was chasing her? But it was Raynar's story.

And so the earl's son came to the heartstone, down in a hollow.

There is always a fane, an enclosure of holy ground, about a heartstone, sometimes a ditch and bank, sometimes a hedge or a drystone wall or a fence that is no more than heaped stones, sometimes only widely-spaced boulders, marking out a circle. This one had a scattered ring of large squat stones, hardly to be noticed among the trees, and it was not a fane tended by any folk. The sacred yard within was not cleared, but grown up in mature oaks, and the tree of the stone—the one that would always have been left standing with the heartstone beneath it—was a great red oak of centuries, older than any of them. Raynar did not tell me this at first. I interrupted, more than once, to drag such details out of him. I wanted to see the place in my mind's eye. To know it.

The heartstone was grey, tall as two men, roughly shaped; it bore an incised carving of a horse, and a human figure with the broad horns of an aurochs, and no other sign. The lines were very worn.

Raynar told me this, when I asked, but I wondered why the man had noticed details of the stone at all, given that he found his mother dead there. Newly dead, and a man crouched by her, bloody knife in his hand.

"Describe him," I said.

Raynar frowned. Shrugged. "Tall. Light-haired—brown, or blond—the morning was still dim. Very pale-skinned, like Islander folk or Coastlanders in winter. I took him for a forester or the like. I didn't understand what I saw. But his hair was long, I saw that much. It wasn't braided. Knotted and matted and his beard a wild bush. Dressed in rags. Rotten rags, my lord, nothing better. He saw me and sprang to his horse—"

"This red horse?"

"Red as a fox, and a cream mane and tail. A stallion. A big horse, and as unkempt as he. No harness on it, not that I saw. But they leapt the stones and vanished among the trees."

"He didn't ride at you."

"He had no weapon."

"What about the knife?"

"He couldn't attack a mounted swordtheyn with only a knife." Raynar swallowed. "It was my mother's own knife he had used, a hunting knife."

"What about her horse?"

The earl's beast had been there. Raynar couldn't remember, when I asked, if it had been loose or tied, the reins trailing or fastened up. Grew snappish, pretending he couldn't see why it mattered. Finally said that the horse was tied, my lord, that his mother had obviously been Forest-wildered as he was in the night's fog, had chosen to rest the night at the heartstone, been surprised there by the wild man, and murdered.

"Why?" I asked. "Did he rob her? Did he rape her?"

"How do I know what he intended? No. He took nothing, except the knife. He didn't have time to rob her. She was dead, dying there in front of me. He'd fled in fear."

"Dead or dying?"

"Dead. Damn you, she was dead, he'd stabbed her to the heart, a great wound in her breast. She never spoke. She never knew me. There was blood on the ground, on the fallen leaves. So much blood."

Lady Rikenza, through all this, sat with head bowed and eyes shut. Now she looked up. "Her arm was cut."

I asked what she meant.

"Defending herself," Raynar answered.

"Cut," Rikenza said, as if in contradiction. "Her wrist. Her left wrist. The inside. I saw, I helped the lychmother lay her out."

I thought about that, about how little someone might bleed, with a knife stopping their heart. A knife, or a sword? Yet there had been blood on the ground at the stone's foot, they claimed. *So much blood.*

More likely it was the back of the arm that would be cut, if she'd flung it up against an attacker's knife. Rikenza met my eyes, flinched away, weaving her hands together on her lap.

Nothing they said went against what the Queen's eyes-and-ears quacksalver had said.

Nothing they said sounded like the act of a reasonable outlaw, some swordtheyn or spearcarl disgraced and banished from his earl's lands for an unlawful killing, say, and living wild and desperate, as such people did. All he would have had to do was ride away, if the earl had come alone upon him. Or if he meant to rob her of what she might have had on her—what, a few rings, a bow and quiver, maybe a flask of drink, a luncheon? He had his own horse, no need to take hers. He had found her dismounted, resting—she'd had knife and bow, since she was hunting, and if he'd overcome her he could have taken all he wanted without killing. If he were armed, why kill her with her own knife, and if he were not, then…he overcomes her and takes the knife off her, and then…no need to kill.

I was tired, and hungry, and thirsty, and my head hurt.

So I sent sister and brother away. I had no proof they lied, no proof they had given Harilan his orders, and though the Queen might kill at a whim, I knew she would demand more of me.

~LANNESK~

"Hey." Anzimor bumps shoulder against him. "Wake up. Take this."

His brother hands him a stoneware jar, its wooden stopper sealed with a twist of rag, another longer rag strung in a loop through its handle for easier carrying. Anzimor's wearing a garland of fir twigs and has bound a spray of wizened rosehips to his spear. Lannesk slings the jug over his shoulder like his shield. He's bound a collar of fir twigs to his own spear. Huntersnight, and there had been deep snow in Bloodmonth. There is all of true winter still to come, as if the sun, which even tomorrow will rise a hair further back towards the east and begin to lengthen the days—or so promise the Singers, whose wisdom measures such things before even Forest-cunning can tell it—must drag by force the world, slow and heavy and months behind, back into its light. Huntersnight, the counterweight of which at the summer solstice is Kingsday.

It's a time to remember the dead, the long dark of Huntersnight. A foreshadowing of the Dark Beyond, to which the Mothers Below will call even the best and brightest-burning of them all, in the end.

There are so many to remember, this cold night. Next year...which of them will come whole and alive through what the new year will bring?

Some folk slept, once the early sunset came and the day's preparations for the feast to come were done. Others sat by the fires and kept a waking vigil; some spoke of their dead. Lannesk has sat in the shadows of a cold bench against the wall, far from the fire, listening, and telling over, to his own memory, the little he remembers of their father; telling over their mother's life, and Swanlight's brief two years, and the story of Brux, who loved their mother and gave them a home. It seems important, this year's end, to hold them close in mind. Anzimor had fallen asleep against the wall beside him, and woken to pat his shoulder, and rolled up in his cloak and skins to sleep once more. Later Anzi woke again and wandered off to some warmer place, slipping silent as if he thought Lannesk slept in turn and feared to wake him, but now they're out in the dark, the stars clear and cold above, and they've found one another.

"All right?" Anzimor asks.

Lannesk nods, leans forehead to forehead with him a long moment, eyes shut, making it, in his own mind, a prayer. Keep him safe. Mothers Below, Dark Mother who holds us all, don't take my brother from me.

A bell sounds, high and sweet like a sleighbell, which it might be, and what has been a confusion of lights, torches and horn-paned lanterns bobbing and wandering, makes a slow pattern, pulling into a skein, unwinding, a ribbon wavering away into the night. Skin hand-drums pound a slow heartbeat. Bells patter over that pulse like falling water. He's heard tell that once the Singersborg was itself a fane, but the anchorstone was thrown down long ago and they hold no rites there; the Singers have come down from their stone walls and the folk of Arrunstead have climbed the steep track that twists around the bluff slantwise and lashes back to the new walled camp, Mair Arrun, to follow the Singers. Now the warband of the camp falls in behind those landfolk. The ridge rises dark to the east, but their way takes them to the northwest, into hills less steep, into Forest.

No speaking now. It's the time for the long silence before the dawn. He and Anzimor find their place behind Lord Ekkard and his uncle, old Theyn Asa. Hennis, the brown-haired spearcarl who gave them cider, comes to walk with them. She and Anzimor have mittened hands clasped together, casual down between them. Lannesk notices that when her foot skids on the icy tramped track and Anzimor lurches, bracing her. Ekkard looks back and grins at them. Ovan and Tolla are there by him and Theyn Asa, carrying torches. Ovan gives Lannesk and his brother a nod, as if he never tried to murder them. Not friendly, exactly, but not unfriendly, either. Allowing their existence. The others are about them, nearly all their band, nearly all garlanded, festive, wearing what they may have that's bright or new.

A wolf—no, only a dog, surely—howls, and among the cabins and longhouses, some of the dogs answer. Heads turn towards the deeper woods that climb the hills. It's a chill, bright sound, but it goes through him like fire. Fool. All along the procession, there are only the drums and the chiming of bells—strings of winter harness-bells, deeper cow-bells—ringing to make a chain of sound, binding them as the torches do. Wolf howls again, far in the distance. Like a summons. There are no wolves on the Holy Isle.

Dogs, excited, bark. Some that have followed the procession run off into the night. For a moment Lannesk has an impulse to do the same.

A horse paces alongside, great feet crunching snow, off the track. The rider carries no torch.

The Wild King. He seems hardly there in the wavering light they carry, shadow turning to bright copper, and then only the darkness of night and trees again. When seen, his garments are supple deerskin, nothing warmer, and tall boots, a red cloak, and his hair and beard are copper-red as his horse's flank, his eyes dark. He rides bare-headed, carries no spear, no sword or shield. In the cradle of his arm, his harp.

No one else is looking at the King, not even Anzimor. Ekkard is looking back, but his gaze is on Anzi again; he's mouthing something, a word unvoiced. No, not a mockery of Lannesk, only keeping the due silence of the vigil. What he's said is, *Later*. And Anzimor nudges Hennis and they lean together and Ekkard nods and faces back up the track.

They've not glanced over at the Wild King. He's not there. Lannesk is dreaming, waking, walking. Seeing things.

The King plays, soft notes and then louder, clear as the sleighbells, each note ringing alone and they sound like warm silver. How do they not hear, not turn, each and every man and woman in that procession, to see that the King rides with them? How can that music be lost in the crunch and scuffle of their feet for all but Lannesk?

He can feel it, the music. Feel it in his heart, as if he would give it voice, wordless notes. Feel it in his finger's tips.

Just for a moment, the Wild King is beside and glancing down. At him, he who alone of all that company seems to know that the King is there. The Immortal nods, as if he is any ordinary companion of the camp greeting a friend and not one of the sacred Immortals, one of the greatest of them. Then he smiles, knowing, amused, or maybe Lannesk only imagines that. The King is more distinct than he should be in the firelit dark, as if he rides in the bright snowlight of the full moon, and it's only a third quarter now, just rising, faint bands of light between tree-shadows on the snow, so maybe after all this is dreaming, or vision. But Lannesk grins back, because what else can he do, and the horse breaks into a trot that leaves him behind. Shadows flow in the Wild King's wake. Ghosts, or like ghosts, like reflections in water. The Riders. Men, women, dark and pale, riding horses as varied, or striding, jogging, carrying spears and bows, and some not even human, horned or antlered or with the ears of foxes, or small and slight as children, faces dappled like leaf-shadow, the fayling-folk on their white ponies. The pack follows after, dogs, wolves, shadowy, silent, and some among them not shadows, but dark solid shapes, ones that have come out from the camp, trotting along among the rest. And then, riding a white mare bareback, head bowed as if on the edge of sleep or dreaming, the white-robed Seer, who is no Immortal but a mortal human born with a great Forest-blessing, claimed and educated by the Singers, among whom Lannesk would have expected to see her walking, far ahead. She looks up—startled, he thinks. A woman little older than he himself, tawny-skinned and light-haired, with a crooked nose as though she lived a rough and brawling childhood till her gift came upon her; her eyes seem wells of shadow, and her gaze holds Lannesk frozen. Shadows flow over, through her, and she fades into the dark young spruces behind, like river-mist burning off in the sun on an autumn morning. Is gone. She, the dogs, the wolves, all the Immortals. Not a track mars the snow.

Only—Lannesk hears the wolf call again. Shivers, shakes himself, looking around. The procession...is far away, climbing a steep hillside, lanterns and torchlight glimpsed and lost and twinkling again through trees, and the throb of the drums faint, the bells cold and distant. He's alone among the trees.

Lannesk turns and goes scrambling down a bank, up again under pines, chasing the procession. A chill sweat drying on his face, making him shiver. So one becomes Forest-wildered. So one might be lost, wandering a Forestway alone. Or called to join the ghostly Riders?

That's another song.

He leaps a narrow stream, climbs a steep hillside, swift under bare poplars, and comes slantwise into the procession again, dodging along through bodies, till he has Anzimor in sight. Not looking around for him, not noticing he's wandered off and lost himself. Eyes only for Hennis. Or maybe Ekkard. Well, what does Lannesk expect? A broken-voiced mute he may be, but he's hardly some unfortunate trapped ever a child, to be a burden lifelong at his brother's heels. He needs to find himself a lover, a friend. A life that is not all halves with his brother.

Anzi looks back as he catches up. He frowns, as if Lannesk has only just now dropped behind, or his absence just now been noticed. Lifts his chin in question. Lannesk shakes his head. Whatever's in his face for his brother to see, it's nothing. Nothing of Anzimor's concern.

And so they come to the fane, one of several holy places within easy reach of Arrunstead and the Singersborg. A ditch and bank mark it off from the wilderness, with rounded boulders regularly set atop that bank, snow-shrouded. The anchorstone itself is a great boulder hunching like a bull near the northeastern edge, tall and long as the King's red horse, and the tree is a three-trunked birch over it. The most recent light snow has already been trampled down by the first-comers. The bonfire is piled high near the centre of the circle, a little to the southwest of it. Some, who can write, push slips of birchbark into the cold dark stack, scratched with prayers, promises, pleas. Some tie ribbons or scraps of rag, locks of hair, which all mean the same. More, maybe, than in an ordinary year. Lannesk has clipped a strand of Anzimor's hair while he was sleeping, wrapped it round his finger. He goes to the waiting bonfire now, and wraps the strand of ruddy gold tight around a twig of rough lichened bark, to hold it fast for the fire. A prayer. Let him be safe. Let him find his way home when this is over, wherever home may be. He deserves that. Safety, home, happiness.

For himself—just let Anzimor be safe. My brother. If you need to take one of us to ride in your train of ghosts—a prayer to the Wild King, who may be here in some dreaming truth, as the Mothers are said to be in all places, or who may be only a dream of Lannesk's own—let it be me.

There's a young person wearing grey robes and a wolf-mask. Musicians follow them as they pace a slow circle around within the fane, drums and flutes and bells.

The wolf-masked youth begins to dance.

A man leads the singing, a deep voice, and they all raise their voices, breaking their silence, to make the proper responses to him. There's always an eerie beauty to the singing, Huntersnight and Kingsday both, but this is like nothing Lannesk has ever heard. Maybe it's because of the Singers, a solid core of voices striking true together, which the rest of them, spilling out of the fane and along the procession-way, can cling to as guide.

One of the voices is suddenly that of the Wild King, who stands among them, his hounds about his feet. His voice is everything Lannesk remembers.

No dream or vision. The King is real. Others see him. Voices fade, falter, silenced by wonder, and then rejoin, swelling in strength, finding true notes.

Their song is an offering. They give themselves to the Forest, by their words, body and soul, heart and faith.

Lannesk sways to the music, feels the beat and the swell of it in his throat, the taste of the words in his mouth. Doesn't embarrass himself trying to give them voice. Anzimor sings for both of them.

A paleness, a thinning of the night, and even singing, they watch the sky, what can be seen though the black bare branches. The stars washing away in the east, the first faint colour, primrose pale. The edge of fire. A shout, and torches are thrust into the bonfire. It kindles swiftly, good omen, rising cracking and spitting, fed with fir and pine and thorn. The masked wolf-dancer whirls through them, a torch in either hand. Others leap out, join the dance, singly, in couples. The Wild King strides to the anchorstone and stands there, hands flat against it, head bowed as if he prays. Does he remember his own sacrifice, or is that mortal man he once was long washed away?

Wolf howls, close, and with a shout the King spins away into the dancers, and the Grey Hunter is among them. Wolf, woman, naked to the cold. She leaps, she whirls, she dances through them, wild and beautiful as the sun rises, woman, wolf, woman, leaping high through the flames, and the masked wolf-dancer pulls their mask down, a young Singer, laughing, no role left for them. Folk run with rakes to pull apart the fire, to spread it into a lower hedge of flame, as the naked dancer rises again, becomes a white falcon like an arrow into the sky.

More are making their own personal pledges and prayers at the stone, some pressing a drop of thumb-pricked blood against it, in token of the King's blood shed to free them so long ago. Other dancers are whirling, running, making the leap over the raked-down fire, which blesses them and blesses the village, or family, or tribe, or here, Lannesk supposes, all this company. Some hold hands and jump in couples. That's a thing for lovers, or for promises, more common at the summer sunset than the winter dawn. Others watch and cheer and make remarks. Children run and shriek and chase. Someone stumbles in leaping the fire, trips, yells, but they're hauled clear and rolled in the snow. Bad luck, that, unless they make the leap again. Lannesk climbs up the bank, leaning against one of the stones that ring the fane. Cold striking through between his shoulders, but it's a good vantage point. He's lost Anzi. There. Dancing, whirling, between Hennis and Lord Ekkard, that's where his brother's gone, and they're passing a flask between them, which reminds Lannesk he's still carrying that jug, so he pries out the wooden stopper and takes a long drink of the strong winter ale, looks around for someone to share it.

The Grey Hunter takes it from his hand. Grey eyes, gold-flecked, and she grins like a wolf, hair tumbling half over her face. Drinks long, passes it aside to someone, a dark-skinned swordtheyn, a stranger to him. A Rider, he thinks, which is as good as to say, a ghost, but the man drinks and hands the jug on to a little fayling with the nubs of horns poking through her hair, golden eyes, and she grins with teeth sharp like a fox and scampers off hugging it to her chest. Lannesk blinks at the Grey Hunter, who's still there by him, solid and real.

She's barefoot in the snow, and wearing now only a long green tunic too large for her, pulled on over nakedness. She hasn't fastened the ties of the neck and it's slipped down, a pale brown shoulder in the growing grey light. For a moment he's lost, just the shape of her collarbone. Her smile laughs at him for it, but not unkindly.

"Look," she says. So he looks where the three of them are running, Anzimor and Hennis and Ekkard together, and leaping the fire in a scramble, hand in hand in hand, Anzimor in the middle between them, colliding in their landing, laughing like children, arms about one another.

"He's all right," she says, as if Lannesk's been worrying. Maybe he has. But...Lord Ekkard. And he hopes, Bright Mother please, that they are taking care, using the ointment of bitter barrenleaf, because the last thing they need is another child with a complicated claim on the lands Tannis thinks are hers and her daughter's, and if Hennis has a baby and nobody knows whether it's Ekkard's or Anzimor's, things may be very complicated indeed, especially if it's a girl.

He worries too much. Anzimor says so. He always replies, and Anzi understands him, that somebody has to.

"He's all right," the Grey Hunter says again. "But you, my wordless, dream-touched singer..." She leans in and kisses him. Not open-mouthed and lustful, but nonetheless, mouth to mouth and burning. "Tegnor speaks of you," she says, matter-of-fact, but he does not know who Tegnor is. "She says..." She shrugs. "Well, that time is not yet come." And then she whoops, and howls. It's Wolf's howl, not a woman imitating a wolf, and she leaps away down the bank in the swelling dawn light, weaving through dancers, and the fire roars up hot and bright and eager around her as she runs with the Wild King at her side, his flame-red hair catching the light of flame, and they leap flying, run dodging, to lose themselves in the trees, while the Seer in her layers of white robe dances alone to welcome the rising sun, a pattern that weaves through them all, mortal and immortal, a pattern that shapes, Lannesk begins to think, some summons, or pleading. Perhaps she invites the trance of her dreaming. But then she too is gone, between one breath and the next, as if she too has been only his dream.

Dream-touched.

No. He is no Seer, not even a poet; he is all impotent of words. Spearcarl, outlaw redeemed by miracle. Vision should not come to him.

Lannesk goes down into the dance, and the winter wind is cold. Jerrah, who is one of Myrild's shipcarls, the shipmaster's nephew, he thinks, though he's never been certain of the tangled kinships among the ship's crew, claims him for the rest of the dancing, and a jar of ale and a spiced venison pie shared between them, with sweet maple-cakes to follow, and back in the camp one thing leads to another under blankets shared as well, while the short wild day falls into the long cold night, and winter settles heavily over them.

An early night of it, after the vigil and the festival day, too little sleep, too much…everything. Ale, food, heavy heads and unsettled guts. Unease they only pretend they've set aside, for the King come among them. It's not the common thing, for him to be drawn to the rites of Huntersnight or Kingsday, even at Singersborg on the Holy Isle, or so goes the talk among their folk and the Singers and landcarls. It is, in the end, not the best of omens, to be noticed by the Wild King, and all there are touched with an unease, that the uncanny has come among them.

What the Seer says of it, if anything, has not yet found its way to the common gossip.

Lannesk feels the weight of the long night, the long waiting winter, falling cold. Jerrah's gone back to his own place among the benches, but he lingers in remembered warmth, in the clutch of hands like bruises. Anzimor snuggles deeper into their blankets, makes some little noise like a contented purr, though it's Hennis asleep now in Lord Ekkard's arms nearest the fire.

Lannesk stalks sleep and it slips away. Lies quiet and still and close by his brother and waits for it to fall on him, and it circles out of reach. Tendrils of cold wind their way in to find skin. He slides from beneath the blankets, tucks them against Anzimor where they've been lying side by side, head overlapping chest, sharing warmth. Anzi catches at his hand, not waking.

Idiot, he thinks, and tucks the hand back under the blankets, pats his brother's shoulder. Gropes for boots, the fur vest he's used as a pillow, worming it out from beneath Anzimor's shoulder without waking him. Cloak off his feet, mittens and his hood tucked into the boots. Shivering, clothing cold and dank against the skin, in the change of air. The fire is sunken low. He walks softly, avoiding a couple of sleeping dogs. Slips through into the porch, where spears lean against the wall and shields are stacked. A nod of greeting to the two sisters of the ship's crew on watch there, huddling shoulder to shoulder on the bench with a brazier at their feet.

"Cold night to go wandering," one says.

He shrugs, finds his own spear and shield.

"Good luck," the other wishes him as he hauls the door open a crack, edges through in haste, letting in as little cold air as he can. She'll be thinking he's off for another, warmer bed.

Deep breath, harsh air catching painful. He coughs, white clouds. The night is clear, the stars bright, sharper than they ever look by summer, though eddies of smoke trail across even as he thinks that. He stretches, loosens joints. Quiet, till a horned owl calls from the tall pine behind the longhouse and somewhere beyond the palisade its mate answers. Heads to the privy, as if that might settle him, though why then bring his spear, here within the walled and guarded camp…

With nowhere to go after that, he starts walking, past the well, past the bakehouse, the trampled path slick in patches where the strewn ashes have blown away. Sleeping halls and bowers, smoke stretching southward, smearing the sky, a bit of breeze rising from the north.

Restless. The way you get when there's something forgotten, something undone. Something half-heard, troubling sleep…

A scent on the wind. There's nothing but the smoke of the fires, a whiff of horses from the barns. The gate stands open, a glow of firelight in the windows of the watchtower, which is only an enclosed platform raised high on four great posts that still gleam a fresh unweathered yellow where the bark has been stripped away.

"Who's that?" a man calls down, hearing the scuff of his boots on the icy lane, and Lannesk waves, moving into the spilling light of a lantern.

"Oh, it's Ekkard's Coastlander, the mute one." That to some unseen companion of the watch. "Where are you off to?"

He waves vaguely eastward and walks on. The road curves along the bluff above the river. Takes the track that branches off, climbing among more scattered trees, rather than dropping down along the river into the meadows and pastureland. The northern sky is alive with burning sheets and arcs of green and violet, pulsing and sliding. There's a sound like distant rain, like the hiss of damp wood laid on a fire, which is the whisper of the sky. The crunch of his own feet as he abandons the rutted ice to walk aside in snow. The wind then, stronger, creak and clatter of trees, rattle of the dry, clinging gold leaves of a young beech, water-rushing song of spruce and pine.

The headland of the ridge is mostly bare of trees and the wind is stronger yet. It smells of ice, of Yearsturn snow and bitter cold. He skirts around the stone wall of Singersborg, not sure where he can go from here. The gate stands open, and even at this hour there will be a fire in the Hall of Song, and perhaps someone to share one, but…he goes on. A narrow path climbs higher, northwesterly, towards where a swell of hill rises from this reaching claw of the fells. Climbs onward, through cedars and tumbled rock. Nothing up here save wandering Forestways. And the Seer's tower.

Quiet thump and crunch behind him and he spins about, shield to his arm, spear dropping down—horse and rider and as swiftly he swings the point up again. The Wild King, with three wolves and a pair of big dogs come pushing through young cedars to crowd about him. Real, no dream. Solid, heavy warmth against him where a dog presses close. The largest of the wolves is the Grey Hunter—he knows her—

him—by his eyes, grey flecked with gold. Wolf stands crouched a moment, hackles bristling, before leaping ahead and dwindling, flashing in the blink of an eye into the white gyrfalcon, speeding low.

The Wild King watches her go. Glances down at Lannesk, seeming unsurprised to see him there. The King carries no spear this night but wears his sword. A leather case that must hold his harp is tied to a ring on the saddle, close behind his leg.

"You," he says, thoughtful. "Again. Tegnor said there were dreams unborn in you. What calls you here tonight?"

Lannesk shakes his head. No dreams, no vision. He's nothing, only a restless and ordinary fool, and he shouldn't let himself feel what he feels, when the Grey Hunter's eyes hold his.

"Come, then," the King says. "Let's see what it is that calls us out of this night."

So Lannesk falls in beside him, walking at the red stallion's shoulder, and the pack surges on ahead.

Seerstorr is nothing like the comfortable, homey tower of an earl, no fire and warmth, neither smell of cattle nor hay nor baking bread. It's only a round stone shell pierced with a few small windows. The platform of the roof, where the Singer may go to meditate, to invite visions in a sacred fire, or to dream beneath the stars, is its purpose. A cold night for it.

There's a man filling the tower doorway, which is only a narrow opening at ground level under a lintel made of a single slab of stone. A burly shape wearing a fur cape and hat that make him look half a beast. His long-hafted axe leans against the stones beside him; his lantern, set on a little shelf of stone that might have been made for that purpose, seems a small and feeble spark of warmth. He's speaking to the Grey Hunter, who stands as a woman, naked in the cold wind. She looks upward, frowning. Lannesk wants to offer his cloak, but isn't sure it's his place to do so.

"Gwion," the man says, familiar as if the Wild King is merely some swordtheyn serving the Singersborg, but he gives a little bow of respect, too. "Is there something wrong? Tegnor's sleep was troubled. She came seeking vision." His glance strays, curious, to Lannesk.

"My Hunter's sleep was troubled, too," the Wild King says, and he takes a dark bundle from behind his saddle where his harp is slung and tosses it to the Grey Hunter, who shakes out the cloak, long and heavy, and wraps herself in it, setting her shoulders to the tower wall. Barefoot, but that doesn't seem to bother her. She leans at ease, sole of a foot raised against the stone.

"Perhaps Tegnor's dreaming will be clearer than mine," she says. And to Lannesk, "Good evening, my harper."

The axecarl frowns at Lannesk, clearly puzzled, trying to place him among the Singers of the Hall. Lannesk shakes his head. The Hunter chuckles. Tilts her head back to watch the stars.

They seem to settle there, the Grey Hunter and the Wild King, the red horse, the wolves and dogs. They don't fade, become ghostly, but— the land seeps into them. They might be stones, trees deep-rooted. Part of the place, and only the Seer's carl and Lannesk, shifting awkward as cold leaks in, fingers and toes beginning to feel chilled, left as living, breathing creatures. He squats down to put his back against the stones of the wall, folding his cloak over hands and feet, huddled around his own warmth. One of the dogs—it's a wolf—stirs from its stonelike stillness and pads over to settle curled beside him. Daring, he pulls a mitten off to stroke its head. Even rubs behind its ears, when it only lids its eyes in content at his touch. A wolf. This whole night is dreaming.

Roar, not thunder but the rushing crash of stormwind, of snow-slide, of earth and rock and tree, a hillside falling, and he lurches up out of the drifting edge of sleep. Sudden barking of dogs, a man's shout of alarm. Above, a woman's voice cries out and they crash together in the narrow doorway, he and the guardian of the Seer. Lannesk flattens himself and the man, a head shorter than he but nearly half as broad again across chest and shoulders, thrusts past, feet thumping on hollow wood. Lannesk follows, throwing off both his mittens. The Wild King has leapt from his horse, is at his shoulder, dogs, wolves, surging past. Black dark and he stumbles against the bottommost stair. A hand catches his elbow and there's—not light, but the dimness of the Forest by clouded moonlight, maybe, enough to see the wooden stairs that climb the curve of the inside wall, the occasional rough-barked beam crossing empty space. The tower is only a hollow shell. The King lets him go and pushes past, but by some shared Forest-blessing he still sees enough not to pitch over the railless side, taking the stairs two at a time in the Wild King's wake. Trapdoor already flung open; they surge up onto the platform of the roof.

Snarling, writhing confusion of bodies, grey and white and glittering silver, a knot he can't untangle in his eye. The Seer, though, is white and dark and on her knees, trying to rise, trying to speak, but her axecarl has cast aside his weapon and has his arms about her, trying to hold her, trying to staunch the darkness that is blood soaking her heavy robes, a wound beneath her breast. The dogs and wolves mill about, leaping in to tear at whatever it is the Grey Hunter grapples with. They're lashed away, snarling, yelping. An iron brazier had given the Seer warmth; now burning wood and charcoal lie scattered in a long arc, smouldering on the planks of the roof.

"Kallyn!" the Wild King shouts, and the knot breaks apart, the great wolf rolling, almost somersaulting, tumbling over burning coals and twisting to his feet, rising human, briefly, skipping backwards.

"Spear!" she snarls, thrusting out a demanding hand, and it's barely a human word. Lannesk gives it, and his shield, too, and snatches up the axe. The Grey Hunter is bleeding; something has ripped at the skin of her jaw, her arm, her shoulder. Her mouth is smeared with blood to the eyes. She grins, showing bloody teeth, fangs too long, too sharp, for human.

Get the Seer away from here, Lannesk wants to say, and tries, hoarse croak-whisper. "Down!" But the carl doesn't hear or doesn't dare to move her, holding some dark bundle of cloth tight against her belly—her white cloak. Lannesk puts himself ready between them and whatever the creature is that has wounded her, leaving the way clear to the stairs, and the axecarl sees that; Lannesk catches movement in the corner of his eye, the man gathering the Seer up.

"Ice," the Seer is saying, or something that sounds like that. "Ernst, tell them—the ice, the ice—"

"Take the Red," the Wild King says, without looking back. Yes, get the horse, flee to Singersborg and whatever surgeons or physicians may be there, but a wound like that—

The Wild King is moving, slowly, watchful, sword in hand, shifting back and forth, gauging his distance, waiting his moment—or uncertain, maybe, what may be its most vulnerable point. The thing coils and shifts over itself like a nest of rats, a mating ball of striped snakes. Rears up to strike and the King moves as swiftly, a great swing, and the creature drops aside, twisting, flaring into something that looks twice the size as it unfolds. The Grey Hunter leaps thrusting with her spear as the wings spread, neck twists, jaws snatch and snap the ash shaft and the dragon's head lashes down again to strike but the Wild King's blade bites, as maybe they intended. Yet the dragon twists so the blow only scores a long gash, dark blood spattering. It shrieks its rage; lashing tail and a blow of the wing set them leaping away to either side, the Grey Hunter again a wolf. The other wolves, the dogs, have backed off. They pace and snarl, guarding where Ernst is carrying the Seer to the stairs, wordless now, though she breaths a ceaseless whimper, an animal's pain, fading with their descent.

And even as the Wild King closes again, Lannesk is there swinging, overlooked. Axe strikes hard against what must be the lower part of the double shoulder of foreleg and wing and the blow jars up his arms into his own shoulder, as if he's struck against, maybe not stone, but ironwood and with a dull axe. The creature is scaled, for all its mane of silver fur down the neck, and the scales are armour. It hisses, snarls, whips around and spits—venom, fire—not a great blast of it like in a song but an oily thin spray that burns and clings with pale orange flame to Lannesk's sleeve, the planks of the roof, the Grey Hunter's fur. He beats at his arm, stamping at the flames on the roof; the Wolf bounds aside and the Wild King's sword hisses and strikes and the dragon snarls, the King leaping the blow of the tail meant to knock him off his feet and it strikes Lannesk, sends him stumbling sideways. He recovers, swings for the head, the eyes. It's fast as a frantic darting bird, a minnow from a child's clumsy grasping fist.

All a confusion in the dark. The Wild King's sword biting as the axe sends the dragon wheeling aside, the Grey Hunter springing, jaws snapping, trying to seize and rip the membrane of the wings, but a flailing bony spur strikes Wolf, knocks him back, dragon's head lashing around to spit fire again. Lannesk sweeps the axe at a wing—even the membrane is scaled, fine and glittering, but that armour's not proof against steel and this time something tears. The dragon screeches again. Blow, burst of red pain, the world ripping into shadows and flares of light. Burning ribs. Not on fire. Great clawed forefoot the size of a bear's paw has caught him, swung him rolling along to crash up against the stone parapet. Lost the axe. Can't catch his breath, can't get his shaking legs under him. The Wild King's in close, has the broken boards of Lannesk's shield for his defence, what little that may give. Swift, his sword's edge, swift his blows and the Grey Hunter's lunges, trying to seize, Lannesk thinks, its throat, as a wolf brings down a deer, but the dragon is swifter still and though it bleeds, it does not falter, nor flee.

Hand on the parapet. Pulls himself up. Eyes blurring. Axe, somewhere. Blinks vision clear, sees the axe and grabs it up. Easier to see now, not the strange dim paleness of the Forest-blessing he was granted. Firelight, a ruddy glow, shadows twisting, swinging wild. Planks of the roof are burning. He makes certain of his grip, watches, trying to judge his moment. The Grey Hunter crouches, bloody, panting, ribs heaving, patches of fur scorched. The dragon's wings are tightly furled again, and the scales of its hide, each with its bony nubbled boss, have dulled his axe, though the Wild King's sword has bitten. Does it move more stiffly now, more slowly? The frost-glitter of its pale flanks is stained dark with its blood, its mane streaked and matted. Silver chain swings loose about its neck. Pewter eye, reflecting firelight, bony brow-ridge protecting it—the Wild King glances his way. Lannesk touches his eye, points to the King. Anzimor would understand him. The King nods. Lannesk yells, rushes, axe raised. Hack at the wing, try to break the fine bat-finger bones of it, maybe, and the dragon turns distracted to strike at him and the King hurls sword like a spear for that small target, the eye—

Shriek of rage, frantic beat and twist and it's in the air, too high, even as the Grey Hunter leaps to seize a trailing foot. A wing strikes the sword clattering, skidding over boards, into the fire. The dragon plunges down behind them, landing on clawed hind legs as he whirls and—she is a girl, younger than he, surely. Naked, bleeding from a dozen wounds; some look savage enough to have left her lying senseless. Her long hair is silver-white and swirls about her like a banner unfurling. She's still winged, though they seem smaller, suited to her human frame, and one is held awkwardly to the side, its membrane torn by axe or wolf, leaking blood. She hisses like a snake, and stoops to snatch up a blade in either hand from where they've lain dropped and unnoticed, dark blades, one straight, one curved, and that's a song, the stone knives of a dragon-kin sorcerer-priest, the knives of sacrifice.

The Wild King scoops up his sword again and grins at the grounded dragon. His face is bloody as the wolf's where a claw has ripped his cheek. "Come on, then," he says, and takes a step back, arms spread, inviting.

Because she's between them and the open trapdoor now, between them and the stairs and Ernst descending with his burden. She's standing on the edge of it, poised on her balls of her feet, about to spring.

Lannesk shifts sideways, just a step or two. Let her lunge for the King and he will bolt for the stairs, to hold them against her. Knows that's what's wanted, as clear as if the King has spoken it. The Grey Hunter circles to the other side.

The girl flings back her head and laughs. Slaps the knives into some fastening on the chain and springs skyward, spitting a wash of oily fire over them even as she shifts, flowing into dragon again, flipping in the air, plunging out of sight below the tower's edge. Even the Wild King shouts and Lannesk finds he's whimpering, beating out flame on his clothes, on hair and beard; his face feels like it's burning and he touches something damp, something crumbling away at finger's touch, stubble, skin, and his eye is tearing cold and stinging—

No time for it.

A horse squeals, dogs bark. A man's cry ends abruptly even as Lannesk and the Wild King run for the stairs and the Grey Hunter leaps over the parapet, burning wolf into gyrfalcon.

Embers shower them as they leap down the stairs, and with a roar and a crash a chunk of charred roof falls.

A little ways down the track amid the cedars. The dragon-woman's pale as snow and red as slaughter, kneeling over the bodies. The fallen red stallion is thrashing to his feet again. The Grey Hunter—a wolf lies torn open, unmoving. Brindled tawny, not her-him. The dragon rises, curved knife in her human hand.

"This blood of the Forest," she says, "is offered to Erryth my lady, in token of the land that was her own and will be again." Licks it, watching them run, the King's sword swinging to take her head. She shoves the knife home on her chain and spreads her wings, dragon into the air, and if she flounders graceless, if there's a frantic, limping imbalance to her flight, it little matters. She's a rush of wind and rattle of boughs, and gone into the darkness.

The man Ernst is dead, his throat torn out, his head barely held to his body but by snapped bone and a rag of skin. Tegnor the Seer is dead, and if she yet might have died from the earlier strike that missed her heart, the clean cutting of her throat has made certain of it.

Offering, the dragon said.

The dogs, the near-white wolf, creep close, sniffing and whining.

The Wild King casts about, head raised, like a hound testing the air. Goes warily, as if afraid, in under the trees, but there's a sound, a predator bird's warning hiss, and then a groan, and a small mottled, stained whiteness lost in the white of the snow stirs and unfolds to battered long limbs. She struggles up. Resists when the King tries to carry her—"I can walk, Gwi, I can walk,"—comes limping, arm torn bloody, face ripped and still smeared, the dragon's blood and her own.

Leaning on the Wild King, she blinks at Lannesk.

"Hey, harper," she says, and her voice is a thin hoarse whisper. "Still with us."

Lannesk, because there's nothing else of use he can do, has been soothing the horse, which is sound, he thinks, save for bruises. Struck sidelong and knocked flying into snow. He holds the bridle while the Grey Hunter pushes herself upright from the Wild King, her hand lingering at the last, though, as if reluctant to let go. Their fingers cling, a caress. But then she pulls away to sniff over the bodies, Wolf again. Limp-lopes away down the track without another word, and the survivors of the pack follow.

"Kallyn will send them up for the dead," the Wild King says. He's hoarse too. Smoke, or dragon-fire. Looks to where the tower burns itself hollow. "If they're not already on their way." He crouches down by the Seer and her man, touches them, a gentle hand closing the Seer's staring empty eyes, setting Ernst's lolling head straight, lying like a blessing on the slain wolf's head.

Had he heard the Seer's last words? Vision, she had gone seeking. Lannesk kneels beside the King. Swallows, and his mouth is dry, his throat a rasping soreness. Scrubs hands on his thighs, which may not do them much good, takes a handful of clean snow, which is not likely to do much more, but it moistens his tongue, at least. It's an easy word. Tries it. A hiss, meaningless. Tries it again, shaping breath. Anzimor could take it from his silent lips.

"Ice?" the Wild King asks.

Lannesk touches the Seer's lips, still warm, but cooling. Says it yet again.

"She spoke of ice?" The King frowns. Shakes his head, but not in denial. Puts a reassuring hand on Lannesk's shoulder.

He takes his harp from the horse's harness, a wonder it's not broken. Tunes it, single notes sounding soft. Begins something, a wordless music, slow, strange, like the drip of water in the spring, not yet a song. Only gathering into one. Plays it, leaning there against a tree, as if it might give some comfort to the dead, or to himself. Lannesk shuts his eyes. Lets the music touch him, pull him — stars, he sees. The river of stars pouring out in a white haze, spreading over the black of the sky, the sharp white knifeprick points of the named stars bright among them.

"So. They will come down from the headwaters of the Leda before the spring," the Wild King says, soft, into that. "Over the ice. The

Dragon does not mean to wait for us to muster the summer strength of the earls to carry the war to her."

~Mairran~

"I don't know how to do this," I told Nowa the next day, as she, flushed and cranky, sat by the open window with her leg up, putting an edge on a dagger for Sage. "I just kill people. If my mother really wanted someone to hunt out truth, she should have sent a law-reeve."

"Which she did not," Nowa said.

It was not an entirely helpful observation.

"If she just wanted them dead, she should have told me. And which."

A cold wind blew in, but I'd opened the shutters regardless, and removed the winter window-covering of dried and thin-scraped hide in a frame that stopped the worst of the wind and let in only a weak yellow dimness. The ravens wanted to be able to come and go. Anyway, Nowa kept throwing off the shawl I'd wrapped over her shoulders. Feverish, but the physician, Glinn, didn't seem too worried. She had left a flask of a red concoction that probably involved willow-bark and another of honeyed poppy in snaps, but Nowa was determined to touch neither.

Lord Raynar came to tell me he was taking a company of swordtheyns and spearcarls to hunt for the wild man in the valley of the cedars—would I honour him by riding with him?

I chose not. Common sense—Nowa's frown—said I would be inviting a hunting accident, but it wasn't so much that as a sudden revulsion at being among people. I'd never been good at it. I didn't like it, and I was feeling—harried. I knew that was stupid, when I was safely where I was meant to be, and they could hardly murder me when

I was a guest of their hall. Not as if I feared an attack, anyhow. I might have enjoyed that, if it weren't that I would have had to worry about Nowa and Sage.

I hated not knowing what I should do, what I was supposed to be doing. What my mother wanted of me, what unwitting failure she would find to be coldly disappointed in, what sleeping anger I might wake.

For three days, I declined to eat in the hall, make use of bath or sweat-house, or see the lady and lord again. I sent Sage to the well in the bakery-yard to fetch our water and to the kitchens behind the hall to carry up the bread and cheese and jugs of small ale for breakfast— drawing the ale herself and at suppertime, taking the pottages and pies, the fish and dishes of fermented vegetables, from the common table where things were set before being carried in to the hallfolk, because my mother's remarks on a dish of poisoned mussels came back to my mind. I didn't want to eat at all, myself. That happened, sometimes. The ravens mostly had my share.

The only people I let into our apartments were the physician and her assistants, the young man and the girl. Nowa's fever abated—I did persuade her to take her medicine. Glinn said that the wound was clean and draining as it should, which was good.

Sage, while tending the horses and taking them out for exercise, fetching and carrying wood and water, and generally doing all that the hall-servants should have been doing, learnt that the castle gate was closed at night, but that yes, an armscarl named Perral, who had ridden to Borharbour on some business, had returned, the night we were in Borharbour ourselves, and had gone to the great hall. And before dawn on the day we were attacked, Swordtheyn Harilan and four others, Perral among them, had gone out on skis, quietly, saying nothing of where or why they went, nor on whose orders.

After our arrival, several families had left the castle, almost as fugitives might, with no farewells and no escort, but word was they went to serve at the hall of a landtheyn who was cousin to the late earl. Henning told Sage that he'd heard that generous gifts had been made to them by the lady.

Perhaps I should have sought out and questioned those folk so hastily removed from the castle, though I didn't suppose they would have known much more than that their dead kin or partner had been summoned to some early-morning expedition by Theyn Harilan. Anyway, I did not.

The bodies were not brought back to the castle, but taken to the lychhouse in Borharbour to await the thaw. A strange decision, because the castle or Fairnshore or both must also have had some place to hold the winter's dead. Lady and lord wanted all to forget that those dead folk had come from the castle. To let it become a mistake, either mine, for thinking Harilan attacked me, or the swordtheyn's, for betraying his honour and turning highway robber.

I had Sage return the tokens I'd taken from the dead to Lady Rikenza.

The spray of cedar with the hairs wrapped around it we did not find, though Sage and I both got down on our bellies to feel under the bench-bed and cupboard, and into the dark crevices between a blanket-chest and the settle by the inner door. I very much doubted that the young hall-runner had taken it.

Nowa taught Sage to play the fox-game and nagged me to eat. I ignored her and she sighed at me, but she didn't demand to know what I thought I was doing. I left the warm inner room to the women and lay on the narrow bed in the antechamber unsleeping. I'd have been chasing the dark on the flute again, except it would have disturbed Nowa, and she needed rest.

By the third day, I was not even drinking the ale. Only water, and the kingswort snaps.

I thought I might dream of murder at the forgotten heartstone amid the oaks, of the wild man with the red horse, of the truth of the earl's death.

I slept, eventually, in the dark with the door to the day-bright inner room shut and no candles burning. I dreamt a black wolf, running.

I dreamt of myself.

The Seer warned of ice—I do not know any seers save father and mad dead brother—but it's fire I dream. The blackened stone shells of the towers of the earls, the outbuildings of their strongholds gone to charred timbers and smoking ruin. Dark wreckage of bodies unburied. Survivors, creeping back, whether to tally the dead or salvage what they might, or maybe they're not the survivors but the scavengers, lured from other villages to pick over the bones. All along the coast by the mouth of the Leda, the mouth of the Naar, down to the northern coast of the Lann Laitellon above Laikyn. Earls dead, and their swordtheyns and hallfolk. And the boatsheds, the winter-resting ships, the new-laid keels a-building against summer's summons to war. The timber yards.

"A silver dragon," a woman tells—me. But this is not myself.

I remember her telling me, but I was other, then.

Restless, that woman's dreams were troubled. A touch of the seer's blessing of true dreaming, she thinks, she-who-is-not-I. I think, the grey wolf who runs through my dreams thinks, we think together. Grey or black, he or she…we do not remember which we are.

I, we, remember that woman, the survivor of attack, telling of what she saw. Don't remember remembering. Lost… Is this how my brother Lorne lost himself?

She'd dressed and gone out, that woman tells us in memory, in this dream that remembers what I-Mairran never knew. She'd dressed and gone out, spear in hand, seen it come from the sky.

"Falling," she says. "Like a shooting star."

Burning bright, and it vanished into the boatyard, so she'd gone to see. There had been tarred hulls burning, and fire eating through the roofs, and she had seen the dragon for what it was, then. Wings, long-taloned claws, tail, teeth. Silver-scaled and a white mane. She had hurled the spear she carried and bolted back for the houses crying alarm, and was lucky to be alive, I think.

I remember thinking.

The dragon had been more intent on destruction.

"A silver sorcerer," another man says. Another place, another day. He's dying. Burns have eaten much of his skin away. An outcry in the upper chamber of his earl's tower and he and other household spearcarls run to find her dead and her husband fallen across her body, sword still in his hand. The sorcerer flings a whip of fire over them — not spitting, she calls it with her hand and a word, he says.

"Sorcerer —" Gasping for the breath to repeat that, as if she who stands listening hasn't understood him. Sorcerer, the killer is — she calls fire and they burn, and the sorcerer dives out the window and flies away on a dragon's back. I-she thinks the dying man is trying to make sense of what he doesn't understand. Was she naked, this sorcerer, asks the woman who is and is not myself, and the man says, silver, all silver, her hair, lost in his pain again, and it hardly matters anyway, whether the woman was naked or not; the woman who is me understands that the silver woman must have been so. The tower burnt, the earl, her captain and husband, daughters, grandchildren, towerfolk dead or injured, some terribly, and they beg for healing, those who, but the worst can only whimper, save the one who screams. There's nothing she who is not Mairran, who is myself, can give save to open the way for the slowly dying and let them slip, easy and beyond pain, into the welcome of the Dark Mother's arms. So that, she does.

Earls, captains…ships and granaries and storehouses, that's what the dragon is sent to destroy, and the dragon-kin hardly number a great army, not like the ones that come from lords and outlands south of the Skagga, or over the eastern sea. The dragon-kin can do no more than raid, seize a valley, hope to hold it as a thieves' lair for cattle-raiding beyond…that's all they've ever done, since the landfolk rose up and overthrew the rule of the dragon-kin sorcerer-priests and their stone knives in the days that only the grandmothers of the grandmothers living now might have seen. Since Gwion and I, she who is not Mairran, she who is Kallyn, with the Smith and the Daughter of Snows and the Fox-kin and the Fisher, defeated Erryth the Golden, who had betrayed them, her fellows among the Immortals, to spawn her devoted sorcerer-priests and make herself tyrant and god over all the tribes; since Gwion and Kallyn sang Erryth down to sleep beneath the Lake that had given her birth, and believed they had given the mortal folk of the Forest a peace that would last, and those who held to the ways of the Dragon were driven from the land. Not so long ago as all that, down the years she can remember. Though one spring passes into another so swiftly…she does not often count the years.

Kallyn doesn't know the silver dragon. There had been lesser dragons, she thinks she remembers, but they were lost so long ago…

I don't want to know of the silver dragon.

I don't want to remember what I saw, before the silver dragon struck and flung me into the trees. The man's head all but torn off; the playful young wolf I'd called from her pack dead. The mortally-wounded woman, the Seer, rousing, weakly, helplessly, trying to crawl, and the dragon-girl takes a fistful of hair to hold her head and slices her throat, her face so set and still, and the blood spraying over it…

Kallyn-I who saw that. Dreaming Mairran-I who remembers.

Kallyn crosses to the Warnavon over ice. The upper third of the Lake has frozen. Are they, she and I, dreaming two made one, are we hunting the dragon…?

Burst of terror. Mairran-I can't fly across the Lake, not so far. Sometimes we travel, Nowa and I, take ship from the Holy Isle to the mainland, ride the roads, lose ourselves, and then Nowa camps alone and I run, but sometimes it's given out that I lie ill in my tower for weeks. The Queen's carrion crow, her fey darling, mad as his brother, maybe, or sickly, cursed with the burden of the blood of sacrifice I've shed. A raven can't overfly the lake. But a raven can make it from Arrunmouth on the Holy Isle to the mainland coast, crossing east. I've done it. Not a long-distance flier, not goose or pigeon or falcon outrunning the snow. But a good day's journey, a good night's rest, always some wolves' kill carrion to scavenge or small incautious beasts to hunt as they raise furrows beneath the snow. It gets me there.

Gyrfalcon flies straight, the Lake…but the Lake is frozen. I forgot. Even for a raven, it's safe.

Raven. I'm no falcon.

Can't…can't remember, what we are. Who we are meant to be.

~LANNESK~

Ice. The Holy Isle is fringed with it, thick enough to bear a man's weight inshore, thinning and wave-broken further out. But there is no sending messages to the earls by water, even so. Possible to drag a small boat over the ice, break a path through where it is not bearing, to seek open water, but wave and spray will freeze on oars and ropes, on sail and spar and planks, on clothing. It will build and build thicker, and if the crew does not die of cold and freeze solid themselves as water and ice suck heat and life from them, it won't take long till the ice can no longer be chipped away and the boat becomes only a drifting ice-shrouded tangle, dead wood crewed by the dead, and is crushed and smashed to kindling when the Lake-ice finally holds it. Such wrecks wash up along the shore every summer. Those who've dared the water too late.

The burns on Lannesk's face are healing. The Wild King has ridden by ways that mortal folk cannot follow, or at least, he is gone from the Isle. The Grey Hunter has flown. The Lake will freeze by the end of Yearsturn, the weather-wise say; until then, the coastal earls and their warbands have only the warning the Immortals have gone to carry, the warning the dragon-kin would have slain the Seer of the Holy Isle to prevent. Beware the ice. In the north where most the earls need this warning, the Lake may be already frozen hard even far from shore, and the dragon-kin who hold the Upper Lann Leda, with the frozen Leda an easy road to the coast, may already be on the march along the western shore towards the valleys of the Lann Laitellon, raiding up the ice-bound creeks and rivers.

The captains gathered on the Holy Isle can't set out themselves, even once the iceways freeze. They're a few hundred spears, not an army. They need to muster the scores of earls scattered throughout the Forest, a land that could hold a dozen, even a few score kingdoms of the Southlands. They need open water, need to gather the warbands into an army, their ships into a fleet. Winter is not the season for warring.

Scouts and messengers can be sent, once the iceways to the Lann Krada and to Laikyn and to the south freeze. All they can do until then is wait. And watch—ice and sky both, they watch. Lady Lauran has ordered an outpost built at North Cape to watch over the Lake's freezing, so that they may send to Laikyn and the Laitellon as soon as may be. She has set archers in towers over the camp of Mair Arrun, over the Singersborg and Arrunstead, and the Lakeside village at Arrunmouth. The silver dragon will not come on them a second time unchallenged. The building was finished by the end of the twelve First Days. Not well, but well enough.

Some among the Singers warn of danger. There are lesser seers among them, true-dreamers whose dreams are troubled, though only by shadows and night-terrors and a waking unease, nothing they can define or describe or make into a shape to be grasped even in a song. Which is in itself troubling. It suggests the ill-wishing of some power against them, and people ask, when will the Wild King return, and the Masters say, the Immortals come as they will.

"What are we doing here?" Jerrah demands, as if someone might have a better answer than what they all know, and he rolls over on the bench, where he's been lying propped on his elbows, head to head with Lannesk and the fox-board between them. He pulls a fistful of blanket up over face. "Wake me for Pasturetide, someone." He's lost yet another game, that's his problem. Pulls the blanket down. "You. You're a dragon-kin witch, Lannesk, admit it. You've ill-wished me to make all the wrong moves."

Jerrah's just too reckless, that's his problem, but Lannesk doesn't think he can get that across. He just grins at the shipcarl, because that'll annoy him more, and sets the pieces out again, switching them so Jerrah plays the foxes who guard the fayling earl-piece.

"No, I'm done," Jerrah says. "Really, I am. Three's enough. Trounce your brother some instead, why don't you?" He gives Lannesk a smile, no sting meant, takes his blanket and goes to a farther bench, kicking off his boots, rolling himself up to sleep. Anzimor's been sitting closer to the fire, darning socks, his and Lannesk's both. He stows the mending away and comes back to their sleeping-bench.

"Game?"

It feels late, though it's only a couple hours past sunset. Too early to sleep yet, save for Theyn Asa, breath labouring, lying closest the fire. Every so often someone goes to check on him, adjust his blankets, replace the hot wrapped stone at his feet, try if they can get a little more broth into him.

"Let's have the board here," Granna says, and nudges her sister. Gillesh comes to claim it, gathering up the carved wooden pieces, much used, the black and red stain mostly rubbed away, the blue glass earl-piece from another, grander set chipped. Fair enough; it is Granna's board. Anzimor flings himself down in Jerrah's place with a yawn. Glances away at Jerrah, looks back, doesn't ask, not even by a raised eyebrow.

But, "What's with you and Jerrah?" Anzimor did ask, when they were out alone that morning—not their day to patrol, but checking snares.

Nothing to tell. It was a Huntersday tryst, and that's frost in the sun, as a song might say. Jerrah plays foxes-and-ravens with him, or with Anzimor, or any of them, smiles his broad and cheerful crooked-toothed smile; sometimes he speaks to Lannesk and strives to figure out his answer without looking to Anzimor for it, but he's never invited Lannesk to share a blanket again back at Mair Arrun, and hasn't made any effort to get close to him here at North Cape when they're all about their fire in the long evenings, beyond playing foxes-and-ravens, which doesn't allow much for cuddling. Doesn't sit by him, when there's ale and songs going around in turn to Lannesk's harping. Doesn't watch him, the way Ekkard watches Anzimor, or did, till their company drew the short straw for the first fortnight's watch at the new-built outpost at North Cape, and Theyn Asa chose Anzimor and Lannesk as part of his dozen carls, telling Ekkard, bored and wanting to join them, that a lord and captain's place was to stay in the camp and attend Lady Lauran's councils.

Anyhow, Lannesk might ask Jerrah to bed again himself. Might show, at least, that he'd be willing, if Jerrah was. Anzimor would thump him on the back and trade places happily enough, and in this little cabin that is the North Cape watchpost the long black night is all the privacy anyone gets, not so different from the longhouse, at that, though in the camp couples do tend to find quieter corners, or retreat to the lofts and outbuildings.

He hasn't. He can't even tell himself why. Suspecting the answer would be no? Maybe, but it just feels easier this way. As if growing to care for someone who might become more than a comrade in arms would be a burden too heavy.

And maybe Jerrah sees that in him. Maybe it's Jerrah, assuming the answer will be no, and not wanting to risk himself.

"Give us a tune, then," Anzimor says. Because Anzimor, who doesn't gamble, having nothing to hazard save what Lord Ekkard has given them, went to the Singersborg and won him a harp at dice, or so he claimed when he handed it over, just before they set out from Mair Arrun. Lannesk wonders. Not sure how he should feel about a gift that was most likely bought with coin begged from Ekkard.

It's a six-string one, not the seven of their mother's, the bridge carved of antler, and undecorated until Anzimor scrounged a little dark-red paint to draw a vinelike tree rooted below the bridge, its tendrils and heart-shaped leaves weaving over the maple soundboard, climbing up the arms and twining around the tuning pegs on the yoke. It sounds well, and "Yes," Granna calls over. "Sing, Anzi. Give us 'Earl Harriny and the Fayling.'" They claim remote descent from that Earl Harriny of the lower Naar, Granna and Gillesh, and maybe from her alleged fayling lover. Certainly they're short, neither taller than Jerrah's shoulder, and light-haired, with darker skin than many and odd yellowish eyes. No horns, though—of course not all faylings have horns—and no magic or Forest-blessing that they've shown, though they're deadly accurate with a bow.

So Lannesk sits up and fetches the harp out, cradles it close to tune it, and Anzimor rolls over onto his back, hands behind his head, shuts his eyes. He'll sing, eventually—in turn they all will—but he'll give Lannesk this space, first. He always does. The others have less tolerance for a wordless music that strives to encompass something he can't quite find. Echoes of night, of dark trees, of stars and black Lake. Of the Wild King's music, but not quite. Something of his own.

"Earl Harriny rode out on a Kingsday morn—" Gillesh sings loudly, drowning out what he would make.

"Gill," Anzimor says in protest, and Mirawan, a thin, quiet woman of Ekkard's spearcarls, "Gillesh, don't, I was liking that, whatever it was."

"Let him finish," Jerrah adds. "It's..." Waves a hand out of his blankets. "Just be quiet and listen properly."

"Noise," Granna says. "Wandering around, that's all. Someone take that harp away from him and give us a proper song." But Lannesk shakes his head, changes his tune, taking a slip of worked quill harpnail from where he carries several woven into the stitches hemming his cuff. Gives her the simple chords she wants. Doesn't want them bickering, since they're cooped up here together for another week at least, and if she can't hear his music, she can't. Anzimor makes a sympathetic face—but there's no stopping Gillesh so he sits up, joins the song, louder and truer and a relief to Lannesk's ear. Gillesh has a quavering edge to her voice that grates on Lannesk's nerves when she's not swamped by the others. He gives them three songs, passes the harp over to Anzimor, and it goes to Jerrah, to Granna, and so around.

Theyn Asa makes a vaguely wakeful noise, so Gillesh goes to take him up, cradled against her breast, carefully spooning a thin gruel to his lips, coaxing him like a baby to eat, murmuring over him, he's fine, he's getting stronger, come morning he'll be demanding ale and fried black pudding, so he will.

And the long evening passes, and the wind finds every chink in their hastily raised walls.

Cold grey morning after a long night and rose-hued light spills along the south, over the black jagged treeline of the coast behind them. It snowed in the dark hours, and the new fall hisses with every gliding stride. Fresh snow makes the patrol more dangerous, too, hiding cracks and fissures and the deadly patches of slush where churning of waves or upwellings of warmer currents have kept the ice from freezing solid yet. A bank of fog hides where open water may lie. They go roped and widely spaced, the four of them who are striking out to the north, Lannesk in the lead, the most dangerous position, with Anzimor and Gillesh and Jerrah following in his tracks. The daylight won't last. They'll make a long circuit, west to east, before swinging back; they check the condition of the ice, how far out it's bearing. The weather-wise among the Singers say the deep waters between the Holy Isle and Laikyn should freeze over by the beginning of Snowsdeep this year. Sometimes it will be early in Yearsturn, sometimes later, but always by mid-Snowsdeep the greater iceways are possible. Neither safe nor easy, but possible. Once the Lake freezes, scouts and messengers will set out to the north, to Laikyn, the Warnavon, even beyond, to the lands where they fear the dragon-kin may be moving. Messengers of the Singers have already been able to cross to the east, to the Lann Krada and the Merkal. Winter is not the season for war, but who knows, once the Wild King and the Grey Hunter return, the captains and the Masters may even summon the warbands of the earls—Laikyn, the Warnavon, either would make a good base for a winter mustering, to strike northward over the ice-roads, before the dragon-kin do so themselves.

Lannesk passes a spruce sapling stuck upright, frozen in. It warns of where yesterday's patrol hit thin ice. The open water's retreat is marked by a line of them.

"Lannesk," Anzimor calls. "Look there!"

Lannesk, who's been looking down, watching the tips of his skis shearing through new snow, watching for the telltale darkness of seeping water, flings up his head, looks around to Anzimor, away to where he's pointing.

Up the Lake, out to the fog rising over the open water as the air cools, the sun slanting with the low light of evening, though it's only a little past noon.

"What's what?" Jerrah asks, cupping his hands to shade his eyes. Their shadows stretch long.

"Ice," Gillesh says. "Just an ice-raft, Anzimor."

"Pretty big one to have broken loose. No wind last night."

The bank of milky fog is shifting and stirring, hiding and unveiling. A whiteness beneath, at horizon's edge.

Ice doesn't grow that way; the deepest water holds warmth longest. It's spring breakup when the great rafts of ice wash out of the rivers or break loose and form islands in open water, at least in the Fairnmere, and Lannesk doesn't know why the Lake itself should be any different.

"Ice?" Anzimor asks, and he agrees. Ice, and there's a chill crawling over his skin, though he was warm enough a moment before.

Lannesk starts towards the open water. He goes slowly, lifting each ski, stepping it forward rather than sliding, weight on his rear leg, ready to rock back off his leading foot if he hears ice start to crack, feeling his way with the butt of his spear. Anzimor behind him will shout out if water begins seeping into his tracks, if they hit slush—though he could be already sinking by then. They nearly lost Theyn Asa so a few days back. Spared drowning by caution and the rope; it's the cold, which froze his furs and leathers and chilled him to the bone, that's laid him low with fever. It's a journey of two days at best and likely three, back around the central fells to Mair Arrun. Too far to drag an ill man on a toboggan in the bitter cold, Lannesk and Anzimor decided, when Mirawan first asked if a few of them should wrap up the fevered swordtheyn and head home. There's nothing more could be done for him back at the longhouse, nothing they're not already doing, keeping him warm and dry, making sure he has all the broth and gruel they can get into him.

Lannesk doesn't know how he and Anzimor have ended up the ones the others look to for such decisions, given that they're all Earl Tannis's folk here at North Cape and none of Brux's.

Black of open water ahead and that bank of fog hanging above it. And no doubting it now, there's ice beyond, the water like a channel, a strait between two shores.

Some warmer current. The Lake will never freeze into the unbroken smoothness of a pond, those who live by it say. It heaves and grinds, makes ridges of jagged ice-fangs, ranges of blue-ice boulders. There are places where it never does freeze, frost-fringed, fog-plumed stretches of open water, known by those hardy few whose trade takes them venturing out over the winter Lake. Places where the water wells and stirs as if some great spring is rising far beneath. Perhaps this is one of them. But they should have been told, if so. In the Singersborg, in Arrunmouth, if anywhere, there are those who know the Lake even by winter.

He feels the give before he hears the creak. Stops, a hand flung out and behind they stop, keeping the rope taut.

There's a trick to moving backwards on skis. Lift your foot, curl the toes upwards so the leather strap over your boot doesn't slip off and your heel's forced down against the board, holding the ski on. Shuffle back a step, careful not to dig the end of the ski in and fall; the thump of your weight onto your hip if you do is likely to break what little still keeps you from drowning. Ease your balance over, go back with the other. Hold your breath, as if that might help. It won't. Back on your own tracks, watching the water seep up to fill them, eating the snow. Not slush beneath, which would show a faster rise of water, reveal its porridgey texture, but the water welling through where weak ice has cracked. Back a little farther, and then he dares to turn, fanning about step by step. Anzimor's braced, holding the rope taut. Gillesh, who's been dragging a scrawny little spruce they hacked down on their way from the cabin, plants it in the snow.

Now they should make a long sweep back towards the Cape, avoiding a rough and broken icefield that's more like a landslip of jagged stone than anything, all ridges and furrows. The day they have to turn back without finding the limit of the ice to the northwest, up the long centre line of the Lake, that's when they send to Lady Lauran and the Masters.

Or maybe that day's today.

Safe on thicker ice, Lannesk stands, watches the fog over the open water and the whiteness beyond. There's something there, something—

He half turns, quick gesture, and Anzimor has his bow strung on the instant, and Gillesh behind him.

"What?" demands Jerrah at the rear and he silences him, a hand slashing the air.

Grey shapes thickening. Five, six. Standing, as they do. Watching. Someone there, on the ice beyond the open water.

Hiss past his shoulder and the impact is quiet; the arrow hits glancing, burying itself in snow and he's dropped flat. Slap of bowstrings, Anzimor, Gillesh loosing. No cry from the fog. The range is long. He's crawling, crouching awkward, but you can, without losing your skis. The others have done the same, neither archer wasting further arrows. There's no cover. Make a small target, don't turn broadside on. Looks back under his arm to see the fog eddying thick again, the black water become an edge with no shore beyond, so he tugs the rope of which he's become the tail and stands, and the others look, and stand; spread out, they retreat till they're past the marker of yesterday's patrol, when without discussion they all swing in on him.

"Hunters?" Jerrah asks doubtfully.

"Hunting what?" Gillesh is scornful. Someone might chase a deer or moose out onto the ice, but no one would come out this far looking for quarry, and ice-fishers don't shoot at looming figures in the fog.

Nor do honest earls' messengers, which those might be thought to be, come over an iceway from Laikyn or the Lann Lathrun, if the Lake has frozen early.

Lannesk grabbed the arrow as he crawled past. He holds it out now, and four heads bend over it. Black, white-shafted goose-feather fletching. Long, slender point. Not metal, not stone, which the faylings are still said to use. Pale carved bone.

Which means dragon-kin. They prize metal, any metal, even more highly than cattle and grain and children in their raiding. No iron and little copper in the mountains of their northern exile.

There's a sound in the wind and he raises a hand for silence, Jerrah and Gillesh arguing over whether bone could pierce heavy leather, which he isn't keen to test on his own back.

It's faint, but someone's singing. A woman's voice, rising high, and maybe another weaving under it. It crawls under his skin, the sound, prickling, burning. He wants to scratch at himself, to claw at his arms, as if it's something foul he could slough off. Anzimor's shoulders hunch, he rubs at his arms, face tight and pained. He's hearing it too.

"Are they singing?" Gillesh asks. "What's the point of that?"

The fog's thinning behind them. Is the black band of open water narrower than it was? He gestures in the direction of the shore, takes Anzimor by the shoulder, shakes him.

"Yes," Anzi says. "You hear it too?"

"Are they calling their dragon?" Jerrah asks, and Gillesh nocks another arrow, scanning the sky.

"Dragon-kin," Anzimor says. "Sorcery, I think—don't you feel it?"

"It's Mothers-damnably cold all of a sudden," Jerrah says.

"Sorcerer-priests," Anzimor says, and looks to Lannesk's nod. "Yes. We need to go. Swift as we can."

They've covered a mile, maybe, over the snow-covered ice, when, checking behind yet again, he sees them. Skiers. Six. This side of the open water. Is there a narrow spur of ice bridging that distant gap? Can water freeze so swiftly?

Sorcery, indeed.

He whistles to demand the others' attention. They've loosed themselves from the rope, here within the arc of their patrol route, not fearing thin ice. They look back.

"Mothers Above," Jerrah says. "How'd they get over that channel?"

Not going to try to explain what he thinks he glimpsed or the chill of that song. Lannesk points to Anzimor. Go, he mouths. He and Anzimor are the swiftest, long-legged. Anzimor hesitates a moment, as if he might argue. Then nods.

"Stay with Lannesk," he tells the others and sets off, a sprinter's pace.

Advance patrol, that's what those dragon-kin behind them are, and they'll be wanting to overtake or shoot down him and his, to stop warning coming to the Holy Isle.

Better the dragon-kin scouts don't carry word back that the captains are warned. Though, how many will have ventured out onto the Lake, and from where? Have they seized some base on Laikyn?

Better to kill them than to merely outrun them. Better yet to take one alive. The captains will have questions. But the open ice is no place for ambush.

The long range of ice broken and piled and frozen by the unseen churnings of the Lake that bars the straight run for shore is half a mile distant. Anzimor is heading to swing around the eastern end of it. Lannesk points, even as the other two set out behind him, keeping close together now. Sketches the jagged ice in the air, an archer shooting.

"Yes," Gillesh says. "We'll have them there."

Not that they won't be expecting it, the dragon-kin behind them. He would.

Anzimor has skirted close to the ice ridge and a long patch where the wind has blown the snow clear, by chance, maybe, or knowing what Lannesk, following in his tracks, would need. So soon as they've put the rising chunks of ice, frozen in place despite whatever forces smashed and reared them, between themselves and the pursuit, they kick off their skis and slither across the windswept bare blue ice as if skating, scramble up into cover clutching spears and skis, find hollows filled with snow, good footing, to crouch in. Anzimor is far in the distance, but is clearly one person alone. The dragon-kin will guess the rest of them have turned aside, even if they've left no tracks on the bare ice to show exactly where they've gone to earth. So to speak.

Him, if he were the pursuer, he'd send some of his spears to pick a way over the jagged ridge, here at the eastern point where it's narrow, and come at his would-be ambushers from behind. He taps Gillesh's shoulder for attention, beckons her and Jerrah farther into the jumbled slabs, climbing upward, skis abandoned down in a trench like a shallow grave. No help for it, they leave a track of disturbed snow to be seen by anyone who climbs in searching. Wind whines and stabs around corners, driving snow off the drifts and ledges to sting against faces.

It takes longer than Lannesk would like and he begins to sweat, afraid. He's made a mistake. The dragon-kin aren't anticipating an ambush after all. He's going to miss his chance and the dragon-kin scouts will be around the eastern end of the ridge and on Anzimor's tracks with no one to stop them, and if Anzi falls, breaks a strap or worse, a ski, they'll—

He slips, falls, sliding, comes up hard with a grunt at the bottom of a dark-shadowed pit. Jerrah's there, though, dropping the end of the rope coiled over his shoulder, and he and Gillesh brace as Lannesk scrambles out. Furious at himself. They've no time to waste.

More cautious, going on, his heart still singing, haste, haste, haste.

Singing rasp of skis on snow—dragon-kin closing in on the ridge from the north, he was right after all. Gillesh goes scrambling past him, climbing like a squirrel up a tilted slab. He slithers around, Jerrah going the other way.

Take out the sorcerer, the woman we heard singing, he would tell her, pointing, but there may be more than one woman among them, or more than one sorcerer. He'll settle for any lessening of their numbers.

Gillesh is perched precariously, a knee up on a knob of ice, a leg braced, leaning out sideways a little. He wouldn't try to shoot from such a position. The wind is gusting, but at least they're hidden in shadow, the long slanting sun behind them.

Gillesh has nocked an arrow, holds another ready. She wears archers' mittens, slit above the palm so she can uncap her hand and have her fingers free. Her face is gone still, her eyes intent. They're above the patrol, and aye, it's dividing, three turning towards the ice-ridge, towards where they hide, three going on around the end of it following their trail.

Close enough to see faces, and they look…just ordinary, like folk you'd rub shoulders with at a fair and never glance at twice. He'd been expecting something less human, like the silver dragon and her wings. A few scales, at least. But the dragon-kin are human, most of them. Not true kin to Golden Erryth, only her followers and worshippers. Two of them wear their hair in many long braids knotted with swinging pale beads, spilling down out of their hoods. A woman like that leads the three who are carrying on in the tracks, a man the ones turning towards them. The braids mark a sorcerer-priest, he would be willing to bet, and he puts a hand on Gillesh's ankle to get her attention, but her focus is that of a hunting cat and she doesn't look down. Shoots, and the woman drops. He pats her boot. Good.

The second arrow flies and the braided man, who's running on his skis, bent forward, falls, doesn't move. Third—another man stumbles, Gillesh dodges back and slithers down beside him, knocking him low just as an arrow whines over his head, shattering on ice.

He edges up again to look, more cautiously, and the two who've clustered around the fallen sorcerer-woman have turned towards the others. They think all four of their quarry are up here in the ice.

Come on, he thinks. Come get us. He'd rather fight them up here than out in the open. They're three and three now, and no one to sing ill-wishing against them, broken bowstrings or unlucky falls, if the songs tell true that the sorcerer-priests can do such things. No one to weaken the ice beneath them, a chilling thought.

Will they turn back, decide to take warning to their own captains, however far up the Lake they may be? And should he chase them in turn? Folly, that.

The dragon-kin hesitate. They come on.

"Good boys," Gillesh purrs, and shoots again, but her bowstring snaps and the arrow tumbles in its flight. "Dark Mother take you," she spits, and sucks stinging fingers. Chance. He couldn't have ill-wished her, thinking of it.

The three below are running, skis kicked off, and the snow is not deep enough to hamper them. Lost to view below the rising edge of the ice-ridge, but he can hear them—scramble, slither—hear panting breath. They've been pushing themselves to overtake; they're winded now. Afraid to go back to their captains, to say they've let enemy scouts get away?

He moves, slow, cautious, spear held shortened. He can hear Gillesh moving above him, following a higher path. Not sure where Jerrah's got to.

Shout, a word without meaning. Slither and tumble and cry. Changes his grip on the spear again and springs up and over a chunk of ice stained sunset rose with the falling light. Slides down, using the slide to launch himself, spear thrusting, stabbing deep and the man crouching below him bucks and flails as he jerks his spear free again, leaves his victim weakly rolling aside. A dead woman comes sliding down away to the left, leaving a smear of blood on a smooth ice-face.

"To your right, Lan!" Gillesh cries, and he's heard the scrape of movement, is turning already, a man coming down from ice above striking his spear aside with an axe that hits blunt-side on, so it doesn't break but he loses his grip, the mitten, sheepskin with the hide outermost, clumsier in its grasp than naked hand would be. The man slips, unbalanced by his swing, and Lannesk wrenches the axe from him instead of going for his own dagger, kicks him in the chest and knocks him sprawling down on the dead man below. Flings himself after as Gillesh slides down with her knife drawn, gets there first and wrenches the man's hands around. There's no resistance. Gillesh pushes, warily, with her foot, rolling the body over, its head flopping, as Jerrah scrambles down to join them.

"Broke his neck," Jerrah says with satisfaction. "Good kick, Lannesk." But it had been falling that did it and he had wanted this last one alive. The captains at Mair Arrun could have questioned him.

Done is done and dead is dead. Less trouble on the way home, anyway. They pick their way back over the ice to their skis, though Gillesh takes a quiver of the bone-pointed arrows. They're of a length with her own.

Shadows of the hills stretch long out over them and the hollows are pits of darkness, once they're back on open ice and gliding in Anzimor's tracks, keeping close together now. Night has fallen by the time they clamber up the shore and onto the path beneath the trees, but the waning moon has not yet risen.

The others haven't left the cabin, though they're partway through packing up, loading the toboggans.

"He won't survive it," Mirawan is saying, grim. "We can't drag him out into the night."

"He won't survive waiting here," Anzimor says. Looks around at Lannesk, who's come in as Granna goes out with a bundle on her shoulder. "Tell her, Lan."

He nods. Shrugs, because he has no argument to make that Anzimor hasn't used already, and it's Gillesh who says, "I killed two sorcerer-priests, if those were what the fancy braids mean—"

Lannesk nods, because he thinks it must be so, and Anzimor says, "Human fingerbones, they tie into their hair." That's a song, but it seems like truth.

"—and if they send sorcerers out with mere scouts, they must have plenty of them. Even if there's nothing but a larger scouting force following on, Lady Lauran and the Masters need to know. Come on— make a couple of firepots. They can keep Asa warm and we won't have to waste time starting fires on the trail."

"We don't know where they came from," says Finch, an older man. "They could have been sent to check the ice in case we've been fools enough to set out north. The dragon-kin could be, who knows, on Laikyn, or still in the Lann Leda, even."

Lannesk sighs, loudly, deliberate.

"Then no harm done but that we rush back to tell the captains the Lake's frozen and the dragon-kin are sending spies south," Anzimor says. "Which is, I thought, what we were here for?"

Lannesk hadn't thought of spies. If the sorcerers took the bones out of their hair and pulled it back decently, if they discarded their bone-tipped arrows, they might pass as hunters, merely scruffy and woods-draggled. Say they strayed Forest-wildered, being out on the Lake, horizons all distant and grey; they could circle around to Arrunmouth and claim that, and maybe be believed. If they didn't sound Outlander in their speech.

"But if we're right and they're the scouts of some attack on the Holy Isle, we've got no time to waste arguing over maybes," Anzimor continues. "This is what their white dragon killed the Seer to hide."

Reminder of the dragon seems to convince even Finch. Mirawan is wrapping Swordtheyn Asa, who wakes and bats feebly at her hands, muttering something about it being too early to get up.

"Hush," she says. "Dragon-kin on the Lake. We're going to Lord Ekkard." That seems to settle him. Swaddled in quilts and furs, with a well-wrapped firepot at his feet, the old swordtheyn is the last of the bundles they strap to a toboggan. Granna goes ahead of them carrying a lantern. There's fluffy new snow from the previous day over the trail, once they leave the cabin behind, but beneath it's packed firm from the passage of oxen and timber-sleds when they were building the outpost, almost a road, and even by night they can travel more swiftly than on a Forest path. But they'll be two days at best skirting around the feet of the central fells, even travelling through several hours of darkness each night, and how many days behind is the main dragon-kin warband likely to be?

He hopes Anzimor's suggestion is the truth—they were spies, not scouts. Even if it does make the pair of them look easily spooked fools.

Bright Mother send them luck and blessing. Let him not be killing Theyn Asa by this harsh journey.

~MAIRRAN~

*T*he sun sets in a bloody smear of cloud, and there is blood on the ice. There is a man, a boy. He offers himself. Kallyn sees it. Shaking, the boy drinks the cup to numb his fear, and he walks to them and their stone knives, the bone-braided sorcerer-priests of the Dragon, and he kneels, and for all he is drugged he shivers and his eyes run tears, but he is too weak to rise again, to run as Kallyn wants to cry to him to do, and they cut his throat as the drums rise to a frenzy and their song with it, a language I don't know and yet the words feel like fire spreading, calling me—

They sing, and they sing, patterning their faces with the spilled blood as the body is wrapped and lifted and carried away into the dark to what disposal Kallyn doesn't know. They force, with their words, a knife of cold. Their will seizes the water, the air...they struggle. One falls, an old woman, her heart stopping. They do not falter though she lies among them; they sing on.

Kallyn can hear it, see it, the shape their song makes in the world. Slowly growing, spreading, like a river flowing. Water laps at a fringe of ice, so thin, so fine, you could break it with a finger tapping. Freezes there, thickens, stilling. Silent, in its advance. Slow. A gibbous moon, waning, is only a smear of light behind cloud. The air smells of coming snow. They cook on small braziers on their sleds; the companies sleep on the ice, now, lying packed tight together in furs. Come the morning there will be the plodding tramp of booted feet, the hiss of runners. They will move in battle array, armed, under banners. Warriors to the fore, archers, spearcarls, axes and swords. Behind, their baggage train of sleds, some towed by teams of men and women, each to a rope, and some by reindeer they must have captured from the folk of the upper Lann Leda. Maybe there are captives among them, pressed into service. Or maybe *there were folk of the north Lann Leda herders who were secret dragon-kin. It happens.*

There are songs that tell of this, their exile, those they seduce to join them. And I remember...

Kallyn is Wolf, among them. Grey he-wolf. He seizes a singing man by his neck and throws him, tearing it. He crushes a woman's throat. He bites deep, hot blood, a third singer silenced, and they are on him with the stone knives of their priesthood, and their warriors answer the sorcerers' cries with sword and spear, but she's gyrfalcon in the air then, gone, lost in the dark. Maybe that will slow them, disrupt them. Profane this night's unclean offering and destroy their sunset working, set them back one day, at least.

There is a woman among the sorcerers, slight and fine and silver-haired, wearing a cloak of white bearskin, hide outermost, carrying a bow. Her face is bruised and scabbed with healing wounds.

She looks up to find Kallyn, circling in the night, pale falcon where a falcon should not fly.

She sets arrow to bow and draws.

Kallyn falls. Out of night. Out of dark. Out of dreaming, even as the silver woman flings herself on the falcon, long and lean and silver-scaled, and Kallyn, Mairran, I flail away into Wolf—

I think there is blood on my face, but it's only sweat. Or maybe it's tears.

Maybe I'm remembering what is to come.

~LANNESK~

Their second night. Something's behind them.

They camped late and set off early, took a break at noon to cook up some gruel for Theyn Asa, who wakes by times, and seems to understand what's afoot when he does, which is an improvement. Maybe taking him out of the smoky cabin into the clean cold air is something they should have done when he first fell ill.

Pushing on into the night again to put some more dark miles behind them before they camp; they'll come to Mair Arrun tomorrow, Lannesk hopes. The night feels like snow. Fingers of cloud are reaching out of the west to cover the stars.

There's something back there, on the trail behind. He can—there's nothing to hear. Only he knows it, feels it, like breath on the back of his neck. Lannesk swings out to the side, tosses his tow-rope onto the toboggan, whistles for his brother.

"Keep on," Anzi says to the others, who have halted, looking around. Jerrah drops back to take up a rope, help Gillesh and Granna with this last of their three toboggans.

They set themselves in the trail, shoulder to shoulder, waiting, as the others hurry on. Neither of them has a bow. No fit light for shooting, but they've been towing the toboggans while cumbered with shields slung over their shoulders. Glad of it now. And yet—

Grips Anzimor's arm, stopping him lifting his spear, when he hears it. A soft sound, a jogging beat with a hitch and drag to it. Not human footfalls; far too quiet for a horse.

The wolf's on them before they see him, looming out of the dark, and they both flinch back, even though Lannesk, at least, is expecting him. Her, as Wolf becomes woman, panting as the wolf was panting, chest heaving, limping, and there's a dark clotted furrow across her face and black scabbed wounds on her arms, too.

"I take it those scouts were your work," she says. "Well done, my Coastlanders."

"Are they out there?" Anzimor asks. "Is the dragon with them?"

"The silver woman. Yes. I failed, again, to kill her." Hair, blood-matted, hangs lank across her face and she swipes it away with the back of her hand, like a dog using its paw. As if she's uncertain what body she inhabits. Sways on her feet; Lannesk and Anzimor both reach to catch her, both stop short of touching. She steadies herself, gives them a weary smile. "We had no idea that golden Erryth had spawned an heir. If the girl is that, and not some feral half-human dragonling out of the far wilds they've tamed to their use. Dangerous, even so. She's sorcerer as well as dragon. But I don't think she commands them. Not yet."

"How long till they reach us?" Anzimor asks.

"They're maybe two days behind, now. Two thousand, armed. They must have emptied their valley in the ice of everyone fit to carry a spear, and left none to hold the Lann Leda behind them, either."

"They're freezing the Lake?" Anzimor asks. "We saw —I thought it was a raft of ice floating free, at first, but that patrol came off of it. Lannesk felt it, didn't you? The working of their sorcery?"

He nods. But it doesn't make him a witch. The Grey Hunter only nods, as if it is an ordinary thing, that he should have felt the making of magic.

"They froze a bridge over open water," Anzimor says. "They were singing."

"I saw. I came over the remains of it, jumping floating piece to piece. It was barely thick enough to bear them and the wind's broken it now. But that was just a little thing. They have a hundred sorcerers, or near that, behind, and they're making more than a footbridge. Building it nightly out of song and offerings of death. What you saw was just the thin leading edge, flung far out ahead of where the Lake's freezing to their road as it would to the cold stone of a shore. I killed a few of their sorcerers, but not enough, and they're willing to kill themselves, anyway, as well as sacrificing their followers, feeding their sorcery. And now I'm grounded."

Lannesk is moving to offer her his fur cape, but she's the falcon, then, flapping clumsy, flight feathers ragged and broken, all grace fled, to his outstretched arm. She walks up to his shoulder.

He strokes the back of her neck, as if she's Anzi's goshawk and needs soothing, heart thumping at his own presumption, but she doesn't snap at him, only hunkers down low, exhausted, as they turn and set off in the tracks the others have left.

Two thousand in arms, and sorcerers. They're only a few hundred at Mair Arrun.

~MAIRRAN~

I dream a grey he-wolf, running through snow. I dream a black wolf bitch, running by the grey wolf's side.

What is he? *I say, and in this dream we speak without voice, mind to mind.* The wild man. What is he? Did he kill the earl?

Does it matter? *the grey wolf asks the black.*

It should, *I say.*

The grey wolf huffs aloud, like a human snicker.

We come to the lakeshore, a headland where the wind sings in pines rooted in the cracks of grey rock. It's the Lake, vast as a sea, not the Fairnmere. I don't know the place, but we often come here when we run together dreaming, the black wolf and the grey. Maybe Kallyn likes the view. She stands, a woman, naked. Her skin is a light brown, only a little lighter than my own, her eyes are grey, made warm with flakes of a colour between gold and copper about the pupils, and her tangled hair is brown and silver, though her strong-boned face is not old. Not young, either. Pale scars mark her. Teeth, blades. Old wounds. The worst are over her left shoulder, front and back, deep and knotted. Sometimes she rubs them, as if they pain her. My shoulder aches. It bears scars as well, echoes to hers. Once I fought a bear. Training, my mother said.

I nearly died.

I am sorry for the bear.

I don't think, *Kallyn says*, that he was ever dead. Only lost in the Dark.

Who? *I ask, but the wind has blown her to dust and there are only white bones lying at my feet, an empty human skull. Wolf, bereft, I howl, but there is no answer.*

Human, I pick up a bone, a broken half from a forearm, and in my hands it's a flute, my fingers settling into place, over the wide broken end that is smoothed now, over holes bored ready for the left hand. I put it to my mouth and play, and what I play is the song that eludes me in the dark, but it runs through my mind like water and I can't hold it, though some part of me half-waking tries to remember, and the bone turns to dust and my mouth tastes of ashes.

I'm afraid. The light is slanting long and yellow, and the yellow grows and grows, till all is brilliant gold, but I stare into silver, spinning, swelling, a drop of water on a twig's tip. I put out my tongue to lick the water from the twig, to taste rain and an ordinary dawn. Gold shifts and stirs within the drop, a tiny thing and filling all the world, sparking harsh glints of light, then softly luminous, then glittering with jewel-like depths. Something vast is passing by, coiling, twisting, turning. Something has come closer. Something stands, as I do, looking through the Dark between us. Then there is a slit of blackness in the gold, darker than night. It watches me, as I watch it. The blackness grows, till the bead of water holds the night sky, and the stars and moon and all, and there is moonlight on grey stone.

I see the red horse, a rider, distant, passing among trees. Grey trunks, russet leaves still clinging.

Kill him, *my mother says, and the water drips, falling, freezing as it falls, and I fall with it, into the Lake. Into the sky.*

~LANNESK~

Snow, great fat feather-flakes of it, falling slow, gentle, hissing into the light of the cresset fixed at the head of the ladder. So quiet you can hear them. Only breathing, the wheeze and sniff of runny noses in the cold, and the creak, rasp, of leather, scuff on stone, as someone shifts their weight foot to foot. Distant cedars are dark, jagged, against the faint greying of the clouds, a promise that the morning will yet come to devour the night.

"They're coming," Anzimor says.

Lannesk slips off his mittens, which are on a string over his shoulders, under the vest of heavy leather, fur still on—bear, it is—that's all the armour he has to cover his quilted tunic, throws his cloak off to hang on the birch rail at the back of the rough wooden fighting-platform—the stone walls of Singersborg had once had a wooden wall-walk built along them, when this was a fortress during the unsettled years that followed the defeat of Erryth the Golden. Dragon-kin had striven then to take back the Holy Isle from those who followed the Wild King, but the wall-walk and most other defences are long gone. They've done what they can in the couple of days they've had, building hasty platforms of split logs at intervals between the crumbling corner towers, throwing up some makeshift hoardings to shelter behind, in place of the crenellations the wall lacks.

He strings his bow. Going to be warm enough soon.

Torchlight, moving, in the distance. No concealment. Open threat of a river of light, winding up along the frozen Arrunlinn. The dragon-kin have been camped in the woods to the northeast, too vast a camp to attack, the captains decided.

The Grey Hunter had wanted them to strike at the sorcerers in the night. Suicide, the captains said, wary of offending the Immortal, but unmoving. If the Wild King and his Riding were here, it would be different…

So the first move has fallen to the dragon-kin.

At least they're not such fools, here on these scattered platforms along the wall, there on the tower-tops, as to be thinking that the torchlight shows the vanguard of the assault.

From the tower at the southeast corner of the wall there's a bolt of light like a shooting star, a fire-arrow, aimed not at the distant advance but striking down the steep slope of the ridge to the tumbled and broken stone, overgrown with thorn and juniper they didn't have time to clear. The thorns may prove their friend.

A cry, cut off, and the light flares, juniper catching, which might be the Immortal's blessing, helping it along. Black shadows writhe and scurry like a nest of disturbed rats. Burning brush casts light on more, creeping, climbing, up the ridge towards the wall, and the bows begin to sing.

Dragon-kin die in the dark, driven up the steep slope below the wall by the burning brush, but those who've kept their wits scatter off into the dark to the north, either to try a different section of wall or to retreat to the main force, still hanging back. The Grey Hunter's up on the southeast tower, wolf's eyes piercing the dark. Outcry behind, off around to the north. Dragon-kin have got up the ridge somewhere. Here on this fighting-platform, the little band under Anzimor's command rests; they warm their hands; they shiver as sweat cools, lean together, cough, rub stinging eyes. The wind drives the smoke to them, but the brushfire below is dying. That was nothing. The first scuffling, a bit of shoving between the benches after too much ale. The knives haven't even come out.

"How long do you think we can hold?" Anzimor says softly, chin on Lannesk's shoulder, not for the others to hear.

He shakes his head.

"Aye." Anzi straightens up, stretches. "Me too."

A girl, maybe twelve or so, clambers up the ladder, lugging a basket, and a younger boy comes behind her with a jug and a few cups. Still-warm bread, chunks of cold roasted pork, blue-veined cheese, ale to share around. The children stare over the hoarding of the platform, trying to make out anything at all below.

"Don't," Hennis says. "Keep your heads down."

But the boy stands on tiptoe, heaving himself up to hang over the top, points. "Is that a dead man? Was he a sorcerer?"

"Where?" says the girl. "Liar. You can't see anything down there. It's too dark." But she pushes up beside the boy to look.

Lannesk grabs the pair of them, jerks them back. The boy yelps, falling on his rump. Arrow streaks over. Still a few dragon-kin out there, hiding in the scrub that hasn't burnt. Watching.

"Get back to the kitchens," Hennis says, and swats the nearest behind. "Go! Before you end up dead men yourself!"

The children go, chastened, and the dozen or so of them here eat while they can, sharing the cups around.

Dead sorcerer, no. It won't be sorcerer-priests sent within easy arrow-shot merely to try their strength and watchfulness.

Not a glimpse of the silver dragon. Maybe the Grey Hunter did wound her badly enough to keep her out of the action. Lannesk counts the fires that begin to bloom, seeded by the wavering torches where the dragon-kin army has halted. Abandons it as too disheartening. Looks like the enemy advance isn't going to push on against the Singersborg right away; they're setting up another camp, sprawling over the road, down to the bank of the frozen river.

Feels like they've been watching, waiting, weary days on end. Only yesterday, though, that they finally burned what was left standing of their own houses and halls and barns down below, closed and barred the gate of the Singersborg. Smoke still rises sluggishly from the ruins of Mair Arrun, the ruins of Arrunstead. All the warband has retreated up the ridge to the stone walls, with all the stores they can shift, and many of the cattle and geese, the sheep and goats and swine of Arrunstead, and its hay, and what they could drag of Mair Arrun's palisade and longhouses, both to build new huts and sheds and to deny the timber to the enemy. The landcarls of Arrunstead did not all join them. Some families loaded sleds and toboggans and set out down the river to Arrunmouth, thinking they could cross ahead of the dragon-kin advance, get over the Lake east to the Merkal, as many from the harbour were said to be doing; some have just fled south to shelter in the forested hills, as if they believe the battle will be swiftly settled and they can return and rebuild. Others have chosen to trust to the walls of the Singersborg, in hope of the Wild King. Better if they hadn't. They're only more mouths to feed.

Night sky fades to morning grey. Wind picks up, and the snow falls more thickly. Have the dragon-kin truly made a closer camp and settled in to take their time over a siege, Lannesk wonders? Fires are an easy deception. Snow hazes the distance like fog. Can't see what the enemy's up to now, less than they could make out at night: the fires are hidden. Here, spearcarls and archers stamp, huddle. Hennis steals a kiss from Anzimor, shifting places to take her turn at watch. Most of them go down the ladder to where there's a fire in the lee of the wall, out of the wind. Ekkard, with Theyn Asa and Tolla and Ovan, is among those set to guard the Hall of the Masters away towards the north of the borg. There was some fuss there; it holds a library of precious books and the Singers fear to lose them. But it's a stone hall with a squat square tower, far from the walls, and judged so safe they've gathered the younger children and frailest of the elders there. He overheard some talk of moving the library, but where they think they can move it to, he doesn't know. Can't care, if truth be told. But the children—they should have all been sent away, not penned in here like autumn bully-calves, to wait.

Five days since Lannesk and his patrol made it back to find camp and village seething like an anthill dug up and turned over in the kaleyard. Wolf had run on ahead the first morning after overtaking them, still blood-matted, still lame, though Theyn Asa, against whom

Kallyn had lain in their hasty brush-hut like a great grey dog, woke clear-witted and clear-lunged, as if Wolf's warmth against him had given some Forest-blessing of healing.

But dragon-bites don't heal swiftly. Broken feathers don't heal at all, and it's not her falcon's season for moulting, the Grey Hunter said, when Lady Lauran's cousin, who has a reputation as a physician and had tried to clean the Immortal's wounds, dared to ask.

And where's the Wild King? Where's word of what the earls may do?

The Ways the King may ride are—twisted, the Grey Hunter says. She has called him, but he cannot hear, he cannot come to her, nor she to him. Sorcery is worked against him. It's no secret kept to the Masters and captains; all the folk within the walls know it, and it's a weight pressing down on them, a burden of fear, because if the King cannot come to them, and if the earls do not...

No matter how plentifully provisioned, no matter how deep the wells, do they dare believe they can hold here till spring?

The Grey Hunter wears anger like a cloak. She prowls, dressed in soft shoes and a heavy hall-gown, along the coping-stones of the wall between the new fighting-platforms, prowls the roofs of the towers; she's up there again now, on the southeast corner, standing on the parapet as if she's invulnerable to arrows, which Lannesk knows she is not, watching over the enemy encampment.

"Tomorrow," Anzimor says, looking to where the Immortal perches, human in form, but like the falcon in her watchful stillness, snow blowing around her, settling white on her bare head, on hunched shoulders. She looks ready to launch herself into the empty air. "Or..." He shrugs. "We won't see Snowsdeep in, if they send their dragon."

The Wild King will come. He must. He'll find a way. Make a Way, through Forest, over ice. Come beneath the stars, his red horse running on the wind. That's what their mother would sing. The silver dragon fled him at the Seer's tower. Lannesk wishes he had his harp out of the hall, could make a song of it, as if that might prove a promise, or a spell to summon him.

A swelling sound, like a wave, like the rush and roar of a river ice-dam breaking. The Grey Hunter leaps backwards. The bell of the Masters' Tower clangs, wind-jangled. They scramble for the ladder as the wind hits in storm-fury, a nor'easter of his childhood, gusts like hammer-blows hard enough a slipping boot might send you to the ground. They make it up to the fighting-platform, both of them, and the others who were below come behind, helping one another. Crouching below the wall, behind the hoardings, trying to peer out, but now the snow is driving hard and blinding up the valley. No shooting in this. Can't see more than a few yards, if that; nothing at all to see but the stinging white. Nothing to hear over the roar of the wind.

"This is sorcery!" Anzimor bellows in his ear. Nothing blows up that swiftly. If it's cover for another dragon-kin advance on the walls, they won't know till it's on them. It should pin the enemy down as well, drive them to shelter. Lannesk doesn't expect it will.

Heavy, shushing sound overhead, like a crow, a goose going over, slow and heavy and almost lost in the wind. He slaps Granna's shoulder, points where he thinks he can track it, shadow, sound, some sense, and she yells, "Dragon!" slapping in turn an arrow to her bow, drawing—but it's gone, and she doesn't shoot blind, to have the arrow come to earth somewhere within their own walls.

Shouting, and the bell again, but now tolling with intent.

Something shrieks, not in pain but anger, or maybe it's triumph. Can't see so far as the Masters' Hall through the snow, but he sees Wolf racing low, swift shadow, in that direction. Hennis starts for the ladder but Gillesh grabs her back and Anzimor bellows, "Don't leave your post—watch the damned wall!"

His thoughts will be on Ekkard too.

Growing light from the north end of the village and it's not the sun. Red glow flaring and dimming. Even the storm can't utterly hide it. Fire. The bell is silent, now, its warning given. Or silenced. If there's outcry, uproar, they can't hear it, lost in the howl of the wind. It's worse than the night, knowing, not knowing. And nothing moves below, no rush to storm the section of wall they can still see. Nothing for them to do.

Screaming, bellowing of cattle, ragged bleating of sheep. Shouts that carry even over the wind. Those are horses, the screaming, and pigs. That's from the southwest, where makeshift corrals hold what the barns cannot, near the main gate. By the barns themselves. Glare of fire there, too, and it's rising, growing, a roar they can hear as the hay catches.

"Mothers Below," Anzimor mutters. Lannesk grips his shoulder. They have to stay. They can't go rushing off to help. Could be what's intended.

"I know, I know," Anzimor says, but his teeth are set.

"'Ware above!" Gillesh shouts, and out of the fireglow the dragon bursts, shadow within the snow. They draw and loose as she hurtles over and the wind flings their arrows to the four quarters. They see only too late the smaller shape that harries her, clawing and rolling away, falling and floundering in the air, so just as well every shot went astray. He thinks he sees that the Grey Hunter's talons are shredding that silver armoured hide where she strikes, dark tears opening, but they're past and gone; he can't be sure.

The shrieking and bellowing goes on, and dies into the lowing of unhappy cattle, so some beasts have survived. The storm too dies as the daylight grows stronger, till there's only a few half-hearted flakes drifting down. Clouds dissolve to grey rags against the brightness of the blue.

The barns still burn, animals loose and bunched up among the houses and halls towards the south, still fearful, save the swine, which have set out foraging through the yards and lanes as if nothing has happened. Orange flames climb through the cedar-shingled roof of the Masters' Hall. There's folk fighting the fires of the burning barns, throwing snow and water. At the Masters' Hall there's a chain of pails being carried from the well to the roof of the tower, but the fire of the hall below is fierce and what's flung falls hissing into steam.

Children cry, little ones too young to have been set to work in the communal kitchen set up in a baker's yard. Some are being taken away by people who might be family, but still, he doesn't think there's enough of them there, bunched up together like the cattle, some taller figures trying to get them chivvied away to new shelter. Surely they got them all out, surely there was time, enough warning—

A yelp from someone on the southeast tower roof, but it's a false alarm. The Grey Hunter crashes down among those on the roof there, floundering, falling out of the air, and Wolf flings out the tower door moments later, loping, limping, leaving bloody spatters on the dirty snow of the paths, through the yards, towards the burning Masters' Hall.

The children have vanished into some new shelter. A woman is wailing.

Nothing, absolutely nothing, to stop the dragon coming again. Nothing to stop the sorcerers turning the wind and the sky against them, if the Singers' songs are not enough.

Noon, and they trade places with another small squad. They should go back to the overcrowded hall, once the home of some Singer and his family and apprentices, which now Lord Ekkard's company shares with a band of shipcarls from Head of Rath. Get some food, some sleep. They don't. Anzimor leads them to join those working at the smouldering shell of the Masters' Hall, shifting timbers with rakes and hooks, carrying water to what still burns. Searching.

Jerrah's dead. And Mirawan. And others not of their company, both here and among the barns. Hennis ends up with a blistered welt across her face, winces and flinches when Anzimor tries to dab the soot away. They're all soot-blackened, red-eyed, coughing.

Ekkard has survived, blistered and coughing, and Tolla and Ovan.

Jerrah is dead. Someone tells Lannesk this, again, as if they think he didn't hear the first time. It's like when their sister died. A pain strange and remote. Something missing and you don't yet quite understand it.

A falling beam struck him, their shipmaster Myrild his kinsman says, through fits of coughing that seem as if they might tear his lungs out. Broke his back as he ran with his arms full of squalling children down the stairs from the upper gallery where they'd put the little ones, far from the draft and the nightlong comings and goings through the porch. Mirawan, who'd been on the tower roof, was set alight with dragon's flame and fell burning to the yard below.

Anzimor's watching Lannesk. Comes over, puts a hand on his shoulder. Yes, he knows. But there's nothing can be undone, and work to do, and if something's gone sick and hard like a bruise in his chest, he's hardly the only one.

Should have gone with Jerrah again. Should have asked him if he wanted to, anyway.

They drag out what bodies they can. Charred beyond knowing, most of them. Not even sure what's a body, what's a beam, sometimes, till your hook breaks it and there's bone.

Not as many as they fear, though. Or they've been burnt beyond recognizing as anything human. Unless they're in what still burns, under the north gable end, away from the tower.

Turns out there's a cellar beneath the south end, filled with rubble now, and broken beams, and puddled ashy water that steams as it slowly drains away. They're trying to clear it, because someone might have tried to shelter there, but a Master, weary-faced, soot-blackened, comes to tell them, leave it be. There's nothing there, she says. No one. Come away.

The dead they've found are carried to an outbuilding that can serve as lychhouse. They're butchering the carcasses of the dead animals, slaughtering those too badly injured to survive long. In this winter weather, the meat can hang frozen till needed in some unheated shed or cellar. Better, in truth, than keeping it on the hoof, eating what's left unburnt of the hay. They won't be starved out for months. At least till the thaw spoils those larders.

The Singers are gathering in one of their halls to make a song against the dragon-kin priests. Someone says that's what they're doing, anyway. There are those among the Singers who are sooty, battered, weary as any of them. They weren't all hiding withindoors, as some grumble. Lord Ekkard tells off a shipcarl who says so.

The Grey Hunter prowls among them as Wolf. People move out of his way.

Eat. Rest. Sleep if they can. The sun is setting, and Lannesk and his band have the watch from midnight to dawn again. Lannesk eats. Anzimor is watching him, to be sure he does. He takes his harp, though, when he's had all he can stomach, which isn't much, and goes out. Anzimor follows. They walk, in the falling dark. Restless, though his body's crying for sleep. Heat beats off the ruins still. Shadows moving there, within the hollow ruin of the Masters' Hall, the dim light of horn-paned lanterns. Shadows coming and going from that tower, a light bobbing down in the pit of the small cellar.

"You shouldn't be here," a white-haired man in a heavy gown tells them. One of the Masters of the Singers, standing as if on guard, leaning on a staff. "Go to your beds. There's nothing here outsiders can help with."

Outsiders, not Outlanders, but Anzimor snaps, "Our friends died here. Can we not give them a song in parting, or are mere Coastlanders fit only for dying on your walls?"

The old Singer holds up his hands. "Peace, my friends, peace. No insult meant." He hesitates. "There's a child unaccounted for. His mother... We're searching..." He shrugs, meaning, they have no hope.

"Can we help?" Anzimor asks, because what else can he say, though Lannesk does not want to be harrowing the debris again and wondering if every pale gleam the light finds might be Jerrah's armbone, his thigh, to find the socket of an eye staring. His was not among the recognizable bodies; they only thought that one blackened, twisted form might have been his, because of the two smaller ones beneath it and Myrild saying he'd been carrying little children when the beam fell on the stairs.

"No," the Singer says. "Thank you. Go to your beds. The morning will need your strength."

"Come on, Lan," Anzimor says, and puts an arm through his.

If he wanted to make a song for Jerrah, the hearth of their hall would be a better place for it anyway. Warmth and light and the friends and shipmates who knew him better than Lannesk ever did. But that isn't the restlessness that drives him. So he walks, and Anzimor lets himself be led.

Wonders what the Singers are really doing. The weak yellow light of a lanthorn's not going to be much use in finding what daylight did not reveal.

It's a comfort, to have his harp, like a child hugging some little wooden toy, but there's no song to make for this night. He lets Anzimor turn their steps back to their hall, and fire, and the few hours' sleep they can take, before they wake their little band again and go back to watch on the wall. Lord Ekkard breaks the rest of the company, the survivors of it, into smaller groups as well, and sends them out to other duties as Lady Lauran requests, there being no more Masters' Hall to guard.

The days and nights in besieged Singersborg fall one into another, and if the days are growing longer as the month of Yearsturn passes, it's only a very slow creeping of the light, and the winter's cold deepens. There are too few children; there are old folks missing, and some say they died when the Masters' Hall burned, and some say the Singers sang them a Way under the stars such as the Wild King might ride, and why cannot they then lead all the folk to some safer refuge… But that's fool's talk. It's only that those who are able keep withindoors more, for the cold, and fear of the silver dragon, which has not returned.

Not that walls have proven much shelter from her.

The restlessness doesn't leave Lannesk. There's a heavy weariness seeps into your bones, watching, waiting, but it doesn't give you sleep. There's hard work to be done, too, repairing and making. They're extending the fighting platforms into a wall-walk; they're wetting and icing the roofs so that their own hearths and dragon-fire alike may only make them too wet to burn, or that's the hope. Trampled lanes grow icy, rutted from the passage of sled-runners and oxen, dragging timber and barrels of water.

The dragon-kin shift their camp, break it into three: east of Singersborg, southwest amid the ruins of Mair Arrun, and down below the bluff, along the river in what had been Arrunstead.

The dragon-kin have no engines to throw shot or great spears against them, but neither do they have any such thing themselves. The Singers' Council talks of building engines; they summon shipwrights, find beams among the salvaged timbers of Mair Arrun, but the dragon comes, floating on silent wings, soft and unheralded by any assault, and the timber-yard is burning before the watch on the west has sounded the alarm. They lose two more halls that night as well, one of the wooden towers, and a long section of their new wall-walk. Lives, as well. The unshrouded dead are piled like cordwood in the lychhouse.

Comes a bright noon that the dragon-kin march bound prisoners up the road towards the gate. Hands tied, roped in a long string. Lady Lauran, some of the captains, some of the Masters, go to the gatetowers. Lord Ekkard and Theyn Asa are among the captains summoned, and Anzimor and Hennis their escort, with Ovan and Tolla. Lannesk, not included when Asa picked out spearcarls, trails as Anzimor's shadow, spear in hand, shield slung at his shoulder, harp in its bag under his arm, because they'd been at a meal when the summons came to their lord, and he'd been playing, as Ekkard had asked. Doesn't like to leave it in the hall they share with the shipcarls of Rath, who've taken to borrowing it without seeking leave. No time to shove it into concealment under Ekkard's bed-platform in the loft above.

The captives are some of the folk who went downriver to the harbour and didn't make it. Likely they've family within. Lannesk can't think what the dragon-kin may ask for, unless it's the surrender of the Grey Hunter, her life for theirs.

But there's no herald sent forward, no demand. Only a crowd of the sorcerer-priests with their bone-braided hair closing in about the captives, and the Grey Hunter suddenly among the folk on the northernmost of the paired gatetowers, Wolf to naked woman, saying, snarling, "Kill them. Shoot them now, give them a clean death, Mothers Below, now, before—" And she cries out, a scream not human, high and agonized, and falls to her knees. Lannesk drops to catch her and does not see what's happening. Someone shouts and archers do shoot. The Grey Hunter, staggering, claws herself upright by him, her face dreadful, as if something twists and tears her within. Trying to support her, trying to stop her flinging herself over the wall—as if she's forgotten her injured wing and how it hampered her last time she fought in the air—he can see, then, what's happening below.

Curved stone knives slashing, red soaking the stone, the prisoners falling. Sorcerer-priests are cutting throats, sorcerer-priests singing, voices swelling, triumphant and the clear winter air grows heavy as if with brewing storm, even as arrows strike and some of the priests fall among their victims. But dragon-kin archers draw and send a ragged volley in return, while the Grey Hunter falls again and writhes, white-eyed and frothing, as if whatever sorcery they weave out of death and song has set a poison in her. Lannesk shields her with his body, wraps her in his fur cape and is picking her up—light, he thinks, unreasoning, as if the weight of her ancient years should have made her a thing of stone—when someone falls against him and he drops heavily onto a knee, still shielding the Hunter, as she still twists and snaps teeth at nothing, blind and senseless. It's Hennis who's fallen on him and she rolls aside, fumbles onto her hands, half rising, slumps again, hand slipping in her own pooling blood, and the arrow pushes through below her shoulder.

Lannesk gathers the Grey Hunter up again and gets her down to the next landing of the stairs, lays her down there and tries to steady her against her thrashing. Out of sight of the priests, he thinks, but that's not enough; he can hear the sorcery still, the drums, the singing, one voice rising over the rest in a harsh demanding word that is answered every time by a new spasm of her body.

No spell to set against them, and if the Singers above have any to offer—he hears a single flute rising, a little unsteady, fear tainting it, and maybe there is song amid the cursing of the archers—they seem powerless.

No voice. And even if he had his speech, he's no Master Singer, to know the magic that may be spun from song. If there is true magic held in the mysteries of Singersborg at all. But he has nothing else, either, so he fumbles out his harp and strikes a chord, and lifts the Hunter's head off the cold boards to his lap, and another chord, and then the strings running, up and down, and settles, finding a shape of something where he had only had panic, before. Names her what she is, Immortal of the

Forest, Hunter, wind-rider, snow-runner, ancient and wise and wild. Finds his way, notes clear and bright, a dance of them: a falcon on the wind, a wolf dancing shadow-dappled, sunlight, moonlight, tree-bough swaying, water's song. He catches her with it, tries to draw her away from the thing they've cast into her, the poison they've made, their sorcery, Erryth's foul blessing. Tries to make something clean and strong to stand against the death-summoned death set against her.

Her thrashing struggle stills and he thinks they've killed her, but then he knows they have not. He can feel it, feel her, as if he holds her, or his music does. It's a rope, a path, a Way that is hers, and she follows it, as if she struggles out of drowning bog to find herself on solid rock again. Rolls over, pushing herself up, blinking at him. Is Wolf, panting, fangs inches from his face, drooling froth. Is woman once more, shuddering, wiping her chin. He hardly dares to let the music fade, but she sets a hand on his, cold as winter and shaking, but so is his own, when their fingers fold together.

"Who in the Mother's name ever taught you that, my harper?" she says. Her voice is faint and rough, and he helps her struggle up to sit by him, pressed side to side. He feels her shivering, shoulder to hip. Tries to get his cape pulled up over her again, without setting hand to her skin, feeling too intensely aware that she is naked, and beautiful. Which—even leaving aside that she has the Wild King, whom she claimed and took from the Golden Erryth herself, and neither needs nor wants such attention from a boy—is something he should be ashamed to be noticing of any woman or man in such a situation.

The Grey Hunter's head is on his shoulder. Not lover's affection. Only warmth. Friendship. A moment's stillness, for both of them.

Deep breath. She stands, pushing herself up, hand on his shoulder, his cape falling away. Her left arm is deeply gouged, a wound scabbed over but swollen and festering. Ill-wishing in it, against its healing. She's an Immortal of the Forest; such an injury should surely not trouble her so long.

"She's coming," the Grey Hunter says. Cocks her head as if listening to what a dog might hear. "*They're* coming." He is Wolf, bounding up the stairs, stumbling on the lame leg only a little.

Lannesk slings the harp-sack over his head and shoulder to bump against his hip and reclaims his fur cape. Spear dropped up above. He goes to find it, running up the steps two at a time.

There's a roar, down on the road, a clashing of spears on shields in threat, the drums pounding, throats shouting. There's a roar in the air, a rising wind, and the silver dragon riding it.

The dragon-kin come.

~LANNESK~

The silver dragon's come and gone, driven back by arrows like a swarm of wasps, leaving another section of the new wall-walk burning along the east. Dragon-kin have stormed the wall over there with the fire's dying, coming with grappling hooks and ladders and an arrow storm of their own, shooting high to arc down inside. Attack rises and ebbs at various points along the wall like a tide, but here at the gate it comes unrelenting.

At first it seems a madness on the dragon-kin, warriors rushing with spears and axes against stone and iron-studded oak under the cover of their archers, who force those on the tower roofs to crouch below the parapets, shields raised over their heads.

The sorcerers have fallen back or scattered from the charge of their own spearcarls up the road, which flows over the dead as if they are just so much dung to be trampled into the snow. The first volley of enemy arrows spent, up on the tower roofs the Forest-folk put their own bows to use in turn, shooting down into the attackers, who hack at the gate-timbers as if they have any hope of getting through. Stone axes as well as iron. It's not that the dragon-kin have lost the knowledge of the working of metal, only that it's scarce among them, and hoarded for the most valued tools. But they've smiths, and forges, and scrap to smelt, captured from the harbour village; the glow of their smithies has been seen. Maybe they've been casting sorcery into their weapons, Anzimor wonders aloud. Singing, quenching blades in blood to make an edge that will not turn or dull. That's a song. Lannesk isn't sure he doubts it.

He has a bow. Shields stacked aside. Arrow to wood and draw, duck out, sighting his target as he does, shoot, and back behind again as Anzimor shoots. They find a rhythm to it. Their archery's improved, both of them, since the summer. Dire need. The Grey Hunter, with someone's cloak draped over a shoulder, scant decency and no protection at all, has claimed a bow and picks off sorcerers as they follow the rushing advance, every arrow finding its mark, despite the festering wound in her arm. The dragon-kin fall back and for a moment there is space to breathe, to take stock. Anzimor is pale, smears of dirty red on his face, as if he's wiped a bloody hand across it. They've had to drag the bodies of several arrow-slain out of the way, no time to carry them below. Hennis among them. Lannesk pulls his brother close, to say what words could not, even if he had them. Lord Ekkard comes over to lean between them, silent. Anzimor puts an arm around his shoulders.

"Ram," Theyn Asa says, and Lannesk doesn't understand what he means at first. Word that makes no sense, till he sees the new crowd of dragon-kin coming, dragging a great trunk on a pair of sleds with some sort of framework collapsed over it, whipping their reindeer along. He puts an arrow through the neck of the foremost beast and the others try to scatter away; they're harnessed each with their own traces, not in pairs, so there's no tangle of living and dead teammates and as others fall dragon-kin spearcarls run to cut them away, roll the bodies aside, take the ropes themselves. More warriors rush with great square shields to protect them.

"Fire," says Lady Lauran. "We need fire of our own, against that."

Lannesk wonders. Throw fire down on them and they may be setting their own gate alight. Swordtheyn Asa and a couple of the Singers are talking of a famous siege in the Southlands. He's heard songs of it, but they've read a history in some book. Various ways to foul a ram. Hooks and chains. Woolsacks. Straw-ticks.

Some of the dragon-kin dragging the ram among the reindeer fall, but its advance never falters; more enemy archers are sent up to loose a new storm against those on the gate-towers and they're forced to cower again, shields raised over their heads, a few shooting when they can. When next Lannesk risks a glimpse below, the dragon-kin have got the beam to the gate and lifted it to hang from its frame of timbers and chains. They're rearing some massive shields over it on more timber frames, so maybe that's what the captains expected when they spoke of needing fire.

Fire is what the dragon-kin send—with a shriek like an enraged falcon the dragon stoops on the southern gate-tower, a hurtling silver bolt from on high. Lannesk swings around to draw on her, he and every archer of the northern gate-tower still with an arrow to hand. She spews her greasy pale fire over the archers of the south tower and wheels in the swarm of arrows to spit at the north.

"Shields!" Swordtheyn Asa doesn't need to shout, and flame splashes weakly, as if the dragon's vomited up all she can; it burns in streaks and puddles. Several rush to beat it out with wet and frozen brooms, someone's forethought. Lannesk is using a mitten to beat out a burning splash on Lord Ekkard's arm; he sees how the dragon dives down low beyond the wall, hurtling along the road. Ploughing into the snow. She thrashes, recovers, staggers into the air leaving a red-streaked furrow through the drifts. Injured. If they could follow—he elbows Anzimor—his own quiver's empty—Anzi sees and takes the shot, but she's gone too far, fleeing to the western camp. Where's the Grey Hunter? A horrible screaming from the southern tower, bodies, more than one, aflame. Lady Lauran sends some of the spearcarls down, to climb the other tower and see what they can do to help the survivors. More arrows being handed out, other makeshift missiles being sent for, burning coals, hot lye. Ram strikes the gate with a dull thud. They've gotten into the lee of the wall, some of the dragon-kin, difficult to shoot straight down without hanging over the parapet. Lye might do something about that.

The Grey Hunter comes padding up the stairs, Wolf to woman standing upright.

"Lannesk." Her voice is quiet, a bit rough. "Anzimor."

"Lady?" Anzimor asks, turning from the wall.

"With me. Come."

"My lady…?" But Lady Lauran's question seems to falter, knowing there's no answer she wants to hear.

"The Wild King may have summoned the earls, for all I know." The Grey Hunter answers it regardless. "Though your guess is as good as mine, as to when they may come. Pray the Mothers protect them and bring them safe over the ice, if you're of a mind to pray. But the sorcerers work against the King's Riding and the Forestways are turned aside from the Isle. So," and she shrugs, "I need Lannesk. And his brother."

She turns away, as if that's all there is to be said, and is Wolf again, going halt down the stairs. Lannesk and Anzimor trade a look. Not sure words are needed. Lannesk takes cape and spear and follows. Anzi's only a step behind.

"Anzimor? Anzi!" Lord Ekkard, calling from above as they turn at the first landing.

"I'll be back, my lord. Don't worry," Anzimor shouts up in answer. Lannesk grits his teeth. Ekkard is not lord over either of them.

"My lord—Ekkard!" Theyn Asa. Clattering boots.

Lannesk looks back. Ekkard, and Swordtheyn Asa hard behind him, turning the corner, and Ovan and Tolla on their heels.

"Lord Ekkard, you cannot take your people from defending the gate!" Lady Lauran is shouting.

"You don't command my lord!" Tolla shouts up the stairwell.

Lannesk turns on his heel, shakes his head. Mouths, no, at Ekkard, who isn't looking at him, of course not. They can't start breaking up the command here. He and Anzimor are the Grey Hunter's to call as she will; they swore their oath to the Immortals. The others only answered the summons to war. It's not the same, and those owe their obedience to the captains they chose to set over themselves and to the Masters of the Singershall. If each lesser captain starts choosing their own path now, the walls won't stand another day. Anzimor…he takes his brother's arm, shakes his head again. To say all that.

"I know, I know," Anzi says. And then soft. "He's young, Lannesk. He's lost his leman. He's hurting. Don't look so fierce." He runs up the stairs to Ekkard, hesitating above. Puts arms about him, while Ovan rolls his eyes and Tolla bares his teeth at Lannesk as if he's about to declare their long truce over. Anzimor is murmuring, strong words, from the look on Ekkard's face, and he bows his head to Anzimor's shoulder.

"Go on, then," Anzimor says. So they kiss, and Ekkard turns back up the stairs, ignoring Theyn Asa, ignoring his shieldcarls. Anzimor watches till he's round the bend again. Comes back down to Lannesk leaping two at a time.

"Young fool," he says, as if the pair of them aren't of an age, as if he hasn't lost his own leman too, and just sent another away, going down to meet—whatever the Dark Mother may send.

Shoulder to shoulder, they follow after the Grey Hunter.

~Mairran~

"My lord. My lord, Nowa says, the sun's set and if you don't get up and wash and eat something and—I'm sorry, she said, stop acting like a sulking child, she's going to send me to tell Ermintrud to come from Borharbour and fetch you away on a sled."

"That would be unwise," I muttered, without opening my eyes. I didn't know what Sage was doing in my dreaming. I was cold. Shivering cold, for all that someone had piled a smoky sheepskin cape atop my blankets. "Don't listen to her, little vixen. This isn't sulking." My throat was dry; my voice croaked.

"You're not a Seer," said Nowa, shambling over, propping herself on a spear as if it were a walking stick. And to Sage, "He thinks his father was, so he takes fits of chasing dreams. He makes himself ill and learns nothing by it."

"Shut up," I said, and coughed, and took the cup Sage handed me, which was only water. "That's not true either. Has Lord Raynar come back from his hunting?"

"Yes, my lord," said Sage. "Just before dusk. And you've been sleeping since yesterday noon. I thought—but Theyn Nowa said to leave you. I was afraid," she added, indignant. "I thought you'd been poisoned."

"Not this time," I said. "Raynar didn't find his wild man."

"No."

"He won't." I sat up, too quickly. Things went red and ringing and hazy for a moment. "Get me something to eat and drink, would you?"

"Buttermilk," said Nowa. "Don't give him ale when he's in this state. He'll be sick."

"She bullies me," I said. "Have you noticed? And I won't be sick. Pour me ale."

"Yes, my lord."

But she didn't. There was sharp, thin buttermilk, fizzing a bit. There was bread, and strong crumbling old cheese, and sliced cold black pudding, which was meant to be strengthening. There was a basin of water heated in a kettle at the fire. I stripped and washed away the sweat of the ride and the fight for the first time. I stank. Surprising that Nowa had missed the chance to point that out. Dressed myself in a clean shirt and my best winter hall-gown, dark green trimmed in black squirrel. Nowa, nodding approvingly at that, chivvied Sage into the knee-length gown a youthful shieldling might wear to serve their lord in the hall, something outgrown by the harbour-reeve's son which her foresight had bought in Borharbour. Watery blue, not the best dye, but it looked well on her with a black hood laid back over her shoulders. Muttering, Nowa combed my hair, which needed a wash, but that would have to wait. Instead of the hunter's braid, the single long plait with the sides woven in, which I preferred, she put it into one of the court arrangements, all loops and twists up and down a thick cascade, and bound it with knotted leather thongs, a desperate last measure to keep it tidy the length of the evening. There was no ribbon stood up to my hair for long. Then she combed Sage, for good measure, and tied a pretty bit of braided ribbon for fillet about her brow.

Brought out the little locked chest that never left her most careful guard, when we carried it with us at all.

"We don't need to go that far," I protested.

"We do. High reeve, and you haven't dined in hall since you came here. You stand for the Queen, tonight."

I wasn't in the mood for an argument I couldn't win, so I stood submissive, like a milch-cow being trimmed up fine to be blessed on Pasturetide. I would have preferred garlands of flowers, like a cow. Less worry if I lost bits and pieces. Or when, Nowa might say. That night it was the entwined strands of beads, bluestone and jet and bloodstone, opaque deep green with crimson spatterings, about my brow and a collar woven of the same stones for my throat. Nowa claimed the bloodstone brought out the colour of my eyes, but it wasn't often that I wanted attention drawn to that dark and murky green, more fayling than human. An oval brooch in jet and silver closed the neck of the gown. There were pendants to my ears of strands of tiny irregular lake-pearls and jet beads, heavy golden bracelets chased with ravens in flight—my mother's humour and a gift from her on my eighteenth birthday—and several random gold finger-rings of the sort one might give to reward a skilled Singer who'd particularly pleased, not that Laikyn was likely to have any Singer I would want to guerdon or trust to bed. And finally my own signet ring, and more weighty, the bluestone signet of the dragon, the Queen's token. I did not dress the prince often. I hated the weight of all that metal and stone. Didn't mean I couldn't be as a gaudy as the next lord when I had a mind to.

That night I felt like I was wrapped in chains.

"We're going to dine in the hall?" Sage asked, watching the glitter of that small treasury with something like awe, and, I hoped, not a mind to pilferage and flight. Unworthy thought. Though I'd have let her go with anything short of my mother's signet, and wished her well.

Aloud, "We are," I said. "Or I am. Can you serve me? Not good manners for you to sneak crusts yourself—get another chunk of bread and pudding into your belly now, but they will keep back some portions in the kitchens for those who serve, for after. Just keep an eye on what the lady and lord's folk do and try not to spill wine down my neck."

"Don't let him drink too much," Nowa said, and fished out a smaller mate to the great brooch, likewise jet and silver, and pinned it at Sage's throat. "Water his cup well."

"Thank you, Nowa."

"Leave the ravens here."

"The ravens come with me." And Lightning came down from the top of the door to join Thunder on my shoulder as if thought had called her. Perhaps it had.

"You look dangerously happy, my lord," Nowa said.

"Oh, I am. I'm going to tell Lord Raynar I shall ride with him to find his wild man after all."

"What are you going to do with him once you find him?"

"That," I said, "would be telling."

I only wished I knew.

~LANNESK~

Lannesk and Anzimor are not the only ones summoned by the Immortal. There's a dozen and half again of them—a company of strays, he thinks. Some of the others he knows for fellow outlaws and exiles; a few are unexpected, men and women he'd thought spearcarls of this lord or that lady, but they've bound themselves by some vow to the Wild King or the Grey Hunter nonetheless. Two of the men are silver-ring Singers, one, an older woman, has the golden ring of her seven-years' study. They gather in a small house, just the one open room and the loft above, the home of Heron, the older Singer. No sign of partner, child. She lives alone in an untidy mess of wood and tools, a maker of instruments. Warmth, ale and stew and bread brought from one of the communal kitchens. A striped cat prowls around, rubbing its head on some, ignoring others. They eat sitting on the bed, the hastily-cleared workbenches, the floor, crowded together. They trade names, tell where they're from, little more. Not the stories of how they've bound themselves. Even names hardly matter, Lannesk thinks. The Hunter comes in and the cat, ears flat, skitters out; the Immortal has dressed herself in borrowed clothes: trousers, tunic, boots, a long vest of sheepskin. Carries a sheathed sword.

"The dragon-kin have been pushed back from the gate," she says. "For now."

Burned and blinded, if Lady Lauran has found the lye she wanted.

"But they're coming at the east again. We can only hold..." She shrugs. "...till there's some failing. Or till someone decides their own kin are among the hostages? There was no reason to slaughter them on the road like that, nothing necessary to their sorcery. They only meant to make sure we saw. How many will it take before someone slips over the wall in the dark, and comes back with a plan to open the gate? Waiting for the earls—assuming the Wild King was able to reach them, before he was trapped in the Ways by the sorcerers—might mean holding out another month. It might mean holding until the spring floods have passed and there are good roads and sailing weather again."

"What do they want with us so badly?" a woman asks. She calls herself, with a rueful laugh, the one-time earl of Forshyn, which is who knows where. Her accent is of the west, south of Long Sound.

Someone huffs disbelief, that she should ask.

"No, really," she says. "Why not hold what they had in the Lann Leda? They may take the Holy Isle, but they'll have cut themselves off from their home in the north and whatever reinforcements might have come. Even if they take the Singersborg, how can they hold here, come summer and all the earls against them?"

"The Holy Isle," Heron the gold-ring Singer says. "It's not just a name. Hold the Holy Isle and you hold the heart of the Lake, the heart of the Forest. It was here the Dragon was defeated and bound, when the King first rode." And she takes up a harp, gives their listening silence a fragment of the longer tale called *The Wild King's Riding*, the verses where he calls the dead to rise against the sorcerer-priests at the fane of sacrifice and drive Golden Erryth, riding against them in the shape of a woman seven-foot tall, into the Lake, where she lies bound and sleeping still.

Lannesk doesn't think that's an answer.

"Defeated and bound," the Grey Hunter says, "For now."

The Singer breaks off and bows her head, acknowledging that.

"What is made," the Immortal says, "may be broken. What is bound, may be loosed."

"What is anchored," the Singer says, as if it is some rote answer, "may be cast free."

"Aye. This was a fane, and a place of sacrifice. And here," the Grey Hunter waves a hand southerly, towards the river, "we fought the dragon-kin. Here we fought the Dragon. At the anchorstone here the

Wild King made the song that bound Erryth the Golden in sleep beneath the Lake."

"They want to capture that anchorstone," Anzimor says.

A nod.

"Can they use it?" He asks what Lannesk is thinking.

"They might. Our song...needed an anchor." Her smile is crooked.

"They mean to wake the Dragon?"

"It may be they think they can."

"What can we do?"

"The sorcerers work against the Forestways," she said. "They trap the Wild King's Riding, by song, and by blood. So. We free the Ways and let the Wild King ride."

"How?" someone asks.

She shrugs. "Kill sorcerers," she says, as if it's so simple. "And— make a new song, to set the Ways aright again, and call the King to us, that he may prevent the Dragon's rising."

The Singers look...like folk told they must work a miracle. Like Sahlin Lark, who had to raise a tower in a night, to win her husband back from the Daughter of Snows.

"My lady," the elder singer says, "I don't have the skill you ask for. I think—there was Yasper-Van of Arrisnaar, but they died last winter. Among the Masters of the Hall, there might be one or two—"

"No," the Hunter says. "We'll leave the Masters. They have their work here. And no, it's not you I look to for the breaking of spells, though you'll need to lend your strength."

"Lannesk," Anzimor says.

"Aye. You do hear it? Your brother has taught himself what many Master Singers never learn, the way of weaving power into song. Call it prayer. Call it making. Call it magic. I need him. He'll make a Way for the Wild King to ride, to come to us here. Perhaps, to come in time. Perhaps we may yet prevent the Dragon's rising. So." She nods, as if all is decided. "Put a good edge on your blades. Then sleep a little, my hunters, if you can. Come nightfall, we go over the wall."

What? Lannesk grabs for the Grey Hunter's arm—the right, not the left, which is bulky with bandaging now. Shakes his head. He knows nothing of Singers' magic and if he must learn—he needs to hear from some Master among them how he may do such a thing. Better yet, lay the task on a Master, if there are even one or two who have this gift. If he made a music with some power in it before, there on the stairs of the tower with the Hunter fighting for her life against dragon-kin sorcery, that was only desperation and luck, and he cannot think to do it again; she cannot, must not put her trust in him, put all their lives and hope on his working some ancient magic out of a song.

"Hey," she says, taking him by the shoulders. "My Harper." Her tone makes it a title. Touches cold fingers to his lips, silencing the denial he shapes. "My Wild King and I, we know our own. Trust yourself, your strength, the truth of your soul. We do."

She leaves him to Anzimor, settles on the hearth. Taking her own advice, stretching out her legs, borrowing a stone from one of the outlaws to whet her sword. A few others do likewise, passing whetstones hand to hand, renewing edges on spearheads and daggers, the few swords among them. Anzimor takes Lannesk's weapons from him, sits down again with their own whetstone. "Check your strings," he says, and Lannesk, after a moment, nods. He settles back to back with his brother, running careful fingers along the harp's strings, checking for what might be fraying, wearing, checking the cords that bind the tailpiece, checking the tuning keys, one of which he had to carve new himself after someone carelessly knocked it off the bench one night. There's a sick hard knot growing in his belly, twisting hotter and tighter. It rises, choking, so he can hardly swallow. Anzimor leans back, a little shove, like the nudge of an elbow. All right, Anzi's saying, to what must be crackling off him like winter sparks off a cat's fur. Lannesk shuts his eyes, lets his breath find the rhythm of Anzimor's breathing. The Immortal's trust terrifies him.

Tells himself, trust her. Remembers the weight of her head, lying in his lap. Remembers how it felt, finding the shape of the song that called her back into herself whole. As if he flew.

So he opens his eyes again, Anzimor's warmth against him more sure than any rock. He makes certain of the flattened, worked ends of quill that are his harpnails, which he carries thrust through the stitching of his cuff, though he thinks this will be a song itself, and not a strummed foundation laid for another voice. It must be plucked, built note by note…stone by stone…anchor to anchor. To lay a road, over Forest, over Lake, under sky… He begins to play, not making the song, not yet, only finding the feel of what it might be, in soft, muted notes.

The fire has died to coals and the daylight through the hide-covered window has died with it; Anzimor has an arm over his shoulder, kneeling by him.

"Time to go," his brother is saying. "You awake, Lan? Time to go."

He wasn't sleeping. Only, sitting, silent, eyes shut, wrapped about his harp. Dreaming, Brux used to say, when he was making one of his wordless songs. It felt like dreaming, sometimes, but the sort of dream that on waking leaves you knowing you've never been in that place, seen or known that…whatever it is you've dreamt. But in the dream it was all known, familiar, ground and truth.

Yes, he nods, and takes Anzimor's hand to rise.

The three Singers come to walk by him. Singer Heron has a harp; the two silver-ring men, Hazel and Tamly, a wooden flute and a hand-drum. He would be wary of their jealousy, but they know it's a burden, not a prize he's been given; there's nothing hostile in their looks.

"You lead," Heron says. "Never fear. We'll follow."

He nods. Gives a hand to them each to clasp in turn. Whatever peace he found in his — call it dreaming — is slipping from him, drifting away like streamers of mist on the wind. He can't recall, now, what shape the music took in his mind, can't feel the strength of it, the surety, that for a moment he thought he held. Shivers.

Anzimor doesn't say anything, but he's there, nudging in through the Singers to walk beside him.

They don't go over the wall after all, but through it. There's a small gate in the most northerly reach of it, no more than a doorway, not wide enough even for a single cart. Singers armed as swordtheyns lift away the beams that block it, bars across and others bracing it. Once through, it's obvious why there's been no assault here. A narrow lip of ledge above a deep ditch hacked in the stony ground, or maybe a natural gully, angling up along the ridge. They slither down, not so silent as they might hope, but there's an outbreak of shouting from the gate-towers, a volley of fire-arrows shot arching high towards the dragon-kin who keep watch on the road. Maybe there's no close watch here on the north, or maybe that's enough to draw the attention of any patrol or picket away. New moon; it won't rise till near the dawn. Starlight on snow isn't much. They keep within touch of one another, letting eyes adjust, as the gate creaks closed above them, shutting them out from what was only dim lantern-light, no torches to blazon the gate's opening against the dark. The Grey Hunter sniffs the air, gives a satisfied nod, and leads them on.

Cold, crisp night. Under a full moon it would be beautiful, the sort of night that would call you out for winter roaming. They try to go softly, but snow squeaks and crunches.

A circling route, down off the scrub and barren rock of the ridge and into woods again. Once the Grey Hunter halts them, chooses three of their number, outlaw brothers and sister, leads them away. Not long before they return.

"Picket," the sister says.

"Dealt with." No satisfaction in the younger brother's voice, only a necessary task done.

Lannesk maps the land in memory, lays it over the darkness they traverse. They've swung south, heading downslope, and are on a hard-packed path now. Quieter, so long as no one slips on ice. They've come behind the western dragon-kin camp, he thinks. Smell of smoke. Trees thinning on the edge of what was Arrunstead pasture; they can see the fires away to the east and south of them, the camp spread through the ruins of Mair Arrun. They keep on their way, lying close and hidden under a bank of hemlocks when the squeak and hiss of skis warns of an approaching patrol.

They mean to go down the bluff, but not by the road. A precipitous path that would never have seen use but in summer.

Ruins of Arrunstead below. There's another camp of huts, which must have been built from charred and salvaged timbers; there are tents, too. Smoke rising, red light showing though the gaps around door-curtains, through smoke-holes. Snow contrasting with dark walls, dirty paths. A stockade. A corral for the reindeer, he thinks, at first, but no, there's a picket-line, as for horses, the deer dimly to be seen.

Someone's coughing, there within the solid wall of spiked pales anchored in a ridge of earth and ice. The sound carries up to them. Prisoners. There's no fire within, only darkness. Maybe a few tents.

"After," the Grey Hunter says, near voiceless murmur, and doesn't need to add what the erstwhile earl of Forshyn does:

"Mothers grant we should live so long."

The biggest hut, round and built of timber roofed with birchbark and fir-boughs, leaks red light as someone pulls back a curtain of hide. Faint murmur of sound, pulse of a drum, voices that might be singing or chanting. Four figures duck in under the low lintel. Space of a moment, and four come out. They stand. One raises arms and for a moment Lannesk thinks of a sorcerer seeing them, shouting some word of power against them, but the person is only stretching. Another seems to yawn, hand against their mouth. Leans to bump shoulders with a comrade. They go off arm in arm. One sets off solitary in another direction. The last stretches again, looking up at the stars. Wanders away, leaving the doorway unguarded. Why should it be, safe in the heart of this camp, with the main encampment up above the bluff, straddling the road, well between them and their enemies?

How many sorcerers inside the hut? If they sing to keep the Wild King from returning, and don't want to break their song… Shifts of four trading off. Eight sorcerers, a dozen? That roof could hold more, though to judge by the light, they've a hearth of some size in the middle of it. He has no idea how many voices such a working would need.

He's supposed to work some magic against what they've made with only three to support him.

The Grey Hunter's beside him. "Listen," she says against his ear. "Do you hear? Do you feel it, the shape of their making?"

He's not certain. There's something. A darkness in the sound. Maybe? He tilts his head. Listening... Falling, the night grown thick around, heavy, as if it's smoke he drags into his lungs, but so cold. Thorns reach, hooking him, pulling—he flings out a hand for balance. Anzimor seizes his arm.

"Aye," the Grey Hunter says, satisfied. "So. Do what you may, once we begin to break their unity. Call the Wild King here to me. Make a new Way, if they hold the old against you. Trust—he will hear you. He will know, and answer. Only lay the path before him."

Lannesk nods. He's terrified. He can't do this. She puts too much on him.

And yet...he tastes it in his mouth still, the darkness. It hurts, as if he's bitten a mouthful of thorns. There's blood when he swallows.

So, aye. He can feel it. The shape of what the dragon-kin do. What he can do in answer...maybe?

"Get under cover," the Grey Hunter tells him, so Lannesk goes a little along the edge of the bluff to where there's a thicket, dense and dark, fine twigs bristling, tangling. Silvery bare honeysuckle, he thinks he remembers, growing along here. He pulls off his mittens to dangle on their strings, takes his harp from its bag. Blows on his fingers, which doesn't help; the cold stings almost at once. If you have to have bare fingers for some task, it helps to have something wrapped snug around the wrist and palm, to warm the blood as it passes, a bit of Forest winter-cunning. They have only what they begged and scrounged, he and Anzimor, not hunters' mittens to free his fingers, and he'll have to keep sleeves pulled down over his hands as much as he can, that's all.

Anzimor's tearing cloth. "Here," he says, and wraps Lannesk's wrists, looping up around his thumb and down to cover even the back of his hand and a part of the palm. Tail of his shirt. He makes flat knots on the back of his wrists. "Too tight?"

It will help. And it feels fine. Lannesk wriggles fingers to say so, gripping Anzimor's own already-chilled hand. The Grey Hunter counts off Anzimor, Breykon the elder brother of the outlaw siblings, and a silent woman named Falleen to stay with the musicians. The rest follow her away.

Lannesk settles into place under the arching twig-tangle, down on one knee on his shield to keep off the snow. Wet clothes will kill you. Spear laid beside him. He left his bow behind in the Singer's house. Most of them had. It's going to be close work that matters. He can still look out, down onto Arrunstead below. The other Singers join him, finding places as sheltered as they may, not to be silhouetted on the bluff's edge against the sky.

One by one, the dark shapes of those following the Grey Hunter are lost over the edge. Silence, but for their own breathing, which sounds too loud. Sudden scrape. Someone's slipped. Rattle, pattering that fades. Stones, frozen clods of clay falling away. They freeze themselves. Lannesk's heart, at least, is racing, but there's no sound of any alert below, not even the bark of a dog.

Maybe it's some magic of the Grey Hunter's, that they move through the camp like a drifting breeze, a shadow stray firelight does not find, and no scent of them carries to the picketed reindeer or sets a dog to sound warning. Up under the honeysuckle thicket, they're all leaning out, watching below. Nothing to raise the alarm.

Lannesk shuts his eyes; he can't watch. Vision's a distraction, an imposition. He'll lose the shape of the makings, dragon-kin and his own both. Tries to calm his breathing, his heart. Anzimor's hand on his shoulder. Anchor.

Cold. Air sharp, every slow breath riding the beat of the sorcerers' deepest drum, which sets their pace, a light one rattling swift around it, and their voices, rising, falling… Words of binding and turning; they snarl and knot and twist back on themselves; they are thorns and jagged teeth and they do more than turn the Ways, they break and shred them, rear spears of ice and steel and stone, a jagged range upthrust, a fanged jaw closed over them —

Shriek. The deep drum stutters. Slaughter, among the sorcerers.

Let it begin.

Think of a road, a Way, a Forest path. He needs more than that. He plucks a chord, soft, almost tentative, but it's a call. It catches a broken thread, a sung note choked off below in a sorcerer's death. He pulls it into a running ripple, water flowing. There. Drawing it in, taking what they've made and turning it to his own use. He can see the sound, livid, dark, like clotted blood. He picks out notes and they ring clean, they gather and leap, his foot tapping the rhythm of the dragon-kin drum, but he changes it, makes it his own. Now fingers can dance it, the three-pulse beat of the red horse, not racing, but swift, controlled. The loping pack. The riders who follow. The drum carries it now, Tamly his drummer; Hazel's flute finds the path he is laying, soars above it, Heron the harper strums the chord that underlies his melody; she finds the beat of the cantering horses, finds the pattern he follows.

Song. Words rising within him, to find the way, thread a path through the knot of thorns, razor-fangs of steel that seize and hold, ice that freezes, pulling the Riders down, smothering-still. Shapes with lips and tongue what voice cannot sing, gives breath, and if what sound he makes rasps and wheezes it does not matter, the words take flight, in heart, in mind. And Anzimor crouches, ear close, head bowed, arm over his shoulder; Anzi takes the words from his lips, hesitant, as if he fears he may break the song. Sing, Lannesk says, fierce hiss, and Anzimor flings his head up, daring, raises his voice to let the words soar.

Dark is night. Cold is sky, the song says. *The Way lies lost and broken.*

Ride to us. We call you. We call to you, beyond darkness, beyond storm, beyond fire. Do you hear us?

We lay a bridge of song beneath your feet. We make a road of harpsong, of flute and drum and voice; we hold the Way.

Through spear and thorn and ice, through the storm's fury and wind's rage. Beyond the very jaws of the Dragon, ride to us.

Dark is night, and bright the stars.

The spells of our enemies are turned away from you; we strike them down.

The thorns of the sorcerers are burning; we call to you, through their flame. Flame dies, ash drifts as snow, wind calms, the Way lies before you.

The Ways of the Forest are the Wild King's Ways; the Ways of the Lake are the Wild King's Ways; the Ways beneath the stars are the Wild King's, and you ride to us. We call you, and we hold the Way open for your Riding.

Now the King's Riding is all about him, but they are dim and faint as ghosts, as figures dreamed of mist. A gale howls against them; they battle against a forest of thorns that writhe like serpents, strike like barbed whips, and the music of Lannesk's making is a pale fire that rises to consume the thorns, dies, torn to nothing by the dark wind, and rises again.

Song, fierce in his mind, the words fierce, Anzimor's voice that carries them, and now Anzi finds the shape of them without Lannesk leading him to them, as if they spill from him to his brother, mind to mind, tinder taking flame and leaping up, a poetry born between them, till there is nothing but the drum and the flute soaring like a falcon, and the music that runs like water from his hands, echoed and laid down anew by the second harp, and the distant roar of the wind, a river flood-swollen, meltwater torrent tearing through an ice-dam, ripping a way through him as if it spills out in heart's blood —

Another voice, faint, growing stronger, and it says, *Harpsong an arrow's flight, burning in darkness. Call us and we ride. Lay your song beneath our feet. Call us, and hold the Way —*

Someone falls against him and he jerks away, startled, lost, falling out of the place he had found, the stillness amidst the storm, and it's the harper Heron who has slumped into him. A thrown spear; she's down and dying, hand still spread over her harp. Anzimor stands over him, shield raised. Frantic close fighting, two men crashing together on the ground, knife and knife, and Anzimor drives spear's blade into a rushing shape and strikes back at another with the butt even as he jerks his weapon free.

"Finish it!" he screams, over the wail of the rising wind, which is howling up the valley off the Lake and roaring down from the fells and buffeting them from all directions, snow riding it. The drummer crawls over to cower down by Lannesk under Anzimor's shield, takes up his driving pulse again and Lannesk strikes a chord that catches loose flying threads of sound, calls the wind—he doesn't have the words, doesn't need them, can feel the shape of his making, see the Riders and the Wild King at the head of them, the storm become the Way beneath them, and he calls, voiceless, calls, *Here, we are here,* and Anzimor's down on one knee beside him then, another leaping through the dark to stand there, sword swinging as Anzimor leans on him and the Grey Hunter calls, "Gwion! To me!"

Lannesk—reaches—a hand, a thought, flings something of himself up along the shadowed star-bright thread of his song, harp-song an arrow's flight through the sorcerers' storm, feels it caught like hands clasping and the wind hits them like a wave, a wall, and they fall, even the Grey Hunter, clinging to earth.

Thunderclap fall of a tree, and a man screams, run down, run through—horses, a bull aurochs, a wolf passing, turning, some out over the empty air, horses half seen shadow-smoke-shape in the night, but they take on form and weight, they carry the smell of sweat and leather, dog and wool and smoke, their breath rises steaming, snow crunches beneath sharp hooves, steel sings. Dragon-kin—a patrol has come up from the sorcerers' camp to silence the making of magic here amid the honeysuckles—they flee, and they die, the dragon-kin, and the snow falls steadily from a starless sky.

Distant roar, a sound hard to understand. Not a river, not the dying windstorm. Under it, the slow deep beat of another drum. The ram battering at the gates of the Singersborg. A sound rising into an outcry, and a dragon's triumphant shriek.

"Singersborg," the Wild King says, and the pale-maned horse wheels about. For a moment the King is by him, the horse reeking of sweat, blowing froth, the man's face lost in the dark, but Lannesk sees the Wild King bow his head, raise his sword in salute. "Harper," he says. "Singer."

And he calls, "We ride!"

Once more they sweep past him, over him. Out of the sky, Lannesk thinks, but there is a great trampling in the snow. Men, women, horses, hounds, wolves, a bull, faylings, beings stranger than those, and some have plunged down the bluff, horses skidding and sliding or trampling the air, and below there is shouting and screaming and the baying of hounds, hunting the sorcerers or freeing the prisoners, but most have gone the other way, up the track through the empty dark fields, towards the dragon-kin camp at Mair Arrun and the besieged Singersborg. Tamly the drummer is gone, following them, and Falleen the woman whose story he never learned, and Breykon the elder brother of the outlaws lies slain with a dead dragon-kin warrior under him and Hazel the piper beside...

Why isn't he following them?

Anzimor's leaning on him. Anzimor's spear has slipped from his hold and he's leaning on Lannesk, head on his shoulder, arm around his neck, hand hanging limply. He reaches his own hand up, grasps cold fingers, his own burning in the joints with cold and numb from the second knuckle, stiff, painful to bend.

"Hey," Anzimor says. "You did it." His breath comes short.

Lannesk shifts out from under Anzimor's arm; he can hardly feel his hands but what he can feel is not only cold, but wet from Anzimor's grip, and sticking. Anzimor turns his head, laying his cheek against Lannesk's searching palm, heavy, letting him take the weight.

Can't see in this damned dark. Silence of the dead about them; only the wind hissing in the brush, snowflakes soft, wet, melting as they hit his face, only their breathing, and Anzimor is panting quick, shallow breaths like a man in pain.

"Where?" Lannesk demands, aloud, and it's a wheeze, a huff of inarticulate sound.

"Kicked, I think," Anzimor says. "Winded. Jus' let me catch my breath."

Lannesk gets Anzimor's shield-arm free, warms his hands in his armpits a moment, starts feeling him over. Anzi winces away almost at once: swollen lump on his temple. Lannesk takes his brother's helmet off, carefully, and the thin woollen coif beneath, but there's no other damage there that he can feel and he gets the coif back on against the cold. Keeps searching. Torn sleeve, and that's where the blood on Anzimor's right hand is coming from, a gash in his forearm. He doesn't think that's the whole of it. Gets a hand inside Anzimor's sheepskin vest, feeling over his chest, up to his neck, down his belly, around his ribs. No warning wetness. Anzi doesn't flinch. No bruising, not kicked. Yet still his breath catches, and he doesn't squirm away, make some joke about tickling. That's...bad. Lannesk coaxes him to lean forward, and Anzimor winces then, head on Lannesk's shoulder, as he works his arms around.

Mothers Above and Below, no. Wet to his groping hands, down about his lower ribs, and for a moment he doesn't try to say anything, doesn't move, just holds him there, Anzimor leaning into him. Presses his face to his brother's head.

"Bad?" Anzimor asks.

There's so much blood, soaking cloth, soaking the leather of the sheepskin and it's warm, still bleeding. He can't find—and then he has it, torn edges through tunic and shirt, questing fingers and his teeth clench, he hisses, finding the wound beneath. A small thing, swollen and ragged. Anzimor makes a muffled sound, a faint grunt, that's all. Lannesk uses teeth on the knot of the rag wrapped around one hand to pull it free, folds it into a pad and works it in to press against the wound.

He can feel the blood soaking it.

"Bad," Anzimor says. And then, "I'm really cold, Lan." More of his weight slumping onto him.

Lannesk's not going to strip him to get at the wound, not going to let the killing cold sink claws into him; he gets Anzimor to lie down over his lap, fumbles off his own heavy cape and fur vest and tunic, peels his own shirt off. Shivering, snow settling like kisses, like tears, on back, on shoulders, he tears it into strips, folds most into more pads, feeling his way against Anzimor's skin to the wound again, stacking them, pressing hard, tying lengths about his ribs to bind them in place. A last one kept to tie over the gash in his arm, over layered sleeves and all, for what little difference that may make. Reminded, he scrubs his hands in the snow to clean them, finds Anzimor's mittens and pushes them onto his brother's hands, which are clumsy and unhelpful as a little child's. Gets his tunic back on and lies down with Anzimor, curled over him, his vest under their heads, his own cape shared over them both. He can feel the shivers running over Anzimor's skin, unless they're his own.

"Wha' was it?" Anzimor says, faintly.

Spear, he tells him, whisper against his ear. He thinks it was. Stabbed and withdrawn, some dragon-kin spear, and whoever wielded it dead, he's fairly certain. He remembers the Grey Hunter looming in as Anzimor staggered down, her sword swinging. There are bodies all about them.

"Din't even feel it," Anzi says. Long pause. "Hurts, now. Aches. Thought it'd be worse. Maybe not so bad, eh?"

Of course it hurts. And Anzimor's a liar. It more than aches, he can feel it himself, in his brother's shuddering, in the way his breath comes in little panting gasps, shallow and rapid like a fevered dog.

Fire. Warmth. But bringing dragon-kin down on them here among the dead will do no good at all; they wouldn't bother taking a gravely wounded man prisoner, and not one who'd been part of the foray to slaughter their sorcerers.

He needs to get Anzimor away, into some better shelter, before the dawn. They'll be plain to see here once the sun rises. Lannesk tucks him up more warmly, feels over Heron's body for the clasp of her long cloak, rolls her off it. He'll need something to put under Anzimor when they get wherever they're going. She didn't bleed much.

She's cold already.

"Don'," Anzimor says, when he pushes his harp aside, off into the snow, one more burden not to carry. "Don't, Lan. Please. You need it."

So he shoves it into its bag again and slings it about his neck to hang bumping in front of him. Makes sure of dagger and knife and that he has his purse, which holds flint and firesteel and a little box of tinder. Anzimor's trying to push himself up. Lannesk fastens his own cape on again, wraps the cloak over Anzimor's. Remembers to put his own mittens on, before he freezes his fingers for good. Kneels down, takes Anzimor's arms about his neck. Anzi grabs on. He doesn't protest that he can walk. He can't. Tried to get up while Lannesk was doing his bit of looting and couldn't make it to his knees. Gets Anzimor's legs up, wrapped around his hips. Grabs his spear and uses that as a staff, clambering upright, using his free arm under a leg, clutching the cloth of the other. Can't trust to Anzimor's fading strength to hold himself on. Sets off, leaning forward like an old man. One step, another. Not up towards the Singersborg, where still there is that distant rushing-water noise, distant grackle-flock clamour, of people struggling to kill one another. Down along the lip of the bluff. There's trampling enough to hide their tracks, he thinks. Hopes. One step, another, steadying himself with the spear. Head down. Anzimor's like him, all lean long bones, and no more than an inch or two shorter. His grip slips and the off leg falls, dragging, Anzimor sliding, making a little whimper, but not able to help. Lannesk lurches, grabs, get hold of cloth again and they stagger on. At some point Anzimor's arms about him fail, slide limp and he barely lets go of leg and spear in time to catch him, stop him sliding right off.

Nearly there, nearly there, nearly there. Step, and step, and step. A belt of dark spruce running up the edge of a little stream that comes down to plunge over the bluff in a deep-gnawed channel. But the path they've been following is veering northward, some track where dragon-kin have gone off up the fields. Maybe a patrol-route, scouting up to the farther pastures. Nothing for it. He tramps, dragging Anzimor's feet behind, through virgin snow towards the trees.

And the light's greying enough to see that, now.

Down slope, into the spruces. Now he crawls, knees and elbows, still dragging his brother. Still breathing; he feels the damp warmth of it on his neck. In deep, in low where the snow-heavy boughs sweep the ground. Like an animal burrowing into its lair. Deep, dense, still night-dark, and there's bare ground, needle-cushioned. He spreads the dead Singer's cloak on the ground and slides Anzimor onto it, rolled onto his side, making sure his cape is well wrapped around him. Pulls his legs up, tucks his arms close.

"Be back," he breathes, shaping the words against Anzimor's rough-bearded cheek, as if he might feel them and understand.

Goes back the way he came and out into the open. Nothing stirs there but that won't last. He retrieves his dropped spear and uses his fur cape to sweep the snow, fresh-fallen and still fluffy, over his tracks.

It won't work, even though the snow's still falling, soft and heavy; shuffling footprints bearing two men's weight have left a deep and dragging trail. Won't take any kind of Forest-cunning, any snow-wise tracker, to see what's been done. But the trail won't shout out to the eye from a distance, and that's the most he can hope for.

He goes back to wait with Anzimor, till his dying's done.

Anzi's awake, propped on an elbow, looking around in a kind of panic. Sighs and lays his head down, seeing him.

"Thirsty," he says.

Lannesk is, too. He goes down to the little stream, chortling and ringing under bubbled ice; he drinks, uses his leaking helmet to carry back water. Anzi doesn't manage to swallow much. Just as well. He doesn't need that chill inside him. Fire just isn't possible here. Might as well go out and shout for the dragon-kin to come butcher them both. Anyway, can't make a fire in under spruces; set the woods on fire over their heads, roast themselves alive.

"Don't leave me," Anzimor says.

Lannesk shakes his head. He won't.

Anzimor shuts his eyes. "No," he says. "Go on. Go. They'll follow. Kill us both. You need to go."

Ignores that. Sits down, helps Anzimor get his head up on his lap. That's no good; Anzimor can't see his face, can't roll over, not with that wound in his back. Lannesk lies down by him instead, face to face.

"Not listening, are you? I said, go."

He manages a smile. Anzimor's gone white, so white. They've always been pale-skinned, light even when summer-tanned. This is white like the belly of a fish, and his lips are grey, and the skin about his eyes. Bleeding inside.

Anzimor. He makes the shape carefully, clear, even in the dim dawn twilight. Anzi smiles.

"Say it," he says. "You can."

It comes out slow, croaking, a slur in the middle of it and the end a rasping breath.

"Anzimor."

"Aye," Anzi says. "I'm here. And you. Looking after me. You always have. You always do."

Lannesk shakes his head. "You," he breathes. Anzimor smiles. It was Anzi who looked after him, kept him alive when his throat was crushed. Anzimor's eyes drift shut. Open again.

"You," he says. "You make songs. Get out of here and make songs. Make all the songs we never sang, you and me. Should have gone to the road. Should have gone. You wanted to. You never said it but I knew you did, and I was...it was easier to stay. Knew you wouldn' go withou' me. Should'a tol' you to go. Should'a gone with you. Sorry." He stops there. Lannesk bares a hand to touch his face, the corner of his drifting eye. Anzimor's focus finds him again. "Sorry," Anzi says, quite clearly.

That's the last he speaks.

The grey lightens into a rose-coloured sunrise. The air is very still, down in this small valley, the chime and gurgle of the stream very loud. Bluejays cry, and a flutter of chickadees comes bobbing and hopping through the branches over them, looking for frozen insects. A woodpecker tap, tap, taps, swooping tree to tree. Blood's soaked through the back of Anzimor's vest, wool stained a dirty red. His panting breaths stutter, limp.

May the Bright Mother ease your going, may the Dark Mother hold you close. That's a prayer. Lannesk doesn't pray.

Gasp. Another stutter. A long sigh. In the dark shelter of the spruces, with the snow falling slow and silent, the chickadees take off in a flurry and whirr of wings.

He's gone.

Cold seeps from the ground, rises like a tide, striking deep into bones.

Stay lying down beside his brother, let the cold take him. He could.

He kisses Anzimor, so cold already. Eases his hand free from Anzi's light grip, tucks his hands in close to his chest. Thinks to take his purse; Anzi carried their whetstone. Lannesk may live to need it. He may not.

Maybe Anzimor won't be found here, not till the spring, and the thaw. Maybe wolverines will have him, if there are any so close to this settlement. Maybe wolves, or foxes. Better foxes than dragon-kin, but Lannesk doesn't want the ravens to come for his eyes, he can't—he can't, not that. He wraps the Singer's cloak tight about Anzi for a shroud, covering his face. Snow will sift down, even through the thick spruce-boughs, to bury him as winter deepens. Could pretend he'll be able to come to back, to take him decent to a lychhouse to await a proper burial in the spring, but there's a cold in him says, come the spring, he'll be lying under some tree himself, going to rot and bones.

Lannesk can't leave him. He's still kneeling, a hand on Anzimor's shoulder, as if he might shake him, wake him. Forget all this, Lan, Anzi will say. Let's go. Somewhere. Anyway. Sing our way south.

Get out of here and make songs, Lan.

He can't do that, either. They're fighting dragon-kin up at the Singersborg. He curls down, rests again his cheek against Anzi's shrouded cheek.

"Mothers keep you safe through all the Dark," he says slowly, aloud, and if it's nothing but a breathy mumble, Anzimor's soul, flying fleet to the Dark Mother's embrace, will surely hear, and know, and understand it. Anzimor always did hear him, and understand, even when he had no voice at all.

Lannesk leaves his brother lie, to crawl out into the morning.

~Mairran~

A foot among riders, sword growing heavy and I'm holding it two-handed now, though my left arm's burning.

There's been fighting all the way. An open hillside, a stony spur thrusting down from higher barren ground to crown it. I think I know this place, the shape of the horizon, but snow is falling thicker, faster, hiding it and there's no time to worry at the uneasy sense that this place should be other than it is. They've swept through a camp and slaughtered what they found, I...she, I am Mairran, I do not remember this, I do not want to remember... I remember. Folk armed and unarmed, scattering, struck with fear flung before us like the leading edge of a wave, and we rolled over them, carried on, chasing—

Chasing what we've found. A crumbling grey wall, gates standing wide, smoke rising, and a killing ground within. Halls, towers—some still hold. There's no order, no command left among our enemies. Whatever captains they followed, these dragon-kin, they've lost any hold over their spearcarls. There's slaughter for the sake of blood, and looting without profit, dragging off the most mundane of things, a straw-stuffed mattress, a churn, a cheese. They're pulling down roofs with hooks, battering in doors and windows, lighting anything they can find at the spreading fires and hurling their makeshift torches through smashed shutters and into thatch. The barns that survived the dragon are burning, beasts screaming.

Too few, the Wild King's, the Grey Hunter's Riders, and they're falling away, not fleeing but fading, gone. Sorcerer-priests somewhere, somehow, Kallyn thinks, are thrusting them back into the Dark from which their souls were summoned. Faylings dying, brave souls, the Fisher falling thrashing, her strong neck opened with an axe. The Smith, the Daughter of Snows—they were lost from the Immortals long ago and no song has ever brought them back.

Even they can die, be put out of the world into the Dark for long and long enough, and when will the black mare rise and run again, when will she hear him laugh, the Fisher her brother, joyous as the woodland waters he loved, and swing her into the summer's dance...

I don't understand any of this.

The Wild King riding, red horse, his red hair a banner, and he wheels and turns back to me, to her where she is running from between two burning buildings, leaping her fallen kin, the broken black mare. Gwion reaches a hand and she takes sword in her right again, reaches to meet his with her left, shoe on his boot in the stirrup and up behind him, perching with a foot on the Red's haunches, arm around Gwion's waist, watching behind.

They're too few. Far, far too few, and they always were. The earls did not follow, did not ride with him. They made promises for the spring. Only a handful sent their sons or husbands, a spare younger daughter, and those who would follow them. A small warband swept baffled and exultant along the Forestways and through the Dark. Mortals, they died, too many of them, in the sorcery sent against the Riding by the priests, before ever they found their way down her Harper's road to the Holy Isle.

Those who went to the autumn muster at the Singersborg are few, too few; they were overwhelmed and dying before the Riding reached them.

Too early, too late. Captains might say, they should have waited, left the island to the dragon-kin if they wanted it so badly, burnt the shipyard at the mouth of the Arrunlinn and let them pen themselves there, for their taking in the spring.

Earls did say it.

They don't understand the danger. They don't understand what the Singersborg holds. What it guards.

Strength in Kallyn's left hand enough to grip Gwion's belt, for all the poison gnawing in the flesh. Not strength enough to fly.

We smash a company that bars the lane we ride. We hit them as a wave and it's the little fayling folk and their white ponies who rush ahead, their spears the leading edge, and we ride, as a wave we roll into what has broken the brave faylings, and there's sword-work aplenty then. I sing, howl, and it seems natural enough, no fear of what they'll think, of Nowa saying—

Dream. It's one of those dreams. It's not my hand on the sword's hilt. A woman's hand, a little narrower, a little finer than even my light bones and not so dark as mine, crossed with scars that aren't my own.

I don't like the feel of my left arm. Her arm. Feels like there's fever in it, beyond the pulling of scabs, the wetness of something weeping. But she grips the Wild King's belt and she perches, swaying easy with the horse's gallop, one knee up, one leg hooked around the King's, braced as if she clings on with her toes, but I'm, she's, wearing soft deerskin shoes.

I want to be Raven, to grip with talons to the cantle, to fling myself rising up and out of here, ride the smoky air to find myself—wherever it is I-Mairran ought to be. Not here.

Fewer of us ride out of the lane than rode in. Ghosts are failing, lost.

How do you kill a ghost?

No time to let wits wander; get myself killed that way.

This isn't me. This is my dream. Her memory.

I hate this dream. I don't want to be here. Not again.

A square stone tower, and the smoke-blackened walls of a great hall. A tide of dragon-kin mill about the tower. I think they're battering their way in, as they broke the gate, but then I realize, as she did, as I always do, that they already hold it. It's the ruin draws their attention.

Small knot of men and women fighting still, holding before the gaping doorway, a fragment of a shield-wall bristling with spears, but they are failing, they are falling.

She/I—we are remembering together—she wants to fling sword away, fling herself on the dragon-kin who surround and beat at them, be Wolf, tear and break, taste their blood.

Her wolves, her hounds, do fling themselves forward. Fewer than ran with the King when he went to the earls. Fewer than came out of the Dark ways on the road her mute Harper and his clear-voiced brother wove. Fewer than ran with them through the gate.

She can't. This maelstrom of weapons is not a wolf's hunting ground, and they are dying, dying, tearing open a gap for Wild King and Grey Hunter.

And she shrieks, the silver dragon. She's been waiting, for Kallyn, for Gwion. Crouched like a brooding hen in her nest, hidden below the parapet of the tower roof, and she springs now to that parapet and cries again, and launches herself to drop.

The Red is veering aside.

I leap. Human, still.

"Kallyn!" Gwion shouts.

I remember the day I first saw him. I…no, Kallyn was Wolf. A morning late in the month of Forest Flowering, and Gwion came riding through the dappled green shade of the new-leafed maples along the Konabrook, below the waterfall. The Warnavon, long, long ago. He was a young man then, and merely human, not yet what he would become; broken sunlight was on his hair and he was singing. His eyes… She stood up in her human-seeming self, the better to watch him. And he left off his song to smile at her.

The silver dragon slams her to the ground and the blade she thrusts up two-handed to the dragon's breast glances aside, treachery of her weak left arm, tearing a long gash through armoured scales but not the blow to the heart it was meant to be. Kallyn feels it when the dragon's teeth meet in her shoulder, I do, the bones grinding, the world washed out in a flare of red pain.

I want to wake up.

Don't know what's happened, only she's, I'm struggling, snarling, trying to get teeth into the enemy, trying to tear free. Tangled. Wolf, thrashing and wrapped in a ripping mess of cloth.

Darkness. Being dragged. Proud cat that's caught the rat. There's shouting, triumphant, furious humans all about. Torches kindled at the fires of some burning building, flaring bright. Madness rides them. The sorcerer-priests most beloved of the Golden Dragon, her chosen.

Erryth steals their dreams and feeds them her own. Her children, she calls them. They aren't. The silver dragon, she might be. Kallyn doesn't know how Erryth's gotten the silver one, though; the Dragon had no child living when they put her beneath the Lake, and her lovers had left her or were long dead before her madness turned her against her fellow Immortals, before she grew half so great and savage, feeding on her own poisoned self-regard and greed.

The priests surround the silver dragon. They try to drag Wolf from her and she won't let him go. Naughty cat. Kallyn is her prize, her victory, the proof she is her parent's faithful child.

The priests beat the silver dragon, driving her on. As if she is not moving fast enough for their liking. Dragging the Wolf, since she won't give him up. Tripping on him. So then Kallyn is woman again, and she's lost her trousers, her boots, which had a knife in them, but the loose belt of her gown is still about her body and the Hunter gets right hand to the dagger sheathed there and stabs for the dragon's throat.

Too weak. Behind, wolves snarl, dogs bark fury, humans scream, dying. The King is there, afoot, fighting to reach her. Low narrow dark place.

She knows where they are.

I know—I-Mairran—I know this place, the rough-squared walls, the coarse yellow stone of the upper levels. The rise where the floor humps over a root of harder stone, the deep-lying streaky-pale and thunder-grey of the fells, of the keep and Great Hall and curtain walls, and the quoins of the lesser halls of yellow stone. It's just before the fork and the left-hand narrow passage that plunges deeper. These are part of the cellars—and the crypts—beneath Queen's Arrun.

The old copper mines, long played out, long forgotten.

After they sang Erryth into the Lake, the Grey Hunter and the Wild King, they pulled down the fane of sacrifice that stood here and raised up the Singersborg in its place, so that when folk thought of the Holy Isle, and the heart of the Holy Isle, it would be the Singers and the wisdom of the Singers their reverence remembered. So that what else lay here would be forgotten.

The anchorstone we put below the ground, not daring to break it, since we had woven it into the binding of the Dragon, thinking to turn that brooding weight, that fell power born of blood and terror and death, against Erryth, who had nursed it into being and drew strength from it as one might take warmth from a fire.

The dragon-kin should not know of this place. Few among Forest-folk do.

Secret dragon-kin among the Singers. It was always a rumour.

They've fled here, folk from above. The Singers had sent the children down, days before, to save them from the fires. Kallyn heard them crying their fear in the cave they call the upper hall. I can't hear them anymore.

Here is a dark, narrow place. The lower galleries, where the stone is dark and sharp; it wasn't always copper they hunted, those ancient miners.

She knows what the sorcerers mean to do. I know it. I've dreamed this dream too many times. I remember it, now.

She tears herself free at last and scrambles away, but she falls. She's lying in cold water, too weak. Struggle just to raise her head. Bleeding into ice-cold water. Pool fills half the cavern. They ended the passage here, those ancient miners. Found what had called them.

Anchorstone, aye.

Bluestone. Mined in the Lann Lathrun, but there was a vein here beneath the Holy Isle. The faylings found it long ago. They mined it, following it deep. They found and revered the anchorstone of the Isle and in later years, when they had retreated to the high fells, the humans mining copper in the yellow-grey sandstone above found the old deep fayling workings, and the great bluestone, and brought it out into the sun, for honour of the Bright Mother and her son. It was beautiful, till Erryth made it her own, and defiled it. Then Immortals and Singers brought it to its home again, out of the daylight green and snow and sky and the deaths that had washed over it, back to the dark where it was born. To hold the Dragon down. To lie forgotten, a thing of the Dark Beneath, in the Dark Mother's keeping, till the long years should leach it clean once more.

Mistake.

Human hands like claws on her, no longer fearful. The silver dragon has been shoved aside. Sorcerer-priests dragging her through the shallow water, into the far dark where the roof drops low. Red light swims on the black water's surface. A torch is dropped, sizzling, hissing, cloud of white steam.

Fighting like a mad thing. Wolf, woman, clipped and flightless falcon, she, I, we don't know what we are. Only claws and fury, rage and pain.

Terror, such as we have never known.

This isn't me. I am dreaming. It's the grey wolf dying.

And I the black wolf am thrashing and I bite and I can't wake up.

The anchorstone's an upright boulder of bluestone, and if covetous Outland eyes ever saw it...

The faylings worked it, smoothed it, polished it, as if it might be by running water. Carved a face, a thing of lines and shallow curves, the secret face, kind and wise and stern, that is all the Mothers, Bright and Dark, Above and Below, looking down on them all... Mothers, help me, she cries.

Mothers, hear me.

Mother, I cry, No—

Head pushed under and Kallyn struggles up choking, coughing, air gone from the lungs. Can't fight, can only hang limp in their grasp, coughing up water, wheezing. Not freezing, not down so deep, but the water feels like ice, biting to the bone, numbing.

The silver dragon, white-haired girl, a greasy fur cape thrown over her nakedness, pushes through the sorcerer-priests. Some reach to put her back. She snarls, showing inhuman fangs. Threatening to spit. Those crowding around, wading to their knees, boots flooded, hems draggling in the water, give way, sullen and muttering. A little afraid. The ones who've caught the Grey Hunter don't let her go.

She, the silver dragon-girl, who takes the knives.

She's hardly more than a child. What have they made of her, these priests?

They've dragged Kallyn back against the stone that stands here, where she and the Wild King set it, wedged upright at the back of the pool, where the water seeps down the wall.

Takes only four of them to hold the Grey Hunter, so weakened is she. The silver dragon meets her gaze and Kallyn is thinking, no, don't. Child, you don't need to serve them, you don't need to fear them, but it's Erryth the girl serves and Erryth she fears, and Kallyn can't find the strength, the breath, for words, I in my dreaming can't…

Mother, please…

It's the dragon-girl who at the last blinks, her mouth twisting, grimacing. She stabs with the smaller flint blade, swift, cold punch; she it is who makes a sound, not Kallyn. A gasp, a moan, almost a sob. And follows it with a dragon's shriek, standing over the Grey Hunter with blood on her shaking hand.

Roaring in Kallyn's ears. The sorcerer-priests, their words and their wishes and the shape they make of rending, of unmaking, of loosing what was bound; her blood, failing. Golden Erryth, waking, summoned, the binding anchored on the great bluestone washed away in its maker's blood, and the silver girl falls to her knees so they are eye to eye, and she—she watches the Hunter's dying, silver eyes gone black in the firelight, and leans to dabble a hand in Kallyn's blood, and smear it over the stone, and dabble again and lick her hand with a dragon's flickering tongue. And then she slashes at the stone with her curved knife, and a chip flies and tongue darts, jaws snap—girl, dragon, thing between—fast as blinking.

Old priest snatches the curved knife from her human hand, not seeing what she has done. All smoke and shadow and lurid flame to failing human eyes.

The curving knife. That's their rite. That's what they think they need, more than her heart's blood shed. The ritual of a throat cut. As if that matters. It's life's blood either way, given to the stone. To the Dragon.

Pressure, that's all Kallyn feels. A pressing weight, when cold keen blade of flint rocks against skin.

Makes no difference. Already falling away, and the Dark opens warm, welcoming, to take what is Kallyn, woman, Wolf, Falcon all one and almost Kallyn-we understand again the true names of the one Mother who is All, which only the dead and the unborn can know. Doesn't matter, how they kill the Grey Hunter. It's done.

Gwion's gained the cave, at last. Too few of his Riders with him. She, I, Kallyn, Mairran, we hear his cry. We hear our name. Breaks our heart.

Sorcerers die.

Out in the Lake, water, ice, erupting, shattering.

Erryth rising.

~LANNESK~

Grey sky now, heavy, low, and the flakes fall like sodden feathers. No breath of wind to disturb them as they settle on every twig, every grass-head and seed-stalk. The air too is damp, strikes cold through clothing.

Not nearly so long a trek back along the bluff as it was carrying Anzimor. Back to where his comrades and dragon-kin lie together, the snow blanketing them already, bodies stiffening, freezing. Beyond helping. He's here only for what he needs, which is his shield.

The camp below seems nearly emptied. A few huts are burning, the stockade standing open, the reindeer cut loose and straying. Aftermath of the Grey Hunter's foray or the assault of the Wild King's Riders. Not total disorder. People are rounding up the reindeer; someone is— praying, he thinks—over bodies laid in a neat row. Sorcerers? Not very many of them. Someone sees him, shouts; Lannesk flings himself flat as an arrow whistles over. Crawls further from the edge, stands and runs, a heavy, slogging run, his harp, slung over his shoulder again, bumping at his back.

Slows, working his way uphill, around through hedges of the pastures and orchards among which Mair Arrun was set. He sees patrols, lone wandering warriors, an archer riding a reindeer in haste down towards the lower camp. No one shoots at him again, or calls out. He's just one more bent and trudging figure glimpsed through the thick-falling whiteness of the snow.

Nothing to tell dragon-kin from Forest-folk at a distance, not the ordinary dragon-kin, who don't tie their hair full of knots and bones, who wear fur and leather, carry spear and shield...the most obvious difference is that few wear helms, and those are mostly stolen, he guesses. Mostly they cover their heads with hooded fur shoulder-capes, or with thick round fur hats. Could have taken a hat from the dead about the drift of honeysuckles, but the snow is falling thicker, faster, white curtain shutting out the world. Forest-folk, dragon-kin, no one will be able to tell friend from foe till they're grappling together now. He gets into the woods higher up, crossing the track they followed to the fane on Huntersnight, and then the road to a timber-camp. Hides, a few times, from patrols that he hears before he sees: grey shadows, lost in the heavy snow. Can't tell who they are. Needs to get to where he can see the walls of Singersborg, the gate. Do they hold, has the Wild King's Riding put the dragon-kin to flight?

Too few, too few, too few...

Smoke rolls down from the Singersborg, stinging the eyes, catching in the throat, darkening the snow-thick world to dusk. The gates stand open. There's coming and going, dragon-kin. Sounds of fighting. Lannesk finds his way along in the ditch below the wall, which is shallow on this southwestern side, overgrown with sumacs and drifted with snow. Not sure what he's doing. He should go to the woods. Run. Nothing left here to fight for.

The Wild King, the Grey Hunter. He can't run while they still fight.

Nothing to run to, anyway. No one to run with.

Not sure what he's doing, but there are dead dragon-kin in the ditch, snow settling over them. Arrow-shot, mostly. His own cape has no hood, so he sheds it and drags off the hooded cape one of them wears. Pale wolfskin, not too grimy. Pulls it on himself, tugging the hood forward to mostly hide his helmet, which he might yet need. Goes along and the air grows thicker. Coughs, muffling it in cloth. Between snow and smoke it might as well be twilight. Comes to the causeway crossing the ditch. A running group of people pass, shouting. Strange accents, but random words he can untangle. Nothing of any use. Dragon-kin.

He scrambles up and follows them and no one cries out against them.

Fire. Smoke. Knots of folk running, hiding. A group, mostly unarmed, scuttle for the gateway, carrying bundles. Belongings, children...he can't tell. Looters or folk of the Singsborg in flight. Dragon-kin crowd around the door of one of the stone-built halls, a pair of axemen taking turns to hew at it—fighting at the foot of a tower, fighting in the ruins of the Masters' Hall, and a clamouring crowd gathering there, surrounding sorcerer-priests who sing and raise their arms.

The dragon, they say. Or maybe it's the Dragon.

She comes—

The red stallion, riderless, comes careening into them out of the smoke and snow. He sees a warrior try to grab for the reins, looped up to the saddlebow, and go down under trampling hooves. The horse kicks and plunges through them and there's a shout, a surge of people out of the ruined hall, a tall figure vaulting to the horse's back, sword whirling, others following, spearcarls and swordtheyns and a handful of other horses, hardly there, almost formless, shadows in smoke and snow, and they seem to fade even as he watches, the ghostly Riders. Priests, singing—voices rise sharp, hard, weapons against the Riding. The Wild King does not sing. The Red plunges in among the priests and the King sets to cutting them down, a fury that takes no heed for guarding himself, and the close mass of the mortal warriors who follow him are buffeted apart by a new dragon-kin assault, scattered, put down one by one.

Lannesk, running, leaping to the top of a foundation wall to run along it, to leap down among the priests, hot spear-work then, till he's driven back against the Red's flank. Dangerous, he'll fall under the horse's hooves or hamper the Wild King's swing but the sorcerers and their defenders are falling back, looking away, staring upwards—

Sound of a stormwind, like the rushing roar of rising water.

"The Dragon!" they cry, words like enough the Forest tongue he understands their meaning. "The Dragon! Golden Erryth comes!"

There is a stillness, then, even the singing of the priests fallen silent. And then a roar, voices crying out, screaming, running. It's not only Forest-folk who flee for the shelter of walls, of what roofs still stand.

It's not all their own who flee, either. Some gather to the King. Silent, grim. Battered, wounded, smoke-reeking. Spearcarls and swordtheyns, Singers and vagabonds. Theyn Asa, he thinks he sees, and Ovan. A handful of faylings. An old woman armed with only a staff. Another woman, small and slight, with the ears of a fox, wearing a scale shirt like some of the faylings, and armed with a spear. There are dragon-kin all about them, more coming now up into the cellar of the ruined Masters' Hall, into a trampled mess of ice and charred beams and fallen bodies. Up from a dark stairwell, back towards the tower, which still stands. So now he has an answer to the lights that he and Anzimor saw. There was something more beneath. A passageway. Buried secrets.

"Kallyn is dead," the Wild King says, as if to himself. He looks down at Lannesk. "They slew her. The dragon's daughter gave her blood to the anchorstone, and broke our binding. Erryth is free."

Lannesk nods, to say he understands. Not the words, but the stunned loss in them. The King leans down to clasp his shoulder.

"My harp is broken," he says, and Lannesk sees it is so, the stiffened leather bag hung behind the cantle cloven as if by an axe, and splintered wood showing through the gash. But it took the force of the edge, and the saddlepad beneath is uncut, the horse unharmed.

Thunder, growling louder.

The King is reaching back to untie the thongs that still hold the wreckage of his harp on. He shakes the bag partway off the harp. Broken wood, tangled strings. Rubs his thumb over the split sound-board. Then he tosses harp and bag from him, into a sullen fire of wreckage that burns against a broken wall across the lane. A moment, and then the flames brighten, rise, eating oiled wood.

The Wild King watches it burn. Dragon-kin watch, too, uneasy, as if expecting some new magic to rise against them from the flames. The leather starts to smoulder.

"Lend me yours, Lannesk," the King says. And then shrugs, and his smile is crooked. "Or—will you give it to me? I don't think I am going to be able to return it."

Lannesk doesn't think he's going to be getting out of here to make any more songs, himself. How did Anzi think they were going to be sung, anyway, without his voice? He hands up the harp that Anzimor gave him. The King takes it in his left hand, and reaching over, passes down his sword. Lannesk has to drop his spear to take it.

"Guard me," the Wild King says. "So long as you can." And he knees his horse around, reins loose, settling the harp into his arm.

A blue-eyed girl creeps from the cellar, wearing a torn, bloody tunic with over it a heavy leather vest meant to fit a grown man, a hooded fur shoulder-cape. What he can see of her face is smeared with soot and ashes and the blood of wounds that couldn't be her own. She takes up his discarded spear, nods to him as if he'd offered it. He shakes his head at her. She should be back in the underground refuge, for what little safety it might give. But he can't spare attention, and anyway, who's he to tell her not to seek some death of her own choosing, rather than a dragon-kin knife?

The dragon-kin are backing away from the King. There's a grim purpose to him, a reek not of smoke, but of gathering storm. Lannesk pushes the wolf-skin hood back, catches up with the King in a few long strides, crossing behind to walk at his right, to have room to use the sword. There's a tattooed man with an axe come up on the left. A stir, a pushing up of others, out of shadow and smoke, falling in behind. A guard forming about the King.

Lannesk does know the sword. Brux did not neglect that, in the education of his stepsons. They'd have been their little sister's swordtheyns, her captains, if she had ever lived to be earl. Hadn't carried such a thing, out on their spying. Spear is a more practical weapon in most situations, and he's always preferred it.

The Wild King's sword is longer, a little heavier, than the ones he's used before.

It'll do.

Thunder, the clouds tearing. Snow whirls blinding, rising, snow and ice and stinging ash, and she plunges from the sky, Erryth the Golden, who once was numbered among the Immortals, who once was revered as a guardian of the Lake and the Forest along with the Grey Hunter, the Smith, the Fisher, the trickster Fox-lad whose death was her first act of betrayal...

She's nothing like the silver dragon, who was no bigger than a yearling filly. Her body alone is the length of three great bull aurochsen; her neck reaches another bull's length, and her tail two. Her wings stretch over them, darkening the already dim sky. Snow melts, landing on her glittering armoured hide. She could close one taloned foot about a big man's chest and haul him into the sky. Drag him from the saddle from above and neither sword nor axe nor any spear would reach her, and their archers—there's shooting from more than one tower still held against the dragon-kin below, but Erryth fans an irritated wing, nothing more, crouched amid ruins, waiting. Arrows did little even against the young one.

She raises the crest on her head. In the confused light and shadow, the blink of snow hitting the eyes, she's darkness, with glints of gold and scarlet where her scales catch the light of the fires. Her eyes are golden as her hide and she blinks, a pale third eyelid like a bird's sliding over. Grins, sharp-fanged.

The King rides on. Lannesk and the axeman keep pace, the others following. He's afraid. Of course he's afraid, but fear seems to have become a strange, hard thing, which he can take up like a stone and set aside, out of the way. He can feel it's there, but...*there* is somewhere else, outside of himself.

"Will you?" the dragon asks, and her voice is a deep rumble. Lannesk feels it in his ribs. "Oh, Gwion, will you be such a fool as to try again? Your leman is dead and what have you gained, the two of you? It was always going to end like this."

"To end," the King says. "Aye." His head is bowed. He flings his head up then, plucks a chord that breaks into a rippling run of notes. And he sings.

It's not a spell. It's only a song of the last Riding, of warriors and Singers, dying to defend the Holy Isle, of oath-bound Riders and faylings. Of the Grey Hunter flying on the roads of the wind—but they come rushing, then, dragon-kin with spears and axes, shouting, crying Erryth's name, as if there might be after all some magic in the words that could throw the Dragon down again, and Lannesk can't listen; words, music are lost to him, in the clamour and the fury. He needs to keep the Red's withers near to the back of his left shoulder, keep them from reaching the horse's flank, from striking at his neck, strike aside any spear that thrusts in—it's been long months since he was in the yard with Anzi, Brux hopping around them, shouting—because he always grew excited—sweating in the Haymonth sun. But what you've sweated into your muscles isn't easily forgotten. The sword is swift in his hand, and there's a dead man at his feet, and a woman, and another man, and a dragon-kin swordsman tall as himself nearly has him down, clambering over his fallen comrades but he catches the man on the jaw, striking with his shield's edge, knocking his blade aside. He thrusts and kicks him off and catches his balance against the horse, driven back, an axe splitting his shield but someone slashes low, another swordsman has leapt in amongst the dragon-kin, and the enemy axeman falls. Lord Ekkard, soot-blackened, whirling about to put himself at Lannesk's side, and Tolla, who throws aside a broken spear and grabs up the axe.

The song changes. It crackles like lightning, words carrying power. Thunder rumbles under it, and the music circles, like a falcon wheeling on the wind before she drops.

Names, the Wild King sings. Lost names. Men and women raised to be kings, given to the Dragon. Given to bind the Forest under her. Given to the Dark Beyond.

From the Dark, he says, they call her.

In the Dark, he says, they will hold her.

By their blood—

Erryth hears it, the shape of his making, the power that gathers. She rears up, roaring. She coughs fire and folk scatter shrieking, burning, folk fall dead and dying, hers, theirs, she does not discriminate, but the fire breaks where the Wild King sings, as if his words raise a shield before them—only it is not enough to defend them all, and between fire and death and flight, nearly all about have chosen flight. As who would not, faced with a burning death.

So they advance, the few who are left about the King, and there's a dozen on this side with Lannesk, there's the girl with the spear, who keeps close behind, as if she would hide in the King's shadow, and Ekkard, and Tolla, and others, women and men he doesn't know or doesn't see to know.

The Dragon leaps, then, pouncing like a cat and sweeps them aside with a blow of her bony-armoured head, left, right, and then raking claws. They scatter; Lannesk dives forward, low, rolling on his shoulder. He sees Ekkard fly through the air and flip and bounce, hitting the ground, like a rat snatched and tossed by a terrier. The Red lunges, teeth snapping and the King's voice is a shout, holding the power still, but fighting hard to do so. Lannesk comes up under the Dragon's head, stabs into the hollow of her throat, but even there she's armoured. Sword skitters; he twists and drives it, biting, deep between scales and she hisses and bats him down, claws raking, tearing through the layers of leather, but he's bundled thick and she kicks him tumbling over rocks. Winded, he's lost his helmet, thumped his head, can't get himself up, but he does, something burning in his left shoulder. Grabs the sword again, dark with smoking blood. Arms still work, both of them, legs still hold him even if he does lurch sideways, dizzy.

The horse is afraid, sweating and blowing, ears back, eyes rolling white. He won't go closer and it's the Wild King's will alone holding him there—he'll break, poor frightened beast, even he. The Dragon is— backing, a little. Blood stains her golden scales. Something builds, in the song. There's a weight in the air, a thunder-gathering heaviness.

But the horse—Lannesk goes to take the reins below the bridle, to lead the Red where the King would go, but the King twists to swing a leg over the horse's neck, still holding his harp, and Lannesk is in time to steady him as he kicks his foot free and slides down.

Lets the horse go, which is the King's intent, and snorting, the Red stands, fidgeting foot to foot, and finally, ears flat, wheels away.

"Go," the King says. "All of you." And he raises his voice again. They are swords, he sings. They are spears. They are knives, the forgotten names gathering in the Dark. And again he sings them, and every name is a flame and every flame a piece of the Mother's darkness, and it is as if night has fallen, the sky opening about the Dragon, black as forgetting and bright with impossibly distant stars. They stand high on the lip of a well and the ground tilts and spills them. Erryth shrieks rage and fire; the King shakes loose of Lannesk's grip that would prevent him and strides forward singing, down into the rushing black. The Dragon's flame engulfs him.

Lannesk, knocked to his knees when the King tore loose of his hand, sees him. Sees him burning, falling, his hair gone to flame, clothed in Dragon's flame and his arms spread, harp silenced, burning, fallen to flakes of light and the King gathers the flame as he falls and the Dragon, wings wide, screaming—he embraces her, flaming, Dragon, golden woman, golden woman wings spread wide, and Dragon again, and they burn together, and the black and the stars that are not the stars of the night fold around them.

Names, he sang. His Riders. One of them was Anzimor's. And the last were Kallyn's, and his own.

Shrieking voices. Lightning strikes a tower. Stones falls. Wind howling and the snow driving blind, and they're scattered, lost. Lannesk finds himself in the lee of a wall, crouched, sobbing. For Anzimor, for Kallyn, for Gwion the Wild King. For himself, maybe. Howling of a lost dog, that's what it is, though it's only a painful, tearing, scar-stifled gasping in his throat that leaves him coughing and tasting blood in what he coughs up, and he can't—he can't—Anzi would be shamed by this.

Well, he wouldn't be, but he can tell himself so, and so get a grip on himself. But the best he can do is be silent, and huddle shivering and chilled to the bone. Gashes ripped by the Dragon's claws through to his skin through so many layers; they're not deep, just seeping, scabbing. Burning. Remembers how the Grey Hunter's wounds festered. But that had been a bite, he thinks. He pulls the wolfskin hood up again. Finds his mittens still dangle on their string, through all that. Thirsty, so thirsty, and only snow to slake it, and that tastes of ash and blood.

Night sinks over them. Fires still burn. The snow's gentler now, but it's still shaping to be a three-day storm.

He hears voices. Dragon-kin, the accent. Cowers down so he's nothing but a darkness; they pass without seeing him.

Needs to get out of here. Doesn't want to move.

Go on. Get up. Go.

Reaches for the spear where he'd have lain it and of course he doesn't have it; he has the Wild King's sword, with its rune-written blade and gilded hilt and the lump of bluestone for pommel that's wealth some would kill for. And no scabbard.

Better just to leave it lying, let it be buried in ash and snow till spring. Wishing trouble on himself, to keep it. But to leave it doesn't feel right, so he wraps the grip tight in knotted strips of rag unwound from what he still has about one wrist, and wraps and knots and wraps and knots again about the pommel till it feels covered, to his touch, and secure. Isn't even sure where he is. Over towards the northeast corner, he guess.

Makes it to his feet at last. Starts walking, feeling his way through what is becoming a storm with the sword as a stick. Stumbles over what might have been uneven ground, but isn't. Fallen bodies. They stink of charred meat, even in the cold and wind, and his mouth waters and then he's sick, crouched by them, though there's nothing in his belly to come up but the bit of water he'd had by swallowing snow.

Dark Mother, Bright Mother, Sun Ascending in Glory, hold them safe and dear, remember their names.

Feels his way over them, not to fall again. Cloth crumbles. They're only part-burnt, not beyond recognition, if there were light. He touches a face, settling towards icy stone-hardness, flinches away. But she has a sword.

He hesitates. But he can't wander around with an unsheathed sword, if he's going to carry it with him at all, especially not this sword, with the Smith's markings like birdtracks inlaid on the blade. He gropes, finds that the dead theyn's sword is slung on a baldric, and it's intact, so he gets it free of her and lays the theyn's sword back naked by her side. Sheathes the Wild King's, which is only a little too long for it, and settles it over his own shoulder.

Lady Lauran carried her sword by a baldric.

Mothers Above and Below keep you, he wishes her. If it is her.

Mothers Above and Below, keep me. Anzi, watch over me, if you can.

He's trying to find his way to that northern postern up the ridge. Not sure who, even, will hold this battlefield ruin, come the dawn or, more likely, come the ending of the storm, a day or two hence. But better not to be penned within, if it's the dragon-kin. Their Dragon is—gone, if not dead. Taken, sung, into the Dark Beyond, and burning. If that can harm a dragon. But are there any left to contest the dragon-kin claiming the Holy Isle? He doubts it. Elders and Masters of the Singers, in some hidden fastness beneath the borg? But the dragon-kin seem to have known of that.

Realizes he's only thinking, he'll get out, go back to Anzimor. As if he's only left him sleeping, wounded...

Think, he tells himself. Anzi won't thank you for dying with him.

But he's so tired.

Of course he is. He's been on his feet, marching, fighting—by harp or spear or sword—since nightfall the day before. And nothing to eat since yesterday, either.

Cold'll kill you. Hunger only makes cold fall heavier, bite deeper. He's got Forest-cunning enough to live, or to know what he needs to live, and it starts with flint and firesteel, which he has, and any number of other things, most of which he lacks. A gaudy sword, no matter how sharp its edge, is not on that list at all.

Go on then, he tells himself in Anzimor's voice. What all do we need, and where are we going to find it?

~MAIRRAN~

It was a long hunting.

They had no choice, Rikenza and Raynar, but to accept that their mother's shield-companion, the man who had been a father to them after the death of their own, had either for his own reasons chosen to turn highway robber and waylay my comrades and me from ambush, or had mistaken my small party, if not for a solitary wild man on a red horse, than for brigands ourselves. That there had been no rumours of outlaws threatening the folk of the Borlinn valley to draw Theyn Harilan to lay such an ambush was not something they or I brought up. Forgiveness all around. A terrible misunderstanding.

I did not offer to pay any blood-fee for the killing. They did not ask it. A quiet forgetting, a salving of the honour of the dead in calling the attack mistaken on both sides, was the best Rikenza and Raynar could ask; it was that or admit to having ordered their liegeman to treason. Panic without time for more reasoned thought, was what I suspected, at that sudden word of my imminent arrival, but now there I was, their guest and their responsibility, the Queen's only living child, and not so easy to make away with, if they did not want to find just how swiftly my mother might muster the earls and swordtheyns of the land against them. And I was in accord with them—I wanted the wild man taken.

"Alive," I said, and repeated that, nearly every time we rode out, to be sure that each swordtheyn and spearcarl and hunter of Lord Raynar's retinue knew it. And once, when a spearcarl had loosed a wild arrow at what turned out to be no more than a startled cow moose crashing through alders with a half-grown calf trailing her, "Alive, because this Huntersnight Laikyn will provide the sacrifice to the Forest on the Queen's behalf, one way or another."

They did not shoot at shadows, after that.

Lord Raynar sent to a village called Elmtellon, south of the Borlinn, for an old woman and her grandson of a family of hunters, who were Forest-blessed witches, he said. They came on skis, the white-haired grandmother as fleet-footed as her grandson, who was my age, and they joined the hunters, sniffing the wind, dowsing with a wand of secret-keeping hemlock, and, the old woman, seeking vision in water mixed with a drop of her blood, all held in a pearly mussel-shell.

They had no more luck than the dogs in finding so much as a direction to ride. I sent them home after a week. I didn't like the way the old woman watched me.

For a fortnight, we quartered the hills north of the Fairnmere and both sides of the valley of the Borlinn. Nowa fretted, sent Sage to practise her archery, set her exercises to build her strength, taught her proper manners for a lord's attendant, and hobbled about leaning on a spear being bad-tempered. I thought it wasn't so much the pain of the healing wound as fear for me, but I was fairly certain that sober second thought on the part of the late earl's children meant I was safe enough, for now. At least while I seemed to be just as interested in capturing the wild man as Raynar was. And little though I liked weighing myself down, I wore my byrnie, with the addition of plate over breast and back, and appropriated some boiled leather part-armour for Smoke.

One evening I went into Rikenza's chambers, while everyone, myself included, ought to have been dining in the hall. There was nothing of interest in the lady's room, which had, presumably, been until recently her mother's. In the antechamber to which my arrival at Mair Laikyn had driven her brother I failed to find the three light-coloured hairs for which I was searching. Not surprising. Perhaps Raynar had given them to his witches to wrap about their hemlock wand. I browsed through the lord's shelf, too, but resisted the temptation to pinch one of his books.

I did ask, the next evening, to borrow one for Nowa. But when Raynar invited me to take my pick, the particular dark and worn spine, the miscellany of old lays and ancient poetry on which I'd had my eye the evening before, was no longer there. I took her a translation of a Southlander treatise on fortifications and sieges instead. More to her taste, anyway, though I don't know how much of it she actually read.

Winter's fangs began to bite. I had bad dreams. Snow fell, the wind whipped away the final clinging leaves of the oaks, and the nights stretched long. We were in the last few days of Slaughtermonth by the time Nowa's wound had turned to a knotted purple scar and she was fit enough to join us in the hall without doing her leg further damage. She was still limping. She would limp for the rest of her life.

The hunt had shifted to the hills north of the Fairnmere by then, but there was little enough daylight for it, not much over six good hours, so we rode out late and returned early in the red twilight. Lady Rikenza spent most of her days among her clerks and law-reeves, setting the accounts in order for the high reeve—that meaning, for me. I had utterly no interest in such matters, but she was determined to present an accounting of every peck of grain and bale of fleece and cord of firewood, as if I'd been sent to question her mother's remittances.

At supper in the hall the lady was quiet, leaving it to others to tell over the tale—dull enough, usually—of the day's futilities. There was a woman who wore a three-winter Singer's silver ring and played harp or drum, and her younger partner who played the fiddle or sang a high, sweet descant over her. They were working their way through the cycle of tales of the wars against the invading Southlanders, those nights, which didn't much hold my interest, though they were meant to flatter me. Tales of my mother riding to war... I'd rather have heard of the Grey Hunter and the Wild King and the Riders in the days of the wars against the dragons and the dragon-kin who came out of the Dark Beyond. Or perhaps only from the ice-mountains of the north. No certainty in those songs.

Dragon-kin lies. You know it wasn't that way at all.

Rikenza, too, did not seem much engaged by her minstrels. Sometimes she would linger, when the singing and storytelling began. More often she withdrew, with only her serving-woman Enith, a cousin of some sort, to attend her. She seemed, day by day, to be shrinking into herself, as if her grief grew rather than lessened. Grief, or guilt.

A cold night, and Raven, I went out the window. Nowa woke and saw me going. My tame ravens slept, and Sage, sleeping limp and curled small like a kitten, did not stir.

So I went out the window, covered only, a compromise with Nowa, with a heavy curtain, on a cold wind, and through chimney-reek beneath the stars, over sleeping halls and frozen water, far beyond the smoke of sleeping Fairnshore, to where the Forest was still and silent beneath the star-thick black. Tasting, if one could call it that, the wind. Listening, maybe, for I could not have told what, and I found the warm silver thread of it and let it draw me, feathers swish, swish, swishing the air, a sound like the quick lapping of small waves over pebbles, and then I was Wolf, running over the snow. There was a swathe of spruce and fir, dark and sharp-scented and to the southwest the moon in its first quarter sliding, a broken silver coin, sidelong into the Fairnmere. Ragged streams of pale green swelled and faded, reaching towards the crown of the sky, stirring like waterweed on unfelt currents, rooted in the north. I might have been dreaming. Perhaps I was. Perhaps I lay beneath the quilts in the servant's narrow bed in the antechamber of our rooms, and the chill wind through the window found me, carrying the scent of the Forest. Carrying dreams.

Maybe I was Kallyn, dreaming Mairran's dreams.

There's Wolf, running, beneath the heavy spruce, the sweet fir, following a path the little deer have made, and a white hare startles away, but she's not hunting hare. She's out beyond the dark evergreens where silver maples line a stream: shaggy trunks, sinuous reaching grey boughs, and elms stand as if they hold up the sky. There's a scent on the wind. Smoke. Cattle. Horse. A mare though, not the red stallion.

Ashes climb the hillside, and juniper crawls between them. Poplar, birch. It's all straight trunks rising and rising, pale against the sky, dark against snow. There's a track, packed hard by hooves and the runners of a timber-sled. Smoke against the stars. Some logs, timber for building, for frames or splitting to planks, and the long poles, coppice-harvest, stacked to age for firewood. A wattle fence, a longhouse, low, sod-roofed, with the forester-family in one half, cow and calf, the pony and oxen and hens and all, in the other. A dog barks and is silent. No light flares, no door opens. Hardly a wild man's lair. Hooves have cut the hard surface of trampled snow: the oxen, the pony, a larger horse. There, that's her quarry. It has trampled about at the gatepost, and a stone is set there, a small boulder, the sort of thing folk living isolated set up, making heartstones of their own, a place to leave small Forest-offerings, imploring grace, and safety beneath the trees. It's been brushed clear of snow, though there's nothing there now. Whiff of bread. The track winds on by, and through the more open woods where the foresters work, coppiced trees and tall mother-trees standing scattered between, and on, and Wolf runs.

Wolves are howling, away to the north. Wolf doesn't answer. She's a stranger here. It wouldn't be wise. But there's another track, and it peels away north, and the land rises, climbs steep. There are oaks, saplings growing among the maples and here and there a dark spruce, and then as the land rises and grows drier the oaks are wild, untended, unharvested, untouched. Holy. They loom thick-boled, old, grown pale with lichen, and the path winds between them and falls into a hollowed way, worn by who knows what passing travellers over long, long years. Wolves and wild things. Ghosts. It's a Forestway, of course.

A red horse.

He's waiting there, watching. As if he heard her coming, smelt her on the wind. Wolf smells the horse, no ghost. Smells him, human, smoke and sheepskin and bread. Sweat, memory of confusion, terror, old blood. Fire and pain, bone and dust. Smells wolf, and dog, faint, as if it's long since they passed by there, but for a moment I see them, memory of them, as if they're made of shadow and starlight and the green banners of the northern sky. Moving, milling about, passing by, and gone.

Very far away, wolves howl.

Not dressed in rags now, but worn sheepskin boots, patched trousers, a tunic too short for him, a sheepskin vest, and his cloak is only a striped blanket folded over his shoulders. Breath puffs white in the air. He carries a spear. It's *a knife, lashed to a stave of ash. The wild man considers me and nods once, clicks his tongue to the horse. The horse nods, and turns, and walks on. Bareback, and head bare.*

Wolf still, I pad after them.

There's a heartstone, with red oaks about, and the fane marked by grey stones, snow-capped. The rider skirts the place.

There's a hillside, climbing higher, steep. The fells, Brother and Sister, loom to the north, a black absence of stars.

There's a darkness beneath the roots of a fallen tree. A bear's den, in some other winter. Passage worn smooth. Stones, earth. A hollow, out of the wind. He drops down from the horse, the wild man, and from the breast of his sheepskin he takes a loaf and three russet apples.

Gift of the foresters, left out—perhaps for the memory of faylings, perhaps for him, as perhaps was his clothing, which is poor, worn and ill-fitting, but even a lord couldn't call it rags. A wild man, an outlaw, a holy hermit. What's the difference to such folk, so long as the outlaw doesn't treat the folk of the assarts and villages as prey?

The wild man sits before the entrance to the den, where there is a stone with the snow brushed away. The fire in the stone-lined pit, stirred to life, is fed again among its ashes, and there is meat, a grouse hung high, drawn and plucked and now to roast. Long silence, with only the crackling of the fire, the hiss of burning juices, dripping, mouthwatering, and the wind. There should be music. A song. A tale. There is not. But the man strokes my black head, as if I am his hound, and I lay my head on his knee. It seems the natural way to be, there in the night. Then bread to eat, and eventually the bird, and the apples, and I'm fed from his hand. Bones to pick clean and feed to the fire. The red horse, after the apple cores and a heel of the loaf, has drifted away, but not as the wolves, the dogs, or the memory of wolves and dogs, have done. Hooves crunch snow. It snorts. It digs through crust, finds something to eat there, rips at twigs, chewing. Its ribs show beneath the winter-shaggy coat. The man's face is gaunt. He's no ghost, no Forest-memory.

The wild man builds the fire carefully, to hold its embers till the dawn, and crawls into the den, which is snug, and filled with a deep bed of bracken and sweetfern over fir boughs, like a nest, and he burrows into it, with the sheepskin vest and the blanket wrapped about him. He pats the bedding next to him, inviting.

I whine. I turn back on myself in that narrow place, and slither out again into snow and night and stars and the moon long set and the north-banners stilled. I shake the dirt from my coat, and beneath the stars, Wolf runs, as the wind rises.

~LANNESK~

They come on Lannesk in the woods on the coast halfway to North Cape. Tolla and Gillesh, with Ekkard herded between them, Ekkard clumsy and awkward, as if his limbs are not his own. They tow a toboggan looted—scavenged. Lannesk himself has been scavenging. He took skis and several worn quilts from a forester's abandoned cabin, along with a store of dry smoked venison from their smokehouse, and a leather bag holding frozen balls of trail-meat, which is jerky pounded up with clean fat and whatever fruit was to hand, dried blue-honeysuckle berries, this batch, and rolled in peameal. He doesn't want to think about why the foresters would have left behind something so laborious to make and so essential for winter travel, when they had to flee into the Forest. But flee they must have; the hearth was cold, and wind had scattered the ashes, though there had been no sign of violence about the cabin.

Now, an arrow drawn on him, while Tolla moves round to come at him without getting between. He watches Ekkard, trying to plead, not realizing yet that whatever is left of Ekkard, it isn't the young man he knew.

Lannesk is exhausted, though the feverish dragon-wounds are healing, smeared with balsam-gum. He has been circling along the coast, meaning to gather what he can and strike out to the north-east, across the narrowest stretch of ice to the Lann Krada shore, now that all the Lake has frozen by nature, not dragon-kin sorcery. Go who knows where, after that. Maybe down south to the Rath. Maybe right past the Falls, along the Bay of Fogs and out to the Coastlands, the homeland he barely remembers. Away. Can't stay on the Holy Isle. Dragon-kin patrol the woods, though in whose name, he doesn't know.

"It's Brux's mute, and all alone," Tolla says. "And he's stolen himself a sword."

Was Tolla there, among those who guarded the Wild King to face the Dragon? That band of heroes, any song would say. If he was, he'd been there only because his one virtue was loyalty to his earl and to her son. Not that the man's likely to feel any comradeship born out of it, or have any more respect for Lannesk than before.

Tolla drags the sword off Lannesk, and takes the dagger and knife from his belt, as well. Lannesk, too late, stirs to fight despite the arrow, because taking his knives means leaving him to die.

"Get out of the way, you motherless son!" Gillesh shouts, but Ekkard bolts out, grabs Tolla's arm, and then, when the spearcarl steps back, flings his arms around Lannesk, making a little whimpering noise that seems to be all the sorrow he can express. The fight goes out of them all. Lannesk holds Ekkard's face, tries to look into his eyes, understanding, then, that something is very wrong with him.

"Cracked his skull," Tolla says. "Knocked the wits out of him." He grabs Lannesk by the belt and slices the straps of the purses, shoves both deep into the breast of his clothing. And while Ekkard still clings to Lannesk, Tolla's ally all unwitting, he explains,, as if it's entirely reasonable, how Lannesk is going to help them look after Lord Ekkard, or be left here to die.

Lannesk doesn't get his blades back. Tolla bundles them together with the sword, wrapped in a singed cloak they seem to have been using as a sack, and straps them to the toboggan, which is laden with other scavenging, including lengths of smoked sausages and a frozen, butchered pig, from which they hack cuts of meat with an axe every night.

Doesn't draw the sword or unwrap the grubby strips of cloth weaving their tight knots around the hilt, though. Doesn't recognize it, maybe. Or does, and fears it.

"Earl Tannis dotes on him," Tolla says. "She'll find physicians, healing-crafty faylings, whatever it takes. Send for surgeons of the Coastlands, even. They have such skills in Goslack."

"We can't look after him, just the two of us. He's witless as a babe and wilful as a toddler," Gillesh adds.

Tolla doesn't contradict that. "He goes wandering away the moment you take your eyes off him. You can keep on serving your rightful earl's son in return for the mercy she showed you, or we leave you weaponless and without supplies, and you can take your chances with the dragon-kin. It was you and your damned brother seducing the boy got us into this disaster in the first place."

Which is a lie. All of it a lie, and they never swore any oath to kin-slaying Earl Tannis.

That there are nearly three hundred miles of frozen Lake between North Cape and Laikyn does not make Tolla see sense. Maybe he has no clear idea of the distance, never having been one much for listening to Singers' tales. Lannesk draws maps in the snow, remembered from the big almanac at Brux's tower, the book out of which his mother had woven stories for them, though she'd never found the time to teach them to read for themselves. He draws a route east to the Lann Krada. Draws a ship. Get off the Holy Isle, wait for spring, then sail across the Lake to Laikyn.

Tolla's having none of it.

"If the Mothers-cursed dragon-kin can come down the length of the Lake, honest Forest-folk can cross it."

There's no leaving till he can get back his means of making fire, or at the very least a blade, an edge with which to shape a fire-drill.

And abandon Ekkard, for Tolla to defend alone, against Gillesh? More than once she says, if he dies in his sleep, the earl can hardly blame us, a head-injury like that…it's what he'd pray for himself and you know it. Leave it, Tolla answers, without any great offence or passion. Bored, as if it's a weary old debate between them, not to be taken seriously. Lannesk fears it shows her true thoughts.

So Lannesk teaches them what he can of the Forest-cunning he and Anzimor learnt from Brux's hunters, who knew their business better than Earl Tannis's spearcarls seem to.

They're going to die regardless, is what he thinks, and he wonders if he can lead them along the coast of the Isle, steal Ekkard from them, hide with him in the Forest on the west of the Isle till—when? Forever? Steal a boat, come spring?

But at North Cape they find that the dragon-kin missed the cabin of their little outpost there, or were in too much haste to loot it, as they themselves had been in too much haste to clear it properly. There's bedding, rope, a couple of clay dishes which he has a use for, and tallow candles likewise. And, most useful thing yet, an iron-edged wooden spade, though Tolla and Gillesh don't value it as they should. With the sack of oatmeal Tolla and Gillesh have...acquired, and their supply of fat bacon, sausage, cheese—he suspects the steading they claim to have been deserted was only temporarily abandoned for fear they were dragon-kin, though perhaps the folk who fled it were wise to do so— they maybe have a chance.

A slight one.

They burden the toboggan further not with firewood—which won't last more than a few days out onto the Lake anyhow—but with cedar and fir-boughs, and the carcass of a deer Gillesh shoots to replenish their fresh meat. The boughs are because he's managed to convince them he knows how to make a proper snow-hut, which it seems, by the clumsy lean-to they made the first night they were together, they do not. That knowledge, and the spade, will maybe save all their lives.

They take a bearing by the stars at dawn, and check it by the sun through the day. When they can. Try to keep on in the overcast, though he knows they waver. The danger is pointing themselves up the length of the Lake or at Long Sound, so that they never come to shore at all. They ski, spread out, with Gillesh always watchful, bow strung, as if she still fears he'll take off on them, or maybe that the silver dragon may come hunting. Ekkard does what he's told, follows close behind Tolla, though he tries to cuddle with Lannesk at night, which is horrible, thinking that the man is trying to find Anzimor in him, but he's like a little child, Lannesk tells himself, only wanting comfort, warmth, a friend. And they all sleep in a close heap anyway, on the platform inside the hut hollowed out of a packed mound of snow, with the boughs and quilts to keep them off the snow, more quilts above them, and a candle burning in a dish. Inside the thick snow walls the little heat it makes is enough to keep them through even the deepest cold of the night, when they lie practically atop one another, sharing all their blankets, cloaks, and the shorter, heavy capes. They melt a jar of ice-shards and snowmelt for drink, steeping fir-tips and cedar in it to make winter-tonic; oatmeal can be softened overnight in the water, cheese warmed, strips of frozen venison toasted, eaten seared and mostly raw. They break the long-bones of the deer; the marrow is a feast. The others have the sense to leave the jerky and rich trail-meat that was Lannesk's contribution to their stores, and the sausages, for once the heavier fresh stuff is eaten. He's trying to keep back the bacon, too. They'll need the lard off it, once the candles are gone.

Never a campfire plume to draw the eye of any wide patrol out from the Holy Isle, if there are such. Only their breath and the little thin smoke of their lamp rising up the chimney-hole. Not too much of a trail. Wind scours their tracks away.

They wait out a two-day storm lying close together. Tolla and Gillesh bicker over whose turn it is to take Ekkard out to relieve himself. They don't trust him not to get lost, alone. Don't trust Lannesk with him, still. As if he hasn't kept them alive for two weeks now, in this great white wasteland. Which is two weeks longer than they'd have managed on their own, if they'd done as they planned and trusted to what they could drag for firewood and a lean-to, out in these great winds that sweep the vast expanse of the Lake.

They've grown gaunt, all of them. Hungry, all the time. The toboggan weighs more every day, not less. Ekkard eats only when Tolla or Lannesk sits coaxing him. Left to himself, he doesn't seem to have any appetite, as if that part of him, too, is gone. Gillesh ignores him. Lannesk remembers her tender care for Swordtheyn Asa when he lay ill; Ekkard's witless state seems to disgust her.

Is there anything of Ekkard left inside his mind? Gillesh is right. But sometimes he takes Lannesk's hand, and holds on to it, and he thinks, whatever is left of Ekkard is remembering Anzimor, and so there are two of them mourning, and not him alone.

Such a weight of grief.

Open water. There are fissures, where ice seams fracture and fret. And places like ponds, where the water stirs uneasily, and steam rises in the dawn. Warmer waters welling up. The fresh meat is gone, and the sausages, and the cheese. He's sparing of the fuel for the fat-lamp, has to defend it. Tolla says, a bit of heat to melt water will do them no good if they're too weak to keep moving. They nearly came to blows that morning, the others sharing out chunks of frozen bacon fat to gnaw on. But open water—he demands his purse of Tolla, gestures—hook, casting a line…

"You want to fish?" Tolla is disbelieving, shaking his head. "We can't waste time. There could be another storm any day."

"No, he's right," Gillesh says. "We need food, Tolla. What good is pushing on and starving ourselves?"

So tired, all the time. As if his bones have turned to stone, and the others must feel the same. The cold, the labour of forcing their way on, bent under the ceaseless wind. Even Tolla, who carried a little weight about his belly, is hollow-cheeked now, and Ekkard's face is shadowed like a skull, his eyes bruised. Often he stands with a hand to his temple, where the hair is still matted with black crusted scabs, as if it pains him.

Tolla, grumbling, takes out the stolen purses, makes a show of checking one, then the other. A few coins, maybe, Lannesk doesn't remember. Their flints and firesteels, the whetstone, gut strings for his harp, which he could maybe make a snare of, but there are neither hares nor squirrels out here, the quill-ends of feathers to be trimmed for harp-nails—each examined and put back, Tolla enjoying taunting him with his stolen possessions. Finally, folded into a scrap of soft leather, fishhooks and a coil of line, carried so long. He and Anzimor hadn't even fished, that last good evening they camped by the beaver-meadow where the fat trout would rise in the deep pool behind the decaying dam. Tolla hands him the hooks and line.

He uses a scrap of frozen bacon-fat as bait. Gillesh makes him a rod from a thick bit of their fir-bough bedding, and another for herself. Ekkard becomes cheerful, not to be pulling the toboggan. Or maybe he remembers some happy time, fishing in the Forest back on Laikyn.

Possible to get quite close to the edge of the water. The ice doesn't reach out in a thin sheet; it's rounded and thick, a lasting shore on some warmer upwelling. They squat there with their lines, heads hunched into hoods.

Tolla grabs at Ekkard, who goes too close. Has to tug him away.

It's a good place. Fish gather, Lannesk guesses, because the rising warmer water is going to draw up whatever it is fish eat in the deep winter. Bits of water-weed. Snails. Whatever. Each other.

Gillesh's little fir-cone float bobs first. She jerks the line to set her hook, pulls up a thrashing silvery char. Not a big one, but fat.

Tolla comes to clean it. Ekkard chuckles, delighted.

More char, both of them, till they have two dozen, and some of them a fair size, ten pounds or more. A big grandmother trout. And then something that fights and nearly breaks Lannesk's line, but Gillesh gets Tolla's spear and manages to stab it against the ice-edge. They haul it in, a pike four foot long, and still fighting, till Tolla clubs it. But Lannesk is water-drenched from the struggle, not soaked through but the outer layers of his clothes freezing. Enough. The char have moved off or stopped biting anyway. They get the hut built, and he gets out of his wet top layers and rolled in quilts, while Tolla goes foraging for driftwood, of which there is some around this patch of disturbed water, to make a proper fire on the ice. They hang Lannesk's dripping clothing on poles to dry and roast four of the fish. The fire hisses, subsiding into damp ashes; they pile wood above the growing puddle on the surface till there's no more within easy finding and they've made a water-filled hollow in the ice beneath the half-burnt foundation layer of the fire.

Another day, like the last, and another. Some nights there's enough wood to be gleaned to make a fire, roast fish. Sometimes they just hack them apart and thaw them a bit over the lamp. Snow is piled deep, packed hard. Drifts rise, wind-sculpted, to curl in knife-edged waves.

They clamber up, flounder down. Wind scours ice clear and skis slither sideways on blue-green-grey that seems to glow in the sunlight. Impossible depths.

Snow-glare gives headaches, sears the eyes, threatens them with ice-blindness. One gets used to going with frosted lashes slitted against the dazzle.

Ice rears in ridges, broken boulders. Long detours around, or dangerous climbing over. Ekkard, clumsy, as if he can't quite control the movements of arms and legs—he's always losing a ski, falling—slips and tumbles down one such ridge, and lies silent at the bottom. Lannesk slides down after him, heart hammering, no no no, and at the same time, please, let it be over, so swift, so clean, and can he get a knife off Tolla when he comes down—since they don't trust Ekkard with one, guessing rightly Lannesk would get hold of it—deal with Tolla—but Gillesh first, she's the one with the bow—

What's become of him, that he's planning murder?

His life's forfeit, if he comes again into Earl Tannis's lands. Tolla seems to have forgotten that, or doesn't care, so long as Lannesk gets him there.

But Ekkard hasn't broken his neck after all, blinks up at Lannesk, when he gently turns him over. Puzzled, tears leaking from his eyes. As if somehow the fall has jarred something, just for a moment, back into place. Just long enough for him to know he's lost it. Lannesk takes his hands, helps him sit up, checks him over. Nothing broken. Tolla slides down and together they help Ekkard climb up.

That's a long day, clambering through that jagged terrain where sheets of ice have ground together, a great rough seam, a scar. And the toboggan and their skis to lug, without losing any of what they need to survive.

Bitter wind, that night. And the next. And they struggle on, slow, slogging. Still taking their mark from the stars, northwest to Laikyn.

~LANNESK~

A raven. Lannesk watches it, long enough to be certain, eyes narrowed against the glare. Watches Tolla, Gillesh. Maybe they see it, maybe they don't notice, trudge-shuffling ski and ski, left and right, one and two, breath and breath, head-down, all of them, even Ekkard, with a rope to the toboggan looped over their shoulders. Neither points it out, or seems to watch.

Raven. Two, flying together. Out over ice, searching, maybe, for what may have strayed to some death there. He doesn't think that ravens fly out far from shore.

Grey horizon, ice meeting blue sky. But it's there, the coast. The ravens say so. He watches, till they're faint black specks heading northerly, nothing more.

Tolla and Gillesh can't chase him if he runs away in the night; they've got Ekkard to look after. But they—Ekkard being the one he cares about—won't die now for his leaving them, as they would have at the start. And they don't keep a watch anymore. Far from the pursuit of enemies, and all lying so close together, Tolla seems to have decided that there's no need to fear that Lannesk can rob them unnoticed, though the spearcarl carries the bundle of the Wild King's sword in every night, and lies with it beneath his arm. A prize he's decided is for Earl Tannis alone, Lannesk figures. Gillesh eyes it sometimes, as if wondering.

Lannesk doesn't need it. Just a knife, any knife. The sword—is only a weapon. It holds no holiness to overcome the dragon-kin in itself. It's a blade, and he can find another. What he needs is knives, to whittle wood, make a fire-drill; he can start a fire with so little, if need be. Won't risk his life for anything more. Gillesh puts her knife beneath her head. Might be able to get it away, if he sleeps next to her.

Once into the Forest, they won't catch him and if they're south of the Borlinn, or if he can cross it, get down into the lands below the Fairnmere, he'll be safe enough. There are earls of the south of the island would take him on, give him a place as spearcarl or hunter, for Brux's sake. Give him a few month's shelter, at least, till he can get off Laikyn altogether.

Wonders, will the dragon-kin take all the lands of the Lake? Will the earls muster and sail to the Holy Isle? What, even, is the story being carried from the Isle of the Grey Hunter's death and the Wild King's last song, and the Dragon woken from the Lake and cast out into the Dark Beyond?

Mind wandering too far. Knife and fire and enough distance between him and the spearcarls of Earl Tannis. Cross that first bridge. All else follows.

He looks up for the ravens again, but they're gone.

And that's when Ekkard cries out and vanishes.

Tolla and Ekkard were in the middle of their fanned-out towing spread, Lannesk and Gillesh on the outer lines. The three of them are all swinging in, skiing fast. Black water, like a small Forest pool, a spring's upwelling. Tolla's kicked off his skis, down on his knees, the spear he uses for a pole stabbed into the ice, rope looped around it. He's struggling, pulling in line as if to draw up a fish. Lannesk kicks off skis still moving, drops down beside him, lying prone, and they drag the rope hand over hand over hand. Tolla swears steadily, as if to curse the Mothers and Ekkard's murdered wits is prayer.

Gillesh fetches up behind them, leaning on her pole, watching without comment. Without offering a hand, either.

"Get wood!" Tolla shouts, without looking back at her. "Get a fire going. Burn the damned toboggan if you have to, but get a fire going."

A snow-mound hut takes time—time to pile the snow and let it settle and set before it can be hollowed out, time to warm up—but without a fire Ekkard could die before they can do all that. Lannesk's mittens are soaked and freezing to the rope, hands stinging with what is only the first bite of the cold.

Not struggling. Not trying to swim, to fight his way back to the land. They pull Ekkard in like a dead fish. At least the tow rope still about his shoulders lets them do so. And his layers of wool and leather trapped air enough to keep him afloat, those few first moments. Soaking through, now. Heavy. He'll sink like a stone if they slip, dragging him out.

It's like when he fell, climbing through the ice-ridge. Not dead, but just gone passive. Finished. He stares up at the sky, while waves of shivering course over him.

They drag him far from the edge. Tolla's outer layers are soaking, too, and freezing stiff with ice.

"Dark take her, where's—" But then Tolla sees Gillesh, almost a quarter of a mile away, where there's something straggling from the ice, a scribble against the blue-white world. And the first orange tongues of a fire.

They bundle Ekkard into their own capes, sheepskin and wolf, pile him on the toboggan, find their skis—his are gone, floating in the water but they don't try to salvage them then—coil the tow-ropes up short and set off at a shuffling run.

Which at least warms them.

Gillesh has found a tree, a double-trunked spruce fallen or torn from water's edge, not in this most recent autumn's storms, because the bark and needles are gone and the twigs broken away, broken tips of the branches smoothed and rounded. She took the axe with her, hacked some limbs off, made a platform and then built her fire above that. More branches and chips lie ready. They strip Ekkard, who tries to curl up away from them, roll him in dry quilts, get him huddling on more dry wood, with the great log at his back to break the wind. Lannesk gets the jug they use for water, packs it with ice bashed off the trunk, sets it to heat. Get something warm into his belly. Gillesh takes over that, and finds sticks to jab into the snow, hangs dripping clothes to steam.

"Get the shovel, get us some shelter made," she orders. And Tolla, wrapped in a quilt over his tunic, is chafing Ekkard's hands and feet, still swearing. Leaves off to hug him, shake him, goes back to his rubbing of hands and feet.

He cares. Brute that he is, he does care for his charge, beyond that he's the earl's son. Or he's come to care for him, for his own sake, through this need to tend him as a child.

That makes some choices—easier. Or it should.

Lannesk, left without any eye on him to unstrap the shovel from the toboggan, rootles a hand into the bundle wrapped in that singed and dirty cloak and retrieves both his dagger and knife. Shoves them down the neck of his tunic, leather and buckles cold against his skin, since he still has no shirt beneath, gone to bandage Anzimor's wound, but the bulkiness of his fur vest hides the lumpy bulge they make above his belt.

Shovel. There's a high drift like a wave curling around behind the marooned tree. No need to pile up a mound and wait for it to set. He starts digging, a low tunnel rising to a higher floor, hollowing out a domed ceiling, leaving some ledges to keep the lamp from setting their bedding alight. Makes sure of the direction of the wind before he chisels out a vent.

Tolla, meanwhile, has rigged a shelter from a couple of the quilts. They strain like sails in the wind, but trap some heat. He's pushed Ekkard closer to the fire than is safe, beats out sparks that land on his wrappings. Tolla gets him to drink hot water with bacon-fat melted into it. Soup, he says, his hands over Ekkard's, cupping the looted bowl.

"Drink the soup, boy, come on, you need the warmth in you."

Ekkard looks up at Lannesk, standing over him. Such bleak eyes.

Lannesk turns away.

Bright afternoon. You don't ski into open water, dark against the white glitter, in the bright afternoon. Not by accident. Might he have been skiing blind, eyes clenched shut to ease them? Lannesk doesn't think so.

They keep Ekkard by the fire as night falls, roast steaks cut through the pike, pick the bones clean, make porridge with bacon-fat in it and eat that too, crowded shoulder to shoulder, faces to the fire, backs to the driftwood tree. Faces too hot, backs shivering, Ekkard's clothing, hung to dry, beginning to scorch. Gillesh goes to unload the toboggan of their remaining bedding, dragging the battered fir-boughs into the tunnel, lighting the wick of the fat-lamp dish at the fire to start the snow-cave heating.

The moon had been in its first quarter when they set out from the Holy Isle. Yearsturn's gone now and Snowsdeep as well. The moon's a few days past its first quarter again, rising after noon, setting after midnight—startling, to realize they're into the month of Springsturn. They must be within a couple weeks of the balance-day, Lannesk supposes. Certainly the days are growing swiftly longer. No wonder they're so deadly weary, ravenous; they drive themselves on through all the daylight that's offered.

No fear of the Lake-ice melting. The thaw's not so close as all that, though landcarls will be thinking of tapping the trees, soon.

The waxing moon will give him light enough to avoid any more open water, or the hazards of rough ice, but it will make pursuit easier. Half the night. And then the deep dark. Cloudless sky. Starlight and snow might be enough to let him see open water—or at least, to tell darkness from snow, and test whether it's water or shadow before he plunges into it.

He thinks he can trust now that Tolla won't abandon Ekkard to come after him. He won't count Lannesk worth it, now he's got them most of the way to Laikyn.

Gillesh will hold a grudge, will pursue it. Better, maybe, to be sure she can't.

No. He won't murder.

Sun sets, scarlet and rose along the southwestern horizon. They get Ekkard back into his clothes, warm and dry. He's still limp, barely responsive. Still breaking out in shivers.

I'm sorry, Lannesk wants to say. If that was your choice, if there's still something remembering in you to choose, then I'm so sorry we stopped you. He puts his arms around Ekkard, who stands, a quilt over him like an extra cloak. Holds him close. Maybe he'll understand that for a farewell, come the morning. But likely he won't even remember.

"Leave him alone," Gillesh says.

"Leave Lannesk alone," Tolla says. "We'd have been dead weeks back without him."

Tells himself again, they'll be fine without him, now that he's taught them what they need. They'll be within sight of the coast tomorrow, surely. The ravens, the increasing amount of frozen flotsam, promise it.

Gillesh shrugs, not looking at any of them.

They let the fire start to die. They can't sit out all night. Everything's dry. The puddle the fire has made in the deep ice, beneath the platform of wet wood that stops it falling into its own meltwater, will freeze again.

Tolla fusses, getting Ekkard settled in the midst of them, himself and Lannesk to either side, the biggest bodies. Gillesh lies down by Tolla. Feet towards the tunnel, all of them, and that closed with a bundle of cedar-boughs, battered needles still sweet-scented.

They press close against Ekkard. He's not shivering any longer, but he didn't eat nearly enough.

Too easy to fall into sleep. Just one more night, get some rest. Leave them tomorrow night.

No, Lannesk tells himself. Tomorrow night could be too late. Laikyn could be just over the horizon. He forces his eyes to stay open, listens to them breathing, Tolla already deep, slow; Ekkard fast and shallow. Cold, and Lannesk shifts a little closer against him. That seems to comfort him. Gillesh's breath is slowing, falling into sleep. Lannesk drifts.

Jerks awake.

A noise.

He's slept, damned fool, he doesn't know how long, and there was a sound.

Someone grunting, that's all. Breaking wind, whatever. Time to go, if he's going. Listens, to be sure no one else was woken by whatever it was. Ekkard is breathing too rapidly again, little whimpers in it. A bad dream, and small wonder if all his dreams are bad, now.

Silence.

Silence, too deep.

Slowly, carefully, Lannesk lifts the quilts, crawls out, tucking them close against Ekkard.

Something's wrong. He meant to crawl out, take his outerwear and the tunic he'd managed to bundle around his blades to keep them hidden, the socks and boots he'd kept under the blankets to stay warm while they dried of the day's sweat, meant to finish dressing outside, but—

Might be his one chance to get away from them. If Tolla notices the dagger and knife are missing from where he had wrapped them with the sword, if he threatens Ekkard to bring Lannesk to heel—

He won't harm Ekkard. Lannesk has convinced himself of that.

His own stealthy breathing, Ekkard's—

The silence is still too deep. He can't ignore it.

He reaches over Ekkard, touches Tolla's chest—

The quilts are thrust down. And he's wet. Warm, and wet.

He wipes his hand on quilts, finds Tolla's face, shakes him by the shoulder. Ekkard whimpers again, and squirms over towards Lannesk.

Lannesk crawls upright to get the lamp, hold it close.

Stabbed. Dark stain over Tolla's chest, where a knife's been withdrawn.

Gillesh's place is empty.

Ekkard is on hands and knees, staring at Tolla. Shivering, shaking his head.

Carefully, Lannesk sets the lamp back in its place, takes Ekkard by the shoulders, turns him away. Shakes his head. Not me, he means. I didn't do it. Ekkard doesn't think so. He grabs onto Lannesk, shivering, whimpering.

"Shh," he whispers in the man's ear. "Shh, shh." Rocks him a little, till he's silent.

Gets his socks and boots on, the tunic pulled over his head.

The blood was still warm.

"Stay here," he tries to say in Ekkard's ear, but it comes out breathy, indistinct. "Stay."

He doesn't know if he was understood. Hesitates, gives his sheathed knife to Ekkard. Draws the dragger. There's a sound outside, a tapping, rapping sort of noise.

He moves the bit of windbreak of cedar, crawls down the tunnel. Crouches in the dark entrance, letting his eyes adjust to the moonlight.

Gillesh hasn't fled. She's over by the toboggan. Stealing food before she runs. That tap, tap, thunk sound—not sure what she's doing. Lannesk rises, treading softly, but the night is cold and the snow squeaks. Gillesh jerks around. Turns back to whatever she was doing, but it's a hard blow this time, a loud metallic thunk, and she snatches something and leaps to her feet. It's the axe in her hand, raised menacing.

"You can come," she says. "You and me, down into South Laikyn and the earl will never know. Make our fortunes. Or you can nursemaid the idiot to shore on your own and see what thanks you get from Tannis. What's it going to be?" She's swinging the axe a little. She's got a rolled bundle over her shoulders, food inside a quilt, at a guess, and her skis lying ready.

She saw the ravens. She knows how close they are to land. But what did she need to take the axe to?

She waves her left hand, gripping—something, he can't see what.

"Make our fortunes," she says again. "What do you think?"

Lannesk understands, then. The sword wasn't by Tolla and he doesn't remember whether the man carried the bundle in that night or not. And for all Tolla never said a word of it, and Gillesh neither, they'd been among those who survived to the last. They must know where he'd come by that sword, even before either of them took a good look at it.

Lannesk shrugs, arms wide, to show no threat, though he doesn't drop his dagger. Steps aside. Let her go. It's only a stone, no magic in it to wield against the dragon-kin. More power in a song.

"That's your answer?" She seems disappointed. "That's your choice? What kind of a life is this for the boy, anyway? And you know Tannis won't thank you."

He doesn't know that. She's Ekkard's mother.

Besides, Ekkard is improving in the little things. Getting better mastery of his arms and legs, a bit. Watching with more awareness. Like a dog, knowing that important things are happening even if he doesn't understand them, not the vacant look of a new baby. Perhaps he can recover at least a part of what he was. Old folks who suffer palsy-strokes do, sometimes. Lannesk has no right to take Ekkard away into some roving lordless life, steal him from the family who must love him. No desire to, either. Wants to know he's safe with kin and not Lannesk's responsibility any longer.

Not that Gillesh has any intention of taking Ekkard along, wherever she plans to go, even if Lannesk says he'll join her.

Not that she'll have any intention of letting Lannesk live through the first night of sleeping at her side, either. She only left him alive because she could be certain that with Tolla dead, Lannesk would stay with Ekkard and not come hunting her. To try to kill Lannesk would have meant reaching over Ekkard, maybe waking him, warning them both.

"You're a fool," Gillesh says, and shoves what has to be the bluestone of the sword's pommel into the breast of her tunic, sliding toes into the straps of her skis. "Don't try to follow me."

He shakes his head. Last thing he wants to do.

Wordless cry. Ekkard, bolting up out of the mouth of the tunnel towards her, clutching Lannesk's knife. Gillesh yells and hurls the axe at him—he yelps, falling.

Diving for the toboggan, dagger dropped and ripping the abandoned sword from its scabbard, up and running—Lannesk's on her as she grabs up the axe again, raising it for a better blow as Ekkard crouches, hands over his head. Lannesk swings the sword, and Gillesh rocks backward, staring up at him, mouth gaping, and the axe falling from her hands. She falls with it, backwards, not her mouth but her throat that's open.

Lannesk drops the sword, arms around Ekkard, who's whimpering again. Distress, not pain. The handle of the axe struck his shoulder, no worse.

"Good," Lannesk tries to say in Ekkard's ear. "Safe." Can't tell if Ekkard understands, but he calms, though he's shivering, no tunic over his shirt and barefoot, too.

Gillesh is dead, dark stain on the snow spreading around her. Lannesk wants to leave her lie. Not knowing how much of their food she meant to steal…he retrieves his dagger and kneels down, cuts the quilt she used to make her bundle, drags it away before blood can soil it. His venison jerky, the trail-meat balls. Nearly all they have left save for a bit of the pike.

He picks up the axe, tosses it over towards the toboggan. Not something he can afford to forget in the morning. Takes Ekkard back into the snow-cave, hushes him, when he whimpers again at touching Tolla. Gets socks on his poor icy feet and quilts over him. Wraps Tolla's body in the soiled quilt he's lying on and drags him out, crawling backwards. Straightens him out, folds his hands together over his breast. The moon's sliding down the southwest sky. Almost midnight, he thinks. The corpse will be stiff by morning, frozen.

Doesn't think she deserves it, but wearily, he does the same for Gillesh. Because—he didn't do anything for the comrades he left under the honeysuckles, and someone should have. And it will make it easier to move her, if she's not all splayed and crooked. Remembers the bluestone set in the clawed pommel of the sword, takes it from her.

He cleans his hands in the snow and goes back in to Ekkard, lies close against him all night, feeling how cold he is, how he shivers. First the drenching, near drowning, now this chill, and in a man who seems, maybe, to be seeking his own end.

"Mother," he tries to say. "Taking you home to your mother, Ekkard." But it's mostly breath, to any ear but Anzimor's.

Feels tears. They gather, trickle slow and cold down his face. He's had no stillness yet to weep for his brother. Can't afford it now. Needs rest. Needs to gather strength against the morning.

Lies wakeful till the blue glow around the vent and in the tunnel tells him that the dawn has come.

He and Ekkard drag Tolla and Gillesh, frozen, heavy, to the patch of open water. Push them in. They sink, not like stones, but pulled down swiftly enough by soaking clothing. It doesn't hide the evidence of bloody death, though another good snowfall will, but anything that makes murder less obvious, should any hunters or fishers venture out this far, makes him feel a little safer. Ekkard bows his head. Lips mumble.

"Mothers," he whispers at last. Broken ghost of a prayer.

Mothers, yes, Mothers Above and Below be thanked. A word. There's something of a mind left, and it's working. Coming back. Lannesk hugs him, trying by that to say, Aye, don't despair. Don't throw yourself into any more freezing water. You're going to find your way back. Mothers, please.

They load up the toboggan with the least he thinks they can risk, to keep on surviving, and leave the rest in the snow-cave. He wraps the jewel, clasped still in gilded claws but ending in a broken stump, in a bit of cloth, puts it in one of his purses taken back from Tolla's corpse, knotting the straps the man had cut. They rope themselves up, set out, Ekkard carrying Tolla's weapons, using Tolla's skis. Lannesk has the Wild King's sword on its baldric over his shoulder. The balance is off, the broken upper end of the hilt jagged. She must have decided the stone would be easier to carry on its own. Easier to hide from other thieves. If she'd just taken the sword and gone, he'd never have followed.

By mid-afternoon there's a dark, ragged, rough line on the horizon. Trees.

Land.

~MAIRRAN~

The morning of the last day of Slaughtermonth was clear and windless, but when I went out before breakfast to breathe fresh air and turn the ravens loose, a high haze blurred the rising sun and the air smelt again of snow.

Back in the hall, "A day's rest," Lord Raynar announced, standing at the high table, laid out with bread and small ale, maple-cakes filled with nuts and dried berries, dishes of salt butter, cheese, potato-cakes, fermented vegetables, and buttermilk and cold meats. Breakfast for a hard day's riding. He leaned on his hands, looking down over the hall, and his eyes were shadowed. Worn by more than the past days of hunting. Lady Rikenza had not joined us that morning at all.

"A day's rest," Raynar repeated, more loudly, standing straight and raising a hand to draw the attention of the hall, where the spearcarls and swordtheyns on their benches were eating, talking softly among themselves, most dressed already for riding out. And then, throwing a glower my way, "If my lord prince agrees."

Men and women, horses and even hounds were weary. I saw relief in the faces below, and apprehension that I'd say otherwise. "If you wish," I said, and nodded to the hall. "But," I added, aside to Raynar, "I'd like it if you yourself would ride out with me anyway, my lord."

Breakfast was not so formal a meal and no servants stood at our shoulders to serve. My folk were close enough to hear, down on the nearest end of a bench at the trestle tables. Nowa frowned up at me, and Sage went still and expressionless, as she did when she was uncertain what was expected of her. Wary, watchful, and always learning.

"Why?" Lord Raynar asked bleakly. "This is futile. I'm willing to admit it, my lord. He's a witch himself, maybe. Forest-blessed as well as Forest-cunning. He calls the winds to hide his tracks. I promise you, we'll never give up the watch for him, for my mother's sake, but we aren't going to take him this way, and you may as well return to the Queen and say so."

Give up, go home before the Lake freezes, get out of his hair. Raynar might as well have said as much. Only the day before, Ermintrud had sent a couple of her crew to tell me that I had a day or two, no more, to decide on taking the *Snow Goose* out; I'd sent them back to tell her to do it.

"Maybe," I said. "But ride out with me today none the less. I want to see the heartstone where your mother died."

Raynar's whole face stilled, very like Sage in her moments of uncertainty.

"My lord prince—" he began.

I drained my cup and rose from the table. "Let's not waste the daylight."

I saw Sage shove a couple of apples into the breast of her tunic. As bad as the ravens, who left crusts and rinds and bones tucked into folded bedding or inside boots. Instinctive fear of impending dearth. Sage, at least, never left her snacks to spoil.

Raynar brought only one of his shieldlings, a young woman named Pool, and an older spearcarl called Orsten, one of the castle's archers. He might have chosen to annoy me, to see how far he could push, by calling for some of the swordtheyns and carls and denying them their promised day of rest, collecting a company to delay and slow us, and he did not, say that for him. We were over the bridge and heading through Fairnshore before the sun was much higher over the little lake.

We went armoured, Nowa and I, and I'd requisitioned a heavy moosehide vest for Sage once she and Nowa had begun joining the hunt some days before. I no longer expected murder from Raynar's folk but still—no need to be a fool. Rayner, too, went armed and in mail.

I chose not to let Raynar lead the way, but followed the road the ravens took, away from Fairnshore and across the Reedcreek valley, up among the rising hills.

"You know the way, my lord? You've spoken with my hunters?" Raynar asked, when I turned off the narrow foresters' road and onto a track that was little more than a depression in the undulating white, unmarked by any spoor save where a wolf had run, and those big pawprints were mostly smeared away by windblown snow.

"Should I have?" I asked.

Raynar looked at the ravens, going tree to tree ahead of us, and back to me. Declined to answer that.

We strung out along the track, which followed the crest of a rising ridge and then plunged down into a hollow, coming upon the border-stones of the fane before I expected, grey and sudden, the vast trees around still, the wind fallen away. Silent, but for the stamp of horse and creak of harness. Not even a jay called alarm. Raynar dismounted and sent his folk to look about, went within the stones on foot. I followed, with Nowa keeping close. She left Sage mounted and keeping a watch.

Nothing larger than a hare had come through the fane since the last snow fell. The holy tree over the heartstone might have taken six or seven people, arms spread, to span about its bole. Lesser seedlings, mature trees now themselves, had grown up about it, some pushing the boundary stones askew. The ground was rough, hummocky beneath the snow. The heartstone itself was partially engulfed by the tree.

Raynar squatted down facing the stone's foot, arms wrapped around his knees, head bowed. Holding talk with his dead, maybe, if only in his own mind. I didn't think anything of the murdered earl lingered there. No ghosts gathered, drawn to our living warmth. I pulled off my mitten and touched the stone, traced the outline of the only visible carving, which was at head-height. It was as Raynar had described it, a horned rider, or maybe the figure wore a horned crown. A running horse.

"It was an offering," I said, when I thought Raynar had had enough time for his prayers or whatever he was about. Waiting, maybe, only for someone else to break the silence. "Earl Raynellin bled herself. Your sister said it."

Raynar looked up, frowning, as if he didn't quite understand. "No. Rikenza didn't see—what was here. She misunderstood."

"Did she?"

"She was stabbed, my lord. My mother was stabbed. Stabbed to the heart. She did not do that to herself." His voice shook.

She might have. Not what I'd been suggesting, though.

"Stabbed in the heart, Lord Raynar, she would not have spilt much blood on the ground." I leaned my spear against the tree, shifted my sword out of the way, and squatted down beside him. "Yet you said yourself, *so much blood*. Tell me again, how she was lying."

Even if the snow had not been a foot deep over the frozen ground, there would have been nothing to see, to smell. The autumn rains and the hungry earth had taken care of that.

Cold seemed to strike outwards from the stone, but that was only the lowering afternoon sun, ruddy light slanting through the trees, and the winter's dark, and the shadows. Night would fall well before we could reach Mair Laikyn again. Snow crunched, the horses moving restlessly.

"I don't know," Raynar said, impatient, maybe, that I wouldn't leave him in peace to brood. "She was there. Against the stone. On the ground. I didn't—"

"My lord!" Sage's voice, sharp, and I smelt them then, horse, man, and leapt to my feet, to the top of one of the boundary stones as if I'd flown there, and saw the wild man where he had come to the lip of the dell, sitting the red stallion, his rough-made spear canted at ease on his shoulder, watching from among the trees. Light caught in his pale hair, a bronze-lit haze.

"Stay here," I began to say, but with a loud cry, Raynar had bolted to his feet, clutching at his breast as if at some amulet beneath his cloak that might protect him. His spearcarl Orsten had kneed his horse around and slapped an arrow to his strung bow. Loosed.

I thought the carl had missed, at first, because the wild man only stared, though his horse laid back his ears and flung up his head, and somewhere dogs roared their fury. Or maybe the howling and baying was only in my mind. The red horse turned, as if the rider had kneed him about, and the man folded down, slowly, clutching at the long pale mane, and then sliding to the ground.

I don't remember moving. I don't remember thinking. But Orsten was flat in the snow, my knee on his chest, the longer of the two flint blades in my hand, curved edge of golden stone, and I pushed Orsten's head back and cut his throat.

The Mothers Below may hold that weight for me to carry, when I come again to them. My only realization then was the profanation of the knife. That was no reverent offering, only rage and pain, and the black emptiness of something lost.

Blood enough then, though shed outside the fane. Orsten was dead even before he had realized he would die, and my face was drenched with the spray of his blood. It dripped from my helmet and ran into my eyes, filled my panting mouth, hot and wet, salt and sweet. It stained the cape of my hood, the front of my cloak, breast of surcoat, my sleeves. Scarlet, the snow.

The ravens came to feed.

"I said, I wanted him alive." On my feet then, and Raynar with his sword drawn as if he would avenge his man, his shieldling's spear held for casting, yet her look uncertain, between me and her lord and my shield-companion.

Nowa, her spear's point at Raynar's throat.

"My lord!" Sage called again, urgent, and then, a shriek, "*Mairran,* help!"

I shoved the bloody knife through my belt and ran to her.

She was kneeling over the wild man, mittens dropped and her hands bloody as my own, but she had the man over her lap, turned half to his side, and hands clamping bunched cloth over the bleeding wounds. The arrow had taken him below the breast. It pierced him through, wicked point emerging below his shoulder-blade, and blood bubbled in his mouth, stained his beard.

He wasn't dead. That washed out the rage, where even her cry had not. I fell more than knelt at her side, hardly noticed the look of horror on her face, how she flinched and nearly tumbled the man off her lap, nearly flung herself away from me.

Remembered it later. Then, there was only fear that I would lose him yet.

Not his heart. He lived, he bled, he fought to breathe. I was spilling words, I don't know what mad things. Denying the Dark Mother and the Bright. Telling the wild man, I was here, I had found him, I had him safe and he would live, he must live. Hands bloody with what should not have been sacrifice on his wounds, and yet sacrifice felt like what it might have been, while Sage looked at me again, and she was still afraid.

The wild man didn't cry out, nor try to struggle away. Only his eyes fixed on mine. They were greenish-grey, like the Lake under cloud, pupils black, devouring them, and what he was seeing I don't know, but he didn't think it was myself.

"What do we do, my lord?" Sage asked. "What can we do?" She still held him, with my hands over her own.

"Breathe," I said, not to her. "You can breathe. You can." And to Sage, "We get this arrow out."

"He'll bleed," Nowa said over us.

"He's already bleeding."

Spear in hand, but Raynar was at her side and his sword sheathed again. Dishevelled, though, as if they'd tussled. If they had, Nowa had the upper hand of it. Pool was mounted and kept her distance, as if she expected she might need to flee, to carry word of—what, another lord of Laikyn dead in this place?

"Get down here," I told the shieldling. "We need another pair of hands." And I did not want them to be Raynar's. Nowa, I knew, would not set aside her weapons, not there, not then.

I had a flask of snaps—I'd thought we would all be glad of a little of its warmth when we ate the bread and cheese we'd carried—and I sent Raynar to my saddlebags to fetch it.

A narrow, leaf-bladed arrowhead, and more than two-thirds of it emerged from the wild man's back. So we cut the fletching off, and I poured snaps over the shaft, because the physicians who come back from studies at Goslack say that there are poisons in earth and air and the touch of sweaty hands that breed wound-rot, and that strong spirits or fire or soap render them clean, and we pushed and drew the arrow through.

The wild man didn't scream. Jerked, once, and went limp in Sage's arms, though his breath still whined and bubbled. His lips faded to a pallid blue. His skin felt cold as the snow to my touch, and was nearly white as palest ash. I doused the wounds with the snaps, for what that might do, and the scent of blood and caraway together was vile.

The wild man would die, of course. An hour, a day. Drown in his own blood, or fall fevered and festering as he rotted from the wound outwards. But I tore up my shirt into wadding and we bandaged the man over the ruin of what he wore, and wrapped him in my cloak and Nowa's.

He kept on breathing.

We couldn't take him up with any of us, not in his condition, not if we didn't want to batter him beyond clinging to what little life he still held. Nowa had a hatchet among her gear, of course, because she was Nowa, and took thought for such things, and folly to ride out into the Forest without being prepared to spend the night. It did not take long for her and Shieldling Pool to cut saplings, a narrow frame lashed to long shafts, fixed to the pony, the saddle and its breastcollar for harness. A slide-car, as if they dragged fish up from the shore. He'd pulled carts before, Sage said. A good little beast, who wouldn't kick or bolt—she told him so, and he rolled a purple-brown eye at her and sighed, and lowered his head to rub against her.

I never wondered that Sage had caught my urgency, my certainty that the wild man was our care, that he must not die. Nowa, I was sure, was only saving up comment for a more private moment.

I put Sage up on Smoke and led the pony myself, though once I was certain the beast would keep on his way I went to walk behind. As if having the man before my eyes would hold him fast, keep the breath and blood in him. I suppose they thought I was mad to even hope the man might survive to come to Mair Laikyn. And to have killed the loyal man, who had—perhaps justly—brought down his liege-lady's murderer. Accused murderer.

"He was married again, just last summer," Raynar said, casting a look back at Orsten's body, shrouded in the man's own cloak and tied over the saddle of his horse, a horrible bundle that was going to stiffen and maybe freeze into that arched shape before we reached the castle. Then his gaze flung past that, to me, trudging afoot in the trampled snow, only Nowa following behind, watching my back, though Mothers knew, with Raynar and Pool riding ahead, maybe my enemies here were all before me. But there was Sage, leading on Smoke, and at least I would see them coming if they turned on me. While Sage, I could hope, shot them in the back.

"He had a husband," Raynar said. "He had three young children."

"I'd told them all, I wanted the wild man alive. They knew. *He* knew. What orders did you give to the contrary, Lord Raynar? Shall I ask Shieldling Pool?"

"Not to kill him," he said bitterly. "And your wild man's still alive."

Mine now, was he?

Kill him, my mother had said.

"You really think," I asked, "that he'll live to come to Mair Laikyn?" Rage had burnt out; I was exhausted, weary and heavy and grey, and tasting ashes again in my mouth, and still the tang of Orsten's blood.

Carried the scent of him, strong and cloying, soaked into wool and leather and grimy in the rings of my mail.

Nowa brought Thorn trotting up alongside me, once Raynar was facing ahead again, riding hunched and—angry, I thought, and not for Orsten's death. My shield-companion said nothing, only reached a hand down to me. I thought she meant some comfort, till I saw she gripped something fast in her glove, torn ends of a thin ribbon dangling. Couldn't read her eyes, which could sometimes be as deep and opaque as bluestone, so I opened my hand and took what she gave me, which was a little pouch sewn of fine linen. No need to open it; I could feel the shape of what it held, the rough texture of the spray of cedar around which I'd wrapped the three pale hairs caught where a horseman had ridden to kill my enemies.

The moon had risen, swelling gibbous, smeared by high thin cloud. It stood out over the lake, high as it would ever climb in this season, and was fast fading to a faint smudge, with fine stinging snow on the wind, by the time we came finally again to Mair Laikyn.

Against all expectation, the wild man was still breathing, shallow but slow, dragging, wheezing—less blood and froth then there had been, and his body was not swelling against his ribs, the way a lung-wound sometimes would, nor was air bubbling out through the wounds.

The Forest took its due sacrifice, though I had not offered the blood at the heartstone.

And gave blessing in return? That was not how it should be. Abominable to think so, to think one might bargain in death and blood. That was not the truth of the rite.

Dragon-kin perversion.

But still, the wild man lived, with only my bloody, murdering hands laid on him.

All the virtue lies in him. The strength, and the innocence, and the great blessing of the Forest.

Yes, I told her, because sometimes I had to answer, voice of my madness or not.

The need.

My need? The Forest's? My ghost did not say.

He will live. He must.

All the way to Mair Laikyn, the red stallion had trailed us, there and gone and back again among the trees, like an uneasy ghost himself. Even through the lanes of Fairnshore. Only at the bridge he stood, as we followed its zigzag course, and flung up his head and whinnied wild, and then turned and ran, as doors opened, spilling folk and firelight, to see what the stir might be.

I thought I heard wolves howling, but maybe it was only dogs.

I paid blood-fees to the husband and, for the children, the former wife of the spearcarl Orsten, though there was never any accusation made of murder or unlawful killing. Fastest means, Nowa said, to make that whole problem go away. Wasn't sure I agreed—I had warned them, how many times, that I wanted the wild man alive. If Orsten had been given orders to the contrary, which I suspected he had, it shouldn't have been I who had to buy peace of the man's kin—though I paid it out of Laikyn's revenues, not my mother's purse. And in case peace wasn't to be bought with silver, Lord Raynar sent the husband's family, skilled leather-workers, parents and siblings and their partners and children, and Orsten's former wife and their children as well, all away to found a new workshop in the holding of a landtheyn named Rowena, some sort of cousin who held the castle at the ferry landing in the west.

If we stayed till spring Mair Laikyn was going to be rather less crowded, Nowa said.

We put the wild man in the keep to finish his dying, which, the physician Glinn said, was all there was left he could do. He could have done that well enough and warmer in my apartments, but I'd pushed Rikenza and Raynar as far as fear of myself and my mother's name would bear, Nowa said. She was quiet enough saying so that I listened. No damning me and calling me a fool; no, "I'd be well rid of you if it were you someone put an arrow through next time." So my dying wild man was in the keep, and chained by a shackle round his ankle to a staple in the logs of the wall. That was not my doing, but supposedly by Lady Rikenza's order—I presumed Raynar's—the first day, when I'd gone out to demand proper warm bedding for him, which they had refused to Sage. Nowa, of course, would not be left behind, and while we were putting the fear of the Queen and the Dark Beyond into Rikenza's hallmaster over quilts and a feather mattress, swordtheyns of hers or Raynar's bullied their way in past Sage and affixed the chain.

I suppose I should have been glad they did no worse than that to either my prisoner or my girl.

Nowa said, leave it be, for now. At least they didn't take and fling him down into the windowless ground-floor cellar, which they might have done.

So without asking the lady's leave—not that I had any need to anyway—I had Nowa send the groom Henning with a sealed letter to Ermintrud at Borharbour, though snow was falling and travelling on skis as he was it might take him at best three or four days to get there, if he proved trusty at all. Meanwhile, I moved my people entirely out of the rooms next to the earl's heir and into the keep, guarding it as my own hall at the one door, which was up the outer stairs a storey above the ground. I left the gate to that barren yard and the steep, wind-scoured stone hillock to stand open, though I didn't like it. Some courtesies had to be observed. We weren't, after all, under siege among enemies, much as I felt it so. I hired kin of Henning's, his sisters, Violet and Ana, and two men cousins, Vany and Ernar, all unmarried landcarl labourers from nearby Reedford, landless themselves. Service in a lord's household might be an improvement in their lives, if only a temporary one, since I had neither lands nor revenues to pay them out of once I lost my claim on Laikyn Province as high reeve, but for that time I had their fealty and Laikyn's silver to pay for it, and they owed nothing to Rikenza and Raynar. I did hold to all courtesy to the lady and her brother, of course—it was merely that I wanted to be certain there was no further misunderstanding over my prisoner. We dined in the hall, I at the high table at Lady Rikenza's right hand, Nowa or Sage attending me—but we took care that what was carried over to the keep, Sage took from the common dishes.

Dined in the hall, ate little, drank too much, Nowa said, but I could hardly stomach the smell of food, much less the taste, the feel of it in my mouth. Buttered bread and beer, and snaps in the evenings when I took over the watch by the wild man's side. Grey-skinned like a forgotten pot of thick sourmilk going bad, his body near corpse-cold, they said, the Henning-kin who sat with him through the day, while I myself felt feverish-hot through those nights, dream-hazed; it seemed to me that only when I played the flute, or lay half-dozing on the floor by the wild man's pallet with a hand on him, his skin warmed and his slow wheezing breaths and odd little whimpers, like a dog's nightmare, eased.

Rikenza, too, ate little, spoke less, and withdrew early with Enith. After a few days she ceased to appear at all, and it was Lord Raynar who took the earl's carved chair at the high table, not wearing any diadem of lordship, but a collar strung with yellow topaz and garnets that seemed worthy of an earl, and brought warmth to the rich browns of his colouring. Rebuke, Nowa took it, to me, who would honour his table now with no finery and kept grimly now to my everyday dull blacks, unornamented. His sister, Raynar said, had taken a chill, and was keeping to her bed. Sage and Ana nosed about a bit and said it seemed to be true—Enith was fetching her meals from the kitchens, and the little hall-runners, who knew everything, said she sat by the fire bundled in shawls sipping hot water and snaps, reading, or listening to Enith play the harp. Not dead or made away with by her brother, anyway.

It snowed most of that first week of Blackmonth. Not storms, but steady, persistent snows that piled deep, bowed down the branches of spruce and birch. The white lanes were swiftly trampled to icy, dirty tracks, and the ashes thrown out to give boots and wooden clogs some grip on that ice were tracked in everywhere, a fine, grimy grit.

The Fairnmere had frozen. The Lake would follow.

And still the wild man didn't die.

Nowa and Sage and my four Henning-kin turned the main room of the squat keep into a hall, with benches and bedding about the fireplace. No stove. In the upper room, reached only by the ladder up which on our first returning Raynar's folk had somehow dragged my prisoner while I was delayed in the hall with Lady Rikenza, there was another hearth, smaller, and we had made the wild man's bed on the floor as close to that as was safe. It seemed wiser to leave him in that upper room, once he was there, than to risk him again on the ladder, risk moving him at all, or lay him where those wanting vengeance for the old earl could more easily come at him.

I burned the cedar-twig and the hairs in the hearthfire. Whatever witchery Raynar had thought he might work by them — maybe nothing more than to draw the wild man within his reach, though I didn't think it had been Raynar he came for — fire would cleanse it.

Five days, the wild man lay, still and pale and cold to the touch, lips, eyelids, his fingernails grey, and his breath scraping in his throat. We'd stripped him and cut away as much of the first bandaging as would easily come. He was thin, but not starved as Sage had been; he showed stark long bones and lean muscle and faint old scars, silvery burns on his cheek, many faded cuts on hands and arms, a thick hard ridge three inches long below his breastbone which must nearly have been his death. A warrior's service, I thought. He was surely no older than I myself. The hair of his body was curling and light, of no colour in particular, but it caught the fire with a warm glint of gold, and his hair and beard were a streaky pale brown and blond mingled, like the grain in polished wood, with the same way of catching the fire with a glint of warmth. But I already knew that.

Nowa sent Sage away from tending him, not that the wild man was in a state to care who washed his body, or that Sage was anything but sisterly in her nursing. I suspected Nowa would have liked to get rid of me, too, but I wasn't going. We spooned broth into him, and hot water with honey, and, because Nowa and the Reedford cousins believed it a cure-all, buttermilk.

His wounds oozed around the pads of filthy cloth that Nowa said we needed to leave be and not soak off, which had been my thought, but I was not the one who helped the surgeon put a ripped and shredded princeling back together after the bear, so I let her do what she thought best. The seeping made more black knotted scabs and wept liquid that dried to clear yellow crusts, and cracked and bled no matter how carefully we handled him, and crusted again. The flesh around the scabs was red and swollen; I felt the wounds ache and burn in my own flesh, when I lay by the wild man at night. Felt it, breathed it, felt sometimes I breathed for him, lying with a hand on his chest, felt breath match to breath and come easier, and the dangerous reddening faded. Sometimes the wounded man scarcely seemed to breathe and I'd feel my own heart stutter; I'd lurch up in a panic to lay my ear to dry lips, to chest, feeling for a breath, a heartbeat. And again it would come, a gasp and falling into my own rhythm once more, and I'd wrap the man warm again, and put more wood on the fire. The physician came up to see the wild man once more, and said there was nothing she could do; he was Forest-blessed to live, or he was not, and that was between me and the Forest and my knives, which was blunt speaking. I sent her away again.

There will be a man… The Queen's voice. *Sunset on his hair, fire on his blade's edge, a horse as red as flame…* I had thought she meant a red-haired man, which was hardly an uncommon thing, and I doubted she'd meant me to make away with Henning, or his cousin Vany either. But the wild man had borne no blade beyond that stolen knife, and nothing of fire about it.

Kill him.

Ill and keeping to her rooms or not, I went knocking at Lady Rikenza's door and pushed in when Enith would have prevented me. Her shield-companion, who should have been there to do so, was elsewhere. Out seeking to capture the wild red stallion, I supposed. I'd sent Sage to gossip with the hall-runners to make certain Lord Raynar was away before I came up. I showed the knife, from which the wild man had made his spear, to Rikenza, who was pallid and subdued and wrapped in shawls as the hall-runners had said. Not a cough or sniffle, though, not a handkerchief or abraded nose in sight. She didn't smell of illness.

Fear, I thought. Grief. The restlessness of a cage, turned inward. She seemed to have been passing the time not with her account books, but in what some might find the soothing mindlessness of spinning, which reminded me overmuch of my mother.

The knife… Long, single-edged, and razor-sharp, a hunter's tool, antler-hafted.

"My mother's," she said.

I hadn't really thought otherwise.

Nine days passed. The wild man's sparse flesh shrank into his bones, broth and honey and buttermilk not enough to sustain him. Nowa said I looked nearly as bad, like a hungry dog, ribs showing and sunken-eyed, and she chivvied me to bathhouse and sweat-house and fed me porridge with maple sugar and clotted cream, curdled eggs and sourmilk with stewed fruit ladled over as if I were some convalescing invalid. Henning had not returned from Borharbour. Perhaps he had never arrived. The full moon of Blackmonth had passed unseen behind cloud and it was waning, rising late and setting near midday, when it could be seen at all. The snows had been falling heavily, two days and three, a break clear and sunny and the wind piling drifts; more snow. A short month, Blackmonth, which would die with the year at Huntersnight, and we would go into the twelve Firstdays between the years, and mark each with feasting and song, before in Yearsturn all the Forest settled to endure the harsh heart of winter, out of which some, the old and the sick and the small and the lost, would never emerge.

"You're going to kill him," Sage said, when she'd crept up the ladder that ninth night of my vigils at the wild man's bedside. I was sitting by the bed we'd made on the floor, deep feather-tick fit for a lord folded double on a chamber-servant's wooden pallet, close enough to lay a hand on him whenever I had need, to check he was still alive. Playing the flute, something long and slow and rising, water and birdsong, I meant it to be, and until she spoke I'd figured that the highest notes were falling to the hall below and she'd been sent by Nowa to threaten the flute with burning. "My lord, all this to keep him alive, just so you can kill him at Huntersnight?"

"Are you on watch?" I asked, because I'd given orders that someone was always to be wakeful at the door of the keep. I didn't know that I was afraid, only that there was a prickling unease I couldn't shake.

"No, my lord. Ernar's at the door."

"Then you should be sleeping, shouldn't you?"

"Shouldn't you? Theyn Nowa's right when she says you look near a corpse yourself." Sage flushed. "Sorry, my lord. But my lord—are you going to kill him? There's only Lord Raynar's word—" She bit her lip and shrugged, but it was said. Think what it takes, for a landcarl and a child to accuse a lord of lying, and to another lord, a prince, at that. "He helped us. He killed that assassin in the cedarwoods. Maybe saved your life."

"You did that. And I don't know that killing Theyn Harilan had anything to do with saving my life, or anything to do with me at all. Maybe our wild man just wanted the theyn dead."

"Why would he, except that he saw Harilan attacking us? He's *not* a brigand."

So fierce, my little vixen, in the wild man's defence. Nowa would call it calf-love for the tragic outlaw hero of a ballad. I didn't think so.

"The landfolk," Sage said, "the Forest folk—they knew he was out there. That's what Violet says. They knew, and they left him food, and clothes, because he was—he was naked, or the next thing to it, dressed in rotten rags as if he'd crawled out of a grave, they said, and he had that wild horse following him like a dog and upsetting their mares. They say the stallion's not any stray of theirs, nor of the earl's. They say the wild man was Forest-blessed, or a fayling, or even a Rider of the King, fallen from the sky or come up out of the Lake. They thought they'd have a blessing for themselves, if they gave him gifts." A scowl, then. "Nicer folk, these, than the village where I was dumped. No one gave me gifts for their thinking I was a fayling."

"You weren't a big, dangerous, comely man with a horse that was going to be making off with their mares come spring, if they didn't win your favour."

She eyed me sidelong.

"Plenty dangerous," I admitted. Nudged her with my elbow. "You afraid of me, little vixen?"

"No."

"But you were. Were you afraid of him, when he showed up?"

"No." She frowned. Shook her head. "No. He was just—there. And of course I was afraid of you, everyone says you're mad, anyway, and

I thought—you know what I thought. And I was so tired, and so hungry and so frightened of being captured even before I knew who you were that I could hardly think."

"Yes." And, as if it followed, "I shouldn't have killed that fool Orsten. Not like that. I am mad, a bit. I think I must be. It's—too easy, killing people, you know." But maybe it wasn't, for her. It shouldn't be. That my mother had made one of me was enough. I had to do better by Sage. "Is all well with you? I never asked. You shouldn't have needed to do that, Sage. Kill that man, in the cedar-woods. I'm sorry. I'm your lord and you're not a sworn armscarl—you're a child I took to shelter. It's my right, my duty, too, to defend you."

She shivered. Maybe she was cold. The tower was more a ruin than my own at home in the Queensborg, barely kept up at all, little fear of attack from rivals or outlaw-lords here. The others passed the time caulking the chinks through which the wind blew with rags and wattles and a plaster of dung and chaff from the cow-barn, there being no clay to come by in this season; there are worst things than a barnyard smell, snow drifting on the floor being one of them.

"I'm not a child, my lord. I'm old enough I knew what needed doing. That man I shot meant to kill you, and I'm your—fox. What should I have done, my lord? Stood by and let him? And there at the heartstone—you thought Orsten had killed—*him*. The wild man. I thought it. And..." She shook her head, arms wrapped close about herself. "Did he kill the earl?"

I held up the edge of the blanket I'd wrapped over myself like a shawl and Sage scooted in against me. I folded an arm around her.

"I don't know. I—don't know that I care, which is wrong of me, but...he needs to live. You know it, too. You feel it."

She sighed and leaned her head on me. I thought she was falling asleep, until she asked, very soft, "What is he? The others enjoy the stories they make up about faylings and Riders, but they think like Theyn Nowa, really, that he's just some outlaw come over the strait from the Laitellon who meant to rob the earl and killed her, maybe even not meaning to, when she fought him. They don't—they don't need him, the way we do."

Need. Yes. It felt like need.

"Is he a witch, my lord? Is he bespelling us? And you never answered me. Are you going to kill him?"

"I don't know," I said, and which question that was meant for, I didn't know.

Better to put a knife into your own heart. And far less likely. Fool child. Take him and flee her. Run, run, run!

"Do you trust me?" I asked.

Sage took her time thinking about that, watching, in the dim firelight, the rise and fall of the wild man's chest beneath the quilts. Finally, "Yes," she said. "My lord prince."

"If you said, 'Yes, Mairran,' I'd know you meant it. You called to me so, with your hands in his blood." Like an oath.

"Mairran. I do trust you, Mairran."

I sighed, kissed the top of her head, not really thinking how she might take it, but she just stayed snug where she was, warm against me.

"Go on trusting me, Sage," I said. "Little sister. My groom, my armscarl, my fox. I don't quite see my way, but it's there before me. Somewhere. I'll find it. We'll find it. Now, since you're not a child, but you're still very young, go back down before Nowa comes and decides I'm a threat to your virtue."

She snorted. And that, beyond anything, was trust, wasn't it? To disdain even the thought? Or an insult, maybe.

I decided to take it as trust.

And I trusted, too, that Nowa had had some stern words for those new folk of my household, regarding their behaviour to the girl.

Sage slipped out from my side and went back down. I closed the hatch after her, even though that would stop the heat rising from the room below. Slid the bolt to. I would hear anyone but lightfoot Sage on the ladder, but still—I was tired, and the reek of woodsmoke and sour sweat and stale blood was strong enough to mask others stirring about if I didn't stay alert to them. The ravens shuffled and settled again, perched on the woodbox.

When I turned back, the wild man was watching me. I went down on my knees beside him. He moved a hand, slow, feeble, as if it were a dead thing, a clumsy contraption of sticks and twine. Touched, fumbling, the wooden flute where I'd laid it down on the mattress by his head. Eyes fixed on my own.

So I took it up and played for him again. And when he fell asleep once more I stripped off the fur-lined hallgown that was all I had been wearing, curled up against the wild man's side, tail over my nose, and went to sleep myself, with the man's hand resting on my Wolf's head.

It still felt like it belonged there.

Wind in the pines, and the wild man climbing a hill, snow crunching. He's not wearing the ill-fitting cast-offs in which we took him, but tall boots and leather trousers, a cape of deerskin, a crown of woven hemlock twigs, dark-needled. Shirtless, chest, arms, hands bare to the icy wind. I fly to his shoulder. Confused, looking at my own feet, talons gripping leather. This isn't me, isn't Mairran. Yellow-scaled legs. Killing claws. Falcon.

Tell me your name, I want to say, but I'm voiceless and that's such a strange thing to demand, as if I didn't know. But I don't.

He laughs and brushes me off his shoulder and I flap and gain height and wheel back to him.

"Tell me yours," he says, as if I have spoken, and his voice is what I expect of him, deep, soft. Familiar. Warm as spiced snaps and firelight, flooding through me, the sound of it.

My own body, Raven, not a falcon now, as I circle him, and the falcon flies at me and I twist and dart and the falcon grapples with me, claws meeting claws as ravens flirt. It's not flirting, not a fight. A dance, but I can't match the gyrfalcon and the grey wolf has me down in the snow by a mouthful of ruff and loose neck skin, growling. I don't struggle. Wave a black paw, batting at him.

The wild man takes us both by the scruff of the neck, one in each hand, shakes us.

"Enough of that," he says, and there's only me, the black she-wolf, scrambling undignified to her feet, puppy-floundering. "Enough, Kallyn." Frowns. "You're not Kallyn."

The way he lets go and steps back then... That the warm hand that rests on my head isn't for me... I turn and run, leaping through deep snow that drag at me, and the wind is cold and the sun sinking in smoke and blood and I break free of the drifts into the thorn-fenced ring of the Fairnshore heartstone, a great empty fane on a hilltop and a weathered blue-grey stone beneath an ash-tree, stretching long shadows, awaiting solstice blood.

In the morning the wild man was senseless as he had been the past many days, and I had a headache, which Nowa said was well deserved, if I would keep lulling myself to sleep with kingswort snaps, except that I hadn't, that night. But the prisoner looked a more healthy colour, and his breath was softer, deeper, and did not rasp and wheeze. He might, Nowa said, be going to live after all. A miracle and the blessing of the Mothers Above and Below. She didn't seem glad of it.

There was an ache in my bones, as if some winter fever were on me.

Henning returned at last, with six of the *Snow Goose*'s crew on skis, and their spears and bows and a look about them that said they were the Queen's own, not any deepwoods earl's, and they'd be happy to deal with trouble if trouble chose to oblige. I took the groom into my service too, since Henning's own lady was not best pleased with him.

There was never any talk of summoning the Queen's justices of Laikyn, a handful of elder law-reeves raised to landtheyns, to sit in judgement over the wild man. I was there, and I had claimed the man. There was no law that said the Queen's flint-king had to take the guilty. There was no law at all, Queen's or Forest, for the sacraments of the heartstones. Old, old as the ancient kings themselves. And the Queen's voice, the Queen's will, given to my words and hands, overrode any law, even her own.

When I woke before the sun on the morning of the twelfth day since we had taken him, the wild man was sitting up, quilts wrapped about him, watching me by the light of the fading coals.

I got to my feet slowly. Didn't speak. What could I have said, with the man chained to the wall? But that wasn't why. I just—found myself empty of words.

Oh, make that doubting, *Mairran, wordless?* face, but that's how it was. I built up the fire again—the wild man couldn't quite reach the hearth and the woodbox. I dressed, and braided my hair as well as I could on my own, and still the wild man watched me. Thunder and Lighting shuffled guiltily out of my way as I moved about. I won't say they understood they should have woken me when the wild man woke, but—they knew. I opened the shutter of one of the arrow-slots and tossed the ravens out to get some exercise. They would have been quite happy to grow fat as lapdogs through the winter, given half a chance. It was still dark, not even the first grey running over the Fairnmere. They flapped up to the roof to huddle and grumble together.

No witnesses at all, then, so I sat back down, arms wrapped around my knees, as the wild man held his.

"I'm Mairran. I'm to give you to the Forest on Huntersnight, for the killing of the Earl of Laikyn."

I couldn't tell if I was even understood. The wild man only watched me, those Lakewater grey-green eyes solemn, waiting, as if I might be about to do something interesting.

"Tell me your name."

A faint frown, lips parting. Shake of the head, with a deeper frown. Hands flexed. Frustration, I thought.

"What happened at the heartstone? I need to know. I need to, you understand? Did you kill the earl? The woman at the heartstone—who killed her?"

Again, a frown. He licked his lips, swallowed. Shook his head. Reached, as if he would touch me, touch my face, and I flinched back.

I couldn't stand to be there. I went away and left the wild man to Vany and Ernar, who had most of his everyday care by then, and who handled him gentle as a new baby in everything.

"He's awake," I told them, going down the ladder. "Don't turn your back on him. Don't take weapons within his reach. And find him some clothes that fit."

The next morning, I ate nothing, save snaps in water, and that before the dawn, but I took Nowa and rode into the Forest alone. The snow lay deep and the horses, not yet winter-weary, plunged through it eagerly enough once we left the narrow road marked by some forester's timber-sled. I wandered as the lay of the land took me, and Nowa trailed after. Eight days remained before the solstice. There was a thing I needed to do.

Silence, but for the crunch of hooves, the creak of saddles, the blowing of the horses. Not moodiness, though the Mothers knew I wasn't in the mood for chatter anyhow. Like the fasting, silence was necessary to the work. I found a place where birches spilled down a hillside, chose one growing straight and clean. Stood with mittens tucked through my belt and bare hands laid on the tree, head bowed against it, as if I listened to secrets it was whispering, but I only told over the words, a low murmur, the blessing needful, before I stepped back. Words that had no meaning in any other time or place. Foresters spoke such charms before they began the work of felling. No one remembered what they meant any longer, the names invoked. Language flowed like a river, the minstrel named Dove once told me; it left old words behind, meaningless as flotsam cast up on the shore, save to those who unearthed such knowledge out of the muck of forgotten years. That was a part of what she claimed she had been doing in her Forest-wandering; hunting for near-forgotten scraps of song and rhyme, old charms of sowing and harvest, hunting and autumn-slaughter, as if they held some secrets. Landfolk took her for some Outlander version of a witch. Perhaps she was. She charmed me well enough, for all it was my mother set me in her way.

Anyhow, I had learnt those words for the blessing of the tree from the old man who had carried the flint knives for the rites of the Forest for fifty-some years before me. He'd been a Singer, once, and of the gold-ringed rank, before the Queen took him to her service for other uses. I didn't know whence he had them, the prayers he chanted. He'd not been a talkative man, even in those evenings he gave himself up to drink, and he never sang at all, that I heard. I only knew the blessing's meaning in a general way. Some of it was in ordinary language. I told the tree what I wanted of it; I called to witness the Kings, who some now and even then would say were one King, the Wild King and the Winter King and the Lake-Born King before her and the Shadow King and…even the oldest scraps of songs did not remember them all. Called the Kings through all their ages; called the Mothers, and especially the Mothers Below, who cared for growing things with their roots in the earth as well as for the dead, to witness that I made this harvest with all due reverence.

Silent again, I knelt and used the smaller of the knives, which had a straight, leaf-shaped blade of flint the colour of a thunderous sky, to nick the scarred heel of my left thumb, just enough to bleed a few drops, scarlet bright as a red whistler's feather, on the snow. Offering to the tree. Dusted snow off my knees and used the same knife to carefully slice away a square of bark from the living tree, the sort of thing one would never do, usually, wounding the tree and scarring it forever, but for this, it was forbidden to take bark from timber or firewood felled for ordinary use.

I don't know why it mattered, only that it did. The old Singer who came before me had insisted on it.

If my still-seeping palm stained the white bark, that didn't much matter.

Then we rode back to Mair Laikyn. At some point the red stallion appeared and began to follow. Neither Smoke nor Thorn were happy with that; they wanted to turn and argue, but the feral red faded away into the thick evening shadows as we neared the wood-pastures of

Fairnshore again. Nowa did not mention in the barns that we had seen him. Lord Raynar was offering a generous bounty to the one who could bring him that horse.

Nowa would have chased all our household out of the common room of the keep for me, but I shook my head, took what I needed, and went up the ladder to the wild man, so she followed to order Vany and Sage down. I was still not speaking. Or eating, but what I needed, in my judgement, included a jug of water and the flask of spruce-steeped snaps that I'd taken from the castle's stillroom a few days before. It was brewed as a tonic against the winter-scurvy, but it was also the proper spirit for the dark of Huntersnight, and was not supposed to be tasted before then. As the flint-king, I considered that I made an exception.

My folk had found a shirt and a quilted hall-gown long enough to fit the wild man, and woollen socks. Still chained—and though the fetter had not been forged onto him, but fastened with a cumbersome lock, we did not have the key. It would hardly have been safe to let him loose, anyhow. Even unarmed, I did not think he would be safe, or tame, for all that he seemed weak and mild enough for now. He was sitting up in his nest of blankets and quilts watching the comings and goings with bleak interest.

"You're not—" Nowa began. Glared at the man, as if he had any choice in being there. "With him watching? Mothers Above, Mairran, he deserves better than that…"

I shrugged, waved her to the ladder. She shook her head, but left us and went down. She would stand guard below, to be sure nothing short of the keep burning over our heads interrupted. I bolted the hatch after her.

And set about what I needed to do, heating water to soften the bark so I could work with it; shaping it, using the pine planks of the floor as my cutting board. The wild man left his blankets and settled near, watching gravely. I didn't suppose he understood.

It was the mask of the priest of sacrifices. Sometimes they called it the flint-king, but that name belongs to no real Forest King, not a hero of songs or tales, not a person at all, and never was, or there would be a song to say so. The flint-king was a thing, a blade and a deed, a pageant-creature with no place in any pageant but his own. Folk did not make a flint-king, a priest of sacrifices, when they burnt a birch-king on the festival bonfires. Only blood brought him out, the old rite revived and overseen by the Queen.

I cut the eye-holes, making it a ragged-edged thing, this one, shaved long tendrils loose, which might be hair, beard, whiskers, frost-fringe, white flame's edge... Carved the signs of snow and blood, death and rebirth and the year's cycle, into it, the light brown layer beneath the white showing through. Skin through a rent in linen, and blood to follow; I didn't look to where he sat, my wild man, watching. Opened the small scabbed cut I had made in the Forest—all this with the smaller flint blade—and smeared the signs I had carved, which was an offering of my own. Unfolded the linen cloth that I'd carried along all this time, shed feathers of the past summer's moulting, raven black. Cut small slits along the upper curve of the mask, wove the quills in, a wild black feather crest, a bristling mane. Fixed them with a bit of spruce-gum against the wind and dabbed the healing resin on my cut, as well. It would probably end up in my hair and Nowa would have to wash it with butter to get it out. The wild man stretched an arm—I'd not noticed he had moved within reach—plucked a feather I hadn't yet glued, sniffed it, sat turning it in his fingers. Held it as if he would write. When I reached out a hand to ask for it, he thrust it up his sleeve. Grinned at me, a wolf's grin. I didn't know what the man wanted with my feather, but clearly I wasn't getting it back.

That grin...it could have warmed me through, like snaps, like fire, in another time, another place. Then and there...I was cold and sick and tired, and wanted to throw myself out the window, and be gone, lost in the dark.

No, she whispered. *No, no, no.*

Thongs of soft leather with which to tie the mask on, when the time came. And that was it, done. I draped it in a towel and set it upright in a far corner. No one was meant to see before Huntersnight came. Worn once and offered to the bonfire after, and a new one, with different signs, flower-crowned, to make for summer.

There was a wolf howling, alone. But I think only I could hear.

Poured the snaps. Two cups, over-generously, and we sipped it, the scent of the Forest rising, sitting as if companions, cross-legged on the floor, knee touching knee.

"Was it you who killed the earl?" I asked, because I might speak again, then, as well as break my fast. The work was done. And I still had no answer. "The woman at the heartstone. Was it you? I need to know."

The wild man shrugged. Didn't matter, he seemed to think now, or he didn't know. Then he shook his head.

No? Or he didn't understand the meaning of the question at all, maybe.

I'd brought up a loaf of rye-bread, too, thinking ahead—I sometimes do, despite what Nowa might say contrariwise. I sawed off chunks from the loaf and we shared them, and watered the second cup of snaps, which was still too much strong drink, even with the bread. The floor, or maybe my bones, went unsteady, shifting like a slow strong swell on the Lake, sign of distant storm.

"Do you have a name?"

He just watched, then. As if puzzled, not by the question, but by my asking it at all. Or maybe it was only that he had no answer. I touched his mouth—I was drunk, yes, I won't deny it. Maybe I meant the touch to ask, *could* he not speak, or *would* he not. The wild man lipped at my fingers, and I jerked my hand back. Not startled, so much as...I don't know. I don't know what I was thinking, then. I don't know what I meant by it, touching the wild man that way.

He laughed at me, a wheezy noise, another grin.

Caught my arm, when I would have risen. I didn't know where I planned to go and by the way the room swung, not far was a good guess, but the wild man tugged me down by him. I don't know at what point the tears had come, only my face was wet, and my wild man's mouth brushed over mine, over skin, over eyes, tasting my salt.

I went to sleep, naked, human, with the wild man's arm over me, hand wound in loosened hair, fitting to his side as if that could be where I belonged.

There's a wind out of the west, and the Lake is flinging great waves against the rocky shore. Pines bend and toss clouds of green; the needles hiss and whine as the spume flies. Grey water, grey stone, grey churning sky. The Warnavon. I knows this bit of coastline. I don't know it. I'm walking barefoot, chilled to the bone, soaked by spray, trousers, shirt clinging to skin, and my tunic is old and worn, faded to a pale grey, shredded nearly to rags that fly in tatters and my hair is loose and flying in ragged banners too, whipping my eyes as the wind gusts, and that brings tears.

I'm following music. The song of the gathering storm, climbing over the slow slamming drum of the waves, notes flying, torn free by the wind.

He's there, down on the rocks nearly within waves' reach, the wild man, seated on a boulder and a seven-string Forest-harp in the crook of his arm, shoulder turned to the waves to shield it. He's singing. I hear him singing, a voice lost to wind and wave, words I can't hold though I think he sings for me, or maybe I only want to be the one his singing calls, and I know I am not, because I've come to kill him.

The wild man looks up, and now he's plucking single notes with fingertips, not strumming with the quill of the raven's wingfeather he's woven into his hair, and the notes spin free and fly, and fall, like autumn leaves.

He wears a black robe like a hallgown, and a black caped hood lined with white winter-hare lying back on his shoulders, a crown woven of the small white bones of birds.

I have no knives. I've left them behind, forgotten them, lost them, buried them deep in a cairn among the pines, thrown them into the Lake.

So I take the harp from the wild man's hands and breathe out a fire, roaring, snarling, wind-torn and savage, setting light to all the driftwood at waves' edge, almost to the rock on which the man sits.

He watches. I break the harp, snap its frame, throws it down into the hungry flames, where something is waiting to be born. It burns, and the wild man watches, flames surrounding him, climbing high, and the colour of his eyes stirs and churns like the Lake, and I am falling into the waves.

Falling, I come apart. Black feathers, white bones. I will wash up scattered on the shore and be done. The King can make a crown of my bones.

I woke the whole of my little household with my screaming. Had a few frantic moments, trying to get myself decently clothed again, shouting that it was nothing, only a nightmare, with Nowa's fist pounding furious at the bolted hatch.

The wild man was laughing at me, then, rocking with it, faint harsh huffing sound though it was, and his eyes bright and his whole face young and alive.

I didn't know why I put any faith in snaps to stop my dreaming, in this season. It never did.

Seven days, eight, if one counted the holy day of Huntersnight itself. Raynar and his shieldling and a handful of grooms rode out to try yet again to lure the wild red stallion to where they could get a rope on him. No mares in season to tempt the beast; I wished them ill-luck, which they had, a barncarl being thrown from her stumbling horse and breaking her arm, and neither hide nor hair of the red beast spotted.

I thought quite seriously about taking Lord Raynar bound into the cellar of the keep to see what he'd tell there. Me, a fire, my knives.

Better yet, put Raynar there, and see what Rikenza could tell.

Or maybe she had already told me enough.

Short days, and long nights, and Lord Raynar had moved back into his old apartments beside his sister's after I abandoned them. I crept up without Sage or Nowa and searched them again when the lord rode out in his futile hunt for the red horse. I took the thick, dark-bound book of old lays that hadn't been on the shelf last time I'd looked for it. Didn't much care if Raynar knew, now, that I'd been there, but I replaced it with the treatise on sieges to hide the gap regardless. Didn't know what I was looking for, only I felt there must be something, as if I'd caught a whiff of it, as Raynar carried the book away when he first cleared the apartments for me. Probably I was imagining that, merely because Raynar had by chance put it somewhere out of sight when I went that time to borrow something for Nowa. A tight, crabbed, old hand the book was copied in, ink brown and fading, and hard reading. It seemed mostly the usual lays of the Wild King and the Grey Hunter and their Riders, old hero-tales, familiar and stirring, though here and there a different turn of phrase. Nothing that found me a way through whatever thicket of thorns it was I struggled in. Hard to focus my attention on reading. My mind wandered off into half-remembered songs from other lays, or dreams that thinned like fog when I tried to recall anything of them.

A sword, and fire on its edge.

A skull staring empty in the dark.

Cold late dawn of Huntersnight Eve came, in the end. I hadn't slept the night before. I never could. It had been years since I had even pretended to. At home in the Queensborg I might have gone up to the roof of my own tower, but here—I'd been keeping away from the wild man. Hadn't spent the dark hours there since the night we'd lain skin to skin with the wild man's arm over me, mouth tasting my tears, hadn't gone up at all in a week, not since I dreamed of a burning Forest-harp and a crown of bird-bones.

I went up that morning, though.

I'd gone out alone, that night. No one had seen me. I can move swift and secret in shadows when I choose, and anyway, I'd been Wolf, and Wolf had gone over the wall, across the ice of the frozen Fairnmere. The drifts so deep, the night so dark, the stars so high and cold...

I had run, and run, and run myself beyond dreaming, run myself to exhaustion, so I could hardly drag myself back. No grey wolf had come to run with me, even in a waking dream.

Nowa had been waiting by the wall when I came back over, with a quilted hallgown and a heavy cloak, a cup of hot water and snaps. I don't know how she knew, even to where and when I'd come back over the wall. Sometimes Nowa just did know. But Thunder and Lightning were with her, one to each shoulder, which usually she did not put up with, because they liked to prod into hair, and ears, and see what one might have hidden down one's collar. And they had flown out in the grey before the dawn to find me returning and left me when I came within sight of Fairnshore. So maybe that was my answer. Maybe I wasn't the only one in my household talked to birds.

I drank the steaming cup before the first edge of sun broke the horizon in fire. Nowa's strong arm around me, to walk me back to the keep. The day before Huntersnight was a solemn day, a time of preparation, of waiting. I had left coming back till nearly too late. The castle was already well awake, fires blazing, stoves hot, ovens of the bake-house busy as the heart of a beehive, and the steam-houses, and the baths. A day of cleansing, this, as well, but I wouldn't go to join the others. I was meant to keep myself out of sight, and running myself to exhaustion did not bring sleep, only a sharp, careful clarity. A day of lesser fasting, too, porridges, plain bread, pickles, small ale, no meat or fish, neither cheese nor butter, no cooked vegetables, but who had time to do more anyway, with all the festival dishes to prepare against the morrow? I would keep my own fast more completely, a deep fast, as I was taught.

I, and the one who would die.

Already the air smelt of smoke, and of baking. It was sickening.

A short day. A long night coming.

So I went up to where he was. Past him, up another ladder to the roof, wrapped in cloaks and sheepskins, not looking at the wild man as I went by, and I kept my long vigil there, sitting, pacing, watching the low sun, with only the ravens for company. Nowa brought up a brazier, and charcoal to feed it, but no kettle or self-boiler. She had given up trying to persuade me that a little hot water and honey was a permitted necessity on such a watch.

And so the short solstice day wore on.

~LANNESK~

He doesn't want to do this. Arm around Ekkard, taking most of his weight. Staggering along a road of icy, hard-packed snow and trampled dung, rutted by runners, and the sun setting, long blue shadows closing in. Wind hissing snow through spruces, smell of smoke, a straggling row of scattered houses and outbuildings, low, sod-roofed, their backs set to a white curve of ice. Light leaks around the wooden shutters of windows. A door opens, dark figures, two people and a dog disappearing into the darkness of a porch. But there's a burst of song, laughter before the door closes again. Ekkard seems heartened by it, lifts his head.

They've been two days following along the coast, which has been bending towards the west. Lannesk hopes they're south of the Borlinn and the Fairnmere. Someone even in the southern earldoms may recognize Lord Ekkard, or he can—somehow—communicate that they should send to Earl Tannis. And take himself off, leaving Ekkard in safe hands, before any folk of hers can come.

Or maybe they could just keep going south, he and Ekkard together—even two days ago, he was thinking that. Travel south together, furtive, hunting, until the man's healing mind and speech find their way back and he can send his own messages, and understand, too, that Lannesk has to leave him.

He'd rather have done that.

No choice left to him now. Ekkard's fallen ill, shivering through the past two nights in the burrows he makes into a drift, shivering whenever they stop for a rest. Lannesk kindles fires, now they're on the Forest edge again, doesn't keep them small and anxious, either.

They've eaten all the trail-meat; can't go much further on lean dry venison. Boils water, brews spruce-tips and dried meat together, but that doesn't seem to warm Ekkard any. Every child knows that a wetting in winter is to invite oneself to the Dark Mother's hearth. Ekkard's too weak now to share in pulling the toboggan; Lannesk abandoned it the morning before, taking nothing off it but their quilts and the axe. They'd come inland from the shore, heading southerly. Uninhabited Forest, not a whiff of smoke, not even a hunters' trail, and he'd begun to think he should have put Ekkard on the toboggan instead, except he couldn't have pulled it far, grown so weak himself, so burdened and alone.

But they came onto a deer-track, and it merged into a Forestway, easy to follow. It brought them to the crossing of this road, a sudden land of humankind again, rutted with the passage of timber-sleds. So they left the skis propped behind a big elm there—Lannesk means to come back for his own—and went on, walking, on the hard-packed dirty road. Ekkard's been falling too much, and each time, needing to be hauled up to his feet. Not quitting. Just so weak. Tractable. Lannesk can't tell, now, if what he thought he saw, some returning sense, is there or not.

And so to this place. To people. To questions.

A wide path is trampled to the door from which the music sounds. The little village's alehouse, maybe, or just some gathering of friends. Someone of substance, anyway. Two chimneys. He knocks, a mitten-muffled thumping that it seems nobody hears, and lifts the latch, pushing the door open. Snow's higher than the floor, which is bracken and straw strewn over beaten earth, mucky with snow and heat spilling to meet one another. Porch, but not the clutter of wooden clogs and tools of a family home. Music, voices loud in song. He tugs Ekkard in, pushes open the next door; they stumble into the firelit dimness and what seems like blazing heat of the room beyond, Ekkard sagging, leaning more on Lannesk than on Tolla's spear.

There they stand dumbly, because—no words in either of them, and he draped with sword and axe, Ekkard clutching the spear, weapons that should have been left in the porch. Realizes too late how they must seem, outlaws or madmen, dragon-kin, even.

Song falters into silence.

"Who are you, then?" a man asks, getting to his feet. Little wiry man, but no less menacing for that. There's a general movement of hands towards belt-knives, and a woman by the fire, maybe the alewife herself, hefts the poker.

Lannesk holds out his empty arm to show he means no threat, and Ekkard at that moment loses his hold on the spear. It clatters to the flagstoned, straw-strewn floor and he's folding to his knees. Lannesk goes down with him, catching him. Ekkard's breath wheezes and rasps. He's not quite fainted, but barely holding his head up.

"Hey," someone says. "That's Lord Ekkard, the earl's son, isn't it?"

"It is. It's the young lord who went off to the Holy Isle to join the Singers' army. And—you, I've seen you," the woman at the fire says, pointing the poker at him, but not threatening, only that she has it in her hand now. "Just last summer, when I took a wagonload down to the Earls' Summonsing. You're one of the rebel earl's sons."

"Stepson, Gerd," the skinny little man is correcting. "They were Earl Brux's stepsons, the Coastlander boys. One of them was mute." And he frowns. "That'd be you, wouldn't it?"

Lannesk nods.

The man shrugs. "Can't think of his name. Here. Better get Lord Ekkard to the fire."

Should be relief Lannesk feels. It isn't. "The rebel earl" isn't what he wants to hear. Very bad feeling that they haven't fetched up south of the Borlinn after all.

But willing hands help him get Ekkard sitting on a bench, his frosty outer clothes removed, a mug of warmed ale into his shaking hands, while the two women whose house this seems to be disappear into the back rooms to make up a bed. He can hear them talking. *Thought they were outlaws, come out of the deep woods... Dead on their feet, the pair of them...*

A child comes through from the kitchen with a dish of pease porridge and ham hotted up, fermented vegetables spooned over, and

Lannesk smiles thanks at him, feeds Ekkard like a baby because he's too far gone to hold the spoon steady himself. Folk watch. Ask questions, did they come over the Lake, did they see the dragon-kin army marching down, because there's hunters say the dragon-kin have left the Lann Leda empty and gone out over the ice... Only after sacking and burning all of coastal Naar and half the Lann Laitellon, though... They grow weary of his nods, start speculating among themselves. Battles, victories, defeats... Lannesk stops listening, busy getting food into Ekkard, into himself. Another round of warmed ale for both of them. Strong winter keeping ale, spiced with bayberries. Too strong. Ekkard's eyes keep drifting closed. Lannesk's own want to. Speculation has drifted into singing again, songs of the Wild King's riding against the invading Southlanders. His watering eyes puzzle him, till out of weariness he remembers, the Wild King is dead. And the Grey Hunter. And Anzimor, and he's back on Laikyn, and alone. Wipes his face on his sleeve and looks up to see Ekkard watching him, with a bit of the old Ekkard there, but quieter, sadder, than ever he saw him, or maybe he's only wishing for it. The older woman of the couple, Gerd, is there tugging at his sleeve, as if he's deaf as well as speechless. Or maybe she spoke, and he wasn't listening. Drifting on a tide that wants to carry him off, deep, deep sleep, warmth and ale.

"Come," she says. "We'll get the young lord washed and into bed."

Only a couple of folk are left in the front room, and the fire's burning low. The younger woman is Netta; wife, not sister, to Gerd. She chases the stragglers out, bars the door. "You," she says. "Bed — now!" Speaking to the child, and the littler one that's crept out from somewhere. They stare, big-eyed, as Ekkard lurches up, supported between Lannesk and the elder woman, and shambles past.

"Putting you here in the kitchen, my lords," Gerd says. "Not meaning any offence by it, but you'll lie warmer there, close by the fire."

He nods. Big stone fireplace, and a mattress laid over a pallet on the floor, heaped in quilts. Probably the straw-tick from the children's bed. A basin of steaming water, a cake of soap scented, like the ale, with bayberry. They strip Ekkard, and scrub the rank grime and sweat of a winter's travelling from him while he shivers, get him into clean wool socks and a heavy house-gown. Gerd clucks over the old black clots of blood that still mat Ekkard's hair, but Lannesk won't let her untie what's left of his braid. Not tonight. Wet hair will do more harm than good. Netta has been making up a mustard plaster. They tuck Ekkard in, plaster lying on his chest and a warm cloth-wrapped stone at his feet.

"You too, my lord," Gerd says, when Netta comes back from tossing out the dirty water, and she fills the basin from the steaming kettle. So he strips to shirt and drawers and flaps hands at them, shooing hens in turn, till they laugh and leave him. Washes in haste, leaving his hair be. He hangs his clothes with Ekkard's over a bench to air and pulls on the house-gown Netta has left, which comes only to his knees. The women's clogs by the back door won't fit him; he pulls on his boots—so damp, they feel now—to throw out the filthy water, tramping through the woodshed to reach the yard. He pokes his head into the other room to show he's done. The children are nestled into the foot of the big bed there, asleep already.

"Good night, then, and Mothers Above and Below keep you," Netta says. Gerd is murmuring with someone in the front room. He hears the door close, the bar drop again as he retreats to crawl in beside Ekkard. There's still a faint sweet scent of summer in the thick mattress. Quiet murmuring between Gerd and Netta, but he can't make out what they're saying.

Not sure where they are. No one's said the name of the village, and the Borlinn was Tannis's from not far beyond the Fairnmere to the Lake. How far north up the coast are they? How many days to Tannis's tower from here for a messenger on skis?

One night. He can allow himself one night of rest, one day to follow of warmth and good food, one day more of tending Ekkard himself, before he sneaks away. Netta seems to understand care of the sick. He feels Ekkard's forehead. Too hot. But they're unused to warmth like this. Ekkard mutters and tries to pluck the plaster away. Lannesk feels his skin for burning, decides it's fine, makes him leave it be. Doesn't like the thick sound of his breathing.

He puts the Wild King's sword down beside him, puts his purses, his dagger and knife, under his head.

Falls into sleep like a drowning man going down, knowing he shouldn't, too exhausted to care.

Hot food, warm ale, dry clothes, even clean, if very worn, linens begged by Gerd from her neighbours...mostly just drowsing by the fire, spooning soup and porridge into Ekkard whenever he wakes. Lannesk tends the fire for Gerd and Netta, smiles at their children when they sneak in to stare at the pair of them. Ekkard tosses and turns, fever-restless. Netta rubs his chest and back with strong-scented herbs, flea-mint and balsam-gum pounded into goose-grease, makes him breathe bending over a basin of balsam-simmering water. Lannesk darns his worn socks, and Ekkard's too. People coming into the alehouse wander into the kitchen, stand around, looking at him, at Ekkard. The most excitement there's been for months, he supposes. Gerd chases them back to the front room when they start to settle in, make themselves at home.

He's uneasy. One of the men had taken up his—the Wild King's sword, earlier. Part-drawn it, wondering at the damaged hilt, trying to make out the runes inscribed on the upper handspan of the blade. What did they say? He had shrugged and taken it back. He doesn't know himself. The children find him and Ekkard a fascination. The littlest one gets into everything. She climbs onto his lap where he's sitting by Ekkard doing his mending, starts taking things out of the purse he's left open, Anzimor's, to get at the little folded wallet with the needles and bit of yarn. He takes it away from her, thinking of the hazard of fishhooks. She takes Ekkard's knife from its sheath, giggles, runs off. He goes after her but before he's reached the door her brother marches her in, clutching the knife, gives it back. Cuffs his sister across the ear, lightly, and marches her out again. Wordless, as if Lannesk is catching.

A moment alone; he takes the cloth-wrapped bluestone from his own purse, tucks it down the front of his new shirt, against his skin.

Dusk, and thick rich stew for supper, with hot fresh hearth-bread to sop in it. Ekkard chews and swallows as if to do so wearies him, but at least he does eat. Tries to get hold of Lannesk's hand, keep hold of him. Huddles as if afraid. As if he understands Lannesk means to leave him. The front room of the alehouse begins to fill up, not just the handful who've been in and out all day. It must be nearly the whole of the village that's coming now to see the lords returned from whatever disaster—they are all agreed, it must have been a disaster—overtook the expedition to the Holy Isle. They want him to join them, to answer by sign their guesses as to the story, but Gerd keeps them from tramping through to gawk at Ekkard in the kitchen. Lannesk slips back there himself to check on him. Sleeping. Still wheezing, still feverish.

"They're saying you play the harp, my lord," Gerd says, coming in to get another jar down from the shelf. "Pike's brought hers. Come give them a tune."

Ekkard has woken, watching him with anxious eyes. Has caught his hand again. Lannesk frees himself, resting a hand on his cheek a moment. Too hot.

Goes out, good guest, to play a tune for the general singing.

So he's there when the porch door bangs, and then the inner door, letting in a handful of folk and a great gust of cold air.

"Arrek?" Gerd asks. "Who've you brought us?"

The one man was here the night before. Remembers his piebald moustaches. Doesn't recognize the others at first. Been so long. A lifetime.

"Aye," one of the strangers says, "that's the Coastlander, the elder one, the mute. Lannesk."

And like himself and Ekkard in their exhaustion and ill-manners, they've carried their weapons in.

He's dropped the harp aside and is bolting for the kitchen as the man who knew him is drawing his sword. Grabs his fur cape and the Wild King's sword and there's a big woman with a levelled spear in the back doorway. Shouts and cries from the indignant ale-drinkers,

Gerd demanding they take their weapons outside, but the swordtheyn comes trampling in with the carls behind him, spreading out, two with axes and the rest with heavy staves. Ekkard lurches unsteadily to his feet, getting hold of Lannesk's left arm to pull himself up, trying to get protectively between them.

"Lord Ekkard, my lord—stand away from him—"

Ekkard is shaking his head, breathing hard, mumbling. It emerges as, "No no nonono," but then his legs fail him and he falls and Lannesk goes down on a knee to catch him, arm around him, sword raised as if he needs to defend the man, which he doesn't, not from Tannis's own spearcarls.

Spear prods between his shoulders. Axeman tugs the sword from his grasp. Ekkard whimpers, trying to get upright, shaking his head, putting arms around Lannesk.

"Leave them be," Netta shrieks. "Your lord's ill. He's had a head-wound, he's fevered. Brux's man's been caring for him like he was his own brother, you leave them be—"

"There's no enemy here—put up your weapons—"

They pay Gerd no more attention than they do Netta. Peel Ekkard off him. The spear's gone from Lannesk's back so he leaps for the door. Doesn't make it. Swinging stick meets his head.

~Mairran~

The drifts so deep and the night so dark and the stars so high and cold. There's a song begins with those words still. Folk sing it on Huntersnight, on their way to the heartstone. All through the Forest, folk were singing, going out from every earl's borg and landtheyn's hall, every village, whether they lived by tilling or herding, fishing or mining, every foresters' camp and assart, from the headwaters of every river to the shores of the Lake. They would go—singing, bundled against the cold in quilted tunics and lined cloaks, in sheepskin and fur, but festival-fine, trimmed with knots of ribbon, with sprays of rosehips still clinging red to twigs, with amulets in wood and shell and silver, and brooches, rings, chains and circlets of gold and jet and bluestone, those who could afford such things—lighting their way with torches and lanterns, and the offerings carried in baskets or dragged on sleds. Braided nut-breads, maple-cakes, spiced meat pies and honeyed cheese-cakes, shrivelling apples, flasks of strong ale and winter-snaps, all to be blessed by whatever power and grace of the Forest might be summoned on such a night, dedicated to the Forest, a shared feast. There would be pageant-dancers, masked and robed, chosen by lot at each festival for the next and practising in secret, with much ale and bickering and giggling, to outdo the last year's team with their presentation.

And drawn on a low sled, there would be the birch-king, which some provinces called the birch-lady, or the straw-lady, or sometimes it was the thorn-king when made for winter's sacrifice and the flower-king, the rose-king for summer, when it was carried on a white pony mare with a foal at heel. Figures of birch-twigs and straw, ribbon-wound, crowned in thorn or blossom, given symbolic life, given their sanctity, by the blood of any who had any especial prayer or plea to make—a finger-pricked smear, only a touch, before the figures of straws and twigs go to the fire. So different a thing from the Queen's own offering, which was made on behalf of all the folk of the tribes. That alone remained the true sacrifice in the old way, given in her name by her blood-anointed priest, her flint-king—a human life, of which the birch-kings were only token or memory.

You know that's a lie. You do know it. Can you not remember?

The sun sank into a long red twilight. Some might keep a vigil by their own fires; others would sleep. What else was there to do? The pageant-dancers would be gathered somewhere, nervously rehearsing their steps and their verses, taking more ale than was strictly in keeping with even a lesser fast, to keep their courage up. I knew how that went, though it was probably more pleasant in summer, when there was no fasting.

I had a part in a Kingsday pageant once, when I was a child. My mother was displeased; I was not supposed to have run with the other children to draw the marked lots, trying for the roles of fox and crows. As it was, she could not deny once I'd drawn one of the crows, to my delight and no doubt the horror of all the grown-ups who had drawn a dancer's lot for that season and would therefore have the Queen's precious child underfoot and a Queen's swordtheyn standing over them through all their preparation. I wore a black beaked mask and gleefully shook my rattle and chased after the little girl—a fisher's daughter—who wore the fox-mask and carried a wand wound with russet ribbons as we darted through the dancers, pretending to trip them up. We all chanted our carefully-memorized verses that, without ever holding enough sting to give true offence, mocked the follies of the guild-chiefs of the town and the theyns of my mother's hall, and ate too much and sneaked tastes of the adults' snaps, and nearly rubbed from our minds and memories the way the man who had died at the heartstone had railed and shrieked and cursed us all.

A drunkard well-known in his own village, who'd battered his child to death in a rage, so I remembered the sacrifice was, that

Kingsday dawn. Such were the more usual condemned criminals who ended up bleeding at the Queen's Arrun heartstone for the Forest's blessing.

It was cold up on the roof despite the brazier and the heavy shrouding layers of wool but I wasn't supposed to be seen out among the folk through this day. If I'd stayed in the common room of the keep, the household would have had to pretend not to see me. I should have evicted Lord Raynar from his rooms again, is what I should have done, but I felt a reluctance to go far from my prisoner.

Sometimes I played old tunes on the flute, and sometimes I stared into the glowing coals of the brazier, warming my feet and hands and wondering what a proper law-reeve and their officers might have done, to drag some truth into the light in this place.

Wondering if it had ever been truth my mother wanted.

I was tired, half dreaming again. The fire seemed to shift and coil, a dragon's stirring, something crawling just the other side of the Dark.

I heard them come to take the wild man down a couple of hours before dawn. The man didn't fight them. Maybe I'd hoped he might.

Nowa came up to find me.

"Time to go," she said.

So I changed my clothes, checked my knives, and let Nowa braid my hair again, looping it up in the style called frozen waterfall, tight and heavy. Let her tie the mask. Called the ravens, one to each shoulder. Robe of black and grey over all, pieced from many parts, ragged, jagged, fluttering when the wind caught it. Like some dead thing snarled in thorns. Strips of fur, trailing ribbons, the crimson of the quilted tunic beneath showing through. For summer the under-tunic would be blue. I didn't know the meaning of any of it. It was just what was done; what, it was said, had always been done.

Sage was holding Smoke at the gate to the lower ward, his brow-band trimmed with fir twigs and sprays of tiny scarlet hips of white hedge-rose. Nowa's spear and those of the ship's crew who were serving as armscarls had collars of the same, fir and hemlock and red berries, a few with the little yellow crabapple that clings on to its thorny twigs well into Yearsturn. Most of them wore wreaths on helmets or hoods. Silent, their waiting, only the handful of horses restless.

We went to find the assembling procession, all firelight and noise. The pageant dancers, with torch-bearers tramping before, the lady and lord and their swordtheyns, the lesser nobles of their hall, all mounted. Their hallfolk, castle folk, torches and horn-paned lanterns swinging on poles... Drums and flutes and a bagpipe, a couple of fiddles, the Singer and her minstrel riding near the lady, though theirs wasn't the chief music for this night... Swordtheyns had the wild man on his knees on a low farm-sled. His wrists were bound to the bed of it, I thought, from the way he bowed forward, arms braced against the planks. I didn't want to look, couldn't look away. The prisoner was swathed in a heavy cloak, a kindness to a man about to die, and his beard had been shaved, not to impede my knife. Without it he looked younger even than me. They had done a clean job, whoever held the razor. Nowa, maybe. And he hadn't struggled against. Men come to the stone already blooded, sometimes, and their beards patchy, rough-cut. Maybe he hadn't even understood... My mood was bleak enough to wonder if the wild man understood anything at all, if I only imagined any of what seemed to sing between us. Whatever that was.

The stars were fading behind thickening haze in the moonless sky, a fine dust of snow sifting down, sparking when it caught firelight, settling on the wild man. He felt my watching, swung his head like a dog questing for some scent. Looking for me.

I looked away. Gaze fell on Lord Raynar instead. Watching where I had watched: the bound prisoner. A hand resting on the gilt disc pommel of his sword, but his staring—such *hunger*. I hadn't thought his tastes ran that way. Sage said that Henning said that the young woman Pool was lover as well as shieldling to Raynar. Then he saw me, startled, bowed, turned away to speak to his sister.

Lady Rikenza looked ill, wan and dreary.

The wild man was watching the earl's children as well. Predator's stare. Turned again to find me.

Smiled. As if there were some secret held between us.

I suppose there is, at that.

With an echoing croak and a rush of feathers, Thunder flew to the wild man, perched on his shoulder. Guards, even my own folk among them, who were used to the ravens' teasing, shied away.

Someone called out an order, which unloosed a great clamour and clashing, spears clattering, drums thumping, children ringing purloined cowbells. There would be someone besides me with an eye to the stars, a Forest-sense of the sky, or the knowledge to read an almanac, probably Lady Rikenza herself. It was a landtheyn's duty to understand such things, and what was an earl but landtheyn of a tribe? Better to arrive early than too late.

We started off with a shout and shrill skirl of bagpipe and flutes, the pageant-dancers and the first cohort of torch-bearers before us. Not their rehearsed story-dances yet, those were for after, when daylight came and their masked heroes and dragon-kin could do battle with an audience's full attention. They only danced a little, when they remembered, and the hound-masked youths with their rattles—not children, and no mischievous fox and crows, not for Huntersnight— marched alongside without scampering. It was winter; it was cold; it was beginning to snow, and we had nigh on three miles to go. The lady, in the earl's place, and her household about her rode next, and then the prisoner, guarded, some of my shipcarls among those guards to ensure no mischief done, and the hallfolk after, and all the folk of the castle, and torches and singing and already flasks and jugs being passed along, for all that it was not yet time to be breaking the fast.

Huntersnight. Longest night of the year and a cold dark watch to keep.

Castlefolk, the other teams and sleighs, more folk, more torches. And my company winding in at the end, as the procession uncoiled, already crossing the bridge, the ice pale and the wind whistling over it, where there were no trees or walls to break its force. We, silent, lightless—dark shadow to the fire and music. We, escort and flint-king, the priest of the knives, the savage heart of this mystery. The folk of Fairnshore came loud and unruly to join, and faltered, uncertain. They knew what was afoot; maybe they hadn't thought too hard, what it did mean. Maybe they'd thought that in the end, there'd be a birch-king on the sled after all, to be cheered on its way to the bonfire with the usual noise. But there were the guards about the wild man, and there, at the end of the procession, were Nowa and Sage and Solvig of the ship-guard riding, the rest afoot, and myself riding a little apart before them, dark and Forest-masked and no singing among us, and no flasks passing.

The Fairnshore folk fell in behind, since they could not cut in before, and came on in an uneasy quiet.

Hooves, creak of leather, crunch of snow, tramp of feet. Thunder came back to me, a shush-shush-shush of feathers heard before seen, black bird, black night.

The road was well packed down—there had been much coming and going, building the great bonfire all the day past—and the procession made good time, even at a walking pace.

The stars were going out like snuffed candles, the snow driving harder, but soon we were among trees, the Forest closing around us. The bite of the wind lessened, though still it howled and hissed, and the black branches lashed and rattled, the torches blowing sideways. Not all the lanterns stayed lit. The pageant-dancers would not be moved to add extra songs and recitations to draw out their performance.

The wind sang with the voices of distant wolves, the barking of dogs. The Wild King's riding...only geese, Nowa would say, when I was a child and said, I can hear them, the Wild King's hounds, running in the sky, circling the Lake... Only geese, flying high in the dark, and the last would have fled for the south a month and more since. I couldn't ask if she heard them too, but I saw Sage looking around, into the wind, and her black pony swivelled his ears that way, and Smoke, too. A few of the dogs—not the masked dancers but real ones tagging along—bristled and barked.

Wolves, but only wolves, distant, and some village dogs barking. There would be other bonfires in other fanes, other heartstones honoured, birch-kings sanctified by finger-pricks of blood and prayer. Maybe some even at the heartstone where Earl Raynellin had died, though probably not. No settlements near. Only the wild man, in his bear's den. A solitude resanctified after murder by human absence, the cleansing of snow and wind and stars and nearly a month of the moon's rise and fall. My thoughts were stumbling into dream again.

The great fane outside Queen's Arrun, with its triple ring of white stone, my mother riding a white horse, but she wears a mask of the flint-king. The tattered robe is silk, particoloured black and white, and there is a man bound and fighting against the ropes that hold him on a timber-sled drawn by white oxen. I don't know who he is. Some ordinary murderer, probably, who would otherwise have died by an ordinary executioner's axe. She rides up alongside and the wind swirls the artful tatter of her robe, the ribbons of her horse's mane, the ribbons of her long braid, the streamers tied to the horns of the oxen. The swordtheyns fall away. She says nothing, only looks at the man. He shrinks in on himself, stricken dumb. Cowers small, finished, knowing he's at the end of all this bright life he ran to ruin, and only the long waiting Dark before him, and the cold judgement of the Mothers Below.

I did not know, that she had ever taken the flint-king's part herself. I did not remember ever seeing a weapon in her hands, for all that the songs tell of her as a warrior, and dragon or not, herself a fighter of dragons.

Bloody hands and she grins, fangs in a human face, bareheaded, naked, hair loose and wind-wild rising, and her face half-masked with blood and she licks the back of her hand, long tongue, forked, black, and she looks at me, knows me watching, sees me dying, on my knees before her and I feel the stone's knife-point sliding cold hot burning into my flesh and she says, Mother, I give you my son. A fire reaches to hold me, golden bright and searing—

She can't, I think. They can only make a birch-king for Queen's Arrun, not give a life. I have the knives. But of course mine are not the only set of ritual knives; of course there must be blood for Huntersnight at the fane of Queen's Arrun, blood at the dark solstice before the Queen, that all may know she is life, and mercy, and justice, and death, that she holds the Forest and is held by it, bound to it, wedded to it by this sacrament. The Forest's grace, its blessing, given and received. Of course. She makes a pageant, to tell them so. But what, then, am I, and this death I ride to, as true, as real, as potent...

But it is all a lie, anyhow. She would surrender her claim on me to no one, and besides, she has no mother.

~Lannesk~

He's cold. He's always cold.

From the little village of Perch Cove they go by sleigh down to Borharbour, where the swordtheyn and his spearcarls had been posted in a wooden watchtower new-built that autumn to warn of dragon-kin advancing over the ice, from whence they had come swiftly-summoned by a reward-greedy man carrying news of the earl's son returned. From there, Ekkard wrapped in furs, feverish and insensible, they go up the frozen Bor to Earl Tannis's stone tower. Lannesk is bound, all that journey, wrists roped and tied to a cleat, but they let him sit by Ekkard. His head aches, throbs with every ridge and rut they hit, and Ekkard never wakes enough to know him. Ekkard's breath rattles. His face is blotchy, red and pale, lips cracked. Netta railed; Lannesk remembers that, groggily, through the headache. Told the swordtheyn the journey would kill the young lord, fevered as he was, called the man a fool, till he struck her. He is a fool. Eager to win his earl's favour, to be the one to return her errant son to her.

Messenger skis ahead, faster than the horses. Earl Tannis comes to meet them. *Earl Brux, mother, coming to the hermit, down in the hills below the Fairnmere...* That was a long time ago. Lannesk's head thuds and thuds with every hoofbeat and he wanders in dreams. Maybe he's fallen ill as well. They've given him ale and bread and sausage, but he's cold, so cold.

"My son in his folly goes chasing after glory," Tannis says, hard-faced, standing over him. "Chasing after you."

Wasn't him Ekkard had run after.

"And this is the reward of his service to the Singers, to the Immortals? This is how they send him back to me? Broken, fevered, starved, and with no more than you to attend him? Dark Mother *flay* you—what happened?"

She kicks him, turns away. "Take Lord Ekkard up to my own chamber. A bed by the fire. Send for Goodmother Inga."

"What about Brux's boy?" a woman asks as they sort themselves out, shifting Ekkard onto a pallet, unhitching the team to lead them away. Young woman, older than him, with Ekkard's blue eyes in a softer face. "He cared for Ekkard, brought him all the way from the Holy Isle, isn't that what they told you in Perch Cove, Svarling?"

The big spearwoman answers, "That's so, my lady."

"We could—Mother, we could give him his sword and a week's provisions and let him go. Lannesk could have abandoned Ekkard, ill as he was, and no one would ever have known. Instead he brought him safe home. That deserves some favour from us, surely?"

"Safe?" Earl Tannis snarls. "He brought your brother home dying. And that's no more Brux's whore's bastard's sword than he's a lord. Put the Coastlander down in the lower cellar. If Ekkard lives I may let him go begging over the strait to the Laitellon."

So cold. Lower cellar, small and dark, below the ground floor cellar of the earl's tower. Maybe it was a cistern, once. Abandoned, now. Damp. So damned cold, though someone in furtive kindness has brought down a few sacks stuffed with straw to lie on off the cold bedrock floor, and some tattered quilts. He's shackled, chains ankle to ankle, hand to hand. Weighed down, hobbled. They bring him food and drink once a day, a basket lowered down. Scant food. Feels like he's been hungry, cold, forever. No slop-pail, only what he hopes is the lowest corner. No light. At first he tries to climb the sides, tries to find finger-holds in the corners, to brace himself upwards, but the chains are heavy, and the stones close-fitted. Once, he makes it, and finds the hatch in the plank ceiling above him tightly bolted, can't get it to give an inch, and then he falls. He never makes it again, and soon he's too weak to try.

Cold. Damp. Hungry. Headaches that go on for weeks. Even the memories of songs die, gnawed away by the measureless dark. He cries, sometimes, and hates the sound of his gasping. Flings himself against the walls he can no longer scale. Mind goes strange. Thinks Ekkard's down there with him, gets frantic when crawling, feeling his way around the small space, he can't find him. Thinks he hears Anzi, talking to him. Telling him things he needs to know, how to find his way out. He needs to find a way out, a way to where he left Anzimor under the spruce trees, because his brother isn't dead, he's there, waiting, getting impatient because Lannesk is so slow, is so stupid in understanding he isn't dead, it was a mistake.

Thinks the Grey Hunter is there, sitting by him. Not saying anything, just sitting, companionable, a warmth at his side. They've left him his boots, the wolfskin cape. Took his belt and weapons, of course, and the purses. Didn't search him to the skin, beyond taking the last small knife from his boot. So he sits holding the wrapped pommel that was hidden in the breast of his shirt. Bluestone the size of a duck's egg. Few earls own such a jewel. Can't see any way to trade it for his freedom, though. The spearcarls who bring him porridge and water would never keep any bargain made with him and they never come one alone anyhow.

Feels it more like a token, maybe, of something that was. That's all. A memory he can hold for comfort. A child's toy. What do you think? he asks the Grey Hunter, and she says, there's strength in memory.

Hears the Wild King, singing. Far in the distance, somewhere ahead. Needs to answer, to follow. Can't find the words. Can't find the way.

Days, and days. Cold, in the dark.

"My son is dead."

Torchlight sears his eyes. The earl is a guess, a glimpse of some black solidity against the glare above. Her legs, maybe, standing at the edge of the opened hatch.

It's not the glare that brings tears to his eyes.

"Ekkard is dead," Tannis says, and her voice is like a dragon's hiss. Lannesk flinches, throws hands up before his face against her spitting flame. But she's not a dragon.

"He went for nothing, he fought for nothing, he died for nothing. They won nothing at all, the Singers, if ever there were any great threat from a little dragon-kin raid and it wasn't just some plot of the southern earls to bring us all under their rule. Ekkard is dead, and my husband's brother Asa, and what's gained? Not even a warrior's death for my boy. An old man's death, wasting away, coughing his lungs up, and mute and witless as you. You could have given him an honourable end and you didn't. You could have defended him as your lord in battle, and you didn't. Did you hope to take my daughter's lands, you and your brother, once you'd rid yourselves of the kinsman who might have defended her? Did you think Anzimor might have persuaded her to wed him, once her brother was out of the way—he's one who thought he could have any girl he pleased just by looking at her, wasn't he, that brother of yours? I know the type. But even she's not such a fool as to fall for a gawk like you, who can't spit out two words together."

He crouches, arm over his eyes against the light. Ah, Ekkard.

I'm sorry, he says to Anzimor. I tried. I tried to save him for you. If they'd left him to Netta's care in Gerd's alehouse, maybe he'd have pulled through. He was getting better, Anzi, he was. He was starting to find himself, there behind his eyes. His wits were healing. I'm sorry.

"Your life was forfeit, the day you came back into my lands," Earl Tannis says. "Today you die." And to someone, indistinct dark shape beside her. "Get him up here."

It's pointless. It's spite. It's the last snapping and snarling of the beast in the trap. Lannesk goes over to the lowered ladder as a spearcarl starts down it, and maybe they think he's broken, because they take no precautions against him at all. He swings the man coming down off and aside, races up and gets the length of chain joining his wrists about the earl's neck before the fools by her, who have not been standing at the ladder's head as they should, can react. Jerks her head back and up and aside together, with his hip turned to brace into the small of her back. Something cracks, he hears it. Drops her, falls beside her, a blow to the belly that knocks all the wind out of him. Lies just trying to breathe.

A woman screaming, wailing. They're kicking him around on the ground. Earl Tannis's daughter, kneeling over her mother, screaming.

"She's *dead*," Ekkard's sister says. "She's dead, she's dead! He's killed the earl, she's dead!"

Lannesk doesn't care.

"Finish him?" the swordtheyn asks.

The earl's heir climbs to her feet. Not Ekkard's eyes; it's Tannis's cold glare, now. "No," she says. "Not here. I won't have his murdering ghost left here, in my—in *my* tower. Bring him. Bring him to the fane where they seduced my brother to sail off to his death, where they swore their lying oaths. Have—oh merciful Mothers, what do I do? Have—have Earl Tannis laid out in the hall. But bring *him*, now."

What lie? What lie did he ever make, to this family?

They drag him through a storeroom, and then up the stairs to the hall on the first floor of the tower, and out into blinding bright morning and down again into the yard. Dizzy, seeing spots and streaks of light, but maybe that's being kept so long in the deep dark.

Not so deep and dark as the Dark Beyond. But there are stars, in the Dark Beyond, and the Wild King rides the Ways between…

Not anymore, he doesn't. Gone in the Dragon's fire.

Tries, one last time, hurling himself upright, swinging fists together, the two feet of chain between them whirling to strike a spearcarl across the face—

Just kill him, here, now. Let him go. Find Anzimor, Ekkard, Brux, his mother, little sister Swanlight holding up her arms…

Just kill him now and have done with. But they don't.

They bring rope to bind hands and ankles tight together before they take off the chains he's proven to be a weapon. Throw him into a cart.

Warm air. Warmer than the deep cellar. Spring's come, while he was buried there.

He stinks, in the clean air. The world is green and new and he smells like rot, like a cesspit. They hit him, when he tries to sit up.

Will they hang him, like they hanged Brux?

He hasn't heard, nobody's said, what's become of Islyn, of Islyn's baby. It must have been born by now, and if a daughter, she could claim the lands west of the Larchbrook... If she lives at all. There's too much murder in this land. He should never have brought Ekkard back here. Forgets, remembers, he didn't choose it; it was Tolla who set their course.

Should have let Ekkard choose his own death. He did try.

Should have stayed with Anzi, under the trees. Gone down quiet into the cold.

But the Grey Hunter needed him, and the Wild King.

Hey, Anzi. I fought a dragon.

Guess the dragon won, in the end.

You still waiting for me?

Won't be long. They've got me, this time.

There's a song half-formed. The Wild King's in it, and the Grey Hunter. Mirawan, Asa, Jerrah. Brave Singers dying amid the silver-barked honeysuckles, and outlaws, honest spearcarls, an erstwhile earl. Granna's in the song, she who never knew her sister for a murderer and traitor. Hennis and Ekkard, who together loved his brother. And Anzimor, bright and true, rock at his back, hawk on the wind, warmth to fill his heart.

And Anzimor. And Anzimor. And Anzimor.

They put him on his knees, there at the anchorstone where they swore their oaths, he and his brother, six months before. A world just waking, first buds breaking on the trees, sweetflower perfume rising from where the pale blossoms hide among leathery low-creeping tarnished green of its leaves.

It's Ekkard's sister takes the sword—the Wild King's sword, and they seem to think it's Ekkard's, some honour given him, some trophy. It's Ekkard's sister, with hatred making an ugly mask of her face, who sets the point to Lannesk's heaving chest—because he's scared, he's so scared, here at the end, and he hasn't finished the song, he can't find the way of it—she slides the sword's point down so it rests below his breast, the notch between his ribs. Stands, holding it so. Even then he's thinking, she won't, she won't. For Ekkard's sake, she won't, now her rage has cooled, she'll step back and tell him, get out of her lands, get off Laikyn and never come back—

She's watching him, staring him in the eyes, when, two-handed, putting all her strength into it, she thrusts it up and home.

Dying...hurts.

~MAIRRAN~

A nd so the procession came to the thorn-fenced ring of the Fairnshore heartstone on its bare hilltop, torchfire burning, and the shadows heavy, and the wind-lashed snow stinging. We wound our way in, all afoot, horses left behind, tied, clusters of them, among the swaying trees on the lee hillside. Even Lady Rikenza, Lord Raynar, went afoot, and the torches flared and streamed. Only the sleds were led or driven in, unloaded, driven out again, horses, ponies, no oxen here—too slow, and this procession had set a faster pace than what I had waking-dreamed of the Holy Isle. People stamped poles to stand in snow, hung lanterns; people huddled together. There were small fires already burning, pools of warmth and red light sunk where snow had been cleared.

Even I walked. My folk debated who would stay with the horses, decided they'd take turns, not to leave anyone out too long in what felt like it might grow to a storm. Sage, apparently, won or lost whatever their debate was, got the first watch. I was glad. It would keep her till the dawn, not long now. I didn't want her there, though there were children enough inside the fane, running and shouting, chasing and being chased by the pageant-dancer hounds, as was traditional. Not so many as there should have been, given the size of the castle and Fairnshore together. But it was turning to a harsh bad wind and small wonder some of the weather-wise had decided to keep their little ones safe and warm in bed. No offence to the Queen's rites, of course.

Two big timber-sleds had been set up, decorated with birch and fir saplings. Stages for the players and musicians, though the dancers wouldn't stay up there, but leap down among the crowd, whirl and battle through the constellation of small fires, circle the great bonfire that would be lit with the sun's rising, when the time came. A third made a dais for the lady and her attendants, with screens fixed, and a canopy, to give a little shelter, though the way the wind was buffeting it, canopy and screens and all looked likely to take flight. The ash-tree over the heartstone stirred and swept the driving snow.

The heartstone was a tall one. Sometimes they were not. Sometimes they had fallen, or never been set upright at all. Wolves ran over this one, carved with a few spare lines. Wolves, dogs, rising, becoming birds. Well, I thought so. I'd looked…maybe I'd only dreamt I looked, dreamt I traced those lines, nearly lost in frilled lichen. Now I could see no sign of carving. Starless and the moon, just past new, not yet even rising behind the thick cloud. They were walking, tugging, prodding the wild man to the stone, spearcarls of Raynar's.

Always Raynar's, never Rikenza's. I noticed I thought of them so. Him, they looked to, not her. And Lord Raynar there among them, sword in hand, catching firelight as he gestured with it. An old sword, some brief inscription high on the blade, inlaid dark tracks of a maker's mark. A fine weapon, cloud-patterned, mackerel-skied. Dragon-scaled, another poet's name for such patterned steel, and there were few enough swords so fine even among those the Queen gifted to her swordtheyns. As Rikenza's own shield-companion, Raynar should be at her side. Nowa was at mine. Raynar shouted as the wild man stumbled, and I thought—I don't know, that it was a ruse, that the prisoner would have the sword from Raynar's hand, that he would cut some fearsome path through them and be gone, but he was still weak from his wounding, maybe, and the snow hid tussocks and hollows and ice, of course. They dragged him to the stone, and he did not struggle. Confused, uncomprehending. Maybe. Maybe understanding only too well.

Wind tugged at feathers, at the mask, whipped my slashed and ragged hems and ribbons.

Waiting.

They stripped the wild man of the cloak in which he'd been bundled to stop him freezing on the way, but left him clothed, otherwise, tunic and trousers, now, and someone's much-worn boots, not the hall-gown he'd had when he was chained to the wall.

Crown of fir and rosehips, and they bound him standing against the stone. They should have had him on his knees at the stone's foot. Fools. He was nearly a head taller than I, who was meant to cut his throat. But no, they stood him there and wrapped ropes about him, as if he were a straw-man tied to a pole to keep him upright.

Still not struggling and I nearly broke my silence, nearly asked Nowa, outrage, panic, had they drugged him, poured poppy snaps down his throat, had she dared let them...but the wild man looked towards me and I knew not.

He saw in the dark as well as I did.

Saw...me.

Was seen.

So then I knew, or understood what I had always known. I went to him then, set my back against the stone by him, warmth by warmth, arm pressed to arm, as if we leaned companionable on a sunny afternoon, watching the world go by. The spearcarls scattered back. Raynar didn't retreat with the rest, standing close, moving restless, sword sheathed again, but he kept his hand on it, wary, or as if he found the touch of it a reassurance. Nowa put herself by me, watching Raynar, best she could. Firelight didn't reach them. Solvig brought a torch.

The musicians were playing, drums slow, fiddles mourning, and the Singer began one of the traditional wintersongs, a carol that summoned folk into the dance, linking hands, circling slow, two steps sunwise, one back and a pause, a shout, a clash of bells on that, two sunwise, and so around. Circles within circles. It kept them moving, kept them warm, anyway.

Winter sits brooding, the sun has fled. The Dark tide rises in the night of the world...

Who brings the fire, who calls the sun...?

I heard a voice I might have known once, clear among them all. Or one who sounded like her. Enough like that I searched, briefly, but saw only hallcarls and folk of Fairnshore gathered to make the Singer's chorus. Too many bodies, too much smoke in the cold air, to sort one human scent from another. Raynar fidgeted, looking to the south, the east, searching beyond the hard-driven snow for the first grey harbinger of dawn. Of death. The ravens fidgeted and I soothed them. Nudged Nowa, nodded to Raynar, and slipped away. Might have let a touch linger on the wild man as I went, cold fingers finding his. Reassurance.

Glanced back, saw Nowa's hand fall on Raynar's shoulder as he turned to follow. Lost myself, night, falling snow, circling bodies. Hopped up to the bed of the big timber-sled serving as the dais, drifted unseen to the side of Lady Rikenza's chair. Crouched there by her, put a hand on her arm. She jerked, looked, flinched away so hard she nearly had her chair over. Foxskin robe and yet she shivered, hollow-eyed beneath the diadem of a single strand of jet beads that was all the jewellery she wore. Her companion Enith saw me, moved uncertainly. I gestured her to go away, and the wary watching swordtheyns, too, who hadn't seen me come.

"Why do you fear your brother?" I asked Rikenza, soft. The flint-king wasn't meant to speak, not yet. Not till the sun crowned the world's edge.

Rikenza ducked her head down, tried to turn her face away. I set the flat of the curved stone knife to her cheek, forced her to look at me. To face the mask, see what I was, in this time and this place.

"Why did he kill your mother?"

Tears, then. Slow, unaware, freezing on the flint.

"She wasn't meant to die," Rikenza said. "He said she wasn't—I didn't know, they didn't tell me what they planned. He was always— she relied on him. She would rather he had been her heir. I didn't know, till after. He had to tell me, then. She wanted—she only meant—it was to call back a soul of the Forest. To wake a Rider again into the world. To call a champion to aid her, to make Laikyn free of the Queen's rule."

"That's not," I said, "what a Rider is. Or how a Rider is made."

Heroes, the Riders. Swordtheyns of the King, undying, till Erryth the Golden proved even they might die and not return. Not true Immortals, born of the Forest and the Lake, not like the Hunter, the

Smith, the Daughter of Snows. Made, yes. Self-made. Self-sacrificed, in answer to dire need, or through dire service. Deaths dedicated in battle, deaths at a heartstone, deaths cried aloud in some bleak black burning moment... Lives given into death, souls freely offered. It was not an easy gift. I understood that. I remembered...but that was a dream of Kallyn's. *She* remembered...that it was not always accepted.

"There was a grave," Rikenza said, and her voice was so faint I had to lean to hear. "At that old overgrown heartstone. They found it when one of the outer ring of oaks blew down, when I was small. They came to tell the earl my grandmother and we went to see. I remember—like a white rock, in the roots, up in the air. But it was a skull. They gathered the bones and buried them again in the pit where the tree had come down, at the edge of the fane, and a witch bound him down with a lake-stone in his chest for a heart so he wouldn't walk, whoever he was. They said he must have been a sacrifice from long ago, buried there. Hallowed, because of the sacrifice. So when they—when my mother thought there might be coming a time—when—"

"The Warnavon was planning rebellion," I said. "And we have not yet hunted that out to its roots, have we?"

"The Warnavon—no." Rikenza shook her head. Denial of any knowledge of conspiracy, or denial of my interruption, confession like a flow of blood, cleansing. "It was nothing to do with the Warnavon. My mother thought she might call him back as a Rider to serve Laikyn, that sacrificed man, if she offered her blood in the old way. A free offering. Blood for life, not death. But he's a murderer—if he was a sacrifice at the stone he's a murderer, he was before and he is still, and when the rite called him he slew her and ran wild to the woods again, with that horse, that horse—the foresters used to tell stories of it. They say they see it on autumn evenings. A red horse, a ghost horse, waiting for him to call it back."

"If he did kill Earl Raynellin," I said, "it was only justice, for her perversion of the sacrifice of the Riders. But I do not think a little blood-prayer offered by a traitorous earl driven by a fool's dream could have worked such a great summoning. What did she hope for, the claiming of her own petty kingdom? I don't think that could tear a soul free of the Dragon's curse that binds the Riding of the King in the Dark Beyond. And anyway, I do not think it was he who killed your mother. I do not think it was her little mockery of offering that called the soul of a Rider home. A great wound, you said. And done with your mother's hunting knife—no, by your description, it was not. Someone there in that fane had a sword and turned it against her."

"The earl rode armed. The wild man seized it."

"Then why did he not keep it? The earl's sword has never been mentioned. It came back with her, unblooded, never even drawn." Not that I knew that, but no one had mentioned otherwise.

Rikenza looked away. "No," she said. "No. He did not." *He* was not the wild man she meant, not any longer. "He did *not*. She was our mother."

"You lie and you lie and you lie, even to yourself," I told her. "You know the truth, even if you won't let yourself understand it. Raynar rode there with sacrilege in his mind, with murder in his heart. He rode with his mother meaning all along to kill her, thinking to offer not blood but his own mother's *life*, to tear open a path by which he could drag back a soul of the Forest and bind it reborn into himself, not in some ancient dead bones, whatever your mother may have thought."

"You can't kill Raynar," she whispered. "Not now. You can't. I can't—don't you see? He's become—not a Rider. A King. He's become a new King."

"He has not," I said. Hissed, not to shout. The very idea was— appalling. So very wrong.

"He has—he has! He says, it was no Rider's soul that answered their call, it was a King, answering the need of the Forest. He said, we had to find the outlaw, kill him—we must finish the sacrifice—his death, this sacrifice will set the King within Raynar free. And then he will be like one of the old Kings, and kill you and all dragon-kin, and make Laikyn foremost among all the tribes when the war comes."

"He's mad if he thinks so," I said. "Those Kings, they *served* the dragon-kin, until the Wild King broke free and shattered their rite for good and all and ever. Don't you listen to the songs of your Singers?"

And I would have denied the name of dragon-kin that she put on me, but that seemed a side issue, just then.

Rikenza said nothing, only ducked her head away. "Are you going to kill the wild man?"

"I was never going to kill the wild man," I said. "It was the children of Earl Raynellin I came to offer to the Forest, for their kinslaying."

"I wasn't there," she whispered. "I didn't know, my lord, what he meant to do."

"I know."

But she had not even tried, so far as I could tell, to get word of her brother's crime to the Queen. She had been no prisoner; she had still the right to command her own folk. Had still her freedom, even to go herself, if she could not or would not lay hands on her brother and hold him for the Queen's justice. She had not stood against Raynar in anything. Fear, reverence—belief that he was halfway to becoming some sacred soul of the Forest—whether she herself was rebel and traitor to the Queen in her heart or no, it hardly mattered to me. Yet she owed a debt, in this time, this place. She had acquiesced, even if only after the fact, in the worst of kinslayings.

But judgement was mine; I judged hers a weary, frightened guilt, in the end.

So I cut her, a thin line, shallow, clean pressure of the blade. It would heal and leave only the scar, to remind her. Blood was owed for her mother's life, for her silent betrayal of justice, her acceptance of murder, both her mother's and the wild man's—because it was murder, what they intended, to have him slain by my hand, innocent as he was of Earl Raynellin's death, innocent of everything, if her story could possibly be true, for if it were, he had already died for any long-ago crimes and was reborn from the Dark Beyond guiltless as a babe.

"Live," I said. "I give you back your life, Rikenza. But you will never be earl." Which was not judgement of her guilt, but of her weakness.

And if hers, how much more my own?

I left her, leapt down, wove through the dance again, and they parted and reformed around me as if they were the air through which I flew.

I could feel the edge of dawn as if it began to burn in my blood, though its first forerunner of thinning dark was lost behind the clouds and the wind-driven snow.

Raynar stood near the stone, though Nowa was making no secret of the watch she kept on him. It was not chance she put herself between him and the wild man, and barred him with a slanted spear when he would have edged around her, his hand, oh so casually, gripping his sword's hilt, not at all as if he were tempted to shed the wild man's blood himself, to steal the act of sacrifice from the flint-king, of course not.

Solvig, too was watching him, holding her torch more as weapon than light. I slid around them all, nodded to Nowa.

Someone among the musicians had been paying attention to the thinning dark, the promise of greying sky and what was due from them. Music swelled again and voices rose, a song for the Bright Mother and her son, the Sun Ascendant.

Mine, Raynar was, his blood owed and claimed. For the murder of his own mother, for profaning of the rite of sacrifice by which they had tried to call back a soul of the Forest from the Dark Beyond and bind it to serve their ambition. I swung behind him and with a closed fist struck him, hard, to put him on his knees. This dawn, this heartstone, would have the blood owed. I had Raynar by the hair, hood pulled down, and would have rocked the flint blade through his throat then but he flung away sideways even as I drew edge over skin, came up with a yell. I could smell blood on him, hot and sweet—not enough. Raynar was drawing his sword as he rose, and Nowa reversed her spear and struck him reeling with the butt of it, maybe because she recognized him as the true victim and understood his blood should not be shed but by the flint-king's hand, or maybe because in the snow-blinded dimness of that dawn she didn't realize what I was about and thought it only some scuffle between us, Raynar's assertion of rights over the death of the wild man he said had murdered his mother.

Raynar came back up facing me, sword and dagger drawn, staggering unsteady, but he flung a look over his shoulder to the stone, turning as if still he counted that more vital to him, to shed that blood and claim what he thought was owed him, than to defend against any threat I and my ancient knife could offer.

He shrieked a denial, because the wild man was gone.

Raynar spun back, launching himself at me. I would have had him, I was moving aside from the murderer's rush and despite his sword Raynar would have given himself to my knife in all that confusion and the grey storm twilight that was still my own amid the blinding snow, but Nowa trying to defend me came between. Raynar tumbled down under Nowa's feet, weakened from loss of blood or stuck down by her or slipped on snow stamped to ice, I don't know which.

Wind and snow and firelight and slow dull creeping dawn.

Shadows wild, Shieldling Pool swinging a sword and shouting for her lord, her leman, and Solvig driving her back, wielding axe and torch.

I dropped to a knee by Raynar to finish him. There was sticky cold blood on my hand, but it would spray me, drench me; I would smell it, taste it, drown in it, when the sacrifice was truly made, dream the reek of it in my hair, on my skin, for weeks. The ravens were circling, crying warning and alarm. And Rikenza rushed screaming down at us then, yelling her brother's name. Whether she meant her spear for me or Raynar no one ever knew.

Nowa, with the wind-driven snow making all faint and indistinct as night and fog, saw only the dim shape of Rikenza's rushing, the tamed and broken sister, to save her brother, and reached too late, only an arm, not a weapon, to check her. The spear was thrust past my swordtheyn with all Rikenza's weight behind it before Nowa even realized the lady bore it. Found its mark, bit deep.

Felt like a punch to my back. All confusion, after that. All gone to dreams. Cold. Raynar scrambling on hands and knees away, Raynar on his feet swaying and his sword fallen from his hand but he stooped and had it up again. What then? Blue fire burning in a dragon's eye, standing over him. They were singing the sun's own songs and the

Grey Hunter's last riding at the Wild King's side. They had thrust torches into the great bonfire because the sun had touched the sky, somewhere beyond the whirling grey snow, and the year was dead and gone and the Forest turned again...

I wore mail under the flint-king's robe and the ritual red tunic, because I was not utterly a fool, but I'd left off the plate over breast and shoulder-blades. Something had given, rings thrust apart, tearing, tearing flesh. It was cold. I was. Cold iron bitten deep. Why didn't Nowa finish the man, I thought—there was enough blood everywhere by then, surely, to feed whatever hunger slept in the Forest, open whatever paths the Dark demanded, for sun and light and life to walk their way back to us. But she crouched down over me and I couldn't think why she wouldn't help me up, kept trying to hold me still, cheek cold on trampled ice.

And my wild man...he took Rikenza where she had run aside and stood shrieking Raynar's name. She was swinging about, searching, screeching, not seeing her brother down on the ground in the storming snow. A knife in her hand now, and what did she think she was going to do with that? I watched, head pillowed on someone's hand. I had lost my mask, or Nowa had pulled it away, and that was wrong. The flint-king's face mustn't be seen till all was over and I could give the filthy thing to the fire, once they had covered and dragged the body away to the lychhouse to await the thaw and its unmarked grave.

Shadow-hounds, shadow-wolves milled around his legs. The wild man wrapped a long strong hand over Rikenza's face, jerking her back as she tried to run, and he cut her throat with the leaf-bladed knife, the black one, the knife I had given him to cut his bonds with at the stone, and he swung and threw her to the stone's foot where she belonged, arc of blood flying, catching sunlight. No, it was torchlight. It might be dawn, but there was no sun. He came striding over the trampled snow, which was drinking the night's offered blood and then some. He was coming to finish Raynar, I thought, but he dropped to his knees by me, dropped his knife by mine and put a hand on me.

Raynar was nothing, then. Raynar had never held a single breath of a soul of the Forest; his perverted rite had failed, could never have

340 / K. V. Johansen

succeeded. Corruption cannot beget holiness. He was gone, staggered away to die in the dark. Pool had gone with him. And the King was here.

Sage was there where she shouldn't have been, sliding down the shoulder of the big red stallion that had come sailing in over the thorn hedge.

I hurt. I hurt a lot. I would have thought that would have been all I could hold, that pain, but my head was buzzing with thought. I understood so much, or thought I did. Rikenza knew what they were about, her mother and her brother, of course she did, and how they'd profaned a Forest blessing by summoning a soul out of the Dark, and I'd known she knew, and I'd have forgiven her that, because she was afraid of them, of what they were, of what she thought Raynar was halfway become, and I understood that. And I understood that you could love them too, even when you were afraid, even when they didn't love you back. Because you needed to be loved. But I had thought that was just me.

Nowa always did say I was a fool.

Nowa was saying, "Stop that. Lie still. My lord, lie still," and I said, "It hurts," and she said, "Mairran, sweetheart, yes, it does. Just let me—" I didn't know what she was doing, but it hurt and I wished she wouldn't, whatever it was.

"Take him," Sage said, though I didn't know who she was speaking to. I thought Nowa was arguing with someone, with the minstrel Dove, whom she'd never liked, though why fault her for that summer romance or the years between us, when it was I who did the seducing, and no blame to the Islander that it had been my mother's idea. And a fine time was had by all concerned, I did believe, so what business was it of Nowa's, anyway? They were quarrelling, Nowa and Dove, whom I was probably dreaming up out of some random woman's voice, and Sage, too, I thought, over what would become of me, which should have been funny, because it didn't much matter where I did my dying. A spear in my back, that's what it was. Better than being chewed up by a dragon.

Doesn't mean I have to try it, to compare.

Sage was arguing with Nowa, and they both had their hands on me, trying to get up under my armour, trying to stop me bleeding, and the wild man was down there beside me too, his hand resting on my head.

Nowa was swearing, damning them both, damning her fool lord, Dark Mother's curse on them all. She'd lost whatever the argument was.

She wrapped me up like a baby. The wild man vaulted up to the back of the red stallion and Nowa handed me up. I knew I was small, but I was hardly that light, and I thought, maybe I wasn't grown to man at all yet, was still a boy and this was the time I fought the bear...and for a moment I was there again. My mother turning and walking away once the poor bear lay dead. I lay like the dead too, my black fur sodden, blood-drowned and dying, blood and blood and...it was always about blood, wasn't it? Blood is life is Forest, but that was not true, a lie we had made. The Forest is the Lake—is trees is wind is rot and water and green and sleeping snow. My mother, disappointed, because I had so nearly failed her, and she was sure I would die. Waste of effort, bearing me. Maybe that was it. I was a child still after all, bundled up and carried in Nowa's arms, and the flint-king was yet to come.

Settled with his arms around me, the wild man, my head against his shoulder. Cold, but the wild man felt hot as a fire.

And the horse cantered a few steps, and I felt the shift and gathering muscle as if I were horse myself and we leapt the hedge and were gone, weaving through trees, and the wind-whipped snow howling after.

Dream-hazed vision lagged behind. The great bonfire blazing high, and the constellation of lesser fires, and the pageant-dancers on their stage chanting, the wolf-masked woman playing the Grey Hunter declaiming, "Wolves to follow, wolves to guard, wolves to race the sun—"

What does that even mean? I asked, indignant, but I couldn't seem to form the words.

Wolves, dogs, running before us. But maybe that was something I dreamed.

They had seen confusion and chaos and murder, the folk of Mair Laikyn and the Fairnshore, but maybe this was an offering, and it was Huntersnight. A night, a dawn, of blood and loss and the strange time between years, and it was important, it mattered, that they keep the rite as it must be kept. So they finished their play and sang their songs and wove the last dance in the dawn, storm or no storm. And after, they would carry the bodies home.

I hoped they would find Raynar's, lost in the woods.

I wanted, very much, to know that Raynar was dead.

I wanted the sword that Raynar had carried that night.

I should have told Nowa what I'd found in the book of lays I stole from Raynar. I should have told her what I had seen. But I had not known then what I had found.

I remembered the Forest closing around us, and the storm-swallowed grey fading of the night that was the winter sun's rising. And nothing more, for quite a time.

To be concluded in Volume Two
The Raven and the Harper

About the Author

K. V. Johansen is the author of the five-book epic fantasy series *Gods of the Caravan Road*, beginning with the Sunburst-shortlisted *Blackdog*, as well as a number of books for children and teens and two works on the history of children's fantasy literature. She has an M.A. from the Centre for Medieval Studies at the University of Toronto and is a member of the SFWA and the Writers' Union of Canada. Various of her books have been translated into French, Macedonian, and Danish. As Kris Jamison, she is the author of the novel *Love/Rock/Compost*. Her website can be found at www.kvj.ca and she is on Bluesky as @kvjohansen. She lives in New Brunswick, Canada.

Curious about other Crossroad Press books? Stop by our website:
http://crossroadpress.com
We offer quality writing
in digital, audio, and print formats.

Subscribe to our newsletter on the website homepage and receive a
free eBook.

www.ingramcontent.com/pod-product-compliance
Lightning Source LLC
Chambersburg PA
CBHW021441240626
47153CB00001B/234